What they wrote about *The 35¢ Dowry,*
book one of the Mango Blood series.

In Fent's debut novel set in the 1950s, a French teenage girl gets the chance of a lifetime when an unexpected journey to India helps her reconnect with true love. An entertaining coming-of-age tale that explores family ties as well as colorful locales. This is the first of two books in the author's series, and its ending successfully provides intrigue by carefully hinting at what lies ahead for the main players. There are also some dark undertones throughout the book that keep the story from feeling overly romanticized.
– KIRKUS review

The 35¢ Dowry by Maryvonne Fent is true escapism. I loved Minouche; what a thoughtful, sensitive, but strong-minded young woman. I loved to see her character develop and her confidence slowly grow as the story progressed through touching moments but also very dark ones. The moment Minouche arrives in India, the story lights up with a color-ful narrative and really transports readers into a dynamic and culturally different country.
– *Lesley Jones for Readers' Favorite*

I'm just over halfway through with the book, but I had to stop and write a review because it's the best novel I've read in a while! The writing style and narrative really embrace you like a warm Parisian chocolate croissant and frothy latte. It isn't often you can lose yourself in great writing. The best writers, like ballet dancers, make grace and strength seem effortless, and Fent has this same artistry with narrative. Her unpretentious style sneaks up on you. I love how the young but wise Minouche bravely follows her heart while retaining her head, and I love how the story is exhilarating while still being completely relatable. I'm looking forward to book number two in the series!
– *G. Bryant, educator*

I love this book! I didn't want it to end. It's a beautifully told story about the power of love, and how love can inspire us to pursue our dreams. The writing is wonderful and rich, replete with poetically descriptive passages that make the reader feel Minouche's world of 1950s Paris and India, and experience through her eyes her incredible, exhilarating story.
– Christine Karas, painter

This book took me on a fantastic journey. From traveling to the Luxembourg Garden in Paris, to sailing to a far, far, place. The book is written in such fashion that I felt the author was reading her novel to me. Looking forward to the sequel to enjoy this marvelous adventure.
– Emmanuelle Stone, Cordon Bleu chef

The 35¢ Dowry got me hooked on page one. You'll be tempted to read this page-turner of a novel in one sitting, but you'll want to slow down to savor its beautifully expressive prose. The author, Maryvonne Fent, grew up in Paris. Perhaps being French is what has colored her writing with a certain tint of poetic luminescence. Like masterfully applied brushstrokes to a canvas, she paints scenes so vivid that you can see, touch, hear, smell, and even taste the sights and sounds of Minouche's ever-expanding universe. I can't wait to read the sequel! Bring on "Mango Blood"!
– Susan René, Transmitter of melody and rhyme, animal whisperer

The book is written like a well written piece of music. It flows and carries you along. The timing and cadence of the words match the storyline, starting with the very first paragraph where the you feel the confusion of the main character. Just like good music can carry you away, this novel carries you away to a new time and place.
– David Silverman, Civil Engineer and Ninjitsu Sensei

What a great story! Minouche is such a wonderfully human character. She is brave and fragile, simple and complicated. I was on her side from the first page. It was hard to put it down, I just had to know what happened next. I am looking forward to the next book and the further adventures of Minouche.

– *Clare Foley, reader*

Unforgettable characters and story. And I felt as though I'd really been on the sidewalks and in some gritty apartments in Paris, and ridden in an Indian Rickshaw in (then) Bombay.

– *Kimberly Allen, Actor*

The wonderful colorful journey of a young Parisian girl finding and winding her way through a sometimes frightful and challenging world to emerge in a new life in Madras, India.

– *Lars Eric, songwriter*

Fent has developed a cast of interesting and colorful characters. And she has a way with lovely descriptions that bring her locations vividly to life. Throughout the book, she skillfully weaves in shrewd observations on love, relationships, class and race that never stop the flow of the story, but which raise it far beyond a traditional coming of age romance. I loved this book and I'm looking forward to reading the sequel.

– *Amazon review*

I read the free sample (4 chapters) on Kindle and I was immediately pulled into this remarkable book. What I found extraordinary was that the author made relevant in modern times the events her heroine encountered in mid-50's Paris. Minouche is a rare character, especially in a time when women had very limited choices. Looking forward to finding out how she finds her way from her life of near-poverty in Paris, to a new life in India.

– *Marina Rheinhart*

Having traveled to Paris for the first time a couple of years ago, I was able to identify with the settings taking place in this very romantic insight into the life of young Minouche. Maryvonne Fent's vivid descriptions of settings and emotions this young adventurist experiences held my attention from cover to cover. I'm looking forward to the sequel to find what transpires after Minouche arrives in India.
– *Amazon review*

Maryvonne Fent paints elegant word pictures that share the pages of "The 35c Dowry" with an engaging, well-defined female character moving through an epic journey. Minouche is a most compelling character as she summons her determination despite the many challenges that confront her. The sensory experience of Minouche's 1950's Paris and Bombay is powerful and authentic. Maryvonne Fent has created an enduring work of historical fiction that stays with you long after the reading is done.
– *Tom Blomquist, Author of "Silent Partners" and "Devious Thinking"*

mango blood

Copyright © 2022 by Maryvonne Fent

Excerpts of reviews about The 35¢ Dowry © 2022 by Maryvonne Fent
Chapter One of The Dancing Foot © 2022 by Maryvonne Fent
Cover concept Maya Grafmuller after a painting by Greta Elgaard
Cover Design John Ancell
Author's photo Lance Baker Fent

This is a work of fiction. Certain locations and historical events are real.
However, names, characters, and incidents are the products of the author's
imagination, and any resemblance to actual persons living or dead, is
purely coincidental.

All rights reserved. In accordance with the US Copyright Act of 1976,
scanning, uploading, and electronic sharing of any part of this book without the permission of the author are unlawful piracy, and theft of the
author's intellectual property. If you would like to use material from the
book (other than for review purposes), prior written permission must be
obtained by contacting the author.

Thank you for your support of the author's rights.

ISBN: 978-1-66786-860-8 (print)
ISBN: 978-1-66786-861-5 (eBook)

To my mother who worked two jobs to keep me in school, but let me go when adventure called—though many disapproved; and to Lance, my husband, who lovingly gave me the space, and the time, to weave stories.

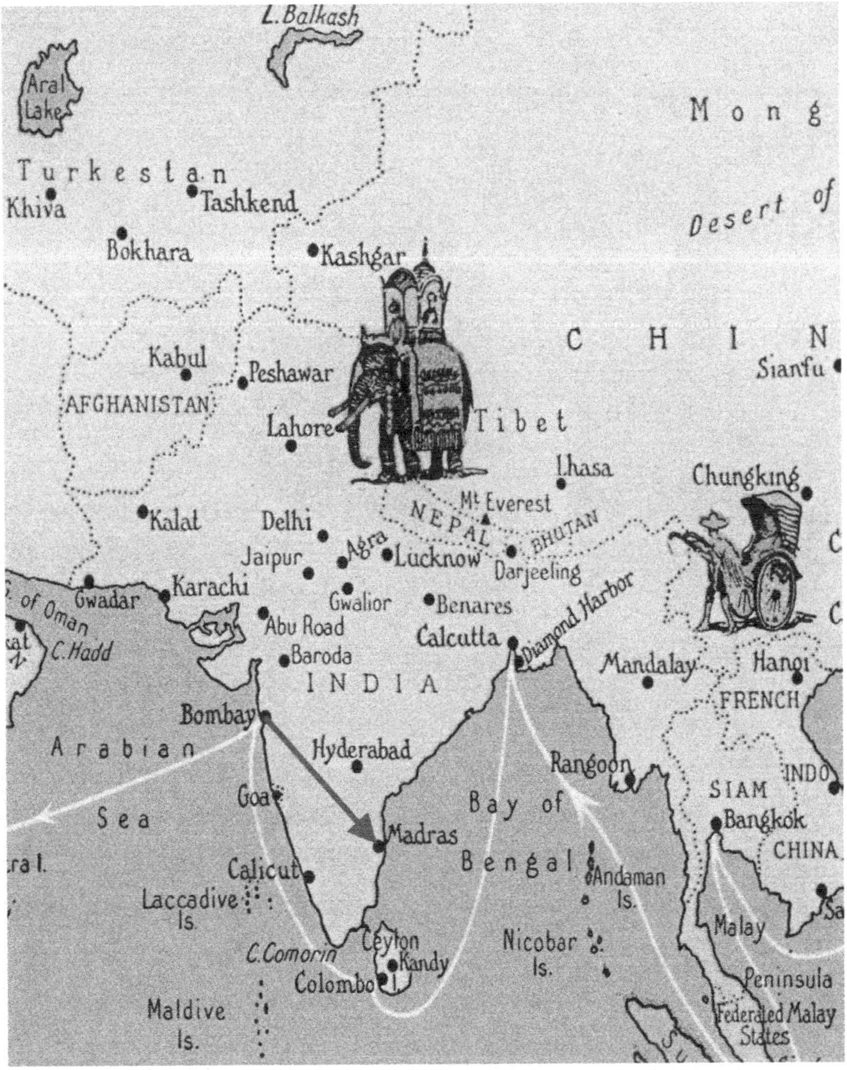

L. Balkash
Aral Lake
Mong
Turkestan
Khiva
Tashkend
Desert of
Bokhara
Kashgar
C H I N
Kabul
Peshawar
Sianfu
AFGHANISTAN
Lahore
Tibet
Lhasa
Chungking
Mt Everest
NEPAL
BHUTAN
Kalat
Delhi
Agra
Jaipur
Lucknow
Darjeeling
Gwadar
Karachi
Gwalior
Benares
of Oman
Abu Road
Diamond Harbor
C. Hadd
Calcutta
Baroda
Mandalay
Hanoi
INDIA
FRENCH
Bombay
Arabian
Hyderabad
Rangoon
INDO
Sea
Goa
Bay of
SIAM
Bangkok
Madras
Bengal
CHINA
Calicut
Andaman Is.
Laccadive Is.
Malay
Ceylon
Nicobar Is.
C. Comorin
Kandy
Colombo
Peninsula
Federated Malay States
Maldive Is.

ACKNOWLEDGMENTS

Forever on my list of thanks is Mark Dahlby, the creator of Writers-On-The-Net, who offered me a judgment-free forum to stretch my wings and writing skills; John High who inspired me to dig deeper on the page; to Shelley Singer, Carrie Bedford, Sue Garzon, Diana Corbitt and Gillian Hobbs for their continued support and the inspiration they impart to me by sharing their own writing.

I'd also like to thank all the American writers and friends who share my passion for story telling: Tom Blomquist, Nick Duretta, Christine Karas, Lisa Coté, Joe Grafmuller, Camille Cira, Mike Jacobs, Melissa DeCarlo, Sophie Cailleux, Jim Hopkins, Ed Markel, Jennifer Boire, Anne-Marie Kramer, Arline Vezina, David Silverman, Susan Inouye, Alan Brackett, Russ Giguere, and Gwen Hernandez, my Scrivener coach, who also writes sizzling romance novels.

Un grand merci also to Danielle Mathieu-Bouillon, Daniele Ohayon and Patrick Fillioud for sharing their work published in French across the Atlantic.

Last but not least, close to my heart, my daughter Maya whose morning brainstorming calls show me the world through her eyes, and my soulmate, Lance, whose love, eagerness, and belief in me, help me pull through the maze of words stories are made of.

mango blood

A Novel

Maryvonne Fent

CHAPTER ONE

1947 - LAILA

The year was 1947, one week before the declaration of India's independence from Great Britain was signed.

The girl was young, barely thirteen but already shapely, almost voluptuous, like the carved stone figures frolicking on the walls of the ancient temple she walked past every day on the way to her dance lessons. She hopped and skipped her way through the mango grove with graceful steps. The colorful glass bangles adorning her forearms chimed crystalline songs answered by the row of tiny bells around her ankles.

Bursting with pride, for she was to be the star of the Ramayana dance drama her school was putting on this year, she balanced on her head an imaginary urn filled with imaginary water and playacted the traditional dance of Krishna's beloved milkmaids returning from the river. She had on a short blouse showing her smooth stomach, and, too young to wear a sari, she wore a long skirt that swayed gracefully under the weight of tiny, embroidered mirrors that reflected shards of sunlight filtered through the leafy canopy.

Right hand raised above her head, she sang to herself and swung her left arm away from her hip as she pranced lightly, practicing the assured gait that village women displayed after years of carrying heavy burdens on their heads.

Attracted by the rhythmical bursts of light her outfit flashed, a bluebird winged lazily overhead and followed her progress through the grove. A little farther, a mongoose raised its juice-smeared nose from the overripe mango it had been feeding on, and watched her pass without alarm.

The girl was pleased to have chosen that route, a shortcut she had learned from her brothers, to run errands to her aunt's house. The long way would have taken her over by the village, along a dusty road shaking under the weight of lorries and bullock carts.

The hum of drunken insects and bees accompanied the dance tune on her lips, as she sang all the names of Lord Vishnu, whose incarnation as Krishna was but one of many.

It was such a beautiful day. The girl's heart overflowed with awe at the feel of her young body moving, undulating and communing with the grove's sweet-smelling air. Forgetting her dancing for a minute, she sighed contentedly and caressed the swell of her small but shapely breasts that felt hard and luscious under her fingers, like the mangoes she suddenly craved.

She reached and picked one that dangled invitingly in front of her face. Squeezing the fruit into her henna-decorated hands, she bit into the warm skin to make a hole and sucked on the sweet pulp with delight. Juice ran down her chin as she gently swatted at an inquisitive bee, careful not to hurt it.

It was then that the girl sensed, rather than saw, a gecko turning sinuously on its tail to slip under a bush. She heard crows caw in alarm as they rose into the air with a flurry of black wings, and she froze as four large figures detached themselves from under the shady canopy

2

and advanced on her.

They were just boys, white boys only a few years older than she was, but they wore the hated khaki uniforms of the British army. One of them carried a jug of rice wine, which he passed around to his friends. Taking off his sun helmet, he bent at the waist in mock curtsy and asked, "Well hello, sweetheart. Whatcha doing here all by yerself?"

"Look! A dancer," said another. "Fucking great! Dance for us, will ye?"

"And what's this ye eating? Come here! Let me lick that juice off yer face!"

They surrounded her, barring her escape, as she spun in panic, darting helplessly, bangles and bells chiming to the terrified thrum of her heart.

After they left, the bluebird returned and pecked at the shiny mirrors on the broken puppet lying in the dirt. From under the bushes, the gecko reappeared and ran across her small hand that was still clutching at her torn blouse.

The air was cool under the thick canopy of leaves which sunlight pierced in places, suspending narrow fans of gold dust through tortured branches heavy with mangoes, carmine, blue, and gold.

Cautious and low to the ground, whiskers alert, the mongoose approached and inspected the dirt soaked with crushed fruit and blood. Cautiously, ready to dart at an instant's notice, it started to lick the sweet pool of mango blood.

CHAPTER TWO

JUL 27, 1959

The muted sound of an efficient air-conditioner purring like a sated cat seeped into my dreams. I rolled onto my back beneath the brocaded coverlet, stretched my arms over my head, and slowly opened my eyes. Under the high ceiling, ornate moldings framed soft white walls. To my right, long gold drapes hung slightly parted along tall French windows. Early sunlight bouncing off a metallic object caught my eye. A ring. A golden ring. On my finger. My wedding ring. At the sight of it my heart quickened. I caressed it and felt my lips stretch into a smile as I remembered. I was in the honeymoon suite of the Arjun Hotel. Next to my head, the still warm pillow was empty, but I could hear the stream of a shower in the next room. I fantasized about embracing Stefan's lean and tanned body under the cascading water, but decided against it. The bed was too soft and comfortable to leave it just yet. Pulling myself up to sit against a fat satin pillow, I breathed in the spicy scent of the red roses sitting in a vase on the nightstand, and gave thanks for the day I had met Stefan, just a year ago. He was the reason my life had changed from sharing a room with my mother in a small family pension in Paris, to waking up in this first-class hotel in Bombay.

After six months of planning and penny-pinching in Paris to save enough money for a third-class seafare passage, I had arrived in Bombay, exultant but broke, with 35¢ in my pocket and no assurance Stefan would be waiting for me. But he had been there to greet me, eager to introduce me to the country he had chosen to undertake his spiritual awakening. For me, it was a dream come true, seeing that from the moment he'd left Paris, all I wanted was to be reunited with him. But still I was stunned when, shortly after I disembarked, he told me that we were to get married.

I'm not sure he would have come to that decision on his own, but on the advice of Miss Petit and Maurice, his seasoned and experienced Bombay hosts, Stefan had realized that it was the right thing to do, as the Indian campus we were heading to didn't allow unmarried couples to live together. I had readily agreed. I hadn't traveled thousands of kilometers to sneak into his room at night to sleep in his arms. And because I had spent the last of my savings on the ship bringing me here, I found the idea of being married quite reassuring, for if the grant I'd applied for to study Indian dancing and Theater Arts didn't material-ize, I would depend on Stefan to support me. I was grateful that money wouldn't be an issue for him as it had been for me most of my life. And on learning that traditional wedding arrangements in India usually depended on hefty financial transactions, I couldn't help but laugh when Maurice joked that Stefan had married me for my 35¢ dowry.

I let out a sigh of satisfaction. As kind and generous as our hosts had been, escaping to this hotel to finally be alone with Stefan had been delicious. After living apart for six long months, we needed that time and privacy to rediscover our chemistry and abandon ourselves, not only to pleasure, but to the sharing of the dreams and spiritual aspira-tions that had brought Stefan and me together.

When he walked into the room wrapped in a long white towel and bent over to kiss me, I pulled on the plush cloth intending to get him back in bed, but he playfully wriggled out of my grasp and reminded me that Maurice and Miss Petit expected us for breakfast in an hour. I wasn't hungry for breakfast. I was hungry for him, but I obediently slid off the soft, springy bed and headed to the shower. To save time, I skipped washing my hair, quickly dried myself, and slipped on my dress.

Though I was eager to discover Madras and the campus where we would live, I was disappointed to leave Bombay so soon. "Do we really need to leave today?" Bombay was this great city the travel guides called the doorway to India. There were so many monuments erected in praise of different cultures, Hindu, Muslim, Buddhist, Parsee, Jain, and of course British. I wanted to see them all and could have stayed in this hotel for days, enjoying sex by night and sightseeing by day, but Stefan had a frown on his face when he answered. "Look, I have to get back to Madras. I've already been gone ten days. I'll need to catch up with Professor Mahadevan's lectures. And I have to move us to larger quarters. The single room studio I'm renting is too small for the both of us."

"You're right, of course," I said, brightly. I didn't want to start our married life with nagging. "But could we come back here during our vacation?"

"Why not?" He opened the wardrobe, pulled out a light pair of pants and a shirt, and started to dress. "You'll see. Between the regular holidays and the mysterious astrological forecasts that close down schools for days at a time, we'll get a lot of extra time to travel. But right now, we need to keep our breakfast appointment and catch our train to go home."

Home. His home. A home I hadn't yet seen.

We gathered the few items of toiletries we had brought with us in

6

an overnight bag. I took a last look at the elegant room while Stefan commandeered a valet to call for a taxi. Minutes later we headed out to Miss Petit's house on Malabar Hill.

On arriving, we were welcomed with some teasing and much laughter from the servants as they served us a simple breakfast of Darjeeling tea, toast and marmalade. Even Maurice and Miss Petit had grins on their faces. In their aging world, the rare presence of a newly married couple was cause for celebration.

Packing Stefan's suitcase took hardly any time, and off we went, dashing to the train station to catch the twelve o'clock Madras Express after thanking everyone and reassuring Babula, their adopted daughter, that we would visit again. Maurice, as always, was generous with advice. And I felt tears come to my eyes when Miss Petit took my hands in hers, and assured me that we now were family. In my mind, her words evoked an image of tiny root tendrils spreading under my feet. Could it be that, possibly, I had started to belong in India? I didn't know what Madras would be like, but the warm shield of our friends' affection, added to Stefan's ring on my finger, told me I could board that train with trust in myself and in the world.

When Maurice first warned me that there were no such things as short train trips in India, I hadn't believed him. I had not counted on cities being half a continent apart, but I had now been on the train for three hours, and Madras was still a night and a day away. To my surprise, the train was very comfortable, maybe due to the fact that, after India's Independence in '47, the railway network built by the British had remained well managed. The first-class accommodations Stefan had booked for us was as good as a five-star hotel and made me feel like an international fashion model on location.

We had a small but entirely private compartment to ourselves. Its aged and polished cherry-wood paneling gave it a lived-in appearance.

It was homey, a small nest inside the long and grimy iron horse we had boarded. Above the deep and comfortable leather seat that ran the length of one of the walls were two stacked sleeping berths, outfitted with linen, blankets, and pillows. A small table was anchored to the floor. I was thrilled to discover we wouldn't have to walk the length of the train to find a toilet, as our compartment was equipped with an individual W.C. and a shower. To top it off, an impeccably dressed and turbaned steward—an obvious leftover from British colonial grandeur—was assigned to cater to our every need, any time, night or day.

But what I loved most about our compartment was that it offered us privacy, something I had quickly become aware was hard to come by in India. Dressed native style in loose white cotton pants and a thin kurta that revealed his tanned chest and neck, Stefan was sitting on the padded leather bench by the window. Legs crossed under him in perfect lotus fashion, he was at peace, lost in *The First and Last Freedom*, a book by J. Krishnamurti, an Indian philosopher. It was the same book he had been plunged into in Paris, as he waited for me at the rank entrance of a metro station or the breezy terrace of a café.

Looking at him now, a wave of desire knocked the breath out of me. I recalled how, not so long ago, anticipation of sex had lit me up and lingered on me like a shimmering coat, making my heart drum in my chest as we hurried, arm in arm, to his tiny mansard overlooking the sooty roofs of the Quartier Latin. It was the only place where we could make love as we were too poor to afford a hotel room. On approaching the old porte-cochere to his apartment building, we would lengthen our stride. The familiar smell of old wax was our ambrosia as we climbed the worn staircase, two steps at a time, to his unmade bed. But why reminisce about the past? Was I not alone with him on a train, with fantasies of wild sex on the Orient Express?

I was stepping out of the bathroom when there was a knock on the door, and Stefan looked up from his book. "Minouche, get the door. I ordered coffee for you while you were in there."

It wasn't what I'd had in mind when I'd gone to freshen up and brush my teeth, but I was ready to jump through hoops for a good cup of coffee. So, I unlocked the smooth sliding door, and the steward squeezed in sideways through the narrow first-class doorway. Impervious to the movement of the train, he carried a large silver tray loaded with a one-person coffee set and a small teapot. He had also brought a light collation of open-face sandwiches. He set the tray on the small folding table Stefan had pulled away from the wall.

"Thank you, Memsahib. Would you like me to pour the coffee for you?"

"Yes, thank you," I said, smiling at him.

"You are welcome, Memsahib," he said, his eyes resting modestly on the tray. "Shall I also pour tea for the Sahib?"

"Yes, please," answered Stefan, without looking up from his book.

The steward filled our cups with a steady hand and slipped back out.

It was strange to be addressed as "Memsahib" which I'd been told referred to a married white woman in colonial India. But "Memsahib" sounded bigger than the "me" I identified with. Memsahib made me feel like an attribute of Stefan's holdings, his chattel, rather than the French girl who had boarded an ocean liner back in Marseille to be with him.

On the other hand, the respectful attention I was getting from servants and waiters was affecting me. It made me feel somewhat above my station. I was jubilant and wished my friends could see me now, but, at the other end of the spectrum, I also feared I might wake up and find it was all a dream. Doubt tugged at me. Could that impeccably turbaned waiter tell I was a fraud, a pauper and a dreamer who had made it to India with 35¢ in her pocket because she was in love?

Stefan looked up and smiled at me over his teacup. He motioned for me to sit across from him. Before plopping down, I took a big swallow and refilled my own cup from the coffee pot left behind by the waiter.

"I'm glad we left Bombay. I was getting tired of the city." Pointing out the window with his chin, he added, "To me, this is the real India."

We were traveling southeast at the bottom of a deep valley nestled between rocky outcrops and plateaux, and the sun was behind us when the train slowed down and stopped after a succession of loud, screeching grunts and sighs.

"What was that?" I asked in surprise, for there was no station in sight, only dusty vegetation growing between scabby rocks.

"Nothing to worry about. The train just pulled on to a siding to let an incoming train use the main rails. You'll get used to it. If the other train is late and we need to wait for more than an hour, the conductor will let us get off the train to stretch our legs. After the other train passes, everybody will climb back on. You'll see."

"Hopefully, it won't be too long before we get going," I said.

This time around, no one was allowed outside, and thirty minutes later a long cargo train coming from the other direction rambled past us. After it was gone, our locomotive coughed a few times, and the train shook and moved again. An hour later, we entered a large valley dotted with villages and fields. The solid blue sky hung like a photographer's backdrop behind rows of water-seeking palm trees. "You're lucky the monsoon is late this year," said Stefan, glancing up. "Otherwise, there wouldn't be much to see."

As we sped through irrigated fields, I caught sight of men at work. Brown and black, heads wrapped in faded turbans, they were clad in loincloths so skimpy that, in the distance, they appeared nude and resembled animated stick figures prodding water buffaloes harnessed to bullock-carts.

The women were the colorful ones. Their saris exploded with juxtaposed shades of reds, yellows, purples and greens. Sure-footed, backs arched, they balanced outsized loads and giant clay pots on their heads effortlessly.

Glued to the window, I was drawn into the poetry of rural India. The sight of these villagers moved me. The way they lived, just as their ancestors had for thousands of years, was both beautiful and inconceivable to my Parisian brain.

Little by little the light slipped away. Dusk fell. Soon night would be upon us, and I was reminded of what Stefan's friend had told me. There were no such things as short train trips in India.

On leaving Paris, I had taken the train to Marseille to catch the *Pierre Loti*, a Messageries Maritimes ocean liner heading to Bombay where Stefan was waiting for me. He had left Paris six months earlier to pursue a degree in Hindu philosophy and find answers to his spiritual quest. I had, at first, lamented the fact that flying to Bombay was beyond my means. But, in retrospect, I'd enjoyed the 12-day sea voyage that had taken me across two seas and one ocean, and given me a glimpse of the people and landscapes on several continents. I would never have seen these from an airplane.

And now, alone in this tiny, air-conditioned apartment-on-rails, I was dying to take off my clothes and get a jump on the lovemaking we had enjoyed for only one night, because Miss Petit and Maurice, our well-meaning Bombay hosts, had thought it important to keep us separate, and celibate, until the big day. But we were on our own now, and darn it, it was our honeymoon.

I kicked off my sandals and climbed on the padded seat to snuggle against Stefan. Impulsively, I took hold of his hand and leaned into him to kiss his neck, but I must have squeezed his hand too hard for he put his book aside and looked up at me questioningly. "Can't you do something—read, write, take a nap? I don't want to upset you, but I'm used to having some time of my own. Being cooped up together in this compartment for hours at a time requires a little adjustment. I'm just asking for a little space, okay?"

What he didn't say was that he had always needed space. I'd known that in Paris, and though I didn't like the way it made me feel, it hadn't stopped me from falling in love with him. It was no secret that he needed a lot of space and wasn't shy about protecting it.

"I don't mean to shut you out," he added. "Just be patient. It will be easier in Madras. I have my eye on a small house for us when we get there." He lifted my hand to his lips, kissed it and looked questioningly at me, as if asking permission to return to his book.

"I'm fine," I said, mouthing a kiss in his direction. I tried to imagine what a small house in Madras might be like, but all I knew were cramped Parisian apartments. I had never lived in a house. Returning to my seat across from him, I leaned my forehead against the window and watched as hues of violet and blue spread across the fading sky. As the sun slipped under the horizon, I contemplated the ebb and flow of the many currents that had conspired to bring me here. I was anxious at the thought of joining a dance school with no qualifications other than my desire to research and learn, but that was getting overshadowed by the anticipation of what my new life would bring, be it good or bad, in this vast and bountiful continent.

Night fell abruptly, and darkness stole my window show. After a while, I started to feel claustrophobic in the isolation of this first-class bubble. I was a product of city life, used to having people around me. When Stefan reached up to turn on his overhead light to keep reading, I jumped up and said eagerly, "Let's not order in. Can we go to the dining car for dinner, please?"

He looked at me over the page he had just read, inserted a bookmark to save his place, closed the book, stretched like a cat, yawned, and said, "Okay. Put on something nice, one of your new dresses."

He didn't have to tell me twice. I slipped on the light blue gingham dress the tailor in Bombay had sewed for me, brushed my hair, and stepped into my low-heeled white wedding shoes.

We didn't have far to walk to find the dining car. A tall and elegant Sikh welcomed us, his long, waxed mustache vibrating with every word he spoke. The ends of his tightly twisted beard reached back under a majestic turban whose saffron color matched the wide belt cinching his white tunic. Stefan had explained to me earlier that Sikhs belonged to the warrior caste, and even though this man was only a Maître d', I was impressed by his virile appearance. His heavy-lidded eyes were watchful under thick eyebrows, and the appreciative look he gave me behind Stefan's back gave me a small jolt of pleasure. It felt good to be a woman and be admired.

He directed us to a booth at the back of the crowded compartment. The seats, upholstered with maroon leather, were soft, and the table setting formal with an intimidating array of forks and knives. My mother had prepared me for such an eventuality. I could hear her voice whispering in my ear, "All you have to do is let someone eat first, and you'll know which fork to choose."

Stefan ordered mineral water for us both. It was fine with me, but inwardly it made me smile. The French friends I had made on the ship wouldn't have enjoyed Stefan's company. Unlike him, they believed a glass of wine was good for your health, and more importantly, good clean fun.

While I looked around at the other patrons, Stefan perused the menu critically and ordered barley soup and poached trout served with boiled potatoes, and the unavoidable British peas. I was delighted to see they served fish-and-chips. I had discovered them during my hitch-hiking days in England, when fish-and-chips, dropped into a cone of wax paper and wrapped in newspaper, were all I could afford. I wasn't disappointed by my choice. It was so tasty I ate every last crumb and would have licked my plate if I dared. I was wiping my greasy hands on the linen napkin when I felt the Maître d's eyes on me as he passed by our table. He waved to a waiter, and the young man rushed to the kitchen and brought back a bowl of lemon-scented warm water which he put in front of me to rinse my hands in. Satisfied, the Maitre d' smiled conspiratorially at me and moved on to other patrons.

During dinner, Stefan told me more about the short trip he had taken to the Himalayas when he'd first arrived, six months before.

"It was a trip to Kashmir arranged by the Students' Council at the university. We stayed in a dorm in Gulmarg, at 8,000 feet. There was lots of snow. Many Indians had never seen snow before. You wouldn't believe the crazy things they did, like throwing themselves down the lower slopes inside tires or simply sliding on their backs or rolling down! It was fun to watch."

"Did you ski?" I asked.

"No, none of us had any gear or ski clothes. But we hiked a lot and enjoyed the magnificent views. I'd like to go back there with you when we get a chance."

"I'd like that," I said, though I'd never taken any vacations in a mountain resort and had no idea what it might be like.

After dinner, Stefan ordered tea for himself. For me he ordered ice cream. It was another of those perfumed confections that tasted like rose water, similar to the pastries Miss Petit, our hostess in Bombay, had served at our wedding, and I couldn't bring myself to eat it. Seeing it untouched on my plate, the Maître d' sent it back and ordered a waiter to bring me mango sherbet. I looked questioningly at Stefan after he'd moved away. "Should we tip the Maître d'?"

"I don't think so," he said. "He's just doing his job, but I think he likes you and surmised you're new to Indian cuisine."

I smiled inwardly. Stefan had noticed.

After dinner we moved to a sitting area where three young Indian men were already settled. They greeted us in a friendly manner and engaged us in discussion. Shortly after, Stefan excused himself and pointed to a section of the dining car that resembled a gentleman's club, with racks of newspapers and deep leather armchairs. "Enjoy your new friends," he whispered to me. "I'm going to catch up on international news."

Happy for a chance to practice my English with someone other than Stefan, I hardly noticed his desertion at the time, but quickly discovered that I might have taken on more than I'd bargained for. Almost at once, I found myself being interrogated by Oxford-educated Indians who knew all there was to know about nightlife in Piccadilly Circus and the red-light district in Amsterdam.

Had I been less naive, I might have guessed their agenda from the way they dressed. Except for the perfection of their dark chiseled features and luxuriant hair, there wasn't much Indian-ness left in them. All three looked like a billboard for the high-class British way of life, from the tips of their fashionable leather shoes to their three-piece suits and striped old-school ties. Their British accent was impeccable. What they didn't have were good British manners.

In a mere fifteen minutes, they had wrung and squeezed information out of me so thoroughly that their inquisition felt scripted.

"Have you some brothers? That's too bad, but at least you have a sister. Jolly good! And your parents are still alive? Good chaps. So, what's your father's occupation? Oh, I see, your mother works. Any aunts and uncles? Too bad really. So, no cousins? That's sad. Tell me, where did you go to school and what did you study? Excellent, Excellent! And how does the degree system work in France? What made you decide to come to India? Why not England or America, and what do you plan to study in Madras? Such a stuffy old city."

Their scrutiny was unexpected and unsettling. I didn't know whether to laugh or get angry at them. Were they for real? But the worst was yet to come when one of them extracted a box of Dunhill from his pocket and offered me a cigarette, which I declined. He nodded understanding, shook out a couple more for his friends, and passed around a gold lighter. He then turned to me, inhaled, and fired the ultimate question in a cloud of smoke: "So, how do you like India?"

I had touched land less than a week ago, but looking at their smirky faces, I got a feeling I liked India more than they did. How could that be? I wanted to defend what I knew about India's art and culture, which wasn't much, but they were more intent on complaining about how poor and dirty their homeland was, and I soon felt drained by their rabid chatter. I'd made a point to answer their questions honestly but was getting tired of their poking and prodding. Was their culture and upbringing so different from mine that they thought it normal to question me like this? I pointed at my watch and told them I had to go, but they didn't notice. They were too busy counting on elegantly manicured fingers all the reasons why they couldn't wait to return to England or Germany, where cars were super cool and music halls, brilliant.

It was sad. They should have been patriots, proud that after 300 years of colonial rule their country had finally become independent. But obviously, their loyalty resided overseas.

I finally managed to escape them and rejoin Stefan. "Indian dandies," he said, distaste in his voice. "I've heard rich snobs like them denigrate India before and won't have any part of it. But rather than telling you, I thought you should experience it first-hand." He looked a little smug about that and I was about to protest, but he was right.

"They have a serious identity problem," I said. "Why would they deny their roots?"

"The rich still identify with the British, I suppose. And getting an education abroad is still an asset to secure important positions."

"How can they be educated and have such poor social skills? Did you hear how they grilled me? I was afraid they might ask me what brand of tampons I used."

Stefan's eyebrows shot up on his forehead. He shook his head. "You'll find that Indians enjoy asking a thousand and one questions.

Especially of foreigners. They are curious about us. Some long-dead guru probably instilled in them that curiosity begets answers, and answers beget learning. It has become part of the culture. They'll also stare at you in public, and no one thinks anything of it. Welcome to India. Things are different here."

"Lesson learned." I sighed. As eager as I was to interact with Indians, the kind of hazing I'd just been subjected to had exhausted me, and I was relieved to retreat to our coupé. When, predictably, Stefan returned to his Krishnamurti book, I smiled at him. I didn't mind at all.

Pen in hand with the notebook Maman had bought for me on Boulevard St. Michel prior to my departure, I gathered my thoughts. I had journaled quite regularly on the ship, but right now I had so much to write about that I didn't know where to start. Or was it that I didn't dare to put my inner thoughts down on paper on the chance Stefan might read them and be judgemental? It was not that I didn't trust him. After all, married people weren't supposed to have secrets from each other. It was just that everything was so new and happening so fast; I needed a place all my own to confide my thoughts.

Brows knitted in concentration Stefan glanced briefly in my direction. I wondered what he was thinking about but didn't dare to pry. Maybe he was concerned about his classes at the University. Maybe the complications my arrival had brought into his previously single and simple life weighed on his mind. Meanwhile, the train rushed on into the night. I would have loved to smell and touch the thick darkness outside the warm glass, but because of the air-conditioning, the windows were shut tight. I didn't know where we were, but obviously, we were far from any city. What I could see of the sky by pressing my face against the glass was a black expanse studded with a million stars, like it had been back on the ship in the middle of the ocean. I wondered if the moon might come up soon. Maybe I would get a glimpse of it by lifting the window and leaning outside.

Guessing my intention, Stefan looked up from his book. "Bad idea," he said. "You'll let the cold air out, and you never know what might get into the compartment, locusts or even bats. And bats can be rabid here. Also, those locomotives run on coal, and you don't want coal dust in your eyes. Coal dust is unforgiving, like glass. You could lose your sight." He paused. "And then, there are the Harijans…"

"Harijans?" I interrupted. "What's that?"

"The poorest caste. The untouchables."

I remembered and nodded understanding. He had filled me in earlier about the caste system in India.

"They jump on the train when we slow down or stop. They hang outside windows and doors or climb on the roof to stay cool." Always a teacher, he paused to make his point. "Do you remember Raji, the fruit vendor across the street from Miss Petit?"

"The one with a limp and the dirty eye patch?" How could I forget such a wreck of a man?

"Yes, that one. According to Maurice, he nearly got killed after jumping a train to go to his sister's wedding. He was working his way to climb on the roof, which is what these people do, but when coal dust flew into his eyes, he lost his grip and fell off. His cornea was so deeply scratched that he lost sight in one eye."

"That's awful. Did he make it to the wedding?"

"I don't know, and it's not important. Just remember to keep the windows shut."

Well, there was no point in starting an argument, even though his imperious tone of voice rattled me.

"Don't worry. I will."

Suddenly I didn't feel so safe in my first-class coupé. I found myself watching the top and sides of the vertical blind that hung loosely against the window frame, half expecting to meet the eyes of a mad hobo hanging upside down from the roof like a giant bat. No wonder Stefan wanted me to keep my clothes on! Maybe privacy didn't exist in India after all, even in first class.

I undressed in the windowless bathroom and slipped on my pajamas. My erotic fantasies of sex on a train had just been killed for the second time. Killed by invisible eyes. My mind, or was it just hormones, still searched for ways around the problem. We might make it a game. Turn off all the lights... but Stefan was not in the mood. Rather than calling the steward to prepare the beds for us, he unlatched the upper berth which was going to be mine, and helped me climb in it. He tucked me in, patted the blanket covering me, and gave me a lingering kiss that raised my hopes, but remained just a kiss. "Bonne nuit, Minouchka. Sleep well."

His calling me Minouchka made my heart swell with the memory of our rambling nights in Paris. I wished he would talk to me again about the stars, the cosmos, and Tibetan Tantric Buddhism. But obviously, that wouldn't be tonight.

CHAPTER THREE

ON THE TRAIN

I thought I heard a knock on the door and opened my eyes to the diffused golden light framing the window blind. Half-awake and strangely disconnected from my environment, I shut my eyes tight to reenter the pleasurable dream I was emerging from. I'd been sitting in a small Parisian bistro near the Sorbonne, telling Brigitte, my best friend, about India's vivid colors, the languid, often irritating music floating on the air, the beauty of the poorest Indians going about their lives, the exotic food I had smelled or tasted, and the yellow, red and blue mangoes offered by street vendors. I was explaining to her that, with a grant in his pocket and his goal in sight, Stefan appeared more confident than ever. And keeping the big news for last, I was telling her how he had talked me into getting married practically off the boat. Dream or internal monologue? I wasn't sure. Images were dissipating like wispy morning mist, but I still could see Brigitte's face, hear her voice, sense her amazement, envy, disbelief. Me, married to Stefan? Then the bistro dissolved, and I was a child riding a glossy painted elephant on the merry-go-round in the Luxembourg Gardens. Stefan's ghostly silhouette had materialized and hovered protectively over me, and I wanted to tell him how happy I was to ride this elephant, but I was spinning round and round so fast that my words were getting lost.

Stefan's hand shaking my arm, and his voice in my ear urging me to get up, finally woke me. I reached for the window wall to steady myself and slid down from the upper berth where I'd slept alone. He was already dressed, waiting for me to move aside so he could close my bunk to make room. I slipped into the silky dressing gown I had received as a wedding present from our Bombay friends, and heard an accented male voice speaking through the door. "Should I come back later with your breakfast, Sahib?"

Stefan turned toward me to check I was presentable and opened the door. The same handsome turbaned steward, or bearer—for that's what they were called here—who had attended to us the day before, pushed a small rolling table through the door. On it were two freshly out-of-the-oven croissants, a silver coffee pot whose steam filled our tiny compartment with a delicious aroma, a smallish jug of thick-looking cream, and two elegant cups and saucers of translucent white china.

I marveled at the exquisite cups. The double espressos I used to drink in French cafés were usually served in tall glass cups, made opaque with scratches from a thousand washes. How did this fragile china survive on a train? It must have cost a fortune. It was slightly embarrassing to acknowledge, at least to myself, that I was currently living above my means.

Tall and erect in his white uniform, the steward exuded modest nobility. I was fascinated by his bearing. There was nothing servile about him. His brown skin was smooth, his nose long, his nostrils sharp, his lips sensuous. Heavy eyelids revealed only the lower half of charcoal black irises. He reminded me of the Moghul miniature paintings I'd admired in library books. With graceful, long-fingered hands, he rearranged the cups on the narrow table and turned halfway around in the cramped space. "May I prepare your coffee, Sahib?"

"Go ahead," said Stefan sitting back down with one of his books. "Cream and sugar for us both."

The bearer scooped out a spoonful of glittering granulated rock sugar into a cup and poured hot coffee over it. He stirred it for a second, and, turning the spoon upside down with the experienced flourish of a first-class steward, he let a stream of cold white cream slide from the spoon's back into the swirling black coffee.

He gently placed the cup on a saucer and offered it to me, "For you, Memsahib," he said, bowing slightly, before repeating the ritual for Stefan.

I accepted the hot cup gratefully. The coffee's aroma was rich and bitter, but the taste was unexpected, for my lips were tasting the coolness of the cream floating on top, while my tongue registered the sweetened bitterness of the hot brew hidden under it.

I must have looked surprised, because the bearer smiled expectantly, revealing perfectly white teeth. He nodded a couple of times and said, "Real Kona coffee, Memsahib."

I took a long sip. "Umm... Delicious. What a wonderful blend of flavors."

The bearer's back straightened with added pride as he acknowledged my remark. "Yes. Very, very delicious." In a conspiratorial tone he added, "It is the absolute favorite of the foreign ladies staying at the Taj Mahal Hotel in Bombay."

I was sure it was, and, in that palatial hotel it was easy to imagine that some ladies might even like it served in bed by this alluring man.

The bearer took a step toward the door but changed his mind. I think he enjoyed telling me about the India I hadn't yet come across. "Kona coffee is quite different from regular Indian coffee," he said. "To make Indian coffee, one must mix coffee grounds, milk, and many, many spoons of sugar, and then boil it all together for one whole hour;

the result is very, very sweet, perfect for our people's taste, but too sweet for…"

"Thank you, that will be all," interrupted Stefan, dismissing him without looking up from the book in his lap.

"My apologies, Sahib."

The bearer's excited smile faded from his handsome face, replaced by a blank expression, and his princely demeanor slipped off his shoulders like an oversized coat. He bowed low as he backed out of the tiny compartment with the empty rolling table, and silently pulled the door closed behind him.

Though Stefan hadn't even looked at me, I felt as if I'd been slapped in the face. The steward's embarrassed exit was disconcerting. "Why did you speak to him like that?" I asked. "He was so nice. He was telling me how the people here make coffee…"

"You shouldn't pay so much attention to the help. They tend to get chatty." He put his book down, pulled me onto his lap, and silenced my argument by pressing his lips against mine. "You will have ample time to sample coffee when we get to Madras," he said. Clearing a loose strand of hair from my face, he kissed my neck and caressed my cheek. "Look, you are new to this country, and of course you're curious. You have to trust that I've a better understanding of the way things work here."

For a second, I flashed back on my dream, remembering how I had felt his presence protecting me as I rode the merry-go-round elephant. I relaxed in his embrace and buried my face in his neck. He was right. I had no idea about the dynamics between people here, and certainly not with bearers, or whatever they were called. As a matter of fact, it was kind of embarrassing to be served so obsequiously. French waiters certainly didn't bow at the waist when they served us coffee, and they were known to get pretty rude when patrons were short with them.

Safe and comforted in Stefan's lap, I resolved to hold judgment as

23

I watched and learned the ways of this new world.

After a while I stood up and he went back to his book. In spite of my resolution, I was puzzled. Had he been manipulative? Kissing me to placate me, or did he really mean to protect me? But protect me from what? Protect me from a chatty person? It pleased me to think that maybe he was jealous of the handsome bearer. But I couldn't help wondering about what Indians thought about imperious foreigners? I saw myself for what I was, a visitor and a guest in an old, extraordinary country, and still wished Stefan had addressed that man in a kinder way.

I finished my coffee and got up to pour myself another cup. I attempted to swirl the cream as the bearer had done, but it wasn't working for me and I stirred the cream in, the only way I knew.

I returned to my seat by the window and pulled out the travel guide Maurice had given me. With nothing else to do, this was a good time to gather information. The booklet confirmed some of the things I had read in Paris during my weeks of research at the library. It said, for instance, that over centuries, the population of northern India, either through commerce or through war, had intermingled with Persians, Afghans and Mongols, and that in 327 BC, Alexander the Great's plans of conquest were foiled by powerful Indian monarchs who repelled his attacks with an army of caparisoned war elephants. I closed my eyes and tried to imagine that battlefield but couldn't. It was too extraordinary. I went back to Maurice's travel guide.

Apparently, the northern invaders failed in their repeated attempts to conquer southern India. As a result, the south is still inhabited by Dravidians, the Indian continent's original race,. Their language, Tamil, bore no resemblance to Sanskrit, Arabic, or the many related languages spoken in the north. Similarly, their literature, poetry, dance, and music, had been preserved and jealously guarded from impurities by Brahmins—the priests' caste. In many ways, southern Indians considered themselves the true heirs and guardians of the old culture. I was glad to be heading to the heart of it. Glad, and terribly curious.

I lay the book down on my knees and looked out as the train pulled into a large station. In spite of the closed window, I could hear the loud metal-on-metal sound of the brakes grabbing the rails as the train slowly screeched to a stop. When it finally did, I saw we were in Guntakal, the station's name written both in English and in a curli-cued script I couldn't identify. Vendors ran along the length of the train raising cool drink bottles and food items to the windows, and I was tempted to open ours, but Stefan shook his head "no" to stop me. He got up behind me, wrapped his arms around my waist, and looked over my shoulder. "When I rode my first train in India, I was as curious as you are. Everything is so new and exciting. But, trust me, you don't want to open that window. It's hot and dusty out there, and you'd be wasting our wonderful A/C."

"Can we at least go out on the platform to look around and grab a snack?" I asked.

"Not worth it," he said. "You don't want any of that food anyway. It's been exposed to flies and who knows what. And this is an express train. It's a short stop."

I put my forehead against the glass and looked at the people rush-ing back and forth on the platform. So many hues and shades of skin. I couldn't see any women. Apparently, they'd remained on the train. That left men buying food items wrapped in leaves, or posting letters in a large red mailbox. Watching them, I noticed some wore khaki shorts, but no one donned a western suit. The tall and fair-skinned men often wore fat turbans, like the maître d' from the dining car. Northerners? They moved around with authority and purpose. Other male passengers donned long white dhotis and kurtas. Most of the vendors running on the platform were Dravidians and wore their dhotis wrapped around their legs like twisted shorts, a local fashion maybe. I was struck by

25

how thin and dark-skinned some of them were.

Stefan had been right about this being a short stop. Soon a series of loud whistles sent the passengers scrambling back to their compartments as the train shook on its rails, and the powerful locomotive huffed and puffed and started to pull forward. I turned my back to the window and leaned on it to read. When I looked out again, I realized that we had descended from some central plateau and were now riding through lush green fields crisscrossed by a network of irrigation canals whose surfaces shone like silver as the sun rose in the sky.

I couldn't believe how much the scenery had changed since yesterday. The dusty villages and hard-beaten dirt roads had been left behind. Every so often, we would come across a primitive kind of merry-go-round pushed by a bull or a water buffalo. From what I could see from the train, the animal was harnessed to a beam rigged to a vertical pole secured in a well. Children armed with sticks prodded the beast to keep it walking around the well's orifice, as small containers of water rose and emptied out into a network of narrow waterways feeding irrigation ditches. It was an ingenious system, probably as old as the rice fields I was looking at, but I was shocked when I spotted a couple of children manning one of these contraptions. My heart went out to them, and a million questions assailed me. How old were they? How long had they been at it? Had their water buffalo died? Were the villagers too poor to replace it? How heavy and hard to push was that beam? How long would the children be able to lean their slender bodies into it, and what would happen when the sun rose to its zenith and heat fell on their skinny backs like a hammer?

Bent low in the wet furrows, men and women labored in the rice fields. As I'd noted yesterday, the dark figures wearing loincloths and cheap head-wraps were men. The vivid bursts of color were women. Swaying palm trees, many stories high, towered over clusters of huts in an otherwise flat landscape.

"We'll be in Madras around four," said Stefan. He put his book down, stood up, and did a few yoga stretches. For the first time since we'd left, I sensed excitement in his voice. "We still have a lot of time but better to take a shower now, while there is still water."

CHAPTER FOUR

ARRIVAL IN MADRAS

We reached Madras by five that afternoon. Our trip had taken twenty-nine hours. The accumulated heat of the day was oppressive on the covered platform as we stepped off the train. All at once, we found ourselves surrounded by an army of beggars. They were Harijans, those untouchables Stefan had told me about, born into poverty and made impure by their menial occupations. According to Maurice, whose educated opinion I trusted, it was to raise these millions of untouchables out of poverty that Gandhi had wrestled India free from the British Raj. Not that the British treated them worse than Indians themselves did. Apparently, the two-thousand-year-old prejudice the higher caste Indians bestowed on Harijans was still firmly in place.

An army of small, dark, snot-covered faces overtook me in well-rehearsed supplication. Five-year-old children in rags carried toddlers almost as big as they were on their hips or backs. The ones closest to me grabbed at my arms and clung to my clothes. Rubbing their malnourished stomachs with one hand, they stretched their free hands out for money, "Baksheesh Ma! No papa, no mama! *Rumba pasikerde Ma!*

Very, very hungry!" I was surprised they knew some English.

Occupied with our luggage, Stefan had left it to me to rid myself of the children. A short distance away, I spotted a few tattered women and men keeping an eye on the campaign of their little soldiers. I wasn't making much headway in keeping the aggressive tykes at arm's length when, all of a sudden, they all fell back in unison and scurried away. A policeman was approaching. In the open palm of his left hand, he purposefully bounced the riot stick he carried. A mixture of grimness and apology was written all over his face.

"Very sorry Mum, those buggers are a nuisance. You better check your belongings. They are excellent pickpockets!"

I thanked him and told him I was fine even though I'd just discovered that the five-franc coin I liked to finger in my pocket was gone. What was I going to do, set a policeman loose on children? They were long gone anyway. One more lesson learned, and this without any help from Stefan.

I kept one hand on our small stack of luggage, Stefan's mostly, because, due to a train strike in France, my trunk, shipped from Paris a week before my departure, hadn't arrived at the ship on time to travel with me. I had been promised that it would be delivered in Bombay on the next Messageries Maritimes ship out of Marseille. From there, I guessed, it would have to be sent to Madras on the very same train we had just disembarked from. I was still upset and sad at the thought that all the favorite books, clothes, and beloved objects I had chosen to accompany me to India where in that trunk. After traveling alone in cargo and going through customs, what condition would they arrive in?

A few feet away, a dozen porters, fighting for a chance to earn a few rupees, fought for the bags as they lay siege to Stefan. He suddenly raised clenched fists above his head and silenced them all with an angry shout of dismissal. His violent outburst made me shudder, as images of my stepfather coming home drunk flashed through my mind. Violence unnerved me, and loud outbursts easily brought tears to my eyes. I recoiled from him.

From the way Stefan acted, one could tell this wasn't the first time he behaved as a Sahib, a white man in a position of power, and I recalled him telling me that he had lived in Tanganyika for several years. Stefan spoke fondly of Africa. The way he had treated these porters just now made me wonder if he was regressing into the mindset of the rich colonials he may have met there.

As if to justify himself, Stefan turned to me. "These porters would rather work for us because Indian patrons will make them carry loads of baggage for a few cents. They get less work and more money from foreigners, but, as you can see, they are a nuisance and need to be put in their place." I guessed he knew what he was doing. I didn't have to like it.

He waved to a tidy old man who had kept clear of the fray. Resentfully, the disgruntled porters backed off. They pointedly ignored the scores of heavily laden Indian families, and actively resumed looking for disembarking foreigners.

After our porter securely balanced our bags on his head, we exited the station. On either side of the large door, the imposing red building spread for several hundred feet. I could see now that it was a grand train station reflecting the British love of railways.

Cabs were waiting at the curb, and in spite of the loud objections raised by the first three drivers, Stefan picked a newer, cleaner car that was fourth in line. I hesitated and looked questioningly at him. "Are you sure? It's not really fair…"

"Look," Stefan snapped, "by Indian standards we are rich, and they expect us to behave like rich people. So, stop worrying about their problems and get in the car. Your days as a professional proletarian are over. You're upper class here, so, act like it."

That stung! I started to enter the taxi but stopped and turned around to face him. I was angry. "*S'il te plait,* do us both a favor. Don't use that tone of voice on me ever again!"

I saw color rise on his cheeks under his tan before I turned my back on him and got into the cab. I guess he wasn't used to people snapping back at him. I felt a spark of satisfaction. This is how my mother would have reacted to his statement, and I was glad to discover a little bit of her in me. I needed it today. I understood that he might be tired, and hot, and preoccupied with getting us and our luggage on our way, but more than his words, it was his attitude that had unsettled me. I shrank back into the far corner of the backseat. I was trying to figure out how the son of a Polish immigrant, whose brother worked in a coal mine, had boarded a plane in Paris and landed as a privileged upper-class man in India.

And what about myself? Would that be me in a year? How would this country change me? Bombay had been exotic but somewhat familiar as any big city might be, and the hospitality of Stefan's friends there had been reassuring. Here I felt exposed and alone. Would Madras put in question who I was, and what my values in life were and would be? What did 'upper class' mean? By the same token, what did 'proletarian' really mean?

Right now, I was as confused about myself as I was about the attitude of the friend and lover I remembered from Paris. He had made some rather insensitive remarks since we were married. Apparently, his new circumstances had done nothing to keep his ego in check. Still, I longed to make things right between us. I hadn't come all the way from France to fight with him, but I wouldn't talk to him without an apology for his outburst.

With my back to him, I lowered the cab window to get some fresh air. The tall brick building that might have marked the center of town was now behind us. The sidewalks here were lined with slipshod bungalows converted into busy eateries and small businesses. Short, dark people milled around and crouched comfortably in front of shabby huts that appeared to serve both as living quarters and stores. Popular music blasted from loudspeakers precariously perched on roofs while, overhead, a heavy web of electric wires hung along and across the narrow streets.

Was this what Madras was like? I was getting more curious by the minute to find out why, of all the towns in India, Stefan had elected to live here. But my questions would have to wait. Ensconced in the back seat of the taxi, I continued to ignore him in spite of his half-hearted attempts at conversation.

The heat was overwhelming, and the lowered window gave me no relief. Gasoline fumes rising from the heated asphalt filled my nose and stung my eyes, forcing me to roll my window back up. The road was so congested that it forced the taxi to a complete stop. Our driver swore and thrust his thin body through his open window in order to pump an old-fashioned car horn mounted on the cab's fender. All the while, searching for an opening in the gridlock, he kept turning the steering wheel with the palm of his right hand. But his honking and expletive-filled exhortations had no effect on the people and vehicles he was trying to push out of his way. Though his insults and body language were foreign, I silently awarded him an honorary French driver title, for, like him, the French were known for their rude language when they drove.

We lurched along through fits and starts, as our driver managed to squeeze the cab into the smallest traffic gap, until finally, the cab emerged onto a wide plaza. I gaped at the sight of a massive structure, a stone temple so tall and ornate that it dwarfed every form of human habitat around it. I couldn't believe I had failed to catch a glimpse of it over the rooftops earlier. I leaned forward and tapped the driver's shoulder. "Stop the cab!"

The man slowed down, let the car idle in the middle of the paved plaza, and, eyebrows raised, turned toward Stefan. I started to open my door, but Stefan held me back.

"Wait!"

"Let's stop for a few minutes, please," I begged. "What's the name of this temple? I've never seen anything like it." Never mind his apologies. Whatever it was that had made me mad at him earlier was of little importance in the presence of the breathtaking edifice.

"That's Mylapore Temple. But listen, I have to make arrangements for our accommodations right away. That takes priority. We can always come back tomorrow."

Reluctantly I pulled the door of the taxi closed.

"Chalo! Go!" said Stefan to the driver.

The driver put the car in gear, and we started moving again. I craned my neck through the open window to take in the amazing sight. Too large for my field of vision, a corner of it rose in a sweeping series of ornate tiers that culminated in a flat golden ledge decorated with a row of spiky globes. It was easy to imagine that, like our French castles and cathedrals, this temple had been the safe haven where panicked villagers came for protection during raids from neighboring kingdoms. Now, the perimeter walls were long gone, leaving the colossal temple to sit alone.

What struck me the most in that first instant was the balance, the absolute mathematical perfection those ancient architects had achieved. I was awed. I pinched myself. What if I were to blink and find myself back in Paris? I turned to Stefan. He was the reason I was here. He was the one who had challenged me out of my Parisian nest and kept the door open for me to come explore the world with him. Forgetting his earlier rebuff, I threw my arms around his neck and kissed him. I had never loved him so much.

For a second or two, I thought he might return the kiss, but, awkwardly, he disengaged himself and raised an eyebrow in the direction of the driver. "No public displays, okay?" but there was a twinkle of acknowledgment in his eyes. I think he was relieved I was no longer mad at him.

I didn't care what the taxi driver might think. It was difficult to remember rules like that in a place like this. As if reading my thoughts, Stefan leaned over the front seat and gave the man new instructions. "I changed my mind. I want you to go around the Mylapore temple a couple of times, alright?"

"Changed your mind? A couple of times? Right, Sir. A couple of times."

"My wife is new here, so drive slowly so she can have a good look."

My wife is new... Was he showing me off or apologizing for my bad manners? All the same, it was the first time I'd heard him say those words, and it sounded sweet to my ears, even if a tad proprietary. I guessed I would get used to it. But more importantly, we were going to drive around the temple.

The driver stared at me in his rear-view mirror. "Your wife, new, new here? Right Sir, I drive slowly, slowly…"

Stefan leaned back in the seat and gave him further instructions. "Afterward, take the bridge over to Adyar, alright?"

"To Adyar! Right Sir, I know that bridge. But first, I go around twice, right?"

"Right."

Turning my head sideways, so the driver couldn't read my lips, I whispered to Stefan, "Why is he repeating everything twice?"

Stefan shrugged. "That's just the way they speak."

The cab started moving again, and we came in sight of the large rectangular wading pool fronting the temple. It was rimmed by a series of steep stone steps descending to the water and swarmed with more people than I could count.

Hip-deep in water, men with shaved heads splashed water over themselves with cupped hands. Unfazed by the crowd around them, they prayed aloud. They wore nothing more than a loincloth and a white thread stretched across their bared chests. Shrieking children ran, skipped, and splashed around them, unsupervised. To one side, a group of chatting women kept an eye on a giant patchwork quilt of saris they had laid to dry, end-to-end, across a section of clean steps.

The lone figure of a wild-looking man drew my eyes. He was leaning on the wall supporting the temple door and was standing on one leg. His other leg was folded against his thigh in a standing lotus posture. He was taller than anyone around and appeared frozen in meditation. His dark body, thickly smeared with gray ashes, was partly hidden by a mane of matted hair that weighed like heavy ropes upon his nakedness. With one hand, he held a gnarled staff topped with saffron- colored shreds of cloth and short strands of dry vine. His other hand stood palm up, his forefinger touching his thumb. Sticks of incense had been lit in front of him and a thin whiff of musk drifted through the car windows as we crawled past him. He suddenly opened his eyes and broke into a loud rhythmical chant that sent chills down my spine and brought goose flesh to my arms.

"Who is that man?" I asked. "What is he chanting? Is he angry with us for disturbing him?"

"He's a *sadhu*, a holy man," said Stefan, following my gaze. "He doesn't care about people. The ashes on his body indicate he's a *Siva* devotee. That's who he is praying to."

Under the greying late afternoon sky, the temple was buzzing with sacred energy. It was a tableau in motion, a choreographed dance involving the sky, the water, the crowd, and one holy man. I was entranced. I felt in the presence of deities, something, someone bigger than me. Suddenly feeling lost and small, I grabbed Stefan's hand resting next to me on the car seat and leaned against the reassuring warmth of his body.

CHAPTER FIVE

THE THEOSOPHICAL SOCIETY

My first week in Madras was an extended blur of introductions to Stefan's many Indian and foreign friends, some from Madras University, others from the Theosophical Society where we were staying. Non-theosophists weren't, as a rule, allowed to live on this groomed and gated campus, but an exception had been made for Stefan because of his studies in Indian philosophy. The fact that he had secured a letter of introduction from an exiled Polish minister in Paris and that our Bombay hosts were old friends of the Theosophical Society's president, also helped. I was not surprised. Cutting through red tape was a gift Stefan possessed and that I admired.

After six months living there, he seemed to belong. He had adapted easily to the no-meat, no-alcohol, and no-smoking tenets rigorously upheld on campus, and I soon discovered that, though all his classes took place at Madras University, and none were tied to theosophy, he was at ease rubbing elbows with the elderly theosophists who had come from all over the world seeking the wisdom of esoteric masters and dead messiahs.

Compared to what I had seen of Madras so far, the beauty of the T.S. grounds was enchanting. It claimed a famous banyan tree whose giant girth and range I could never have imagined until I stood within its labyrinthine shade. The vines hanging from its branches had generated hundreds of new trunks, and it now was a forest more than a tree. It covered the quarter of a square mile and was so unique that a plaque stating it was 450 years old had been dedicated to it. Compared to it, the dates-yielding palms looked spindly against the cloudless sky. On the ground, the air was perfumed by the exotic flowers that bordered a web of meandering paths linking small temples and lotus ponds. Walking the grounds, I wondered if I had landed in the Garden of Eden. But, based on the photographs and rare movies I had seen about India, it was nothing like I had envisioned. I had imagined myself living in a hut, a nice hut, but a hut, all the same, elbowing a colorful sea of humanity, the neighborhood redolent with the smells of jasmine and spices, resounding with strange languages and the slippery contour of eastern music. Instead, I found myself in a studious, almost monastic campus.

We were staying in Stefan's two-room studio on the second floor of the guesthouse, but he had already put in a request for a larger apartment until a separate house became available. Compared to the cramped Parisian hotel room I'd lived in, the guesthouse felt like a seaside resort. It was a long and narrow three-story colonial structure painted white to deflect the heat and had tall, shaded verandahs supported by slender columns that ran the length of each floor. The floor-to-ceiling shutters and doors were a glossy forest green and still smelled of fresh paint. On the ground floor, a large dining room overlooked a wide estuary that sheltered small sandy islands, beyond which the Indian Ocean took on pastel hues at sunrise.

Stefan was annoyed that the rooms weren't air-conditioned, but I didn't miss it and quite enjoyed the gentle air stirred by the long-bladed wooden fans outfitting the ceiling.

"No cooking allowed in the rooms," Stefan had warned me on arrival. "We'll have to eat downstairs in the guest dining room until we get our own place." That suited me just fine. One thing my mother hadn't been able to teach me was cooking. How could she when we'd never had a proper kitchen? Moreover, I hadn't come all the way to India to play house and cook. What I really looked forward to was to visit the dance school as soon as possible, but its director being out of town, I would have to wait until she returned.

Meanwhile, I had no choice but to take it one day at a time as I got accustomed to my new life, the new climate, the new food, and the new people. One thing I couldn't help being curious about were all the older folks around the dining room table. "What are these people really doing here?" I asked Stefan over sticky porridge one morning. I hated their breakfast and would have died for a fresh croissant. "What do they hope to find?"

"The same as me. Realization, nirvana, something like that."

"And can these answers be found in theosophy?"

Stefan took a long sip of tea before putting on his professorial hat. "The word theosophy is derived from Greek. 'Theos' for divinity, and 'Sophia' for wisdom. Its goal was to form a universal brotherhood without distinction of race, creed, sex, caste, or color."

"A worthy goal," I said. There was nothing wrong with that.

"They encourage the study of comparative religion, philosophy, and science," continued Stefan.

"How do you know all this? I thought you didn't study theosophy."

"Well, I went to a few lectures, just to see what they were all about. Among other things, they investigate the powers latent in man. At least, these were the goals of Madame Blavatsky, theosophy's key founder."

"And when was that?" I asked.

"In 1889, I believe."

"That long ago, eh?"

It sounded erudite, but kind of passé and a little outlandish, so I kept my opinion to myself. Personally, I was more interested in studying tangible subjects like people, architecture, art and dance, rather than burying myself in abstract concepts put forth by long-dead Russians or whatever that Blavatsky woman was.

Sensing my reservations, Stefan changed the subject. "As far as you and I are concerned," he continued, "we can live here and pursue our own studies without getting involved in theirs. I plan to rent a small house I have discovered by the beach. It is modest but quite roomy. We'll even have separate studies." He beamed an impish grin at me. In moments like this I wanted to lean over the table and kiss the grin off his face, but that was a no-no at this breakfast table, and I had better behave.

When the distraction faded, the full meaning of his words sank in. My own study? I had spent my whole life sharing space with others. As a child, I had slept in my grandfather's living room and later in my parents' dining room. My own study? Me, who for the past five years had shared a bed with my mother? I had no desire or need for privacy. But he obviously did, for he was annoyed with my moving his books when I sat at his desk to write letters, and hated it when I touched his papers or borrowed his pens.

If Stefan's plan worked, it would be the first time I lived in a house, and the sudden thought of living in a place big enough to afford him his cherished privacy felt cold and foreign to me. I had been looking forward to nesting with him, entwined like kittens asleep in a drawer, and the idea of spending time in separate rooms felt like punishment more than comfort. It was not something I desired, but I would try it if it made him happy. I might even find that I liked having my own study.

I tried to imagine what a study would look like, but all I could think about was the bedroom. I would make it comfortable and intimate with a real bed. No more narrow Indian cots. I would buy a wide and thick mattress and many pillows.

I'd been aimlessly stirring at my porridge, but now, fortified by bedroom imaginings, I lifted my face to him, made eye contact and smiled. "That's great. When can we move in?"

"The house hasn't been occupied in years. It's in pretty bad shape and until it is cleaned, repaired, and repainted we'll have to stay here. Probably two or three months more," he added as we walked back to our room.

From the door of the guesthouse restaurant where we had just had breakfast, I watched Stefan stoop to tie the right leg of his pants with a rubber band and ride away on an old black Schwinn bicycle. He looked smart and tanned in a pair of white pants and short-sleeve shirt open at the neck.

It was two weeks to the day since I'd arrived in India, and it already felt like months rather than weeks. I had a lot of time on my hands and wished Stefan could spend more time with me. There was so much to explore in the city and its surroundings, but he attended daily classes at the University and admonished me to be patient. He promised we would soon go on a significant sightseeing trip together. So I waited.

The morning was mine. I went upstairs to our room, picked up *La Peste*—The Plague—by Albert Camus, the novel I had brought from home, and settled into one of the canvas chaises longues abandoned on the shady verandah fronting our studio apartment. A welcome sea breeze played in my hair and dried the film of sweat covering my body, but the skin on my face was tight. I'd have to start using a protective lotion. The tan I had acquired on the ship would not protect me from the fierce Madrasi sun.

I found my bookmark in the paperback and was surprised to realize that I hadn't read a line since I left the ship. It was a poignant story, but it held no interest for me right now. My eyes drifted to the page but glossed over the words. I fell into daydreaming and was startled when a red-faced, middle-aged man stuffed into a form-fitting safari outfit stopped by my chair and extended his hand.

"Milt Bauer, nice to meet you." He had a thick accent. Not British or American. Australian maybe. "I'm your left door neighbor," he said, pointing to his door.

I shook his hand, which was moist and beefy.

"Minouche."

"You must be Stefan's pretty bride. Welcome! Welcome! We would have met earlier, but, just between you and me," at this, he lowered his voice, "I spend a lot of time playing poker with me mates at the British Club." He raised an eyebrow and nodded conspiratorially, letting me know that gambling wasn't tolerated on the premises. I wasn't surprised, and even felt a surge of sympathy for this rogue theosophist whose clothes smelled of cigar. His flaws gave me hope I might meet more people like him in this apparently perfect world.

He pulled a nearby chair, sat next to me, and went on talking as if we had been friends for years. His thick accent made him hard to understand, and I leaned forward to catch his words.

"Do you know the island in front of us is a wild bird sanctuary?" he asked, passing me the binoculars he carried around his neck. "Take a look and tell me what you see."

Surveying the lowlands that spread out like fingers at the mouth of the Adyar river estuary, I brought into focus a group of tall birds wading in the shallows of a small promontory. They stood still, perched on one leg, the other leg tucked under their vivid pink bodies. The only moving pieces were their long necks and beaks that darted in the water and came out with a flash of silver when they caught small fish.

"Oooh!" I murmured, delighted. "What birds are these?"

"Pink flamingoes," he said. "Aren't they beautiful? Every year they show up here and stay for a few months. Then they're gone."

Fascinated by the phlegmatic one-legged creatures, I was watching their stilted movements, when a sharp report rattled the air. I flinched and nearly fell off my chair, but the loud noise that had startled me had also spooked the birds. They sprung up and rose on the wind as one, circling over their small island, their long wings aflame with sunlight.

"Nothing to worry about, lovey. That will be the exhaust of some old truck crossing the Adyar bridge," said my self-appointed new friend. "Golly! I'd love to stay and chat, but I've got to run to a lecture I signed up for." He mumbled an apology and stood up. "Jolly good, then! Just hang me glasses on me doorknob when you're finished." That settled he strode off, leaving me to my birdwatching.

To my right, the Indian Ocean had retreated from a flat sandy beach and lulled benignly behind low sandbars, waiting for the tide to return. To my left, the Adyar bridge we had crossed by taxi on our way in from the train station spanned the river by way of a few high-reaching arches. Behind me, visible through the back window of our room, stood an impressive building housing the Theosophical Society Library. My new world.

I soon tired of lifting the heavy binoculars and lay back in the chaise longue. There was so much to see without them. I watched the flight of unknown birds sharing the island with the flamingoes until a large Monarch butterfly fluttered on my foot, displaying the kite-like design of its orange and black wings. Above me, racing inland, white clouds chased by some atmospheric winds morphed into phantasmagoric figures. I sighed. This campus was idyllic, and the Indian residents were lovely, but the foreign contingent was far from being my world. In my eyes they were a weird bunch, be they European, American, Australian, or New Zealanders. Most were older women sporting perfect porcelain smiles and short white hair touched with blue rinse. There was one, however, that fascinated me. She'd been born in Poland, but went by Umadevi, an Indian name. Though she was in her seventies, she stood tall and erect in a plain white cotton sari and wore her naturally gray hair braided and wrapped around her head like I wore mine when I was a child. Stefan had told me that she'd lived in the T.S. for decades and had a reputation for being eccentric, but I preferred to think of her as a youthful and free spirit. Having accepted an invitation to have tea with her in the cottage where she lived, I decided to cultivate her friendship. She was so full of worthwhile advice and wonderful stories.

I still hoped to run across people my own age, but Theosophy didn't seem to attract young people. Maybe the residents came here after they were through raising their families. Maybe they came to learn how to die properly and continue in the afterlife? It made sense in a morbid sort of way.

I had a bit of a problem understanding some of them. My ear for English was far from trained, and it was hard to deal with all the different English dialects spoken around me. I learned to recognize the New Zealanders right away because their speech pattern was heavy and monotonous. They appeared to push all their words with equal breath, like toothpaste out of a tube. I took to smiling and nodding pleasantly when I ran into them, letting their featureless dialogue gush over my head.

Occasionally I wondered what they were saying. There was no way to be sure, but upon reading their twinkling eyes, I became an expert at making up our imaginary dialogues.

"So nice to meet a beautiful young girl like you, dear."

All I had to do was smile and nod.

"And young Stefan seems sooo happy to have you here with him!"

Smile again, stretch discreetly to hide a yawn, nod.

"It gets kind of lonely here for a young man, if you know what

I mean."

Conspiratorial wink. Cough. Nod. Repeat.

I liked the Australian group better than the rest. They were more energetic and easier to understand, but they were a loud bunch, barely tolerated by the British residents, who preferred to engage in hushed conversations, something they equated with being civilized.

Overall, I was wary around these older folks, even the nice ones. Only weeks ago, my friends and I would have sworn that anyone above 25 was not to be trusted. At 24, Stefan had barely escaped our critical cut-off. I missed my best friend Brigitte and the gang so much! What would they think if they saw me fraternizing with these antediluvians?

To quell my impatience for contact with the dance school, and with Stefan admonishing me not to go to town alone, I spent time exploring the T.S. campus. It was crisscrossed with shady gravel paths, but few people walked them. This conspicuous lack of crowds felt unnatural to me. During my incursions in the Bombay bazaar district, and in my most recent drive around the massive Mylapore Temple, I had observed more people per square meter than in most European countries I'd visited.

Finally unable to resist the temptation, and in spite of Stefan's warnings, I walked to the T.S. gate, found a taxi, and had it drop me off in sight of the temple that had so fascinated me.

Mylapore was what I had missed inside the gates of the TS campus. Here, India was a sea of bodies adorned with gold and silver, perfumed with flower garlands, clad in cotton or silk, or naked but for a smear of holy ashes. I stood at the edge of the wading pool fronting the temple. I could feel the sun beating on my head and longed to meld into the crowd, descend into the cool water, wash off my alienness, be one of them… But I hesitated. Was a foreigner allowed to bathe here? Women looked at me and smiled encouragingly, their saris hiked high above their knees as they descended the steps into the water. Aware of the nakedness of my bare legs under my layered petticoat and skirt, I didn't dare immerse myself inside the walled-in waters of this sacred place.

Around me, the plaza was saturated with music. Punctuated with drums and oboes, a procession was approaching. Another funeral maybe? Ever-present film music blasted from loudspeakers mounted on trucks and storefronts. The confluent river of songs blending and mixing into one another flowed as a primeval symphony that made me feel alive. This was the India I had come to explore.

After returning from my excursion to the Mylapore Temple, the T.S. campus felt even less Indian to me. It was too green, too groomed, too hushed with the seriousness of its hallowed halls. Part of me liked the studious atmosphere, the respect and friendliness the older residents showed me, but another part of me felt cheated of the real India that lay beyond those guarded gates. And I wanted friends. I had befriended Umadevi, the old and eccentric Polish lady who lived by herself in a tiny bungalow hidden into a thicket of giant rhododendrons, but I needed more. I needed the company of young people to talk to, laugh with and dream with about impossible things just for the hell of it. Discovery. Exuberance. Wasn't it what people my age lived for the world over? Why couldn't Stefan see this? What could I do or say to convince him that loving him didn't mean I agreed to spend all my time inside these gates?

So, the following Saturday morning, when Stefan slipped on the sandals he kept by the front door and invited me to accompany him for another walk through the T.S. campus to photograph some of its founders' mausoleums and attend a free lecture on Annie Besant in the TS library, frustration dug its nasty nails into my stomach. I closed the book I was reading and banged it so hard on a nearby coffee table that, to my embarrassment, my cup of coffee skidded and bounced on the woven coconut floor mat, spilling its content without breaking. Grateful the cup was intact, I picked it up and put it carefully down on the low table. It gave me time to gather my thoughts. I had to get it right to let him know what had made me angry.

I got up, wrapped my arms around his waist, and nuzzled his collar bone. "I'm not interested in spending a morning dedicated to dead theosophists. It's Saturday, and you are free. Can we go to town instead and meet normal people? Please?"

Startled by my reaction, Stefan slithered out of my embrace and held me at arms' length to stare at my face. "What do you mean by 'normal' people?" He looked truly puzzled.

"People our age, who like to go to the movies, the theater if there are any here, restaurants. I'd love a juicy steak and fries once in a while."

"You'd better forego your fantasies," said Stefan, a stern expression on his handsome face. He fingered a loose strand of hair from my face, pushed it behind my ear, and led me to the sofa where he sat down next to me to talk. "Have you forgotten the promise you made in exchange for living here with me? No animal flesh, no drinking, no smoking?"

Cupping my chin, he lifted my face so he could look into my eyes. "Let me tell you about meat. Butchering in India is not a precise science and is far from safe. The sooner you embrace vegetarianism, the better, because not only is it a condition for our stay here, but it will save you from becoming ill."

"I can't care less about smoking and drinking. I never smoked, and you know I loathe alcohol, but entirely giving up meat is a little drastic, don't you think? And do the T.S. rules apply when we go out? The single window opening on the long verandah bordering the guest quarters was wide openaa and I was talking too loudly. Stefan motioned for me to pipe down.

"You can look forward to eating fish or chicken when we travel," he said in a hushed voice. "But while in Madras, it would be rather embarrassing to get caught eating beef." He made a funny face and got a smile out of me.

He was probably right, but I wasn't finished. Shaking my hair down to hide the tears swelling behind my eyelids, I said, "The days are so long when you're gone; the silence is driving me crazy. What about getting a record player and some records? Can we at least have a radio? That's allowed, isn't it? I miss music so much."

Stefan pulled my head onto his shoulder and kissed the top of my hair. "Many people here meditate, and music might disturb them, but we will get both when we move to our house, I promise." He pushed my hair away from my face and, with the side of his hand, dried the tears that had rolled down my cheek.

Deflated, I let out a long sigh. I had never missed Maman and Brigitte so much and would have given anything to run into any of my old friends, even the ones I didn't much like. Couldn't he see how lonely I was? "And then there is the grant," I said, in a small voice. "I took your advice and notified the Paderewski Foundation that I had made it to India on my own, and that we were now married. I also made sure they knew that your address in Madras was now my address, but they haven't acknowledged my letter. Until I find out what they decide, I don't know what to tell the dance school. The wait is killing me."

Stefan took my hands in his. "I understand your frustration, but we'll find a way to get you into that school with, or without the grant, as soon as the director is back in town. And once you're enrolled there, you'll make lots of new friends. I bet that in a few weeks, you'll be as busy as I am with classes." The morning that had been grey and foggy suddenly lit up as a burst of sunlight entered the window. Stefan smiled at me reassuringly and said, "Concerning the campus rules, never forget that we are allowed to live here as a favor. You may not realize it, but it's the best environment to study, remain healthy and get our degrees. Lots of foreigners end up sick in India."

I couldn't help feeling a tinge of resentment about his having the last word. I pulled away, got up, and sat on the windowsill with the sun warming my back. "I know that you are right, and I know we are lucky to live here. It's just that I miss my friends. I miss my independence. Coming and going as I want. Eating what I want. I love you so much, and wanted so much to be here with you, but sometimes, this place makes me feel like I joined a monastery!"

"What would you know about monasteries?" he teased. He seemed relieved to change the subject.

"Not much, except that they are a sort of retreat. A place where people go to escape the chaos and responsibilities of civilian life. I don't want to live in a retreat. For some people retreats may be a means to look within themselves in stillness and silence, but I'm only nineteen. I want to swim in the stream of life. Not stand by it."

CHAPTER SIX

GRANT NEWS

Standing under the shower, I reflected that a month ago, as I traveled to India in a third-class cabin with three other women, I could only dream of a shower, because the third class had no water to spare for such luxury. I examined the spartan shower room around me. It lacked the chrome and custom implements our hosts in Bombay had been so proud of. All this shower offered was a concrete cube with a basic waterspout and a hole in the floor to drain the soapy water. But washing my hair and rinsing the night sweat covering my body was all the luxury I needed. It felt wonderful. I wrapped a short towel around my waist. Outside, I could hear some crows cawing behind the kitchen of the guesthouse where the cooks often left scraps of food for them. I stepped into the bedroom and looked outside the window. The sky was a solid blue. Not a cloud in sight. Stefan and I had talked about going to the beach today, early, before the sun got too high in the sky. I was pulling a comb through my hair and winced when it ran into a tangled knot. "Coming to breakfast?" I called to Stefan, as I slipped on one of the summer dresses he'd had a tailor make for me in Bombay.

After a few seconds he answered from the next room where he was already sitting with a book. He sounded tired. "You go ahead. I woke up with a bit of a migraine and just took my meds to derail it. My stomach doesn't feel good either. I think I'll fast today."

I made an effort to sound concerned, but I hated his fasting ritual. Maybe it was because my stomach was so strong; I could probably eat dirt and ask for seconds. Stefan, on the other hand, was prone to migraines and had a fragile digestive system. I had used his precarious health to enroll Viktor's support when applying for my grant. And, true to my word, on getting here I'd done my best to monitor Stefan's health, but it was difficult because he was constantly experimenting with fasting and new diets. I didn't mind the new diets. What annoyed me was that fasting led him to think of himself as a better, purer person.

"I understand, but can we go to the beach when you feel better?" I asked, although I already suspected his answer.

"Not today, I'm afraid. I think I'll stay home and read."

I sighed, loud enough to be heard, let myself out, and closed the door behind me. It wasn't the first time I had gone alone to the dining room. Descending the wide staircase, I reflected how very Victorian the lobby was, with its lush velvet drapes framing the tall windows, the wood-paneled walls, the damasked bow-legged settees and deep, matching armchairs. Where did this antiquated furniture come from? In my eyes, it was out of place in Madras and would have been more suited to an old-fashioned bed-and-breakfast in England or Scotland. Not that I had ever stayed in a real bed-and-breakfast during my hitch-hiking days. I had only stayed in youth hostels, and those were more like school dorms than tourist inns.

I was about to enter the dining room when the concierge hailed me. He was young and handsome and wore a well-cut western suit. His manner, more than his burnished copper complexion, suggested he was of mixed blood. An Anglo-Indian, as people called them here.

"A letter for you, Miss," he said cheerfully in a British accented voice. He knew I was a married woman, but he made a point to always call me "Miss." With the middle finger of his right hand, he pushed back the gold-framed reading glasses he wore and proceeded to pat his glossy black hair, combed back with brilliantine like an old-style movie star.

The letter lay on a gilded platter in the middle of the reception desk. The slanted morning sun held it in its beam like a spotlight, before flowing, like gold dust, off the heavy mahogany desk.

I stared at the letter uncertainly and wondered why it was lying on the desk and not in the slot reserved for Mr. & Mrs. Polszewski, my last name now.

I still had mixed feelings about using Stefan's family name. Last names were a complicated thing for women, especially for me. Born out of wedlock, I had never shared my biological father's name, and after my mother's disastrous marriage, I so abhorred the use of my stepfather's name that, amongst my friends and unless a last name was absolutely necessary, I identified only with my first name. I was Minouche. Only Minouche. And now Minouche Polszewski? I wasn't the only one who needed time to get used to it. Most people couldn't even pronounce it.

The concierge's lips stretched into a wide smile. "I wanted to make sure you got that letter as soon as you came down."

"It was so very thoughtful of you," I said, flashing a warm smile at him. "News from home means a lot to me."

He lowered his pomaded head and busied himself with some of the paperwork lying on the desk. Noticing his unease, I took the envelope and entered the dining room. Had I acted too forward and embarrassed him, or had there been a hint of flirtation in the air? I couldn't tell. I couldn't read the signs and would have to hone my skills on how to interact with the men around here.

The envelope was oversized and very white, and it wasn't from home. It felt heavy in my hand. The frontal view of an eagle with spread wings and powerful talons was embossed in the top left corner. The eagle looked over its right shoulder, and its beak seemed to point to the name of the sender embossed under it: The Paderewski Foundation of New York.

My heart skipped a beat, and bile rose in my throat. What had I been thinking when I had fraudulently replaced my unknown grandfather with a famous Polish musician to get a shot at obtaining a grant? A grant I had to have, having learned from my mother that, to remain independent, I couldn't afford to be anyone's charge. I'd been desperate, but in my quest to being self-sufficient, had I doomed myself by breaking the law, and, by the same token, endangered Stefan's own grant?

Ironically, it was he who had given me the idea, back in Paris, on the night he'd told me his grant was approved. "Too bad you are not Polish," he'd said. "If you were, you could have applied for a grant like mine."

That thought had stayed with me, and after a while I had started to see how it might work. There were dozens of Polish artists living in pre-WW1 Paris, and I had hunted and found a prominent Polish violinist and composer who fitted the profile I needed. A womanizer who didn't marry the women he seduced, including my grandmother, now dead, bless her soul.

Envelope in hand, my heart in my throat, I wondered if there was any possibility that I may be arrested for fraud, here, in India. With trembling fingers, I tore open the envelope and extracted the letter.

Madam,
Your request for a grant to study South Indian dancing in Madras, India, at the Kalakshetra Dance Academy, as indicated in your application to the Polish/American Board of the Paderewski Foundation of

New York, has been granted.

Please report to the school at your earliest, and upon proof of enrollment you will start receiving a monthly stipend of one hundred dollars, amounting to 477 rupees in local currency.

Congratulations on your recent union to Stefan Polszewski, one of our most promising scholars. We trust that you and Stefan will endeavor to represent the high standards and ideals of our foundation in Madras and wherever your travels take you.

Please rest assured...

I stopped reading and almost broke into a victory dance. I wanted to shout. It had worked. I was so excited I could have kissed the concierge. I was rushing back upstairs when he called out from behind his desk, "I could tell it was important, coming from the U.S. with that eagle and all." Voluble and sleek, he was his old self again.

"You were right. It *is* a very important letter."

I was delirious with relief. I rushed up the staircase, two steps at a time, back to Stefan's studio. I was not hungry anymore.

Hiding the letter behind my back, I rushed into the room. I wanted to throw myself into Stefan's arms, or better, make a trail of my clothes and pull him back to bed with me to celebrate, but I remembered he wasn't feeling well. Instead, I bent over the cane armchair where he sat, book in hand, and was about to sit in his lap when he raised an eyebrow and nodded toward the back of the room to show we had company.

Careful not to let his eyes wander in our direction, the houseboy was assiduously making the bed. He looked frail and old and walked barefoot with a limp as he rolled the mosquito net up over the corner posts of the adjoining sleeping cots. His thin limbs floated under the loose weave of the white cotton uniform he wore, and his dark face looked tiny under the weight of his houseboy turban.

I noted how skillful he was at arranging the oversized net hanging above the cots that had been pushed together under a thin mattress. It was strange to look at this old man making my bed. A few weeks ago, I would have given up my seat for him in the metro or on a Parisian bus.

I pulled a chair close to Stefan. "Hang on a minute while I finish this page," he demanded, heedless of the heat and excitement I was sure to convey.

Ugh! At times Stefan drove me crazy. Like now. Repressing my impatience, I let my eyes linger on the Indian cots, the *charpoys,* with their sturdy canvas straps woven and tied to a bare wooden frame. Except for our short stay in Bombay, I had never slept on anything but these since arriving in India. That cot business would have to go as soon as we rented our own house. I wanted a real bed, a large one with a real mattress. And now, I would have the money to pay for it.

"That was fast. Did you finish breakfast, already?" asked Stefan, without raising his eyes from his book.

Maybe sensing our need for privacy, the houseboy hurried to finish his chores and left the room. I touched Stefan's arm to capture his attention.

"Something came up. I couldn't eat," I said. "How are you? Feeling any better?"

"Yes. The Ergotamine tabs the doctor gave me worked. I beat the migraine before it took hold."

"That's great, because I have something to show you," I said, excitedly shoving the letter under his nose.

Holding it away from his face, he quickly read it and gave it back to me. "Excellent. All is well that ends well," he said, handing the letter back to me.

I was stung. "That's all you have to say?"

"You want the truth?" he said, lifting his head to look into my face. "I wasn't sure at all they'd give you that grant. Yours was a far-fetched story, and, as we both know, a lie."

I stared back at him, feeling hurt by his judgmental assessment.

"Hey! I'm happy for you," he added, noting the moisture threatening to roll off my eyelashes. "What do you want me to say?"

He looked surprised at my reaction, and I was surprised at his lack of one. I don't know why, but I expected a big cheer. Now that I was safe from retributions, my actions appeared brilliant to me. "I thought you would applaud me. It wasn't easy researching and filling in that grant application, and now that it's over, I can tell you that, I too was terrified it wouldn't work."

"What you did was very risky. Risky for you, and probably for me too now that you're my wife. You realize, of course, that I could've been implicated?"

I found myself pacing the room. My heart was beating loudly in my chest. "Okay, okay, so I lied, but my actions are not as far from the truth as you might imagine. Did I ever tell you that, as passed down by my grandmother, my biological grandfather was a rather unscrupulous Russian nobleman who deserted her after discovering she was pregnant with his child? So, in a way, you can look at the grant as life's way to right a wrong."

Stefan sighed warily. He must have actually worried that I'd get caught. He closed the book resting on his lap and raked his fingers through his hair. "Look, I'm really happy this charade is behind us." He took a deep breath and pulled himself straighter in his chair. I could see wheels within wheels turning in his head as he warmed up to the news. "By combining our two grants we'll have more than enough to rent the small house I told you about," he said, nodding thoughtfully. "We will, of course, have to hire some servants, but that won't be a problem." By now excitement showed in his eyes, and color crawled up his cheeks. "After living expenses and tuitions, we'll have plenty of money left to travel," he concluded. He looked pleased with himself.

I was thrilled to finally have his attention. "I can't wait to get the house, but are you serious about hiring servants?" I said, wrinkling my nose at the idea. We couldn't possibly be that rich.

"Absolutely. That's just the way things are done around here; and help is so cheap, why deny yourself the comfort?"

He had that look on his face again. The satisfied colonist. I ignored it and raised my voice to punctuate my request. "I'm fine with hiring servants, but the first thing I want to buy with my grant is a real bed. I'm tired of those uncomfortable Indian charpoys."

Stefan did not respond. I could tell that right now his mind was neither on sleep nor on sex. It was on his train of thought. He raised his eyes to me. "By Indian standards, our combined grants make us more than well-off. I think we should buy a scooter for me, so I don't have to ride a bicycle or take the bus to go to the university."

"What about me?"

"The dance school is next door. All you'll need is a bicycle. You know how to ride?"

"I only rode a bike on vacation, never in Paris," I said, uncertainly. And not very well, I should have added. I had a few small scars to prove it but didn't want to look stupid.

"I'm sure you'll be fine. That's a plan then," he said, decisively.

I noticed how my brand-new grant money was being distributed, and how Stefan used the royal "we" for all things but didn't interrupt.

"Having enough money to travel is a huge plus," he said. "When you came, I was concerned about travel expenses, but considering how cheap train fares are, especially if we go third class, we'll do fine," he said, nodding with satisfaction.

"Where shall we go?" I was dying to go on a trip. Explore India.

"Anywhere we want. The Himalayas, Kashmir, Nepal, Sikkim, Bhutan. Maybe Thailand, Indonesia even." He was feeling grand, gesturing at postcards pinned on the cork board above his desk.

"But when will we have time? Won't we be in school?"

"We would be if Indian schools didn't observe everyone's religious vacations," he said. "As a result, we will probably have a couple more weeks to travel." He paused and changed the subject. "Now that your tuition money is assured, I have no doubt Kalakshetra will accept you as a student."

"I can't wait to start dance classes, but are you sure Kalakshetra is the right school for me? Umadevi, you know, that old Polish lady, told me they are extremely strict."

"Don't let people scare you; you'll be great at it." He beamed a reassuring smile. "Anyway, you can't start looking for another school. You used Kalakshetra's name and reputation to secure the grant, so the Foundation will expect you to study there. Now that you're officially a Paderewski scholar, registering will be no problem." He got up and approached his desk to make a note. "I'll leave a message with the school's secretary and make sure the director sees me as soon as she gets back in town.

"See you?" Why you? Can't I go there by myself with the letter?"

He shrugged. "You can if you want. But I know people there. It'll be better if I deal with them in person."

I certainly didn't need him to do that for me. I wasn't a child. I'd been doing things like that by myself for a long time but reasoned that he meant well. It was nice to have someone looking out for me, but I resolved that, when the time came, I would introduce myself to the director in person.

Holding his hand out, he called to me. "Come here."

I noticed the way he was looking at me. It was a look I hadn't seen in several days. He became playful, and his voice turned husky when he reached down and slipped his hand between my thighs.

"I've always found something sexy about dancers," he whispered. "I can't wait to see you in a *Bharata Natyam* dance costume!"

I smiled uneasily. Joining a dance school looked good on paper, but I wondered what they would think of me. I could waltz, tango, and do the Paso-Doble better than any of my friends, but had never studied modern dance or ballet. I hoped they were not expecting to make a dancer out of me. All I really wanted was to unravel the mystery of the Indian dancers' hand and body language that I might later incorporate into theatre work. I relaxed and smiled at Stefan. He had bolted the front door and the curtain-less windows that opened onto the verandah and hung a large beach towel in front of their naked glass.

Catching my hand, he pulled me to him and started to unbutton my blouse. He struggled briefly with my bra before it landed on the floor, along with the rest of my clothes. He was only wearing a dhoti, which I easily yanked undone. Without a word, we slid the blanket covering the sofa onto the floor and dropped on it, laughing, fumbling, and kissing, stopping only when we heard the passing footsteps of our neighbors cruising past our door.

A while later, we glanced at the back of the room where our two single sleeping cots stood side by side with impeccably starched folds. We giggled. The long-eared servants who loved gossip and always knew everything wouldn't know about our tryst.

CHAPTER SEVEN

AUG 1959 - MYLAPORE TEMPLE

Almost two weeks had passed since I'd received the miraculous news about my grant, and we still hadn't heard from the dance school. Depressed by my forced idleness, I was losing patience. Seeking a reprieve from boredom, I decided to do something to improve my English. While in school, my teachers, all of them French, had done a poor job of it, and though my hitchhiking trips to England had helped, I was still keenly aware of my lack of fluency in standard English, which is what most educated people in Madras spoke. The way I saw it, my first job was to expand my vocabulary. I would tackle Tamil, the local Indian language later.

With that in mind, I sat at Stefan's desk to type a list of authors and books I wanted to read in English. It was slow going, because the keypad of the typewriter he had borrowed from the T.S.'s office lacked the arrangement my French fingers were used to. Instead of AZERT—read from left to right on the top line—it said QWERT, which forced me to find and type one letter at a time.

When I heard the sputtering of Stefan's scooter through the window, I welcomed the interruption and padded barefoot to the verandah to wave at him.

He jumped off the nearly new second-hand Lambretta he had purchased five days ago and pulled it under the twin peepal trees that shaded the entrance to the guesthouse. He brushed the mirror off with the side of his hand, scratched off the dry remains of a dead bug stuck to it, and wiped the smear with his shirttail.

I could tell he was in love with that scooter. He had already washed it and polished it twice, and kept it under a tarp after dark, to protect it from a thousand real or imagined nocturnal dangers, and from the tropical dampness night brought in. But more importantly for me, he looked for reasons to drive it, which was perfect as I was dying to explore Madras and the surroundings villages.

"I heard that Rukmini Devi was back, so I stopped by Kalakshetra," he said, entering the room. "Everything is arranged. They'll let you known when you can come and watch a class for orientation." He must have noticed my stunned expression and quickly changed the subject. "Hey, I'm free for the rest of the day. Want to go to town?" He smiled. A child looking for a playmate.

I raised a hand to stop him. "You went to Rukmini Devi without me? We were supposed to go together, remember? How could you discuss the classes I want to take? That was *my* business."

"I'm your husband. Your business is my business," he said, dropping his book-heavy satchel onto the floor mattress we used as a sofa.

Seething, I said in a tight voice, "You may be my husband but the course selection I wanted to discuss with her is *my* business." My throat hurt with repressed frustration. "And my letter? Did she say anything about my letter to her?"

"What letter?"

"That's exactly my point. You didn't even know I'd attached a letter to my application." In it, I had emphasized that I had no prior dance training and was hoping to only study those elements of Indian dancing I might later incorporate into theatre, specifically the eye, hand and body languages Indian dancers use to convey action and emotions.

"Look, I'm sure she's got it all figured out."

"That's not good enough. I was expecting an answer to my request," I said. "I'm worried..."

"Stop worrying," said Stefan. He picked up a glass and poured water from the pitcher he kept on his desk. "You'll be fine."

Pointing to my bare feet he said, "If you want to go to town, you better put on some shoes. You need to change?"

I exhaled slowly to release my tension. "Non," I said, in my most Gaelic French, and slipped on my sandals.

"Alright then. Ready?"

I was ready but I wasn't fine, and Stefan appeared to have no clue. Zut, zut, zut! His interference was maddening, but there was nothing I could do about it. Why had he gone to the school behind my back instead of letting me negotiate the classes I wanted? What was in it for him? How would he like me going to his philosophy professor to choose his curriculum? I bit my tongue to refrain from starting an argument. "Give me a minute," I said, tying my hair into a ponytail to keep it out of my face while riding, "and let me grab the list I typed."

I took a minute to clear my mind from angry thoughts, threw my list and my camera in my old leather purse worn soft by years of escorting me everywhere I went, secured its strap across my shoulders and pulled the door closed without locking it. People didn't lock their doors on campus.

"Let's go!" called Stefan astride his machine.

I went outside and climbed behind him, wrapping my arms around his waist, filling my lungs with the beloved fragrance of his body. "Can we go to the bookstore first?"

"All the same to me."

Minutes later, we were immersed in a moving sea of people, dodging pedestrians, bicycles, rickshaws, and the occasional mangy dog, as we zipped smoothly around sooty taxicabs and belching trucks smelling of gasoline fumes and burnt rubber.

"How come all taxis look the same?" I shouted, next to his ear.

"That's because most of them are Standards, an Indian economy brand," said Stefan, speaking loudly over his right shoulder.

We made good time, swerving around precarious handcart wallahs, overtaking rattling buses to avoid their suffocating exhaust fumes, and my mood lifted. To my relief, Stefan kept a respectful distance from the slow, cud-chewing Brahma bulls whose long horns swayed danger-ously right and left as they trudged in the middle of the road.

In spite of the breeze generated by our riding, I was hot and leaned back to allow the rush of air to slip under my blouse and whip my ponytail around my head; I could feel my scalp and skin cooling as sweat evaporated from my body. Hanging on to Stefan's waist, I felt invulnerable.

Our first stop was Higginbotham's, an old British bookstore I hadn't yet visited, but I immediately felt at home in that temple of learning. The high-ceilinged store was cool, and I greedily breathed in the famil-iar scent of books, a combination of paper, cardboard and glue; I noted that most books were printed on poorer paper than in France and was surprised to detect the smell of fish glue in some of the bindings, some-thing I hadn't encountered in a book since I was a kid.

I lost Stefan in the philosophy section while I browsed through shelves filled with English novels. Never before had I read a whole book in English. I had only tackled out-of-context fragments chosen by less- than-expert teachers. What I needed now was a special author, someone who would hold my interest with a story while enriching my vocabulary. I located a display of books by Aldous Huxley, one of the writers on my list.

"See anything you like?" asked Stefan, running into me at the end of a row.

"I think I'll get *Brave New World*," I said, showing him the cover of the book I was thumbing. "I remember reading it in French and enjoying it. That will make it easier to digest. I'll also try *The Fox* by D.H. Lawrence."

"You're going at it the wrong way," said Stefan dismissively. "Why pick something you've read before? Moreover, I think you should be reading books written by Indian authors."

I felt like telling him to keep his advice to himself but managed to control my annoyance. "Not for what I have in mind. What I need right now are English tutors," I said. "Huxley and Lawrence are perfect."

Stefan rolled his eyes. "Don't get me wrong, *Brave New World* is a good book, but it paints a depressing vision of the future. Do you really want to read it again?" He shook his head and, without waiting for an answer, walked further down the aisle with the book he had been leafing through.

"Yes, I do," I said to his back, adding a thick French-English Larousse dictionary to the volumes I held in my hands. I had what I needed to get started on my project and was pretty sure my selection would be more entertaining than his dry philosophy treatises.

"To each their own." Stefan said, joining the queue in front of the cash register.

When it came to literature, his opinion didn't matter to me, for I knew the only books he ever read were his textbooks. Come to think of it, I'd never seen him enjoy a novel, while novels were more than books to me. They were my constant companions, my teachers, my friends, and I was pleased with today's selection.

63

"Thanks for bringing me here," I said, catching up with him. "I'm so happy to get something new to read. I finished the only book I brought from France."

"What book was that?"

"La Peste, by Camus. I was lucky it was in my purse when I boarded the ship in Marseille without the rest of my luggage."

"Really bad luck that the French railways went on strike when they did. Can you imagine all the parcels and luggage sitting somewhere in the middle of France?"

"At least there was no food in my stuff."

"No kidding. Have you heard from the shipping company? I could use the books you were bringing me."

"They are probably on their way right now. The Messageries Maritimes ships sail to Bombay every four weeks." I wasn't surprised that Stefan only thought about his books. That's just the way he was. I stopped to think about my belongings. That trunk contained the most beloved objects I owned and had packed for my great adventure—books, records, knickknacks, as well as some warm clothes and boots in anticipation of hiking in the Himalayas. But to be honest, I hadn't really missed any of these things, except for a change of clothes during the week-long sea crossing from Marseille to Bombay. Maybe it was just as well the French novels I was bringing hadn't arrived. It would make it easier to challenge myself into reading in English.

We retrieved the scooter that had been left in the shade under the watchful eyes of a guard sweating inside a short, starched, khaki uniform, and Stefan slid back on his seat and into the dense traffic. Erect behind him, I enjoyed the feel of my chest pressed against the thin linen of his shirt as the scooter swayed right and left to avoid the vehicles racing around us. Aroused by the prolonged physical contact of my hardened nipples against Stefan's back I couldn't help but reflect on what a strange country India was, where the sight of a woman embracing a man on a scooter in plain view was acceptable, but holding hands on the street wasn't.

To distract myself from the sensual tingling in my body, I studied the crowd milling around us. So many people. So many bodies juxtaposed in various stages of dress or undress. So many handcarts loaded with fresh coconuts, green banana leaves, giant bunches of brownish dates and leafy things I couldn't identify. Hand rickshaws pulled or pushed by thin coolies whose dusty splayed feet gripped the ground for traction as they trotted alongside us.

To one side of the road, laborers were dredging a narrow canal. The shallow waterway let out a fetid odor, but the men didn't seem to notice. I couldn't help but admire their wiry dark bodies clad in nothing more than sweat and a loincloth. Like a line of giant ants, they passed mud-filled containers from hand to hand all the way to higher ground.

A little further, a roadside eatery surrounded by a crowd of locals, mostly men, attracted my attention. It was a crude shack built with raw planks and a tin roof, but it seemed quite popular, and the smell of fried dough, onion and spices was enticing. "Looks like a good place to grab a snack," said Stefan. He stopped, waited for me to dismount, and pulled the scooter onto its stand. For a few seconds, I felt the eyes of the men on me, but they soon returned to their conversations. Stefan approached the stained but surprisingly polished wood counter and got the owner's attention. "One *vadai* with mango pickle for me, and two *idlis* with mint chutney for the Mensahib."

Nodding right and left in that strange way South Indians have to acknowledge almost everything, the vendor repeated the order after him, his wide grin exposing two rows of red teeth and gums.

"Betel leaves, right?" I whispered to Stefan who nodded in agreement. "What are vadais?"

"They're deep-fried pastries filled with spiced potatoes and onions," he said. "These," he pointed to a row of steaming snowballs cooling off on a bamboo tray, "are idlis. They are plain but very tasty with chutney. You'll like them."

Instead of plates, these local staples were served in small boxes made out of folded banana leaves stitched with twigs. On getting our order, we settled against the scooter to eat. Around us, people ate with their hands, the right hand I noticed, but the vendor gestured to me and produced a plastic spoon from a box he kept under the counter. He made a big show of wiping it clean with a towel hanging from a rafter, and I discretely finished the job by rubbing it in a fold of my knee-length dress. The idlis were plain, but they were the perfect vehicle to taste the aromatic chutney he had put on the side.

Colas were sweating inside buckets filled with melting ice, but Indian sodas were too sweet for my taste. I opted for the dark and foamy café-au-lait the vendor whipped by pouring it from cup to cup at arm's length.

Most men wore short sleeve shirts and white dhotis, the long cotton wrap resembling a sarong, but short khaki uniforms appeared to be the norm for government employees. In this cramped sidewalk eatery that lacked tables and individual space, physical contact between men was unavoidable, but they showed no self-consciousness about it. Neither did the younger men casually holding hands as they walked past us. So, it appeared that the hand-holding taboo didn't apply to men. They were free to touch. In a way, I envied them. Having grown up in France where people walked arm-in-arm and embraced to greet each other with kisses on both cheeks, I missed the comfort of touching. It was such a spontaneous urge in human nature.

After a while, we got back on the Lambretta scooter and drove in the direction of the Mylapore Temple. While large numbers of men loitered around, the women kept busy carrying perfectly balanced brass or clay pots on their heads as they weaved through this predominantly male crowd without ever coming into physical contact with the opposite sex. Early on, I'd half expected the men to reach out for a feel of their breasts or butts, but the no-touching-women-in-public taboo appeared to be holding.

Self-aware of their privileged caste, the Brahmins were easy to spot with their half-shaved heads and their foreheads painted with red and yellow stripes to display their allegiance to gods I was too new to guess at. One easily perceived the sense of superiority afforded them by the thin white rope crossing their bare chests. It was fascinating to watch how the crowd opened up for them without ever exposing them to the danger of impure physical contact with the lesser castes, including me.

"How far to the temple," I shouted over Stefan's shoulder.

"Almost there," he shouted back. He leaned to the left to enter a side street, took the next right, and parked against the scarred plank wall of a tiny tea stall. He hailed the storekeeper, a thin ebony-colored man whose small head disappeared inside a messy red turban. "Hello boss! Will you keep an eye on my scooter while we walk around?" asked Stefan, handing the man a brand-new rupee banknote.

"Acha! Sure, Sahib. I will keep it like my own, exactly like my own, very safe, like the last time."

Nodding conspiratorially, he pointed at me with the rupee bill and added, "You brought the lady back, yes?" Pleased, the man put the precious rupee in a metal box he kept under the clay stove where a kettle, blackened by years of bubbling over a coal fire, simmered noisily.

Stefan waved the man a hasty goodbye and started to walk away without answering.

"Brought the lady back?" I repeated, as the meaning sank into me. Even though I sensed it might be smarter to let the chai wallah's remark slide, I was piqued with curiosity. "Which lady would that be?" I said, catching up with him. "I bet she was white, 'cause we all look the same to him, don't we?" Sarcasm was a cheap shot, but I was suddenly itching to punish Stefan for his meddling with my dance curriculum.

"Look," mumbled Stefan, "it was long before you arrived. I borrowed a friend's scooter and drove one of the dance students here to take pictures."

"I didn't know they had non-Indian girls in that school. Who was it?"

"Her name is Lycette. She's a ballet dancer researching Bharata Natyam and choreography."

"I remember you telling me about her in one of your letters." My face was smiling but the image of a ballet dancer snug against Stefan's back as they rode through Madras made my stomach lurch with unexpected jealousy. "I'd love to meet her. Looks like we have some common interests."

Stefan must have read the stiffness in my voice. "Don't get any ideas. She's just a friend," he said. Noticing my agitation, he continued. "When I first arrived, I had a little bit of a crush on her, you know, because I was lonely, and it was nice to have someone to speak Polish with. But she set me straight. And anyway, she's married," he said awkwardly.

I took a few long steps to distance myself from him. Jealousy is bad medicine at any time and had led me to act stupidly. I felt confused and somehow diminished by my veiled accusation. As Stefan had said, what did it matter what he had done weeks, no, months ago? It came to me that I was no better than him. Images of Bernard, the young French man I had flirted with during my seafaring voyage flashed in my mind. On the last night of the crossing, we had left the festive ballroom dance celebrating our imminent arrival in Bombay, and sneaked up to the bridge to kiss under the stars. I had refused to go further but had been *so* tempted. Who was I to judge Stefan or be jealous of his friend? I turned around to wait for him.

He looked relieved to see me smiling and took my hand in his for a moment, a total breakdown of the behavior code he was so keen to observe in public. I squeezed his hand back and marveled at how this small gesture was more powerful than any words we might have exchanged. I was willing to forget about his past crush on that Lycette, but I still didn't understand why he had taken it upon himself to talk to the dance school without me. It kept bothering me and threatening to sour my enjoyment of the temple. But then, the alley we were following opened up into a large plaza, and here it was, solid as a mountain, courted and wooed by a tide of half-naked men, sari-clad women, naked children, inspired musicians, ragged beggars, peddlers, saints and sinners, all drawn to its walls like moths to a flame. In its presence, I forgot at once the problems I thought I had.

From a hundred feet away, the massive stone structure looked impossibly tall. It dominated the square with its three-dimensional trapezoid shape revealing tiers after receding tiers of friezes covered with crawling sculptures of brightly painted mortals and gods. A ten-foot enceinte painted with alternating white and orange stripes made up the base of the giant shrine, and the symmetry of these vertical stripes below a wall filled with curvaceous sculptures was incongruous. I pulled my camera out of my purse and wondered how best to capture this enormous structure. I knew, from a postcard I had bought, that the roof featured a golden crest crowned by small gold spires, but I couldn't back up far enough to see them with my own eyes, let alone my camera. I decided to focus on people until I could find a side street or the roof of some nearby building to get a clear shot of the whole edifice.

Fronting that candy-striped wall, a large rectangular water tank enclosed by a sweep of wide stone steps offered precious water to all. Holy Water. Water in which to immerse their bodies in devotion but also to cleanse their skin and clothes; water for all to splash, play in and pray. The lure of the water reminded me of how hot I was. I'd have loved to wade into it myself, if I dared.

A group of male musicians dressed in saffron robes sat cross-legged in the temple shade and sang, accompanied by a breathy, beat-up harmonium. I wasn't surprised. I knew from reading that in India, classical music and dancing were sacred in nature. In the past, major temples had attracted artists. I tried to imagine what it had been like for the temple vestals of past centuries, to perform at the foot of this massive edifice. Clearly the temple had been, and still was, so much more than a place of worship. Maybe the large cathedrals I had visited in Europe resembled this temple a few centuries ago, when actors staged plays in front of them and commoners sold their wares in their holy shade.

We had stopped to take in the temple, and a group of men and women crowded around us, staring. One woman appeared to be talking about me. She pointed at the bangles on my wrists, and another one, nearest to me, touched my hair, smiled, and offered me a string of fragrant frangipani flowers to tuck around my ponytail. She seemed to approve of me, which pleased me, and made it easy for me to direct my camera at her and get a few shots of her and her friends.

Behind us, on the road circumventing the temple, a team of water buffaloes was pulling a tall wooden cart. Horns glinting in the sun, their wide nostrils parched and dusty, the animals edged stubbornly toward the tank, only to be pulled back by their handlers. It made for another great photo.

Noting the direction of my lens, Stefan said, "I can't warn you enough about water buffaloes. They look slow and harmless, but they are unpredictable." For once, his tone of voice was conciliatory without being preachy. I was relieved that he, too, wanted peace. Though we'd rarely had disagreements during the seven months of our relationship in Paris, I knew him to hold grudges against some of his old classmates. His gentleness triggered in me the desire to turn around and touch him, kiss him, act like the lover I longed to be instead of all this decorum, this no-touching-in-public business.

Walking around the water tank where children shrieked and sprayed each other, we arrived at the great doors to the temple. An old woman stood there, her shiny, charcoal-colored face melted into a thousand folds. On spotting my camera, she turned sideways and smiled at me, revealing a toothless hole of a mouth before spitting a stream of red juice to the stone floor. She had been leaning on the wall with one foot. Presently she pushed off, stood, wiped her mouth with the back of her hand, picked up a large basket full of wet clothes which she balanced skillfully on her head, and walked away.

The same ash-covered holy man who had so impressed me on the day of my arrival caught my eye in a corner of the courtyard. Standing utterly still on his left leg, his right leg resting on the opposite knee, he seemed impervious to my lens and the curiosity of onlookers.

"I don't think he's moved or slept since we last saw him."

"Who knows," said Stefan. "Some sadhus achieve remarkable things, like sitting naked on snow for days or weeks. Others walk on red coals without burning their feet, but not all are that adept."

"Do you think he'll mind if I take photos?"

"I don't think he cares. None of us are part of his world."

Careful to keep my distance from the holy man I took a few shots, before following the great wall into which another entrance had been cut. Looking up, I let my eyes travel over the graceful figures carved on it, marveling at the way their curvaceous bodies seemed to animate the very stone they were chiseled in. They were so beautiful, my breath caught in my throat and a sudden pain twisted my stomach. I realized that I was scared. I was way out of my league. Why had I applied to a dance school to get that grant? Had my choice been influenced by Stefan because he loved the idea of his wife being a dancer? A dancer like Lycette, that ballerina friend of his? I hated to think that way. I was after all the one he had married. But why had I applied to a dance school? Why not a drama school which would have matched my experience? I couldn't ignore the possibility that my lack of training was the reason why the school director had ignored my letter? Frozen in front of the dancing stone figures, I wondered if I'd have the kind of stamina and coordination it took to be good at their art. Meanwhile, the loop of unanswered questions squeezed my brain like a steel band.

CHAPTER EIGHT

SEPT 1959 - THE CHURCH

Staring at the slowly revolving wooden blades of the ceiling fan above the charpoy where I lay, I reflected that it was only six weeks since I'd left Paris; four weeks since I'd arrived in Bombay. So much had happened in six weeks that had changed my life forever. First and foremost, I no longer was "a girl." I was a woman, miraculously married to the man I'd dreamed about for months. I also was in a totally new country, having left behind my mother and sister, my only family. I had also parted from my two best friends, Brigitte, an aspiring existentialist poet who loved to mix politics, philosophy, and red wine, and could drink her male friends under the table, and Francine, who had been like a sister to me until she turned seventeen and eloped, only to fall under the spell of a brutal and possessive husband. Except for Stefan's presence, I could never have anticipated my new life. Everything around me was new, the culture, the climate, the architecture, the food, the music, and the people. I was surrounded by the rich spiritual and architectural history of this conservative corner of South India, and had recently met more scholars than I possibly could have in my whole life, including an

elderly Polish lady who called herself Umadevi, which, in Sanskrit, was
the name of the Hindu Goddess Parvati. But one of the greatest gifts
in my new life was to receive the confirmation of the grant I had been
hoping for, ever since learning that there were such things as grants,
manna from heaven, to pay the tuitions of lucky students. Amazingly,
it would pay for mine at the best dance school in Madras. Getting this
grant had made a difference in our lives. Now that our financial future
was clarified, Stefan appeared more relaxed. This was the Stefan I
remembered from Paris, boyish and talkative with a contagious enthusiasm for knowledge.

It was only 8 a.m. and except for the musical call of crickets, all
was quiet outside suggesting that most of our neighbors had already
left for a class or a lecture. Things usually started early here, because
daytime was, as some of the guesthouse tenants loved to kvetch, hot,
hotter, and hottest. Outside our open door and window, the sky was a
brilliant cerulean blue, and not a frond moved in the palms bordering
the graveled path surrounding the building. Out on the lawns, sputtering sprinklers were shutting off. I listened for the birds, but the usually
chatty minahs remained silent, and in spite of being on the second
floor, where we often benefitted from drafts of salty marine breeze, our
one-room studio already felt like a heat trap. Stefan had classes five
days a week, but today being a holiday for some Hindu saint whose
name I couldn't pronounce, he had the day off. So we had an early
breakfast, grabbed our swimsuits and a couple of towels, and lured by
the promise of a cool swim we hurried to the beach before the sun rose
any higher in the sky. We waded directly into the retreating tide. Small
waves lapped and gently died against my ankles as the Indian ocean
slowly uncovered shells, scrambling crabs and shiny rocks in the wet
sand. The green smell of seaweed filled my nose and I shivered with
pleasure as goose flesh covered my arms. Above our heads, seagulls
glided and shrieked as they hunted in the waves and on the sand.

By the ocean the temperature was perfect and we could have stayed there all day, but after swimming and walking up and down the deserted beach for a couple of hours, we felt cooled enough to undertake the walk back to the guesthouse. My stomach growled at the promise of the cold lunch awaiting us there. After lunch Stefan would have to study. As for me, still days away from starting dance classes, I looked forward to tackling the novels I had bought with the help of my French-English dictionary.

As we re-entered the deserted T.S. grounds whose residents were either at lunch or resting, Stefan took special pleasure in pointing out the many small shrines tucked between tree thickets, rock gardens and lotus ponds. Christian, Hindu, Buddhist, Jain, and Zoroastrian, these shrines housed more faiths than I knew about. There was even a newly built Tibetan temple decorated with prayer flags. Some structures housed statues and were large enough for me to walk into, but others were monolithic. Feeling a little light-headed from the sun and the scent of flower offerings and sandal wood floating in the warm air, I suggested we pause a moment on a meditation bench placed in the shade of a nearby banyan.

I had never been very religious and couldn't help feeling a little irreverent as I reviewed in my mind the varied architectural styles of all these temples housing God. Presumably one god, so why the many buildings and faiths? It made me think of a book Stefan kept on his desk; *The Thousand Names of Shiva*. Did Hindus really have a thousand names for that one god?

Behind a tall tamarind tree, we came upon a Christian church. Compared to the shrines we had just stopped by the church was large. Built out of cut stones, it strived for a Gothic look reminiscent of European architecture and stood out starkly amongst the more ornate and colorful places of worship we had seen. To one side, it displayed a square belfry tower, and to the other, a slender gothic spire. Its steeple

75

roof, covered with plain gray slates, looked foreign to me against the date palm trees and surrounding Bougainvilleas.

It looked deserted and, when we stepped inside, we saw that whoever had designed the church had opened up the tall austere walls with large stained-glass windows that poured streams of colored lights over the polished pews. The air was rich with the burnt and bitter smell of incense, the one constant shared by all the churches I had visited around Europe.

"I have an idea," said Stefan playfully, as we walked through the echoing aisles of the plain edifice. "Let's have a real ceremony here, one with a priest."

"You mean get married again?" I asked, puzzled by his statement.

"Your mother is fine with our civil marriage, but you know my mother. In her last letter she accused us of living in sin. She's terrified we will burn in hell unless we get married properly." He made a face and stressed the word "hell."

I knew his mother was a devout Catholic and it made sense that he would want to reassure her. Still, it wasn't like him to extol the benefits of a church wedding.

"It would mean a lot to her and give us an opportunity to take better photos. The ones taken in Bombay by Miss Petit's assistant cook are pretty bad."

He looked pleased with himself. I tried to guess the thoughts perco- lating under his beach-ruffled hair. Even though I owed no loyalty to the Catholic Church, getting married to shoot better photos was incred- ibly impudent. But he had a point. He always had a goddamned point, and here he was again deciding for both of us, just like in Bombay, where, without ever broaching the subject with me, he had surprised me with the news that we were to be married five days after my arrival. And he had done it again when, after hearing I had obtained the grant, he'd decided he would buy a scooter for himself and let me trade his tall Schwinn for a girl's bicycle. That's what he did with everything our new life together touched. I was torn between enjoying his taking charge of our life, and detesting the fact that he swept me along without consulting me. Unsure about how to communicate that without offending him, I asked, "So... are you... asking me, or telling me?"

Sensing my sarcasm, he stared at me, a puzzled look on his face. I softened my words with a smile. "I was only teasing, but it would be nice if you asked my opinion once in a while."

"Okay. Yes. I am asking you," he said dutifully, without a hint of repentance.

"Thank you," I replied graciously, "but I'm already your wife, so, let's skip the church ceremony. If you want better pictures for your mom, let's just hire a photographer."

"Really? I guess I could do that," he said, and burst out laughing. Stefan's charisma was his shield. For once forgetful of the Indian etiquette he so faithfully abided by, he pulled me to him for a kiss. Inside the cool shade of the empty church, I closed my eyes and molded myself against him. It felt so good to be held that way. I wanted to stay there forever.

CHAPTER NINE

THE VEIL

There were no armoires in our small studio apartment, and the few dresses I owned hung neatly in a little alcove I used as a makeshift wardrobe behind a long turquoise shawl I had bought in town to add a splash of color to the plain room.

I had also strung a colorful shawl along the bottom edge of the bathroom sink, but Stefan asked me to take it down. "Better to have a clear view of the plumbing," he said. "Venomous scorpions and centipedes find their way into bathrooms by crawling along the pipes." He was obviously impervious to my desire to make these rented rooms more homey. Using bits of colorful fabrics and scarves was a trick I had learned in my hitchhiking days, when, on arriving at a Youth Hostel, I always threw my favorite scarf on the bed I was assigned to. It never failed to make me feel at home in any dorm.

Centipedes or not, it was the first time I lived in a place that had a shower, and the sheer sight of it was a thrill. I had grown up taking sponge baths, washing my hair in kitchen sinks and visiting public bath facilities, a necessity in Paris where so few apartments have their own "*salle de bain*". It was a novelty for me to step into a shower without first having to ride the metro or a bus.

There was a knock on the door and one of the house boys delivered a dress I had sent to the local laundry to be starched and ironed. It was the dress I'd worn for our civil wedding in Bombay. I was hanging it into the alcove when the veil slipped down from the hanger and landed on the floor. I picked it up and laid it out on the bed where Stefan, propped up on pillows, was reading. He marked the page, closed his book, and frowned questioningly at me. "What's up?"

"I had my wedding dress washed and pressed. It was smart to choose this simple style. I now can use it as a summer dress."

"What's with the veil?" he asked.

I walked to the full-length mirror Stefan had purchased for me after my arrival, fluffed up the veil and held it to my face.

He stared at me playing with the light fabric. "What are you thinking about?"

"My *almost* first communion," I said. I wrapped the veil around my shoulders and sat next to him on the bed.

Stefan frowned questioningly. "What exactly do you mean, your *almost* first communion? Either you did or didn't have a first communion."

"I wish it were that simple, but it wasn't." I sighed. "What about you? Your parents are Catholic, so you had one, right?"

"Yes, my brother and I did, in Africa. A summary affair."

"What was it like? Tell me more."

"What is there to tell? Along with hundreds of others, our father had shipped to England to join the allies in the war effort. There were lots of us, kids, stranded in Tanganyika with our mothers and a wizened old priest. I know my mother would have insisted on communion. For us kids, it was really no big deal, except that I remember having to memorize prayers and put on an ill-fitting hand-me-down suit."

79

"I can just imagine you on that day. Any photos in that suit?"

"I don't think so. I couldn't wait to take it off. We kids were a wild bunch, running with Masai children, roasting snakes on open fire pits and learning to hunt antelopes with spears."

"That sounds incredible. How long were you there?"

"It's a long story. I don't feel like going into it now. Maybe we can keep it for another time, okay?"

He pushed back into the pillows and returned to his book. Resting my eyes on his tousled hair that the sea and sun had begun to bleach I tried to imagine him running with a spear. What went on behind that smooth forehead, behind those pale blue eyes that made me think of exotic seas? What drove him to cultivate such mystery about his past? But I knew he hated to be questioned. He had made it very clear from the beginning of our relationship, so I let it go. It was strange that we had come together at all, for our childhoods couldn't have been more different. Fortunately, I had a whole life in front of me to unravel whatever secrets he held onto.

I pressed the veil against my face and its weightless texture brought back a flood of memories. I was almost eleven at the time, studying for my first communion. My single mom and I lived with my Freemason grandfather who may have been a Christian but hated the church and all it stood for. Despite his objection, my mother who wasn't a practicing Catholic thought it was good for a child to have a religious foundation, so she sent me to catechism.

I liked catechism. It told great and unusual stories. All that talk about conception, immaculate or not, sacrifices, betrayals, miracles, it all came across like some of the fairy tales I enjoyed reading, except for the life of Jesus, which, as we all knew, ended badly.

I must have chuckled, for Stefan looked up from his book. "Still thinking about that *almost* communion of yours?" He pushed his book away and rubbed the fatigue out of his eyes with his thumb and forefinger.

"Oh, that!" I said. "Studying catechism was fun, but the priest who ran the class was weird. Kind of a sadist." I shuddered at the recollection.

"A sadist?" said Stefan. "That's quite an accusation."

"Call it what you want, but we were terrified of him. He affected calm and piety, but he was a brutal man with piercing blue eyes under bushy eyebrows. He looked like someone whose skin never saw the sun, and wore his salt-and-pepper gray hair buzzed short, like some kind of officer. I think he saw himself as a soldier of Christ. When he walked up and down between our desks, everyone cringed. One day he stopped next to me and quizzed me about something. I was so scared of him, I couldn't think. I froze."

"And?" asked Stefan, leaning forward to better read my face.

"He grabbed hold of my two braids, lifted me out of my seat and dangled me above the floor. I thought my whole scalp would tear off and stay in his hands."

Stefan pushed up against the pillows and sat straight up. "That's criminal. Did you report him? Did he get arrested or at least reprimanded?"

"No, I was too scared to complain, even though my scalp hurt for days after that. I figured I hadn't studied hard enough."

Stefan shook his head and leaned back on the pillows. "Is that why you decided to skip your first communion?"

"No, no! I wanted to do it!"

I wasn't sure Stefan understood what first communion meant to my friends and me in those days. For him, suiting up had been an inconvenience, but all we talked about was how beautiful we would be on that day, dressed in white like small brides of Christ. My best friend Julie, who was the same age as me, was short for her age and skinny like a boy. I was plain, a little plump and rather uncomfortable in my budding pre-teen figure, but when we imagined ourselves dressed in long white satin dresses, under yards of fluffy white veils, looking part Virgin Mary and part ballerina, we knew we would be beautiful.

"Doing our first communion was like being presented at a debutante ball. We dreamed of being princesses for a day and spent a lot of time speculating about the traditional gifts we would receive on that occasion, a watch, a pen, or maybe both."

"My first watch was also a big deal," said Stefan. "So, what did you get?"

"Nothing."

"Nothing? Your mother gave you nothing?"

I got up, picked up the veil, placed it on my head, whirled around and said, "No. No communion, no pen, no watch."

"I don't understand. Stop moving around! Come here!" He reached for my hand and pulled me down next to him. "Tell me what happened?"

I didn't like those memories, but I complied. If he saw how open I was with him, maybe he too would become comfortable talking about himself.

"Everything fell apart the first time I went to confession."

"Your first confession?"

"Yes. Remember I was only eleven and frightened to death, alone in the dark, in a tiny cubbyhole behind a black curtain that smelled of incense, mildew and tobacco. The darkness paralyzed me, but the presence of that brute behind the thin confessional screen scared me even more. I could imagine his face through the screen separating us and hear him pull in short gasping breaths. I recall breaking out in a cold sweat and shivering as the muted sound of someone practicing the old church organ floated around like a ghost outside my small prison. I would have run away if I dared, but I knew I had to go through with the confession to do my communion. I was snared, glued to a cold, worn-out bench.

"To be on the safe side of confession, Julie and I had concocted a list of all the venial sins and small truancies we might have committed. Had

I ever cheated at school? Possibly! Kept some change when running errands for my mother? I had. Told my mother little white lies? Guilty. The list was long, but I was not prepared for the priest asking if I had ever played doctor with a boy and touched his "little thing." Or ever touched myself between my legs. And whether I knew what a penis was."

"Did you get up and leave, or tell him to go jerk off on his own time?"

"No, nothing like that. I wasn't street smart and had no brothers to learn those clever repartees from. I was speechless. I had no clue about his line of questioning except that it made me feel uneasy and kind of dirty. And I was scared. Would he come out and lift me by my hair again? But it was the ragged breathing that frightened me the most."

Stefan raised a hand to stop me. "What happened? Did he come around and touch you?"

I let out a nervous laugh. "No! I guess he got tired of my shyness and reluctance to respond to his leading questions. He finally told me to recite ten Hail Mary's and sent me away. Maybe he wanted to clear the confessional for a more interesting child, one who might give him more of a thrill."

"I agree it was a bad experience, but how did that stop you from doing your first communion?"

"Ah! You're going to love this. When I got home, Maman looked at me and asked me what was wrong. So I told her the whole thing. 'He asked you what?' she said, dropping the saucepan she held over the sink where it crashed. I repeated the priest's questions, the ones I remembered. Before I was even finished, she was on the move. Her green eyes had turned steel gray and I never argued with her when her eyes were that color. Gray meant she was dangerous. 'Grab your coat. We are going to pay him a visit.' On the way to the rectory, she was walking so fast that I remember running breathlessly alongside her most of the way."

"Did she beat him up?"

"No, but she got in his face. I think she shocked the hell out of him. 'You are a filthy old man,' she said advancing on him until his back was to a wall. 'How dare you talk to my daughter as you did? Do you like talking dirty to innocent children?' He tried to protest but she leaned over him as if to bite his nose off. 'I've got news for you, priest! You will never, ever see this child again. She is lost to you and your church, and you can burn in hell, you, miserable pervert!' After getting that off her chest, she grabbed my hand hard and dragged me, half running, half gliding, all the way back home."

Fingers interlocked, Stefan stretched his arms above his head and grinned. "I can just see her doing that. I bet you were relieved not to have to see that priest again?"

"I was, until I realized that a first communion was now out of the question. I wouldn't get to wear the long white dress and veil like all my friends. I wouldn't get the watch or the pen."

Maybe the old disappointment still showed on my face, for Stefan pulled me to him. He put his arm tight around me. "Well, you can wear your white dress and your veil any time you choose. And if you want, I will get you a special pen!"

I wasn't sure if he was teasing me or being serious, but it didn't matter. I snuggled into his arm and closed my eyes. I liked it there. If that's what it took to be held, I could think of many more stories to tell as I breathed in the musky scent of sandalwood oil Stefan had rubbed on his forearms and elbows chaffed by the desk he leaned on for hours at a time.

Later that day, it occurred to me that it would be fun to organize a small wedding reception. The stunted gathering that had followed our civil union in Bombay had left me wanting something more festive, but I'd no idea where to start and needed to discuss it with Stefan as soon as he returned from his visit to the library. Who should we invite? What should we do about food? Was everyone a vegetarian? Should we order from a restaurant in town or have the guesthouse restaurant cater the event? How much should we budget for it?

I was still trying to figure it out when a campus clerk hand-delivered a letter addressed to Stefan and me. Without waiting for Stefan, I opened it. It was a joint invitation from the Theosophical Society and the Dance School for a reception to be given in our honor the following Sunday. Obviously, they had belatedly heard about Stefan's impromptu marriage in Bombay and had decided to make it official by introducing us to the rest of the people on both campuses. It was such a coincidence, I could hardly believe it, but my relief at the realization that I wouldn't have to organize the event was followed by puzzlement and a hint of suspicion. Nothing in my past had prepared me for that kind of generosity from strangers. Would Stefan expect such a gesture from people who couldn't be much more than acquaintances? I was waiting for him when he returned from the library.

"Look what we just received," I said, showing him the invitation.

"Excellent," he said, on reading it. "That will save us money and a bit of a headache."

"But don't you think it's weird that people who hardly know us want to throw us a party?"

As I suspected, he wasn't surprised. "I don't think it's weird at all. I've been here for seven months and have met a lot of people, and they are curious about you. I know that the T.S. president likes me. Maybe he sees the future in me, and in us, because we are young. As for the director of the dance school, she's a shrewd woman. You're starting dance classes next week and you're going to be her special student, the one with an American grant. She'll want to show you off."

"I understand they all mean well, but..." I sighed, "I'd trade them all for our families and friends!"

"Don't be so dramatic. We'll organize another reception when we return to France."

"And when will that be? A year, two years from now? It won't be the same."

Stefan tossed the opened invitation on the table and took me in his arms. Lifting my chin, he kissed me lightly on the nose and waited until I smiled. He was right. Besides saving us money, it would allow me to meet the school's staff and students as well as the entire community of theosophists. Life was strange. Six people had attended our Bombay wedding, including the servants and the notary public. I wondered how many would show up for the reception next Sunday. One hundred?

CHAPTER TEN

THE RECEPTION

On the day of the reception, Stefan and I crossed the gardens of the Theosophical Society and entered the adjacent Kalakshetra School grounds. Curious and excited, I looked around this adjacent gated campus where I would soon uncover the secret hand-language of classical Indian dancing. Ahead of us, fifty or so guests had gathered next to a spacious covered verandah where lunch would be served.

I expected to see tables loaded with food but, to my surprise, found instead two long parallel rows of straw mats covering the length of the verandah. A five-foot corridor had been left open between them, and young men were laying long green banana leaves at regular interval in front of the mats. Norma, a youngish American woman I'd met a couple of times in the TS office where she worked, had tagged along behind us and caught up with me. The long white braid down her back could have made her look old, but it didn't. It made her look soft, and kind, as did her pale pistachio cotton sari. She wore no jewelry. She greeted Stefan and me and took charge of me as Stefan joined a group of men. Pointing at the open row between the mats, Norma said. "Don't step in there. The leaves you see are our plates. This aisle is for the cooks and their helpers only, so let's go around to the women's side. As you'll see, the men sit across from us."

I was thrilled at the prospect of a traditional Indian meal but worried about sitting down on the floor. Guests were settling down on the mats and I cursed my knee-length white dress and bare legs. I was in trouble and wished Stefan had warned me. Had he known the food would be served on the ground? Sitting modestly cross-legged on the floor was going to be a challenge.

"Can you manage eating with your fingers?" asked Norma.

A quick look at the mats confirmed there was no cutlery in sight.

"I guess I'll have to," I replied, with more confidence than I felt.

Just then, a young woman approached. She looked regal in a moiré blue and purple silk sari that changed color as she walked. She nodded at Norma. "I'll show her where to sit." She smiled at me and said, "My name is Sharada. Welcome to Kalakshetra."

There was so much going on, a smile and a small 'thank you' was all I could manage. As I made to walk toward the row of sitting women, Sharada put her hand on my arm to hold me back and pointed to a bunch of sandals dumped against the verandah wall. "You had better take off your shoes," she said.

I looked at the heap of sandals piled haphazardly against the wall and hesitated. These were the only dress shoes I owned, and I would have preferred to keep them near me. It must have shown on my face because she laughed. "Do not worry. They will be here when you leave. Your name is... Meenoush, right? Am I saying it properly?"

I nodded 'yes,' and made a mental note to remember that her name was Sharada, an easy name to remember.

"I teach dancing at Kalakshetra, so we will probably see a lot of each other soon." Her lips curled in a wide smile that revealed a perfect row of small child-like teeth, so white, they brightened her dark features.

I immediately took to Sharada. Her bearing was elegant and, although she spoke as Indians did, without the contractions I'd studied in school, her English was musical and clear with a touch of a British accent. I'd have to ask her if she'd lived abroad. I leaned toward her so only she could hear me. "I'm terribly afraid to make a faux pas. Will you please let me know if I say or do something wrong?"

"You will be fine," she said, placing her small brown hand, heavy with gold bangles, on mine.

She led me to a spot halfway down the line and handed me a shawl. "Here, I brought this for you. Use it to cover yourself," she said, pointing at my bare legs.

I was so grateful I could have kissed her. Holding the shawl in front of me, I lowered myself cross-legged to the ground. It was lovely to see how the pleated front of Sharada's sari spread open like a fan as she lowered herself to the ground on my left, all the while making sure her legs were properly tucked in.

"This throw will make your sitting proper and more comfortable!" she said. "Also cover your toes. And, oh! Be sure the soles of your feet are not directed at anyone; Hindus consider that very bad manners."

Across the aisle from me, Stefan was sitting amongst the men. He was busy telling stories and making them laugh. Behind him, the photographer he had hired, a young Indian looking smart in a pair of green army pants, was taking long shots of the gathering. I playfully extended my arm and hand toward Stefan, waving my fingers where the gold of my new wedding band shone enticingly. Stefan in turn wiggled his ring finger, winked at me, and returned to his conversation.

Down the row from me, on my side, women and children sat comfortably behind the green banana leaf plates. I could tell they were curious about me. They leaned forward and stretched their necks to get a better view, and they smiled when they caught my eyes. I looked around for Norma and saw that she'd chosen to sit farther down.

Soon, two light-skinned men appeared. They were bare-chested. A long loop of heavy white string came over their left shoulders and crossed their chests to the right of their waist. As they walked along, I saw that the loop continued behind their back and wondered where the knot was? A length of white cloth tucked at the waist covered their lower bodies and legs the way a sarong would have. They were carrying a large brass vessel between them.

"Brahmins," said Sharada, pointing discreetly with her chin. "They belong to the priests' caste. That is why they wear a sacred thread across their chest."

I had already guessed but thanked Sharada all the same.

Walking between the two rows of guests, the Brahmins scooped small ladles of cold water from the vessel they carried. As I watched, people collected water in their cupped right hands and let it run through their fingers to rinse the banana leaf, after which they swept the leaf off to let it dry. It looked more like a ritual than an actual cleansing method, but I was careful to imitate them.

Soon, more bare-chested, fair-skinned, and often well-fed Brahmins followed the water bearers. Some carried large pots of a soupy concoction, which they ladled into small stainless-steel containers a helper had distributed ahead of them. Others dropped solid food in neat little mounds directly on the individual leaves. The food smelled rich and exotic, and my mouth watered in anticipation. Still, I was puzzled.

"If Brahmins are priests," I said, pointing in the direction of our food detail, "how come they are serving food? Is cooking the right occupation for them?"

"Priests are scholars," said Sharada, sounding professorial in her British-accented voice. "They are knowledgeable about health, so people trust their kitchens. When you eat out or travel, you should always look for a Brahmin restaurant."

"Is that all they do?"

"Of course not. Their professions vary. All Brahmins are not priests. In fact, a majority of them are not."

"It's all rather confusing," I said.

Sharada laughed. "Do not worry. In a few weeks you will have it all figured out."

The food serving was nearly completed. I turned to Sharada.

"Can you tell me what's what on my leaf?"

"It is a typical South Indian meal," she said, with a sweeping motion of her hand. "The dishes are vegetarian. We usually eat white rice with various curried vegetables, chutney, pickles and dhal."

"Which one is the dhal?"

"The yellow lentils next to the rice," said Sharada. "Dhal is important because it is rich in protein. The white liquid in that cup is raita. It tastes like your yogurt, but we prefer it a little sour and spiced with cumin seeds. The short tumbler there contains sambar, a tasty broth made with tamarind paste, turmeric and many more ingredients you probably have not heard of."

"Is South Indian food different from North Indian food?"

"Very much so. Most North Indian dishes contain meat and are loaded with hot chili." Sharada shrugged, showing her distaste. "You will find out when you travel. In South India, we serve condiments and spicy dishes separately. That way you can mix ingredients to your liking. Look at what you got. This is sweet chutney, and these," she said, pointing to a small red pile, "are mango pickles, very spicy, so be careful!"

All around us, the guests had started eating from their leaves, skillfully picking bits from the different food stacks with the fingers of their right hand, mixing and blending bite-size morsels, and using their thumb to push them smoothly into their mouth. In spite of my resolution to learn the Indian way of eating, I found myself looking around for a stray utensil. Stefan, who sat across from me, caught my eye.

"Use your right hand," he said urgently "and whatever you do, don't touch the food with your left hand. I'm sorry I didn't take the time to explain earlier, but I didn't know we would be treated with a traditional Indian reception"

"Yes," confirmed Sharada, who had followed the exchange. "Never touch the food with your left hand." She leaned close to me and whispered in my ear, "The left hand is saved to deal with the private, you know… impure parts of the body."

I was surprised to detect embarrassment in her voice. She had been so self-assured until now. And what did impure parts of the body mean? I had always thought of my body as one unit, not a clean part and an impure one. I looked around and noticed I couldn't see anyone's left hand. It was almost as if everyone was sitting on it or hiding it under the folds of a sari or dhoti.

I didn't fully understand or agree, but it seemed like a good idea to follow suit. I had been too nervous to have breakfast this morning and was hungry. I wanted to eat, even though I'd no idea how to get started without a spoon or fork.

"Watch me," said Sharada, once more coming to my rescue. And she demonstrated how to pick a small bite of rice with her gathered fingers without allowing a single grain to slip through them. She then dipped that bite into the dhal and pushed it inside her mouth with her folded thumb. It looked easy enough. Tentatively, I leaned over the leaf-plate so as not to stain my dress and reached for the food. It was warm to the touch. I did my best to duplicate what Sharada had just showed me but ended up with a slippery yellow glove smelling of caraway spice.

The women around us laughed, shook their heads, and pointed to a finger bowl someone had conveniently placed to my right so I could rinse my hand. Once again, Sharada demonstrated how to prepare a bite and I repeated the maneuver, adding a colorful sliver of the mango

I had seen Sharada slip into her mixture. No words were needed. This time half of the food made it to my open mouth, and I pushed it all the way in with my thumb to a chorus of encouraging nods from my sympathetic audience. I think they appreciated my efforts to eat like them.

All at once my mouth exploded with fire and my eyes filled with tears. At first, the heat of the pretty mango pickle I'd added to the food was unbearable, but I found that after a minute of discomfort, the flavor was worth the pain. Holding back a grin, Sharada instructed me to dip a small ball of plain rice into the yogurt preparation and place it on my tongue. To my amazement, it dissipated the burn of the chili. It took a while before I was able to taste anything else, but I felt good about my first wrestling match with the food.

On both sides of the aisle guests were now watching me, tipping their heads from side to side the way I had often see Indians do, but I couldn't tell what it meant. It looked negative to me, but their encouraging smiles said otherwise and Sharada appeared proud of my progress.

Across from me, Stefan had cleaned up his leaf and was waiting for seconds. Emboldened by my small success, I looked at him with a smile of triumph, and he nodded approvingly. I was eager to fit into this colorful and spicy world. I had taken so many things for granted until now, things as simple as sitting at a table and eating with a fork and knife or sleeping in a normal bed. Now, I had to find sleep on a hard cot under an irksome mosquito net. And last, but not least, I was expected to become a vegetarian, a strange choice for someone raised on horse meat, which was my mother's viand of choice for its lean tasty quality. Judging from the feast I was being served today, I might not miss meat after all.

I took another bite. The food was good, but my legs were killing me. Sitting cross-legged on the thin mat had become a torture. I surreptitiously gathered a thick wad of fabric from the shawl and slid it carefully under my tender ankles. As time passed, the pain turned into numbness, and I became so worried about how I was going to get up that it spoiled the end of my meal. As the guests finished eating and started to lift themselves effortlessly off the ground, I turned to Sharada and grimaced.

"I can't feel my legs anymore."

"You cannot... Oh my! We had better remain here until the rest of the guests leave," she said with a crooked smile.

To kill time and make me forget about my legs, she told me about a Sanskrit drama she was producing using dancing, music, and theater. After I told her about my theater experience and how interested I was in her project, she promised to let me watch a rehearsal.

After the last of the guests had moved away from the banquet area, I was finally able to pivot away from my plate and stretch my legs in front of me. Blood rushing back into my feet and knees hit me with agonizing pain, as if a million flesh-eating ants were crawling all over them, but after a while, and with Sharada's help, I managed to get up and limp away.

When we found Stefan surrounded by a group of teachers and students from the dance school, Sharada introduced me. Most of them spoke passable English and were as curious about me as I was about them. As we talked, I realized they had no idea where France was. In a way it made sense, as they probably hadn't met many overseas students, except for Stefan's friend, the Polish dancer. Part of me wanted to meet her, and part of me wanted to ignore her. But I hadn't come all the way to India to hide, so, to get it over with, I turned to Sharada. "I understand you have a Polish student in the school. If she's here, I would like to meet her."

"You mean Lycette?" said Sharada. "She is in New Delhi and will be back next week." She paused, and her eyes sparkled with excitement. "She is a trained ballet dancer, you know. My best student."

Her best student! It was bad enough to know that my husband had fantasized about this girl, but I hated the fact that Sharada, my new Indian friend, might compare my lack of training to hers. Lycette this and Lycette that. Lycette the ballet dancer; the elegant and worldly ex-wife of—what had Stefan said? A diplomat, no less. I found myself hoping that, maybe, she wouldn't come back from Delhi. After all, one could hope there was, in Delhi, something the amazing Lycette was needed for.

But that negative train of thought was petty and led nowhere so, when I noticed that the photographer Stefan had hired was taking photos of the assembled guests, I pulled my shoulders back and put a smile on my face. I wanted to look my best as I wondered if Lycette and I might ever become friends. Just then Stefan caught my eye and signaled to me that we should go soon. He bowed respectfully to an older teacher, whose forehead was covered in ashes and vermillion stripes and took leave of the girl students in a friendly but formal way. Bashful, the young girls returned his goodbye, glancing up with expressive kohl-lined eyes more playful than their modest words.

Had any of these girls daydreamed about a match with him, the handsome foreigner? Some of the chemistry still lingered in the air, even though, in what appeared to be a predictable South Indian fashion, it was all show and no action. I wanted to reach out and take Stefan's hand in front of them. Stefan, my husband, my mate, but I knew better. Here people touched with their gaze, like these girls were doing.

Reluctantly, I parted from Sharada and some of my future classmates. A lot depended on my getting along with them all, and I felt both anxious and exhilarated about it. When I had joined my theater group in Paris, the actors, director, and stagehands had already been a tight unit like this school was, and I knew from experience that, as an outsider, I would need to work harder than the rest of them to be accepted.

On leaving the reception, Stefan waved to the photographer to join us, and after locating our shoes the three of us left. After my long sitting session it felt good to exercise my legs. We returned to the adjacent T.S. campus and headed for the group of small shrines dotting the luxuriant gardens.

At first, I felt awkward and self-conscious about the camera lens trained on us, but Stefan was all business and urged me to play along. On his suggestion, I posed at the edge of a shallow pond brimming with lotuses and water lilies. We knew that both our mothers would love these shots. A bit farther, Stefan encouraged me to stretch suggestively alongside a voluptuous nude goddess carved into the pillar of a small Hindu temple. I caught a glimpse of the photographer's grin behind the camera.

"These shots are for us," whispered Stefan, with a knowing smile when the photographer was out of earshot. "Too bad you couldn't take off your clothes."

We were walking on a path bordered by large flowering bushes whose names I didn't know, when the strident cawing of a murder of crows startled me. They were flying low over our heads, their blue-black wings stirring a breeze in the turgid afternoon heat.

"Look," said Stefan, pointing excitedly in front of us. "A mongoose family. That's what the crows are after."

Fifty feet ahead, a mongoose was hurrying her furry pups across the empty path. It was the first time I had encountered a live mongoose, but I recognized its long, short-legged bodies at once from images I had seen in books. Above us, the crows circled, looking for an opening to dive-bomb the babies that walked, head-to-tail, under their mother's belly for protection.

Camera at the ready, the photographer jumped ahead of us and fell to one knee. I guessed he was trying for a National Geographic shot, which he got when a crow flew in low and razed the mother's head. Responding to the threat, the mongoose reared violently on its hind legs, red eyes blazing, claws and teeth bared, and hissed ferociously at the winged attacker. It looked so savage that I flinched. I took several steps back and was relieved to see the pups scrambling to safety into the underbrush. Being cowardly, or maybe wise, the crows gave up their kamikaze attack plans, and the mongoose plunged into the leafy bushes lining the path and disappeared.

"That was amazing," said the photographer, getting up and brushing the dirt off his pants.

"I can't believe we actually saw that," I said. "Those baby mongooses were so precious. Do you think we could have some of these pictures?"

"Sure," said the photographer. "It is your photo shoot."

After a while, we reached the guesthouse.

"One last thing," said Stefan, leading the way upstairs to our studio. "As long as you are here, we'll stage a few indoor shots for the people who pay our bills."

"And who would that be?" asked the photographer.

"A Polish organization," said Stefan without elaborating. "Here is what I have in mind. We're going to sit here." He pointed to a bamboo sofa placed under a large, framed poster of the Imperial Polish eagle he had brought with him from France.

"That is quite an eagle. What does it stand for?" asked the photographer, examining it.

"It' a symbol of the free, pre-World War II Poland."

The photographer nodded vacantly, and Stefan didn't bother to ask the man if he knew where Poland was. "Shall we?" he said, inviting me to sit at his side. I complied and sat upright and solemn under the Polish eagle. I wanted to look good to the people who had approved my grant. That was the least I could do.

The camera clicked busily as the photographer danced around us, adjusting the focus of his lens.

"That should do it," said Stefan after a few minutes. "Thanks for taking on this job. Let me know when I can see the proofs."

After we were alone, Stefan and I peeled off our sweaty clothes and took refuge in the shower stall. Standing under the slow drizzle of a cold-water spray with him made me smile as I remembered how nervous I'd been the first time we had showered together at a Parisian bath establishment. I was no longer nervous, but after all the preparations and stress of the reception and the photoshoot, my mind wasn't on lovemaking. The wall thermometer read in the 90's. Naked and wet, I stretched gratefully under the ceiling fan stirring the air over our twin cots. "This small studio is like an oven," I sighed.

Stefan turned to his side to face me. "Remember my student mansard in Paris? It too was like an oven in the summer, but that never stopped us."

That got a chuckle out of me as he climbed onto my cot. Later as we lay apart, sweaty and sated, the reception flashed through my head again. "I think I may have made two friends today."

"I told you, you would. Who are they?" he asked, sleepily.

"Norma and Sharada."

"I know Norma. She's an American ex-pat and is married to Anup, who happens to be the brother of the T.S. President," he recited, as if out of a tour guide. "She's a good friend to have, for she's lived here for twenty or more years and knows everything there is to know about the T.S." He rolled on his left shoulder to face me, and said, "I've also been introduced to Sharada. Isn't she a teacher at Kalakshetra?"

"She is. She mentioned that Lycette is her student. She's very complementary about her being a dancer and all." I waited for his response, but none came, so I continued. "It was really nice talking to

98

her. She was so helpful during lunch, explaining to me how to behave with the food in front of me, and..." I turned to Stefan. He'd had rolled onto his back. Mouth open, he was snoring lightly.

It was only three in the afternoon. All was quiet in the guesthouse and outside. This was the time of day when most living things waited for the heat to subside. I closed my eyes and tried to imagine our future life in the small villa we wanted to rent at the edge of the campus' gentle jungle. I had walked past it and sneaked inside it to get a feel for the place. It was bright and roomy with a red-tiled floor and whitewashed walls. I was excited to see that the cleanup and repairs had already started and prayed no important guest would requisition it and disrupt my plans for our love nest. If all went well, it would be ours in a month.

CHAPTER ELEVEN

TAKITA TAKADIMI

At Stefan's request, Norma had taken me to town to buy saris. She'd suggested I wait on the silk saris that were only worn on formal occasions. Instead, she'd steered me toward cotton saris with traditional borders copied from old-fashioned South Indian designs which appealed to me. To wear with them, we had chosen matching fabrics to be sewn into several bare-midriff blouses known as *cholams* and two long petticoats, which a local tailor had made and delivered to me the next day.

With her help, the following week, I dressed in a sari and left early for the dance school where Sharada had invited me to observe her 7 a.m. beginners' class. Excited and a little shy to finally set foot in that renowned institution whose reputation claimed the highest standard in South India, I found my way to Sharada's class. On entering the long thatched-roof hut where she taught, I saw there were no windows, but the latticed walls let the breeze in, and the room was cool. Facing her students, Sharada was sitting cross-legged on a thin mat. On her invitation, I silently lowered myself on her left. The concrete floor felt cold under my folded legs.

There were no male students in this class. On their feet, backs erect, the dancers first recited a prayer in a rhythmical language which I guessed was Sanskrit. After the prayer ended they waited, feet solidly planted, wrists on hips. As soon as Sharada picked up a short wooden stick and started tapping a simple but compelling beat on a woodblock, the girls came to life like marionettes in a puppet show. In time with the thumping, Sharada's voice rose and fell in a rhythmical singsong of clipped, nonsensical syllables: takita, takadimi, takita, takadimi.

Five rows of brightly clad girls who looked to be between eight and twelve slid gracefully to their right like a flock of brilliant birds veering on the wind. I could see and hear their feet slapping effortless rhythmic patterns across the classroom floor worn smooth by generations of dancers. They moved as one to the driving beat: takita, takadimi, taka, taka, din, din.

It was a new language, precise, demanding, leaving no room for ambivalence. I was amazed by the coordination of the dancers whose assured feet responded in unison to a Morse message dictated by the sure hand of their teacher.

I had been told that most students applying to Kalakshetra came with several years of private coaching before being admitted. Did it mean they'd started dancing when they were four or five? The shoulders and arms of the pre-pubescent girls I was watching were thin. They looked light, yet their frail appearance hid a steely stamina. Compared to them, I felt like a block of marble waiting for a sculptor.

Before I joined the school, Stefan had been eager to remind me that by dressing in a sari I was more likely to be accepted by the students and teachers alike. He had a lot of advice for me. "You'll have to enjoy what they love--their clothes, their food, their music and, of course, their dancing. You'll also need to find a way to sit comfortably on the floor for hours, which may take time. You already learned how to eat with your hands, which is good. If you can respect their taboos and smile at their jokes, even if they sound obscure to you, they'll adopt you in no time." I hoped my theater training would help me get through by emulating what they did.

As I was getting ready that morning, fighting with the six yards of cloth that had to be properly pleated and secured around my waist, I'd told Norma about the first time I had worn a sari. It had been for a costume contest on the ocean liner that had brought me to Bombay. I hadn't won any prize, but letting my Indian cabin mates dress me up in a sari for the contest remained a sweet memory.

The sari I wore today was royal blue with a yellow border in which red geometrical shapes were woven. I loved the way it draped over my body, sensuous and elegant. Glass bangles tinkled brightly on my wrists when I moved, and I had managed to insert a short garland of jasmine in my short, braided hair, but, in spite of all my efforts, I still felt like a clumsy outsider. To make it worse, my crossed legs were starting to hurt at the ankles and knees.

I was pleased when, during a break in the class, Sharada turned to me and whispered, "Aiya! Look at you in a sari! You are a natural! You look like a Kashmiri girl!"

"Why a Kashmiri girl?"

"Because you are so fair. And your eyes are green like some of the tribes who live in the Himalayas."

She might have meant it as a compliment, but I wasn't quite sure how to react. I had heard that fair skin was a valuable asset to negotiate a girl's dowry in India, especially in the south where the predominant Dravidian population was dark, while high-caste Brahmins tended to be lighter-skinned. The Indian caste system was still hazy for me, but it bothered me to think that skin color invited preferential treatment. I had rubbed elbows with African and Indian students pursuing university degrees at the Sorbonne in Paris and had always looked at color as variety rather than a status marker. Brigitte's boyfriend was a Masai, and people accepted him and admired his exotic heritage.

As Sharada resumed her class, and the girls repeated their routines with increased tempo, I reflected that India wasn't the only country with a caste system. In the western world, the power of money, old and new, had created its own kind of caste system. There had always been a power hierarchy, the gentrified families, or the nouveau riche, lording over the blue-collar class. I had stood at the bottom of that ladder in France during the years spent under my stepfather's roof. I hadn't forgotten what it felt like to be ostracized because of poverty. I had cried when passed over for the school play because I couldn't afford to buy a costume. I'd been punished for getting into fights with better-off kids making fun of the hand-me-down clothes I wore. And when my toes and heels blistered and bled inside the cheap galoshes in which I walked through rain and snow, I hid my bloody socks to spare Maman's feelings. I knew she did her best for me with the money she had. In those days, we were the low caste. The Harijans.

I dismissed Sharada's comment about my fair complexion but retained her compliment about the way I wore a sari. In spite of my sore ankles and knees, it reassured me. Her words were an indication that I was on the right track to finding acceptance.

The class resumed and an animated dance sequence brought me back to the moment, but my newborn confidence didn't last long. As I watched the smooth flow of arms and legs, the graceful bobbing heads, the mesmerizing finger language and eloquent kohl-lined eyes, I soon felt overwhelmed by the enormity of my situation. I had assumed the school would let me pick and choose what I wanted to learn, mostly the hand language and emoting to be found in Bharata Natyam, but so far, no one was willing to discuss my class selection with me. It appeared arrangements had been made for me to simply join a beginning dance class. Had Stefan done that? Did it mean I'd have to learn with these children and, most embarrassingly, would I be able to keep up with them to protect the grant I had worked so hard to obtain?

The urgent clapping of the woodblock Sharada used to direct the class was seeping into my bones. I became aware of a scent floating in the room. It was a sweet odor. Was it hair oil from the long single braids swinging down the dancers' backs? It wasn't the fragrance of the jasmine and frangipani flowers woven into their hair. Those scents were already familiar to me. No, it was something else catching at the back of my throat. Coconut oil? I'd have to ask Sharada when I got a chance.

The beginners' class ended, and a smaller group of older dancers appeared and stretched, chatting quietly among themselves.

Sharada, who was sitting to my right, in front of me, asked over her shoulder. "So, Meenoosh, what did you think of the class?"

I swallowed hard. What did I think? I was aware that what I said could be misconstrued and might affect my relationship with Sharada and the school. Better to remain vague and complimentary. "It does look amazing, but… exhausting." The last word slipped out of my mouth before I could stop it.

"That, it is. I will not lie to you." She swiveled around to face me, her back to the class.

"Those girls are so young. How are they selected?"

"Some of them have received private tutoring since they were four and must pass an entrance exam to get in."

"Isn't it a little excessive?"

"Parents are eager to have their children study our almost lost traditional dancing and music," said Sharada. "You have to remember that the British suppressed our ancestral culture for nearly three hundred years. After they left in '47, there was a strong revival of our classical Bharata Natyam, which, in Sanskrit, means 'Dance of India.'"

"Why would the British do that?" I asked, stung by the harshness of the colonial reign.

"It was meant to subdue us. Make us good British subjects," said Sharada. "So, as soon as they left, there was a great resurgence of both. Everybody wanted their children to study the old ways. Because of the demand, many people, qualified or not, set themselves up as music and dance gurus."

"So, it was a good thing, right?"

"Good and bad, I suppose. But Kalakshetra stands unique in that regard, because Rukmini Devi, who started the school, is a famed dancer who set her standards to the highest and oldest canons of dancing, supported by ancient scriptures—some of them two thousand years old." To soften her professorial delivery, she grinned and added, "You will study that in your dance theory class. And that is why you will have to study Sanskrit. These girls are learning dancing the way it was taught two thousand years ago. Nothing like what you see in those Hollywood movies!" Pleased with her little joke, she got up. "I will be back in a few minutes." she said, looking down at me. "Are you comfortable?"

I smiled and nodded 'yes,' realizing I must have been holding my breath, because as soon as she left, I let out a long sigh. Sharada's mini lesson had been informative, but also scary. The prospect of studying only what I needed for any future theater project was getting dimmer and dimmer.

A drop of sweat ran down from my hairline and tickled my nose. Even though it was only 8 a.m., the sun beat down hard on the thatched roof above our heads. Taking advantage of the break between classes, I stood up to stretch and relieve the ache in my legs but found, once again, that I couldn't feel my feet. For an instant I thought I might fall down, and when the restored blood circulation surged up my calves, the now familiar sting of a thousand insects dug into my flesh. The pain was crippling. It was maddening. It hurt to sit, and it hurt to stand. Careful not to put too much weight on my feet, for I didn't know how sturdy they were, I leaned for support on the hut latticed-walls and looked at the young girls whose stamina had so surprised me.

Their dance costumes limp and damp with sweat, they had settled silently on the floor along the back wall. I would have loved to photograph their small faces shining with expectation as they watched the older dancers line up in front of them, but I hadn't thought of bringing my camera. On second thought, it might have been unkind to photograph them recuperating from the class.

Sharada returned and motioned for me to sit back down. I'd noticed that she mixed Tamil and English when addressing the next group of dancers, but she spoke English to me. "This is my advanced class. We are going to rehearse a *Tillana*. It's a difficult piece that requires speed and more technical skills than you have witnessed so far."

I nodded silently. And worried some more. After seeing the beginners' performance, I feared that whatever these advanced students were about to demonstrate would remain forever beyond my reach, but their line-up was so statuesque and colorful that it lifted my spirit. I hadn't come this far to give up before I'd even started.

The advanced dancers wore the same practice outfit as the younger students. Their short cotton sari, or *dhavani,* was the main item and came in various shades. Under it, they wore a bare-midriff blouse, or *cholam,* and a pair of assorted drawstring pajamas cut with narrow legs and an extra wide seat that allowed them to crouch, bend their knees and perform demanding dance moves without constraints.

The color combination offered by the costumes was a tableau in itself. In Bombay I had seen saris cut from cloth that could have come from anywhere in the world: pastel fabrics printed with floral or paisley patterns, animal borders, art deco motifs and even cubist blocs of color. But South India exuded an archaic presence, an unmistakable cachet that bespoke an unbroken tradition. It could be seen in the temples' architecture, heard in the classical tunes seeping from classrooms and tasted in the food I had eaten on fresh banana leaves. And it was present in fabrics in a way I had never experienced before.

The juxtaposition of colors was aggressive and unique, reds with purples and blacks, blues with yellows and oranges. They were strong and ancient hues, passed down over generations by dedicated dye makers. They were not this year's fashionable shades dictated by modern mills. Norma had explained to me that in India, colors illustrated life. Wedding saris, for instance, were blood red, a symbol of the first blood of virgins. And there was the maroon red of the ancient temple saris that covered revered deities in the temples I had visited. There were whispers that, long ago, blood had been spilled in temples. Had that dark red been chosen to conceal the blood of ancient sacrifices?

For the first time in my life, I could feel the pull and power of colors. Today I wore a bright orange cholam under my royal blue sari, even though I'd always hated orange and was tired of blue after wearing too many blue pleated skirts in school. But in Madras, where the rising sun morphed the molten lead of a sleeping ocean into sprays of crimson and gold and caused sculptures on temple walls to come to life and dance, here where flamingoes streamed across the sky like flames, and where sunset skies exploded with equatorial exuberance, colors, as I knew them, were being reinvented.

Taka, taka, din, din, the wooden stick bounced ferociously to signal a momentum in the story enacted by the dancers. I stirred out of the reverie I had fallen into and tried to focus on the stomping and twirling figures facing me. My feet and legs folded under me had gone to sleep again, for good this time. I tried to find a better position, but the concrete floor yielded no comfort. I looked enviously at Sharada who sat straight and prim like one of the Indian goddesses that abounded on the walls of Hindu shrines in Madras.

The dance number ended in a complicated display of hand and foot work, and the dancers, very much in control, pranced gracefully backwards toward the far wall of the room. A single burst of applause erupted at the hut's entrance.

"Brava! Bravissima!"

I turned to the newcomer and saw a tall, slender woman in her dance practice outfit. She looked to be in her late twenties. Her features were sharp, with a straight nose and pointed chin. Her light blond hair pulled back into a simple chignon revealed high cheekbones. Under thick black lashes, her blue eyes were large without any help from kohl. My breath caught in my throat. She was beautiful. Sharada turned to greet her.

"Lycette… good to have you back! We started without you, but you are welcome to join the class."

"Sorry to be late, teacher. I got off the plane an hour ago and stopped by my bungalow to change." Lycette spoke in a bright voice suffused with a mix of accents I couldn't identify. She smiled at me and whispered "Hi!" before rushing to join the line-up. I self-consciously forced a smile back and nodded at her. So, this was the famous Lycette, Stefan's Polish friend. Her hello to me had been friendly just now, and I cringed remembering how the mention of her name had nearly provoked a fight between Stefan and me last week. Who was she? Had she ever been a real threat?

The first thing I noticed was that Lycette was a woman, not a girl. In the extreme simplicity of this classroom, she exuded a sense of confidence and sophistication that commanded admiration as Sharada started on the next dance number. Fascinated, I watched as Lycette slipped into the persona of an Indian dancer, squatting effortlessly in a half crouch, pelvis unlocked, knees open, her feet slapping the unforgiving concrete floor in perfect time with Sharada's woodblock prompting. I couldn't help but feel a bitter admiration for her. She was a professional. It was obvious that, for Lycette, dancing was just an extension of movement, as simple as breathing.

Back in Paris, and without having ever received so much as one hour of dance instruction, I had thought it would be enough to want to learn. I would open myself to the dance and absorb it, by osmosis, especially its hand language, which was unique and fascinating. But now, watching Lycette in this advanced class, my heart sank. What had I gotten myself into?

After the class I had been invited to watch ended, Sharada took me to a small hut she used as an office and informed me that she would be supervising my training, but not teaching me. She produced a sheet of paper with a printed schedule of the courses the school director had laid out for me. It wasn't a very long list. I was pleased to see that I would be studying Sanskrit, a prerequisite to learn dance theory, a topic that also included studying the *mudras*, or hand language I was keen on learning. But my heart sank when I saw that I was also expected to join a beginner's dance class. It would be taught by an instructor named Geeta, as Sharada was busy preparing the advanced students for a dance drama to be performed after the graduation ceremony, months from now. Sharada was kind and patient enough to listen to my complaints about not being allowed to choose my own curriculum, but apparently, Kalakshetra wasn't an institution within which a student could negotiate.

How strange, I thought, that the grant that had made me feel so empowered was now holding me hostage to the decision of someone I had never even spoken with. But there was no turning back, and I couldn't remain bitter for long. I hadn't bargained to become a cross between a gymnast and a ballerina, but I wasn't a quitter and part of me was eager to measure myself against what they would throw at me.

CHAPTER TWELVE

KALAKSHETRA

Three days later, after acquiring four dhavanis, and hiring the village tailor to sew the matching cholams and pajamas I needed to conform to the school uniform, I was officially enrolled as a student and started dance classes at Kalakshetra.

That first morning, even though I had a bicycle, I set out to walk to class. It was only a fifteen-minute walk, and the morning was cool. I could have ridden the new bicycle Stefan had bought for me when his old one—a man's bike—had proved to impractical for me as it didn't have a basket for my books, and I didn't trust myself riding with just one hand on the handlebar. On my way I ran into Sujita, an advanced dance student I had been introduced to the day before.

"Namaste," she said, nodding and bringing her hands together.

Happy for her company, I pressed my palms against each other and returned her salutation. Ever since I'd discovered that *Namaste* meant, 'I bow to the divine in you,' I enjoyed using that greeting. What a nice thing to tell another human being. I liked it better than the kissy-kissy manner French people engaged in when they met.

Colorful in our bright, short saris and pantaloon pants, mine green with an orange border, hers purple and red, we followed the groomed alleys shaded by large neem trees. I carried a Sanskrit dictionary and two notebooks. Sujita had only one notebook and a thin pencil box like the one I had taken to school as a child, but hers was decorated with a blue Krishna playing a flute. I didn't need one for the Parker Stylo I kept tucked inside one of the notebooks.

"So, how do you like our dancing?" she asked, looking genuinely curious.

"Honestly, I didn't expect it to be so demanding."

"It is demanding for me too," she said, "so, I imagine it would be more so for you." She waited a minute before inquiring, "In England you were a dancer also?"

"Not England, France," I corrected. It was funny how Indians seemed unaware of most western countries except for England. "And no, I was not a dancer. I studied theater."

"Ah! Every year we stage plays like the Ramayana and the Mahabharata, but instead of actors we have dancers and musicians," she said, excitedly.

"I heard about it," I said, "and was hoping to get involved with those productions."

I wondered if they would let me. I also wondered why the school director had never answered the letter I'd sent her. Apparently, speaking to my husband had been enough for her.

Stuck as I was with mastering the grueling technique of traditional Bharata Natyam, my nineteen-year-old body was taking a beating. How had I ever fantasized I could master it? I must have been mad or just blinded by my desire to please Stefan at any cost.

We were walking past a large banyan tree when I noticed a small dish wedged between the gnarled roots. It was filled with what looked like milk. I pointed at it.

"Is that milk? Are there stray cats around?"

"Not stray cats… no one cares for cats. This milk is for the cobra that lives under the tree," said Sujita.

"A cobra?" I sidestepped hastily to put some distance between the tree and myself. Sujita giggled.

"Do not be afraid!" she said. She spoke with a lilting Tamil accent, and I noticed that she too wasn't using contractions, the way English and American people did when they spoke to me. She put a reassuring hand on my arm.

"Every day, on their way to school, children walk past this tree and take turns leaving an offering of milk for the cobra."

"And in exchange the cobra agrees to leave them alone?" I asked dubiously.

"Yes," said Sujita. "They do the same in other villages. It is a known fact that cobras love milk," she added.

Great! Just great, I thought. I can't wait to write to Brigitte about that. But she'll have to swear not to tell Maman. She would die of fright if she knew.

The Kalakshetra campus resembled a South Indian village built with rows of neat 40'x 80' huts used for regular classes and dance instruction. All had cement floors and thick thatched roofs. Short concrete walls rose about four feet from the ground, after which they were replaced by thin wooden laths loosely woven like a trellis, to allow air to circulate.

To take advantage of the breeze and cooler temperature, dance classes were conducted in the early morning or late afternoon. The beaten dirt paths separating the huts were filled with brilliant bursts of colors as students congregated noisily before filing into their classes. It reminded me of an aviary.

I said goodbye to Sujita and walked into the assigned dance studio where I met Geeta, my designated dance instructor. Sharada had told me that she was one of the best teachers, having lived in the school since she was eight. She was all the founders expected their star-students to be: beautiful, groomed, proficient and entirely vested in the school's reputation for purity and discipline. Considering all that, I was grateful for her patience and lack of criticism for my poor performance.

I greeted her and took my place at the back of the room so as not to block the other girls, some of whom were half my size and couldn't have been more than ten years old. Being assigned to this class was a devastating blow to my ego. Standing in the back row, I pushed down the bitter taste of humiliation their bright-eyed youth and stamina triggered in me, and stared above their heads at Geeta, who was standing against the far wall.

First thing in the morning, we recited a Sanskrit prayer addressed to Lord Ganesh, the elephant-headed God and beloved patron of artists. It was followed by a prayer to Lord Nataraja, an incarnation of Shiva worshipped for having danced the universe into creation. From the moment I'd touched land in Bombay, I'd felt a deep affinity for Hinduism. Everything I had ever read or heard about Ganesh and Nataraja resonated in me. It was as if they were old friends, and now I called on both of them to help me in the next hour, as I had for the past five days.

The prayers finished, Geeta folded smoothly into a sitting lotus position, raised her wooden stick, and brought it down on the wood-block sitting in front of her, her voice rising in time with the tapping.

Ta...tey...tah...ha.

Dit...tey...tah...ha.

I knew those syllables had no meaning. They were just assembled to build phrases that corresponded to a sequence of steps in a dance exercise.

Ta... Lift my left foot and slap the concrete floor, hold for three more beats.

Tey... Lift my right foot and slap the concrete floor, hold for three more beats.

Left. Right. Left. Right. Over and over. Repetitious. I fell into the rhythm of it, making sure to slap the flat of my foot and not the heel, because hitting my heels hurt like hell. My breath was labored. I wanted to stop to wipe the sweat rolling into my eyes and couldn't help but resent the three rows of girls in front of me who were performing this exercise as if playing hopscotch.

"Minouche!" called Geeta. "Open your feet like in ballet, one pointing right, the other left. Then bend your knees. You must bend further down. Look at the girl in front of you. And keep your back straight. Your bottom is sticking out."

What did she think I'd been doing? I could see the posture of the girl in front of me, but my knees were unable to open at such a wide angle, and if I pulled my rear end in, chances were I'd fall down on the floor altogether.

The slow practice of this step continued unrelenting for another ten minutes and then Geeta moved to double time.

Ta.tey.tah.ha.

Dit.tey.tah.ha.

Ta. Lift my left foot and slap the concrete floor, hold for one more beat.

Tey. Lift my right foot and slap the concrete floor, hold for one more beat. My heart was racing in my chest and my thighs were trembling, but the acceleration helped me keep my balance. It was almost bearable. Time passed and I forgot what I was doing in this room filled with children and a mistress of pain. Then the tempo charged to triple time.

Tateytahha

Ditteytahha

Each syllable required that I slap the concrete floor audibly from the knees-open-crouched-stance and back-straight-and-butt-pulled-in position. I no longer could see anything. Tears of pain and frustration mixed with rivulets of sweat rolled from my hairline. My legs were shaking so badly I was afraid I'd collapse. My lungs were on fire, and I thought my heart would explode any minute now.

Geeta stopped. Everyone stopped. The young girls turned around and smiled at me. They were hardly sweating. To them it was just a warm-up exercise. They whispered in Tamil. Probably commenting on my pitiful appearance. Geeta took a long look at me, bit her lower lip thoughtfully and asked me to sit by her side and watch the end of the class. I dragged myself to the front of the room, sat and crossed the legs I no longer knew I had, did my best to hide that I was dying, and prayed Geeta would forget about me.

After the class ended, I stayed behind until circulation came back into my legs. I wasn't going to stumble and fall in front of them. My Sanskrit class was next, but I was in no shape to sit cross-legged on a concrete floor for another hour. I decided to skip it. All I wanted to do was go home and jump in the shower to cool off and restore my sore ego and bruised muscles after the brutal workout both had endured.

Holding on to the trellised bamboo wall, I raised myself and retrieved my notebook and sandals that had been left outside the door. The air was still cool, and I turned my face into a hint of breeze that felt wonderful on my overheated body. But it was the vision of a tall glass full of ice and tea that gave me the incentive to get moving.

Ahead of me I saw Lycette walking in the same direction, past a mango grove. An open-air dance theory class was starting, and she stopped to watch it.

We were the only two foreign students in Kalakshetra, which made it impossible for us to ignore each other. So far, we had met without engaging in personal conversation but as could be expected, I was aware of a palpable current of curiosity in the school. After all, students and staff had witnessed Stefan earlier in the year, hanging out as he waited for Lycette on campus. His former attention to her must have piqued their imagination, and now they expected drama, some kind of scene, a cat fight maybe, like in a Hollywood movie?

I had such mixed feelings about Lycette. Part of me wanted to befriend her. We probably had a lot in common, more, surely, than I could hope to find with an Indian girl. But I was afraid to find out too much about what had happened between her and Stefan before my arrival.

She saw me approach and acted happy for an opportunity to chat. That threw me a little off balance.

"Well, hello there! How are you surviving your class?" she asked.

I was tired of getting that question five times a day, but the sincere expression on her face prompted me to respond honestly.

"Barely." I raised my shoulders and rubbed the middle of my back with a bunched fist. "I just hope it gets easier soon."

"I hate to scare you, but that's not likely to happen," said Lycette with a sympathetic look.

I loved the way she spoke with an elegant and musical accent that sounded similar but different from what I remembered from my sojourn in Spain.

"I heard that you never had formal dance training."

"That's correct."

"I can't imagine what you're going through," she said, biting her lower lip in a pensive way. "After ten years of ballet, I still have a hard time keeping up."

She sounded sincere, so I accepted her statement for what it was. Apparently, the prognosis was bleak.

In front of us, a dozen young girls clad in assorted dhavanis sat on bamboo mats inside a mango grove. Two boys dressed in plain white dhotis sat a little farther back. The teacher, an old man, leaned comfortably on the trunk of a tree; the front part of his skull showed a new growth of white bristles, and as he turned away from me, I caught a glimpse of the knot of hair he wore at the back of his head, Brahmin-style.

It was already getting hot, and my dance outfit was starting to dry on my body. Spreading my arms to let the breeze envelop me, I smiled at Lycette.

"Not flying away... just drying off!" I said, falling into step with her to move on down the road. The braid on my neck felt wet and I lifted it for a few seconds. It was too short to knot it and get it out of the way with a flick of my wrist as I had seen Indian women do. My stomach growled... it had been hours since I had swallowed the dreaded English porridge the guesthouse cooks called breakfast.

We were walking to the far end of the Kalakshetra campus, our sandaled feet safe from scorpions on the gravel path. As we passed a flowering jasmine bush, I picked a blooming sprig, and put it behind my ear. Lycette nodded approvingly and did the same.

"Jasmine flowers are wonderful. I like them better than perfume," she said.

We walked in silence for a few minutes. Before meeting Lycette, I had hated her on principle because Stefan had been, and maybe still was, interested in her. It crossed my mind that I could hate her now for being so blonde and slim and beautiful and such a good dancer. But the thought of befriending her was more intriguing. It would certainly surprise people. It might even shut them up, which I would enjoy, for I didn't like their scrutiny. But what if she was a flirt? What if Stefan's interest hadn't completely died out?

On the other hand, what if Lycette and I, against all odds, chose to become friends? In France, we probably would never have met, but both being expatriates changed the game. Maybe I should give friendship a chance, and today was as good a time as any to start.

CHAPTER THIRTEEN

LYCETTE

Taking the first step wasn't as hard as I'd imagined. "So, where were you born?" I asked.

"Near Warsaw, not too far from Białowieża Forest where your husband was born," replied Lycette, "but I grew up in Argentina."

I noted how she had referred to Stefan as my husband. It was an adroit move on her part. She had found a subtle way to acknowledge the new order. I replied without revealing my feelings.

"How come Argentina?"

"Like many families during World War II, my parents had to flee, first from the Russians, then the Germans, and Argentina was welcoming immigrants in those days."

I thought back to Stefan's family history, what I knew of it. In 1939, when the Germans and Soviets were allies, the two great powers had annexed Poland and divided it between themselves. Before long, the Soviets rounded up the population of whole villages and towns, forced them into freight trains and forcibly relocated them to Siberia. Stefan's family was among them. They hadn't seen the storm coming. It was that time Stefan didn't like to discuss. "It's hard to believe they deported a million people," I muttered, awed by the enormity of it.

"I know," said Lycette. "They called it "the de-Polinization.""

"You were lucky to have left before that happened," I said.

"Yes, we fled in '38. But fortunately, the Poles who were sent to Siberia got a break in '42."

"You're amazing…How do you remember all these dates?"

"My parents made sure I attended Polish schools in Argentina. They taught us well."

Lycette stared into the distance, gathering her thoughts before continuing. "When the Germans broke their alliance with the Soviets, the Russians allowed 110,000 Poles to leave the Soviet Union. That included 36,000 women and children."

"And Stefan was among them," I said, remembering snippets of things he had said about how hungry the people had been during that exodus, and how he and his brother had scoured the fields to find random onions. A treat for them.

"Those relocated Poles ended up in many places," Lycette said. "Iran, India, Palestine, New Zealand, British Africa and even Mexico. All the able-bodied men eagerly joined the allies to fight the Germans on the western front. Meanwhile, their wives and children were shipped to safe military camps where they stayed until the end of the war."

"I bet you had an amazing history teacher. This was a lot for kids to memorize"

"We were not just kids. We were Polish children. You see, Poles are very patriotic. Look at them now. They've been ruled by the Soviets for twenty-one years and can't wait for Poland to be free again."

Being run out of their country of birth would have given Lycette and Stefan a lot in common. Looking at her now, I wondered what it had been like for her to grow up in exile.

"How old were you when you left? Did your family lose

everything?" Hopefully, my questions would not offend her. We were not friends yet, but we were making progress.

"Let's see, in '38 I was six." said Lycette. "My father was a banker and he managed to siphon most of his money into a Swiss account ahead of time. After the money was safely out of the country, we fled with my mom, my two brothers and my grandmother. Just in time, in the winter of '38. We'd to leave our home behind, but we weren't poor."

"How did you exit the country?" I asked. In spite of myself, I was fascinated.

"My brothers and I thought we were going on vacation," said Lycette. She made a funny face, probably remembering her brothers' shenanigans. "To avoid raising suspicions, my father had only packed three suitcases with winter outfits. We went to sleep, woke up in Gdansk and boarded a ferry headed to Malmö, in Sweden. From there it was just a hop and a skip to Denmark and England. I learned later that he had secured false papers for all of us. We were lucky, but it was not a heroic escape."

She might have been playing it down, but it sounded quite heroic to me, and I surprised myself by blurting out, "When I was fourteen, my mom and I escaped too."

"Escaped? From France? Where did you go?" It was Lycette's turn to be intrigued. She stopped and turned toward me to peer into my face.

"Oh! It was nothing like your WWII escape. More of a domestic war." Lost in the harrowing memories of that day, I shuddered and closed my eyes for a few seconds before telling her how, when I was fourteen, my mother and I, with my baby sister, had fled from my drunken and abusive stepfather.

Lycette must have seen my shudder, because she lay her hand on my arm and gave it a reassuring squeeze. "But you got away okay, right?"

I nodded and sighed. "We did, but we forgot the cat." After all these years, the abandoned cat was still on my conscience.

"Don't worry. Cats are good at finding new homes," said Lycette, kindly. "So where did you go?"

"Here and there, with friends, until my mom could afford to rent a modest hotel room." Surprisingly, it was easy to tell Lycette our story.

"It must have been dreadful," she said, in a sympathetic voice. "How old were you?"

"I had just turned fourteen."

"What about school?"

Ahead of us, two village boys were playing catch with a red ball. When it bounced near us, I put a foot on it, and before answering Lycette, I kicked it back at them. "I had to change school."

"Were you able to stay in touch with your friends?"

I hesitated. "I didn't really have friends. Most of the kids I knew were afraid of my stepfather."

"You must have felt terribly sad and alone," said Lycette. She was a good listener. Her voice, warm and loaded with empathy, told me she meant what she said and drew me out some more.

"More frightened than sad. We were terrified he might return home early and catch us. We threw what we had secretly prepared ahead of time in a small suitcase and grabbed my sister. There was not much to take anyway. He had already sold everything of value in the apartment."

Shaking her head as if to shrug off some memory of her own, Lycette scowled. "Drunks are the worst."

"Uh-huh."

I took a deep breath and blinked away a couple of tears that had sprung from my eyes. "My books stayed behind. They were heavy and took too much room." More than the cat, I still mourned my books. Most had been precious prizes from school, each one a mark of appreciation from teachers whose kind and supportive words had helped me survive my home life.

With an effort I pulled myself together. The air around me was rich with the smell of warm grass and freshly trimmed hedges. I could feel rather than hear the hum of insects under the voices of another open-air class in which the students repeated Sanskrit words after their teacher. I was here now, and this was paradise. I turned to Lycette, "Getting rid of that man had been my goal for years before it happened. It took a lot of convincing to talk my mom into leaving him."

"That's what shrinks always say about battered wives."

"She was a lot more scared of him than I was. In the end though, I was able to make her see that we had to break through. On the day we left, everything became possible for us. Day-to-day happiness, better jobs for her, continued education for my sister and me, and, most of all, meeting Stefan and coming to India."

I covered my face with my hands for a second and raised my palms in a questioning gesture. "I don't know why I'm telling you all this. I usually don't talk about those times. I'm superstitious that way." I turned to her. "I also didn't mean to talk about me for so long. I'm sorry."

Lycette reached out and touched my arm again, the way my friend Brigitte would have. It was such a European thing to do, touching or locking arms. It was something I'd sorely missed since I lived in India.

"We both have lived through hard times, in different places and for different reasons, and we both can appreciate what freedom means, whether it's political or familial," she said. "I am glad you're here now, and glad we are talking."

I was glad too and liked the way she came across, self-confident and open about who she was, and was grateful she'd acknowledged my emotional account without judgment.

After a beat, still curious to know more about her, I asked, "Tell me about your life in Argentina."

"I liked Argentina. We lived in a hacienda and had lots of animals, dogs, cats, goats, parrots. When my father bought land and started raising cattle, which turned out to be a profitable business, my brothers and I got our own horses."

"It sounds like a great place to grow up. Did you miss Poland at all?"

"Not really. What started like a vacation became a way of life. Many of our neighbors were immigrants from Eastern Europe. They formed a tight community around us. That's when we met La Pavlina, an old, but strikingly beautiful woman who had been a celebrated ballerina in her youth. She became very close to my grandmother. I think they enjoyed reminiscing about the elegant past they had shared in the capitals of Europe. It was La Pavlina who convinced my parents I should learn ballet."

"How old were you then?"

"I was eight. She took me under her wing and started giving me lessons. I took to ballet quickly. Perfecting points was easier for me than riding a horse."

We stopped for a moment so I could take one of my sandals off to remove a stone that had lodged under the arch of my foot.

"And you said she was famous?" I asked, replacing the sandal on my foot.

"Quite so. Before the war, she toured with the Bolshoi. But when she fell in love with a Jewish concert cellist and became pregnant, they let her go. Ballet and children were not compatible."

"What happened to her Jewish lover?" I asked, fearing the worst.

"I believe they got married and moved to Paris, but when the war broke out and France was invaded by the Germans, they too sailed to South America to escape from the Nazis."

I let my breath out. "A good ending to that story."

"Not quite. When I was older, I found out that her husband and son died in a fire soon after they arrived here."

Lost in thought, Lycette was silent for a moment. "She paid a high price for her freedom," she said. "Fortunately, her passion for ballet never died. Teaching dance was her way of contributing to our community."

We left the school grounds and entered the public road bordering the Theosophical Society. It was abuzz with mid-morning traffic.

We passed hand-drawn carts covered with flats of live green plants and flowers. Heading in the other direction, bullock-carts loaded with heaps of dates harvested from the T.S. giant palm-date trees were on their way to a nearby market. "The T.S. gardens generate a lot of jobs for the nearby villagers," said Lycette, patting the head of a little girl who had run to her with her hand outstretched for a coin. Instead of money she gave her a piece of gum she pulled out of her notebook. Delighted, the child ran off.

It all looked so exotic. I once again berated myself for not taking my camera with me everywhere I went.

On our side of the road, past a man selling red and blue mangoes, an old woman squatted in the dirt next to a pyramid of fresh coconuts. When she saw Lycette, she grinned widely, showing worn teeth and red stained gums.

"Quite a sight!" I said, turning my eyes away from the disturbing mouth.

"Nothing wrong with her," laughed Lycette. "She's only been chewing *pan* for fifty years."

"No kidding. What's the attraction, anyway? What's in it?"

"Lime paste and shredded betel nuts rolled into a chewable leaf," said Lycette.

I hadn't paid much attention to pan-chewing since arriving in India.

"What does it taste like?" I asked.

"It's bitter and sharp-tasting, and in New Delhi where my ex-husband is posted, some pan merchants add hash into it."

I had heard from Stefan that Lycette had been married, and was curious to know more about it, but feared it might be in bad taste to pry. It was safer to keep talking about *pan.*

"Hash? Like in hashish? Are you serious?" I said.

She shrugged. "Completely serious. Hashish is legal if you are a practicing Muslim. What can I tell you?" She rolled her eyes and chuckled. "I don't think they can sell these loaded pans in Madras, not legally anyway. But as you can see, most villagers are addicted to pan, the way Indios are addicted to chewing coca leaves in the Andes."

Deep in conversation, we had stopped in front of the coconut seller. The woman swiftly lopped off the tops of two fresh green coconuts with a sharp machete and held them out to us.

"How much?" I asked, pointing at the coconuts.

"Ek rupia," answered the woman lifting one finger in front of her face. "One rupee."

I pulled a rupee note from one of the books I was holding.

Lycette looked embarrassed but recovered quickly.

"I'll owe you!" she said. "I don't carry any money on me." With a wink she added, "No pockets!"

"Don't worry," I said, "I've got it. I never leave home without money for a metro ticket."

That image was so incongruous that we burst out laughing.

I lifted the coconut to my lips and sipped on the fresh liquid. It was sweet, bland, and soothing to my parched throat.

After I had drunk my fill, the old woman gestured for me to give her back the coconut. With one clean stroke of her machete, she cut it in half. With the blade, she lifted the tender white flesh from one of the half shells and handed it back to me. The fruit melted in my mouth.

Eyebrows raised, Lycette was watching me. "What do you think?" she asked.

"I've had it before, but never so fresh and good tasting. I like the flesh from inside. Hum! I didn't realize how hungry I was."

"Me too," said Lycette, slurping the last of her own coconut milk. "This one is still green. See how gelatinous its flesh is? Coconuts are healthy, you know, full of vitamins. Can you buy them in France?"

"They're probably imported from North Africa, but I never had one. Maybe they were too expensive for my mom."

We resumed our walk toward the adjacent T.S. campus. I was heading home and assumed Lycette was too, but she kept walking alongside me as we exited the Kalakshetra campus and entered the T.S.

"Going to the library," she said, sensing my unasked question. "I need something to read."

"I just bought a few books in town," I told her. "I wasn't sure I could use the T.S. library. Do they have good books?"

"The best," said Lycette. "I love reading. My father made sure my brothers and I read all kinds of stuff. We had neighbors from so many countries. He wanted us to learn about, and appreciate, everything about the world we lived in.

"Your father was right, and it sounds like your neighbors were interesting."

"Yes, we were fortunate that way. What about you?"

"I wouldn't know. I wasn't allowed to talk to neighbors. When I was a kid, I had a bad habit of babbling stuff neighbors should never know."

"Really? Like what?"

"Well, there was the time when the gas got cut off after my stepfather gambled away all our money, and I proudly boasted that we were cooking on a wood stove inside the apartment! The neighbors had a field day gossiping about it for months and my mother was mortified. After that I was not allowed to chat with them."

We stepped back to let an unhurried water buffalo pass by. Its blue lips were foamy with scud. The man sitting on its thick neck appeared to be sleeping.

Lycette turned her attention back to me. "What about your family?"

"Hmm, let's see… The only two that count are my mother and my little sister. There is also my grandfather. He's getting old and a little forgetful, but I love him. He was like a father to me before my mother got married. My biological father is a nice man, but he has his own family."

Lycette frowned questioningly, prompting me to continue.

"He was drafted into the army and never got a chance to learn that my mother carried his child, and by the time he found out, he was married to someone else."

"How tragic," said Lycette, sympathetically.

"Not really. Let's just say that, *c'est la vie…*"

"No grandmother?" she asked. "Mine was an important part of my childhood."

I shrugged. "I hardly knew my maternal grandmother. She suffered from depression and ended up in an insane asylum when I was five. She's dead now. I have an uncle, my mom's younger brother. He was fun when I was a kid, but he turned into an alcoholic and a wife-beater after doing his military service in North Africa. So, that wraps it up for the family. No one to feel warm and fuzzy about."

"Are you close to your baby sister?" asked Lycette.

"She's my half-sister. She was three when we ran off. She's in a boarding school now. My mom works two jobs to pay for it."

I was amazed at what I had just confided to a stranger, but she was such a good listener. I caught myself feeling as if I had known her all my life. It was me who broke the silence.

"I had a strange childhood. Sometimes I think that, when I was twelve, I was older than now. And look at you. In spite of the fact that your family had to escape from the Nazis and travel halfway around the world to make a new home, your childhood seems strangely normal."

"Maybe it was," said Lycette. "I don't have anything to compare it to. I was just a kid. I went to school, took dance classes every day, chased the dogs around and struggled to stay on my horse! But I was good at ballet. So, when I turned twelve, my father sent me to a boarding school in La Plata, a large town near Buenos Aires. By special arrangement, half of my time was spent on academic studies and the other half at the dance conservatory."

"I think you had a charmed childhood," I said, half serious and half laughing.

"It may look that way but maybe it wasn't quite so charmed," said Lycette. "By the time I turned seventeen, I was very full of myself. I joined a ballet company. The following year I ran off and got married to a dancer who turned out to be gay, so we divorced, and I went back to my ballet company until I got married to another guy. He was going to be the love of my life but that didn't work out either, so I left him and ended up marrying a middle-aged diplomat!"

"Your ex?" I asked.

"Yes... His Excellency the Argentinean Ambassador to New Delhi," said Lycette derisively. "And see where it landed me? In Madras, going through another divorce." She threw her arms up and burst out laughing. "Three in a row. One might say I'm a serial monogamist," she managed between hiccups. "It sounds like a felony--fifteen years to life." She grimaced, and our hilarity increased.

Hands on knees, tears rolling down our cheeks, we were trying to catch our breath when Stefan turned the corner and stopped in his tracks. I couldn't quite read the look on his face. Astounded? Puzzled? Seeing Lycette and me having such a grand time together was probably the last thing he expected. I hoped he didn't think we were laughing about him. I certainly didn't want to hurt his feelings. On the contrary, I thought he might be happy to see that I had finally met Lycette. We could all be friends now. But I couldn't stop laughing long enough to explain the reason for our mirth. I was helpless. Lycette and I looked at each other and laughed even harder.

CHAPTER FOURTEEN

JAN 1960 - RANGA VILLA

Sitting crossed-legged on the thin mattress that served as a sofa in the living room of Ranga Villa, the small house we had finally been invited to move into the week before Christmas, I looked around the large, airy, square living room and wondered what kind of furniture, if any, we should bring into it. A tall mirror mounted in its corner made it look even bigger and emptier than it was.

It opened onto the covered verandah that fronted the house. I loved the villa's footprint. A basic square. On two sides the living room where I now sat opened onto two rooms whose exterior wall had been replaced with a solid wire mesh screen. The screen kept the wildlife out but allowed the breeze to move through the whole house. For privacy in our bedroom, we had chosen the screened-in back room facing a thick wall of trees. On the other side, the screened-in room faced a clearing with flowering bushes and a lush mango tree. It made for a perfect dining room. Eating in there was like eating outside.

We'd chosen the two corner rooms flanking the entrance as our studies. Their counterpart, in the back of the house, had already been set up as a kitchen and a bathroom.

For sleeping, we'd borrowed the two Indian cots and the double mosquito net we had used in the guesthouse where we'd first resided— my longing for a real double bed would have to wait— and on Norma's advice, we'd contacted the T.S. warehouse manager, who had found the two desks and chairs we needed to equip our studies. He had also dug out a long dining room table with four matching chairs. That's really all we needed for now. The rest, I was sure, would trickle in.

The little villa, repaired, replumbed, scrubbed and white-washed, smelled new, and I welcomed the breeze that brought in the heady scent of a nearby star jasmine bush in bloom. After living inside the four tired wallpapered walls and the linoleum floor of a Parisian boarding house, I found my new environment exhilarating and liberating.

Getting up from the mattress to resume some of the dance moves I had been practicing earlier, I yawned and was stretching when the large calendar hanging on the wall caught my eye. I did a double take. January 23, 1960. My pulse quickened as I counted the months on my fingers. Six months. It was the sixth month anniversary of my arrival in Bombay. I closed my eyes and remembered Stefan detaching himself from the crowd and waving at me with an umbrella as he crossed the quay towards the ship. I remembered the burst of love in my chest and the immense sense of relief I had experienced on seeing him there, waiting for me.

And I still could see how an old Indian man disembarking ahead of me had fallen on his knees and kissed the solid ground. I had been moved and astounded by that demonstration of love for his native land. I felt a smile creep up my cheeks as I recalled turning around to watch my young and crazy traveling companions wave goodbye to me from the ship's upper deck. Would they recognize me now? I looked in the mirror above my desk and saw a serious face looking back at me. Green eyes accented with kohl, forehead decorated with a vermillion bindi, and blond hair pulled back into a braid that brushed my shoulder blades and made my Kalakshetra friends smile indulgently. It was short and thin compared to their heavy dark braids, but I got an "A" for intention.

South India was changing my looks and my perception. The flat rice fields punctuated by tall palms and coconut trees no longer felt alien to me. India was now my home and, although, fueled maybe by my inborn French skepticism I questioned the Brahmins' claim to superior knowledge and authority, I got along with my teachers, my schoolmates, and the people I interacted with. The fact that most people spoke basic English made communication easy, and I was gratified to see that my years of English classes were paying off, even though my pronunciation left a lot to be desired, as did theirs.

Above all, I enjoyed the crowded temples and the smell of burning sandalwood, the vivid colors, the roadside restaurants selling foamy chai and potent Madrasi coffee. I still thought about Paris but didn't miss it anymore. Paris was a magical place, an anchor to my identity, but though I was concerned about Maman's struggle to pay the bills on time, I didn't miss the tiny hotel room we had shared and called home. Here I had a real home, a house with more rooms than I knew what to do with. For the first time in my life, I even had my own study.

I was particularly grateful for the large tile-floored living room where I could practice dance steps, for even though I now knew for sure dancing wasn't for me, I had to maintain my grades in that school to satisfy the grant Foundation. But some days were easier than others and today, as I was reviewing the morning's lesson, I found myself hopelessly at odds with my resolve. The weather was hot and muggy, my chest burned with exertion, my knees and heels hurt from the pounding on the tiled floor, and even though my body had slimmed and acquired a certain amount of stamina over the past four months, the sight of myself in a tall vanity mirror I'd placed in the room to check my posture was so unflattering that I wanted to crawl into a hole. I was in a foul mood when Stefan got home.

"Looking good," he said, beaming at me. He entered the room and threw a satchel full of books on the floor. "I see you're practicing."

"Stop patronizing me," I retorted, leaning my back against the wall to catch my breath. "Nothing is 'looking good' and I've had it with this damned dancing. I want out."

"Just be patient, okay. You're doing much better, and it'll get easier as you go along. You just need more time."

"No, what I need is to be allowed to do it my way. To study the theory, not the technique."

"What's wrong with learning a few moves?" said Stefan from the kitchen where he had stepped in search of something to drink, as was his habit when he came home.

"What's wrong? You're kidding, right? I wonder how long you'd last clomping around with a bunch of ten-year-olds."

He returned with two tall glasses of iced-tea and handed one to me. "Don't be ridiculous!"

I took a long sip of tea, trying to get my frustration under control. "You don't know what it's like. It makes me utterly miserable."

I wiped my face with the end of my dhavani and put the tea down. Walking across the living room, I doused the top of my head with water from a metal tumbler I kept on a corner shelf. It was not lady-like, but I was hot to the bones. I turned to Stefan. "All I needed was to learn just enough to work it into some form of modern theater. Maybe the powers that be at Kalakshetra would have let me if you hadn't interfered."

The blank expression on his face didn't fool me. It reminded me of the look in the eyes of my Paris concierge's Doberman when she'd caught it chewing one of her shoes. He knew what he had done. Still, he asked, "What do you mean, I interfered?"

"I know you spoke to the school director *after* I had clearly requested a customized curriculum. I know you did."

"Why do you keep blaming me? You can learn Bharata Natyam, I know you can."

"Give it up," I spat at him. "I am no dancer, and I don't want to continue the pretense." I knew my voice was raised, but I couldn't control the anger I was feeling towards him.

"Hey, no need to be rude. I'm not forcing you into anything. Sure, I like the idea of you being a dancer. Any man would." I could see he was trying to be funny. He grinned and added, "I'm sure you know that in India, dancing is considered an important part of a girl's dowry."

I threw my arms up in exasperation. "Good for them. But you are not Indian, and neither am I," I said. "Why can't you understand my frustration? The young girls in my class are already better dancers than I'll ever be."

"You don't know that. Practice makes perfect," said Stefan, collapsing with a sigh onto a large floor pillow. He looked so fresh and relaxed; it made me even more furious.

"You just don't get it, do you? You have no idea what it's like to be big, white and clumsy in a classroom filled with lithe and bouncy, brown-skinned children."

He propped his back on the wall. "Well, it's a little late to change your mind," he said, in the professorial tone of voice I hated. "You got a grant to study a specific subject. You'll just have to bite the bullet and get on with it."

"And what if I can't. I'll never be a dancer. Lycette agrees with me. She knows that her superb form and stamina are due to her life-long ballet training."

Stefan sat up abruptly, color climbing to his cheeks. "Leave Lycette out of this," he said. "I don't know what kind of cock-and-bull story she's been feeding you, but she's not helping."

"On the contrary. She seems to be the only objective person around," I said, pleased with myself for finally getting a reaction from him.

I could see he resented Lycette's intrusion into our problems. Maybe he feared that by becoming her friend, I had somehow taken his place in her affection. Controlling his anger, he said calmly, "Okay, so, you tell me. What will Lycette do if you lose your grant? Pay for whatever you decide to study next?"

"Now, *you* are being ridiculous."

"Am I?

I leaned over him and stared into his eyes. "Is this all about money? Is that what's worrying you? That I might lose my grant?"

"Shouldn't that worry you too? What will you tell the Foundation if you leave Kalakshetra?"

"I suppose I could modify my agreement with them, concentrate on other subjects. Languages? Dance theory?"

Red in the face, he jumped to his feet and let out a sibilant vociferation. "*Co ty mówisz?* What are you talking about?"

I'd never heard him slip into Polish before and recoiled at his explosion of anger.

He grabbed my right arm in a tight grip. "What if they disagree and cut you off? What if we have to live on one stipend instead of two? I guess you expect me to support you?" A little spit showed at the corner of his lips as he muttered, "I would, of course, but we would be broke, my dear. Broke! No traveling, no scooter, no extra money to send to your mom. Broke. All because you don't feel like making the effort!"

"But…"

He let go of me and took a step back. "Any way you look at it, you'd be going back on your promise to the Foundation, and to me. I know… I know. You don't care about the money. But I do. I have to. I like us having enough money to travel, have servants, keep this house."

Money was important, but I was not sure it was the only cause of his outburst. Maybe his traumatic childhood was. Maybe he had a need to control things. Calling the shots gave him the sense of order and security he needed in his life. I saw now that I had indulged him in that area when we had first dated. It had surprised and delighted me that he wanted to take care of me, but it had gone too far. Starting now, I felt the need to speak for myself.

"You should have thought about all of this before you interfered in my study plans. Just because I let you order for both of us when we go to the restaurant doesn't mean I want you to rearrange my life to fit your fancy," I said, holding back tears.

"You know what? I've had enough of your complaints. You want to do it your way? Fine. You do that."

He disappeared into the bedroom and reappeared five minutes later with a small travel bag. Without a glance in my direction, he made a beeline for the door, came back to grab his heavy satchel, and got out, slamming the screen door hard behind him.

Infuriated by his refusal to take responsibility for what he had done, I followed him outside and yelled in his direction. "Bravo! You're developing a flair for drama." He didn't respond, and it struck me that, maybe, I was the one.

A second later, the scooter's engine came to life, sputtered, and took off. In the new silence, I heard Rishu, our new Siamese cat, meow indignantly. He usually stayed clear of the Lambretta and must have been surprised by Stefan's rushed exit. I loved the way Rishu talked the way Siamese cats do. I stroked his back to let him know I agreed with him, invited him inside and locked the screen door behind us.

Seething with frustration, I went to my study and sat at my desk. What had just happened? Our first fight. What did it mean? Stefan had never done anything like that before. Where was he going? To hang out with some MU friends? I had no idea what else he might do. I had better discuss dinner with our cook. Surely Stefan would be back for dinner.

I wished Brigitte was nearby. I so needed someone to talk to. Talking to Stefan had been like talking to a wall. But at least, I'd had the last word.

CHAPTER FIFTEEN

AT THE FOOT
OF THE MASTER

The metallic sound of the alarm intruded on my sleep like a thousand bells from hell. Shreds of dreams floated briefly behind my eyelids and burst away like soap bubbles. I rolled over and patted the pillow beside me. My heart sank. Stefan's side of the bed was cold and empty. He hadn't come home last night. Plunging my right hand deep under the thin mattress I pulled the mosquito net free and reached blindly for the alarm clock that usually sat on the bedside table. Finding nothing, I reluctantly opened my eyes and peered into the aquatic pre-dawn light. The clunky old alarm clock rang and rang, out of my reach on top of the dresser, where I had placed it the night before. It was 5 a.m.

I jumped out of bed and slammed the maddening alarm into silence. Part of me wanted to go back to sleep but Krishnamurti was giving a talk in the mango grove this morning, and not only did I want to go, I wanted to get there early to sit in the first row, undistracted. On Stefan's suggestion, I had read Krishnamurti's *First and Last Freedom* volume back in Paris. He was a fascinating person, a philosopher, speaker, and writer who had been groomed to be the new world teacher but had rejected this Messianic role. The path he had chosen was limited to giving talks and writing books. His favorite topics included the nature of the mind, meditation, and bringing about radical change in society. It was unlike anything I had ever read; an inward journey that led me to my mostly unknown self. After also being told by Norma and Sharada that listening to him in person was an incomparable and transcendental experience, I couldn't wait to sit at the foot of a man so many people revered as a Master.

Fully awake now, I entered the bathroom. The glaring lightbulb was harsh but necessary to check the concrete floor around my feet. Before coming to Madras, I had scared Maman and myself half to death with tales of tigers and cobras but had since discovered that the real enemies tended to be much smaller, things like mosquitoes, scorpions and centipedes. I inspected the floor and shower drain, shook my towel before replacing it on the towel stand and stepped under the shower. The water was tepid but there was no need for a hot water heater as the pipes usually remained warm from the previous day's heat. I rinsed off the night sweat without washing my hair and was done in minutes. Stepping out, I dried myself, keenly aware of the cool morning air rais-ing goose bumps on my nude body.

Nudity felt good. It was a luxury I could enjoy only when there were no servants around. I felt a little guilty about that servant business. I was, after all, a working-class kid whose mother had needed two jobs to pay the rent. On the other hand, our need for a cook, a gardener, and a cleaning person had a positive impact on the life of the local villag-ers. They needed that small but steady income from us, now that the Raj was no more, and the Brits had gone home. And to be honest, I needed the time to study.

I rubbed myself dry and did a few yoga stretches to warm up the sore muscles nagging at my legs, neck, and back, courtesy of my dance classes. I chose a sari and a matching blouse—today would be a yellow and green day—threw a raw wool Kashmiri shawl around my shoulders and walked out the door just as the first rays of amber light lit the top branches of the giant tamarind tree that stood guard in front of our house. There was a chill in the air, and I pulled the shawl over my head.

Where was Stefan? Longing washed over me. Was this love, or some aspect of it? If it was, it also felt like pain. I wanted to share with him the crisp springiness of the dewy grass under my sandaled feet and the sight of flaming bougainvillea petals leaning on the house like a thousand butterfly wings. I regretted the fight we'd had yesterday, but why did he insist that I should be a dancer? Was it because it made him look good when we went out? Was it just a male fantasy or a whim? Whatever it was, I felt that decisions about my studies and my career ought to be examined and discussed jointly, as equals, and I was proud of myself for having said so.

And what had he done? He had clammed up, packed a bag, and left. There had been talks about some lectures organized by his mentor at a sister university a short distance from Madras. Maybe he had decided to attend it, but I didn't know for sure, as he hadn't said a word. Damn him and his secretiveness!

In spite of myself, I wondered whether he was up already, and if so, what was he looking at right now? Did he miss me as much as I missed him? Double-damn him! I was barely twenty, and life as I knew it was so full of questions. What was I supposed to do? Who could I turn to for advice?'

As if to answer my question, Rishu rubbed against my leg, and I bent over to caress his café-au-lait colored coat. Soothed by the warm contact of my hand on his short fur and the purring sound issuing from his small body, I breathed in and out a few times to release the angst clutching at my chest, picked him up and dropped him gently on one of the big floor pillows in the living room. I then left, closing the door behind me, and started walking toward the mango grove standing between the T.S. and Kalakshetra. I looked forward to the lecture and hoped it would empty my mind of its inner turmoil and make me whole again.

As a child, to escape the misery my stepfather brought into our family life, I often tried to empty my mind. It was a game I entertained myself with, after my mother put me to bed before going to her job at a theater where she sold the printed programs of the running play. In the summer, as daylight lingered after she left, I read as long as I could. But when darkness descended and streetlights came alive and ushered shadows through the open window, I would lie in bed, sleepless, and stare at the cracks etched in the plaster of the ceiling above my bed. There, I rediscovered the familiar shapes of horses, clouds and dragons populating the stories I made up in my head night after night. Sometimes, tired of a story, I would stop the last sentence, back it up one word at a time and freeze its very last word. I would then discard its letters one at a time, until I visualized the very last letter sliding off the tip of an icicle. I'd wait for it to melt and evaporate into nothingness, but it never happened. Letters and words always came flooding back, mocking me.

The memory of my ten-year-old self made me smile. I loved the curious and precocious child I was. The child who, unknowingly, experimented with meditation. Maybe I could learn from her and try that kind of word-melting meditation again.

When I arrived at the designated grove, twenty or so people were already sitting peacefully. Some were contemplative, a few appeared asleep. I quietly folded and refolded the blanket I had brought along and sat on it with my legs folded beside me. Sitting on the ground for any length of time was still uncomfortable but the blanket helped. I took a long breath and leaned into the heat of the rising sun climbing my back.

Far overhead, crows circled. Crows were everywhere in Madras. A few winged over the gathering with raucous croaks. Noise and silence. I let the noise go. Thoughts came and went. I had traveled to India to be with Stefan. He had been the reason I came, but would he be the reason I stayed? In six months, I had made India my own. Deep down, I knew I was in the right place. Maybe India was offering me things I hadn't even realized I was yearning for. Maybe mornings like this one had been my reason to be here all along. To discover a place and time to sit and learn how to listen.

As more people arrived, they lowered themselves onto the grass mats covering the dew-misted ground. I was struck by the respectful silence enveloping us.

Krishnaji, as people lovingly called him, arrived, climbed the few steps to the raised platform that had been built for him and sat down on a thick piece of rug the organizers had thoughtfully provided for him. He looked around, a smile of recognition in his eyes as he acknowledged a few people in the audience. In spite of his advanced age, his features were strikingly handsome. His white hair, parted neatly to one side, softened the matte cinnamon color of his skin. He was dressed in a tan kurta and narrow-legged Nehru pants that revealed his light, almost frail body. His hands, with their long-tapered fingers, rested folded in his lap. He looked mild, but the intensity behind his eyes as he silently watched us was palpable and betrayed the cutting edge of his mental power.

He closed his eyes and remained quiet for a while. When he spoke, his voice struck me as being high-pitched for a man, but it was strong and purposeful. "How do you name the unnamable?" He looked pointedly into the solemn faces of his audience. "How do you explain color to the blind, music to the deaf? I am sure all of us here have experienced grief at some point in our lives, but how do you explain what grief is to someone who has never endured loss?"

There was a long silence as people waited expectantly for answers he wouldn't give to the question he asked. He surveyed the crowd for a whole minute and started talking again, his voice clear and urgent. "Today we'll talk about love. What do we know about love? Can anyone tell me what love is?"

It struck me that I was wondering the same thing. What was love? Was it the need to reach, to touch, to connect? Was it a longing to share? The desire to hang the word love on a chosen face? Stefan's face? Was it a tune that filled one's heart so full, it might burst? In the pregnant silence that followed, Krishnamurti asked if maybe love wasn't the absence of need. And wasn't the absence of need the same as detachment? Ergo, love was detachment.

I shuddered. How could detachment and love not be opposites? I was in love and couldn't begin to imagine standing alone, stripped of wanting to be loved back. But Krishnamurti was saying otherwise. He was saying that true love meant abdicating ownership of the object of one's love, and that letting go brought freedom from attachment. I wondered if that was what Stefan was seeking in his quest for self-realization? But that wasn't my quest, and that notion filled me with a sense of loss and dread.

My nails dug deep into the palm of my hands as I considered what these teachings might mean for our marriage. Afraid of what else I might discover at the foot of the Master, I started to tremble. I wanted Stefan back. Where had he gone? Would he be home tonight?

In the mottled shade of the mango grove, Krishnamurti's gaze challenged the silent upturned faces of his listeners. A crow glided down from high in the sky to settle on a nearby branch and his round, golden-brown eyes stared curiously at me as tears rolled down my face.

CHAPTER SIXTEEN

THE CONCERT

As I approached home on returning from Krishnamurti's lecture, my pulse picked up and my heart did a happy little somersault on seeing Stefan's scooter in front of the house. I rushed up the verandah steps and kicked my sandals off inside the door.

"So! You're back," I said, on entering the bedroom.

He had just stepped out of the shower and was looking for clean clothes to go to class.

"I forgot Krishnamurti's lecture was this morning. How did it go?" He said it as if nothing had happened between us and slid his white belt into the loops of his starched white pants.

I was relieved that he was back, but not relieved enough to hold my tongue. His casual attitude was reigniting yesterday's frustration, and I answered him in an icy tone of voice. "He was fine, but I was not. Where have you been for the past twenty-four hours?"

He finished buttoning his shirt without answering, combed his hair and picked up the Hindu Times on his way to the breakfast table, where our newly hired cook, an older man by the name of Gangan, had laid out some warm toast and coffee.

We ate in silence, and though it was surreal to sit here together, as if we hadn't had our biggest fight ever the day before, I chose not to question him further. Maybe he would tell me later. Right now, over-riding mixed feelings, I was ridiculously happy to just have him back. Maybe he would come around and understand why I was tired of trying to be someone I wasn't just because he wanted me to.

He finished his toast, drank his tea, and said in a neutral voice, "Don't forget we're going out this afternoon." He picked-up the satchel he'd left by the front door and left. There were no hugs or kisses, but that didn't bother me. He was home. That's what counted.

Still, I wondered if the reason he had come home today was because of the personal invitation he had mentioned earlier, to go this afternoon to a house concert organized by a rich American conducting research at Madras University.

I had been excused from my early morning dance class to go to Krishnamurti's lecture but needed to attend my eleven o'clock Sanskrit class. I would have plenty of time to get ready for the afternoon event. After returning home from my class, I showered, got dressed and I told Gangan to take the night off, as we would be out for dinner. I went into my study and had just started a letter home when Stefan showed up, a little after three. I heard him freshening up and getting changed in our bedroom. Soon he called from the living room. "You ready?"

Pleased with my looks, I took a last glance in the mirror hanging on the back of my study door and came out smoothing the front of my light blue Vichy checkered print dress, one of the dresses a tailor had made for me when I'd first arrived in Bombay. It seemed like the proper outfit to meet this American professor.

Looking me up and down critically, Stefan asked, "How come you're not wearing a sari?"

"Isn't our host American? Moreover, it's hot and this dress is cooler than a sari."

"For god's sake Minouche! We're going to a concert of Indian music, not to lunch at the French Consulate." His tone was so overbearing that I stopped, uncertain what to do next. I sighed.

"But you never told me it was a concert of Indian music; you just said a concert. For all I know it could have been chamber music."

"Suit yourself," he said in a controlled voice. "Anyway, we better go, or we'll be late." Turning his back on me as he walked out the door to his scooter, he shrugged, "You won't be able to sit on the floor close to the stage. You'll have to sit on a chair, in the back."

I climbed behind him, tucked my short dress under my thighs to keep it from flying up and, wrapping my arms around his waist, I held on tight as he roared down the road.

So, I would have to sit on a chair, I thought. Fine with me. It's true that I hadn't shown much enthusiasm at the thought of going to a house concert I knew nothing about. I felt tired, sore, and depressed by my lack of progress in dancing. I would have been happy to stay home writing letters and working with my English books, but Stefan had insisted. It was good manners to attend when one of us—and by 'us' he meant us westerners—went to the trouble of putting together a cultural event in Madras.

When we arrived at Professor's Eisenberg's home, I was surprised to be directed to a gymnasium featuring a stage against the far wall and a large area covered by bamboo mats facing it. By the door where I had entered, several rows of chairs waited for those who needed to remain off the floor. Like me. The chairs were neatly divided into two sections, and I wondered, not for the first time, at the reasons why women had to sit on one side and men on the other? I had gone to an all-girls school and could appreciate the fact that the absence of boys had allowed me to study with fewer distractions than the kids going to a co-ed institution. But the people here were adults, husbands and wives, families.

I took a seat in the women's section and was surprised to see, at the end of the row, two Indian nuns, their dark faces sweaty under starched coifs. How could they ever bear the many layers of their habits? A few older Indian ladies garbed in elegant silk saris had chosen to ignore the floor-sitting. Next to them, several middle-aged foreign women were talking and laughing. They waved at me in a friendly way. By the door, an elegant blonde woman wearing tan slacks and a powdery blue silk blouse greeted the newcomers. I took her to be a member of Eisenberg's family or an academic colleague of his.

So, there I was now, as Stefan had predicted, sitting on a hard metal chair in the very last row of this improvised auditorium at the grand house of Professor R. Eisenberg, PhD, musicologist emeritus, and recipient of a lavish Fulbright grant for post-doctoral research. Though we didn't know for sure, his grant was rumored to be ten times the amount of ours, which made him the most affluent and influential foreign scholar in Madras. On the chair I'd found a program announcing the performance of several Indian artists I had never heard of. I hadn't known Eisenberg was involved in Indian music, but it all made sense now. There definitely wouldn't be any Chamber Music.

Listening to the animated conversations of the foreign women, probably American, I suddenly wished I had enrolled at the University instead of Kalakshetra. Madras University appeared more liberal, and I might have been able to negotiate better courses in an international atmosphere. By now I was aware that Kalakshetra was as closed and insular as a convent, if one can imagine a convent inhabited by colorful dancers, shaved-head musicians, and half-naked Brahmins.

We had arrived early, and the show had yet to start. Bored and hungry, I reached for the bowl of assorted nuts sitting on a small table to my right at the end of the row. My new vegetarian diet kept me hungry all the time and I had deliberately chosen a chair close to that bowl. I picked out three more large raw cashews and nibbled on them with satisfaction. They tasted rich and comforting. I knew that I should stop eating them because they were loaded with fat, but I felt washed out and lonely in my sprightly summer dress and eating felt good. Anyway, nuts were supposed to be good for me. Sure, they were fattening, but didn't they also contain the protein I needed?

Accompanied by several musicians, a woman stepped on stage, lowered herself to the floor on a rolled-up mat, spit a few times into a spittoon conveniently placed to her left, had a sip of water, and hummed a note in tune with the harmonium played by one of her accompanists as she prepared to open the concert. When she started singing, I found myself uncomfortably nauseated by the slippery, meanderings of her voice and did my best to ignore her. To distract myself, I looked around, aware of the curious looks some Indian patrons threw in my direction. I didn't mind. I was getting used to being stared at. Apparently, staring was not considered rude in the local culture, and Indians had mastered the art of it.

In front of the chairs, the bamboo mats observed the same segregation, and I noticed Stefan, right there on the floor among the men, shaking his head like a native to the convoluted rhythms of the music. I wished he could have sat next to me, but even in this American home it was taboo. There were too many local rules, and people like Eisenberg and Stefan enforced them all dutifully. How I missed my free-wheeling Parisian arm-in-arm walks with Stefan and my friends.

To come here, he'd changed into white raw silk pants and a long collarless shirt that showed his tanned neck. From where I sat, I marveled at the ease and elegance of his posture, the way he could sit cross-legged effortlessly for long periods of time. Already I found myself shifting in my chair, as my buns were slowly turning numb. Meanwhile my thighs, calves, and even my heels ached from yesterday's prolonged abuse. I needed to do something about this damned dancing. Maybe check if there was a way for me to switch my studies to the university.

I stretched my legs as far as I could under the chair before me and resumed my people watching. On the women's side of the spectators, I noticed several girls I knew from school, including Sharada and Lycette. Cross-legged on the mats, they sat together and moved in a sensuous and hypnotic manner to the glissandos and spiraling melodies proffered by the singer. It made me wonder how the music could have such a different effect on them. From the corner of my eye, I caught sight of Stefan smiling at Lycette as he swayed with the audience. I felt a stab of jealousy at the realization that they had that music in common.

In spite of my desire to fit in, I felt like a stranger in this crowd. I was stuck, glued to a chair, and irritated by the slow winding and unwinding of the singer's nasal melodies magnified by the speakers hanging behind me on the wall. I wanted to leave but knew that if I did, I would have to face a scene later. I had to stay put and force myself to listen to the alien bubbles that slid like stretched rubber bands out of the singer's throat. To distract me from the slippery sound, I grabbed a handful of nuts and resumed people-watching.

Several rows behind Stefan, I noticed a dark-haired man. Even though I couldn't see his face, there was something about his appearance that alerted me. The way he hunched his shoulders, the little flip of black curls resting at the edge of his shirt's collar, the outline of his head. It was all horribly familiar. I found myself leaning on my neighbor's shoulder to try and catch a glimpse of his profile. As if feeling the weight of my eyes on him, the man swiveled his body to look back and I saw that he was Indian. For an instant our eyes locked and then he turned away. I let out the breath I'd been holding and felt my body relax. I knew in my head that my stepfather was eight thousand kilometers away, but his likeness, even in an Indian man, still made me fear for Maman and my little sister in Paris. Weeks before my departure to India she had caught sight of him on the opposite quay of a metro station. Before her own train had taken her out of his sight, he had extended his arm in her direction and pretended to shoot her, leaving her shaken to the bone. It had only happened once, but it was hard to ignore the sense of guilt I felt at the thought of having abandoned her to start my own life.

Annoyed at myself for allowing the past to tug at me, I reached into the bowl and retrieved one more handful of cashews. A few more wouldn't add a pound on me, would they? I pulled on the hem of my short dress. Stefan had been right. I should have worn a sari. The metal chair I sat on was a torture device. It stuck to my thighs and dug into the inside of my knees. I looked at the clock on the far wall. I had only been here for forty minutes, but it seemed as if the music had been going on for hours and it all sounded the same to me. How could that be? If I could figure out what they were doing, all would not be lost.

I focused on the stage. It was covered with a vivid carmine fabric held down by heavy brass oil lamps shaped like peacocks. Looped garlands of flowers ran along the front of it and dripped down on either end. I counted four performers. The singer, a plump Indian woman, was center front. Clad in a green and gold sari, she sat upright and spread her girth gracefully on the colorful floor. I could tell the audience loved her and I renewed my effort to appreciate her singing, but I couldn't get past the nasal quality of her voice. To her left sat a young girl whose tireless fingers caressed and plucked the strings of a long-necked instrument. I was pleased to recognize it as a tambura, like the one the voice students used at Kalakshetra. I liked the ethereal sound of the tambura. It put out a wall of harmonics designed to support the singer's pitch.

To the right, eyes closed with concentration, a violinist sat, cross-legged with the head of his violin pointing at the floor. I watched him listen to the melodic phrases offered by the singer and repeat sections of them with gusto, vigorously shaking his head as he did so. On the opposite side, a drummer hit both heads of a horizontal wooden drum with alternate strokes of his palms and fingers.

In spite of these noteworthy observations, I was starting to feel seriously sorry for myself. This concert was boring, except for the tambura and maybe the violin, for I had studied violin as a child, until my stepfather had hocked my instrument to raise money to play the horses.

By now the audience was totally engrossed in the performance, swaying and nodding, keeping time by clapping their hands on their thighs, but my eyelids were getting heavier and heavier. I leaned back against my chair and fell asleep.

I didn't know how long I'd been asleep when, with a start, I awoke on the wings of a heavenly sound. Without knowing why, I felt refreshed, reborn, redefined. I felt neither French nor Indian, nor awkwardly big and pink and different from the people around me. My heart was entranced by a new sound, the voice of an instrument that talked to me, seduced me.

I stretched my neck to see where it came from. The stage had been emptied of its previous occupants, who were now sitting on the floor three rows in front of Stefan. I could see them, rocking back and forth with the new music.

A slight man dressed in a soft butter-colored shirt and dhoti occupied the stage, accompanied by his own tambura player and drummer. His warm complexion reminded me of dark chocolate. He wore a white scarf trimmed with gold over one shoulder. A flower garland he must have removed from around his neck lay beside him. He was sitting cross-legged on the floor, shoulders hunched over a string instrument that had to be at least four feet in length. I'd never seen such a design up close before, except in books. The wood it was made of looked rich and ornate under the light, but a closer examination revealed that it was simply made of a long, fretted neck sitting on two gourds. To the right of the musician, the largest of the two gourds rested on the floor. The second, smaller gourd was propped on the musician's left knee and above it, the neck ended into a stylized dragon head. That design allowed the musician's left hand to travel the neck to finger and pull the strings, while his right hand plucked at them at the other end of the neck. It sounded amazing and I loved the way the musician conjured and cajoled the notes into exciting tones and rhythms.

Without taking my eyes off the enchanting apparition, I leaned toward the older Indian woman sitting next to me and asked in a hushed voice. "What instrument is that?"

"It is a veena. A very old instrument." Her strong Tamil accent and the way she nodded her head sideways—like one of those celluloid dolls with bobbing heads—made it difficult for me to understand her words.

"Veenas were mentioned in The Vedas two thousand years ago," said another woman in clear English.

"It sounds heavenly!" That's all I could say, for I had no other words to describe it.

"Heavenly is correct," whispered the second woman reverently, "since the veena is the Goddess Saraswati's instrument, and she, the wife of our God Shiva."

So, that's where I had seen pictures of that instrument. On posters of that goddess.

"We better hush," she added, laying her hand on my bare arm as curious heads turned in our direction.

I sat back, transfixed. Music was turning into colors, water, sky, the beat of my heart. I felt myself lifting from my body. I drank the sound through my skin, felt it pulse through my veins and burst behind my eyes. I felt weightless and whole. For the first time ever, I stopped wondering what I was supposed to do with my life. The answer lay in front of me.

CHAPTER SEVENTEEN

RAO

The performance ended, and I woke out of the parallel universe I had entered under the spell of that music. I didn't know how much time had elapsed. In a trance, I stood up and pushed my way through the audience until I was leaning against the stage where the artist was still sitting behind his instrument. I was in a strange state, both shy and bubbling over with excitement. Unable to contain my impatience, I turned my back to the room and the people trying to get his attention and called on him: "Sir? Please?" until he looked my way.

"Your music was… out of this world. I want to study with you. Will you please teach me?" I said in English. I assumed he understood English, and in any case, the few words of Tamil I knew were entirely inadequate to express the mass of emotions churning inside me. Around me, the people who had come to pay their respects to the performer stopped to listen and stare at us.

The musician was also looking at me with curiosity. I think my question had surprised him, but he was gracious enough to ignore my bad manners.

"Namaste," he said, formally bringing his hands together in greeting. He waited for a bit and, seeing as I was at a loss for more words, he added: "I am Mokkapati Nageswara Rao, and you are?"

"Sorry. My first name is Minouche, and my last name is too hard to pronounce for most people. I didn't mean to be rude, but this is really important to me. I have to find out if you'll teach me to play the... the..." The new name was escaping me, so I pointed to the long-necked dragon on his lap, "That."

"And why do you think you need to study *that*, which, by the way, is called a veena," he said, pointing at his instrument with an amused smile as he wiped his shiny brown face with a small hand towel. Limp strands of wavy black hair stuck to his sweaty forehead. He pushed them back, proceeded to wipe the strings of his veena with a clean towel and waited for me to speak.

This was not an easy conversation. Having said that much, I didn't know what to say next. I turned my back on the people nearest me and said softly, "I don't know why, but I know I have to." It was not really an answer, but I was too excited to be embarrassed, and his calm demeanor was encouraging.

He held my gaze for a few seconds as if to penetrate my thoughts, but there were no answers there. Nonplussed, he nodded and reached for a colorful cloth pouch that was lying behind him. He pulled a business card out of it. When he spoke again, there was a curious light in his eyes.

"Where are you from?" he asked.

"France. I grew up in Paris."

"Ah," he said. "I could tell you were not British or American. So, you are French? We do not meet many French people in Madras." He gave a friendly chuckle that took some of my tension away. "Here is my address and phone number," he said, extending the card to me. "I live in the Mylapore district. Why don't you give me a call and come over in the next few days? I will ask my wife to make some sweets and prepare chai. You like chai, don't you? We will talk then."

My fingers closed on the card. On greeting or leaving a friend, it was customary to bring joint palms in front of one's heart, but I raised my hands in front of my forehead and bowed to him respectfully, the greeting one gave to a guru or the gods in a temple. I hoped my formal Namaste would seal a life-changing moment, but who could say? Did one choose a guru, or did a guru choose you?

I was still caught in the excitement of my daringness when Stefan caught up with me. He looked at me suspiciously and asked, "What just happened here and why were you talking to that man? Have you met him before?"

"No, I just met him. But I want to study the veena with him."

"You want to do what?"

I watched his face turn red, and took a step back, afraid he might explode. "Study the veena with him," I repeated. "That instrument is called a veena." I was shocked by the defiance in my own voice and, reading from the card I had just received, added in a more conciliatory tone, "His name is Mokkapati Nageswara Rao," I said, pulling out the business card I had received. "Why don't you ask Eisenberg? He must like him a lot to feature him in concert. Did you hear him play? Wasn't it incredible! I think I had an out-of-body experience."

He gripped my arm firmly. "Forget the veena. You are enrolled in a dance school, remember? You can't change your major in the middle of the year."

I looked him straight in the eyes. "Yes, I can, and yes, I will." I struggled to free myself from his grip. "Let go of me." I was suddenly angry. I felt a rush of adrenaline as Stefan's fingers dug harder into my forearm. Never before had he grabbed me like that, and never before had I stood up to him so adamantly. But studying the veena was not negotiable. Straightening myself to my full five-foot-six height, I stared into his eyes. "I said, let go of me." In a lower voice I added, "Don't make a scene. People are looking. I know I should have discussed this with you, but I didn't know until today what a veena sounded like."

Finally letting go of my arm, he said, "My point, exactly."

I rubbed my forearm where his fingers had left a livid imprint on my tanned skin. "Look, I've never felt that sure of what I need to do. I just know in my heart that the veena is what I've been looking for. You came here because you were drawn to Indian philosophy and the lure of nirvana. I came here to study this music. I just didn't know it until today."

"You're delirious. What could you possibly do with that music?"

"For a start, I'd be happy to just learn to play that instrument, rather than study dancing which hurts every part of my body. As for what I might do later, I don't know, but I'm sure it will reveal itself. I could teach, integrate Indian melodies into theater plays or movie soundtracks…"

The crowd that had filled the large auditorium was now heading to a verandah where refreshments were being served. The dark-haired man I had noticed earlier was approaching, and I turned my back on him to protect myself from his gaze. Was there such a thing as a cosmic twin? This man made me feel as agitated and apprehensive as my step-father had. I held my breath to make myself invisible, as I had learned to do as a child. But the stranger moved pass us, and I found myself breathing again.

Speaking urgently to get my attention, Stefan tapped my arm. His touch was firm but no longer aggressive. "You mustn't give the Foundation a reason to cancel your scholarship."

"You keep saying that, but they won't," I said. "I'll sort it out and find a way to make it acceptable to them. Please, let's not fight about it, okay? Not here, not ever."

"This is not over. We still need to talk," he insisted.

I would have liked to seal our temporary peace with a hug, a kiss. We French expressed our feelings. We touched, walked arm-in-arm, shook hands, and kissed in the street. I reached for Stefan's hand, but he stiffened and pushed me away.

"How many times do I have to remind you not to do that in public? And for the record, I don't agree with your impetuous decision. And, also for the record, you should have spoken with me before talking to this Rao."

"If it were not for my impetuous decisions, I might still be a virgin," I said, trying to cover my disappointment with a tease. "And if I ignored my feelings, I might still be in Paris, maybe dating someone else, and you would have no wife." My lips were smiling but deep down, for the first time, I didn't really care about his opinion.

He motioned for me to accompany him to the verandah where Eisenberg stood, surrounded by friends. Stefan was soon absorbed in conversation with a pundit from the university and our host introduced me to a French woman, a musicologist, he said, passing through Madras. She was in her forties, very plain and already greying around the temples, but her eyes were sparking with life, and I warmed up to her immediately. We started chatting in French and I discovered that she taught at the *Centre d'Etude de Musiques Orientales* in Paris, an institution I was unaware of. She was a great fan of Rao's and visited Madras frequently to research the local styles of music. I couldn't believe my luck at such a fortuitous encounter and looked forward to having her as my guest next time she was in town. I asked for her business card and stored it next to Rao's.

When she got involved with another group of guests, I absently followed the conversations taking place around me, but my mind was on hyperdrive, wondering what the future held for me. I was on a high, walking on clouds. My clouds.

We rode home in silence. It was hard to argue while riding on a scooter. Back at home that evening, Stefan refused to discuss the matter of my newfound love for music any further. Claiming a head-ache, he skipped dinner and went to bed early while I stayed up late, sitting inside a free-standing mosquito net we had installed on the villa's verandah.

After the heated emotions of the day and the sudden revelation of a possible musical future for me, the night was cool as I contemplated the array of stars shining between the trees. Encouraged by the still-ness around me, my mind was reaching for the right words, the words I would need to convince the Paderewski Foundation that as an alumna of theirs, and an accomplished Indian music specialist, of which there were few, I would represent the Foundation better than a mediocre dance student would.

The next morning, I awoke feeling on top of the world. I couldn't wait to find out more about studying the divine music I had discovered. As I got dressed for my morning dance class, I reviewed in my head the beginning of the letter I would draft to the Foundation, and softly hummed a phrase I remembered from the veena's enticing melodies. More alive than I'd been in weeks, I would have sung out loud if I dared tackle that Indian tune. But I fell silent when I noticed that Stefan was again pulling out his travel bag from under the staircase to the roof where it was stored.

"I have decided to go on a field trip organized by the university," he announced. "I hadn't intended to go, but I think some alone-time will help you clear your head."

Naively, I kept hoping he cared enough for me to support my change of direction and, in an effort to stop him from leaving, or to, at least, slow him down, I told him about meeting the French musicologist and what she'd said about opportunities to work at the Centre d'Etudes de Musiques Orientales in Paris if I followed through with my interest in Indian music. But he dismissed all I said and shot down my idea to approach the grant Foundation. With Stefan, there was no such thing as agreeing to disagree.

Stunned by his cold demeanor and the anger I heard in his voice, all I could ask was, "How long will you be gone?"

"Three or four days," he said, carefully folding several shirts and pairs of pants into the bag. "That should give you time to come to your senses and avoid endangering your grant." Next, some underwear and shorts were stuffed in a side pocket, along with an extra pair of sandals.

With a sinking heart, I watched him zip up the travel bag and look for his bungee cords to secure it to the back of his scooter.

There were no kisses and no goodbyes. The front door slammed. The scooter roared to life, and he was gone.

CHAPTER EIGHTEEN

LETTER TO BRIGITTE

Madras, January 30, 1960

My Dearest Brigitte,
It's been four days since, after we had an argument, Stefan left on a field trip. Four days without a phone call. True, there is no phone in our house, but the post-office clerks routinely forward phone messages to the people living on our campus, and Stefan knows it. Four days. Time enough to receive a postcard, but there has been no postcard either. Four days. A short vacation in his academic life. A silent eternity for me. I am stoically keeping up with the program my current school is forcing on me, a two-hour dance class in the morning, followed by Sanskrit tutoring, and dance theory in the afternoon.

He'll probably be back by the time you receive this letter, but how I wish you were here with me now to talk and cheer me up. You never pretended to like Stefan, so you won't be surprised to hear that we had a fight. No, it wasn't about Lycette. Despite my earlier concerns, Lycette is turning out to be a trustworthy friend. My argument with Stefan erupted over my decision to change the focus of my studies from dance to music. He's afraid of the repercussions it could have on my grant. I tried, without success, to convince him that music was the right choice for me, but there is no discussing things with him. He simply vetoed it. When I refused to change my mind, he packed a bag and walked out the door. He's done it once before, and even though he came back the next day, I wonder if it's going to become a repeat pattern.

Because of his absence, I had to postpone my visit to the musician I approached to be my teacher. It wouldn't be proper for me to go to his house alone. He also couldn't accept me as a student against my husband's wishes. That's India for you, where a married woman needs her husband's approval on all things. How do you like that?

I am puzzled and upset by the way Stefan is changing. Where is the charming and elegant prince who kissed my hand after a waltz at your birthday party?

I hope you had a truly Joyeux Noel. Here, Christmas came and went, hardly noticed, because Stefan thinks of it as an old Christian superstition. He refused to decorate the house and skipped the exchange of gifts. For the first time in my life, I missed the joy of walking past the lavish holiday displays of the Galleries Lafayette windows, and the hunt for small, affordable gifts for maman, Violette, you, and the rest of our friends. I can't tell you how much I missed the Christmas Eve dinner, the lamb or venison dishes, the Christmas cakes and rum grogs, the Christmas songs and general cheer.

I was sad for a whole week, as the house is isolated and I am mostly alone, except for Gangan, the hushed and bespectacled old Indian cook who does the food shopping and comes three times a day to prepare our meals. Alone, except for Rishu, a splendid Siamese cat that someone at the Thai Consulate in Madras gave us. We were told that Rishu comes from a fierce line of felines bred by priests to guard the gold and gems of some of Thailand's rich temples. I like to believe that it's true, and that now Rishu guards me.

Unlike Stefan, Rishu is good company. He responds vocally and physically to every sign of attention I give him and never tires of following me from room to room and rubbing his long silvery body against my legs. Since Gangan doesn't talk much, Rishu and I end up holding entire conversations in my isolated radio-less, TV-less and phone-less house.

Feeling thirsty, I left my desk to fetch a glass of iced water from the refrigerator. I walked past the full-length mirror that hung behind my study door and caught a glimpse of myself wearing a pair of faded jeans and a torn T-shirt. I liked what I saw and smiled in spite of myself. If old jeans could talk, they would tell stories no daughter would want a mother to hear! Those clothes had arrived in my lost trunk, which had finally made it to Madras after being delayed in Marseille, held and searched by customs in Bombay, and finally sent by train to Madras.

Upon discovering that Stefan had gotten rid of my old, patched jeans, the ones I had worn on the ship and a cherished memento of my hitchhiking days in Europe, I had hidden the newly arrived pair under my saris in the chest of drawers holding my clothes. Why had Stefan thrown away my favorite jeans? Was he embarrassed by the person I used to be before he'd married me? I couldn't tell, and he wouldn't admit to the deed, claiming instead that they had been stolen by the laundry people.

In his absence, wearing my old outfits had become a new ritual. As soon as I returned from class, I took a shower and put on my pre-Stefan clothes. That small act of defiance made me feel better and almost made me forget that I missed him, at least some of the time, for while evenings dragged on, empty and shadowy, I always felt happy in the morning, which surprised me, as I'd never expected to enjoy being alone.

I mostly stayed home after school. I preferred it to seeking the company of my new Indian friends whose nosy questions about my husband's whereabouts made me wary. Being home gave me time to think things through and catch up with my reading and correspondence. I sat down and resumed writing to Brigitte.

Don't hate me for not missing Paris as much as I used to. India is getting to me in new ways, putting strange thoughts into my head. For instance, when I see my waist-long hair, I try to imagine what it would be like to crop it short, or even shave my head like some Hindus do. It must be so liberating! I've been wondering what my skull might look like shaved, the bumps I feel with my fingertips, the little nooks, the bone geography I may never discover unless I do it.

I think those ideas have a lot to do with my desire to get even with Stefan for his cold, controlling behavior. He claims to love my long hair. Can you imagine his reaction if I were to shave it off?

Dusk is falling again. I'm always surprised by the speed with which dusk happens in the tropics, and by the way it transforms the tamed jungle that surrounds our house into a dark and threatening labyrinth of whispering branches and leaves. You wouldn't believe how fast the reddest sunsets turn to ink.

I stood up to stretch my legs. Earlier this morning, as I sat on the verandah drinking strong Darjeeling tea served English-style with milk by my anglophile cook, I'd spotted a chameleon slinking on an outer branch of the giant tamarind tree outside our house. Chameleons were such primeval creatures, their eyes, protuberant and round, protected by heavy eyelids that rolled down like headlight shutters on expensive cars. Cleverly camouflaged behind a Krishna flower, its front feet anchored into the branch, this one had suddenly flicked its coiled tongue and caught a visiting fly. The next moment, chameleon and branch had turned into a lifeless mosaic of dark grays and greens.

I'd been admiring my small friend's perfect camouflage when an owl had swooped over the branch and lifted off with a few beats of its wide wings. Clamped in its powerful talons the chameleon hung like a broken puppet. It had happened in the blink of an eye. My heart had surged with compassion for the poor beast. Life and death, so far apart, yet so close. I'd mouthed a silent prayer to keep my mother and sister safe. As an afterthought, I'd added Stefan, wherever he was.

The light was fading, and I shivered. Dusk always depressed me. It brought out mosquitoes and bats, both unpleasant dinner companions. I hated that time, the death of day, the receding light when objects melted into one another and set its demons free. I turned on the light and, despite the heat, slipped on an extra layer of clothing to protect myself from mosquito bites. After I was dressed, I rubbed insect repellent on my face and hands and returned to the kitchen in search of a snack.

Because, as was the custom here, Gangan, our cook went daily to the village to buy whatever he planned on cooking for that day, the kitchen cabinets were mostly bare, save for a few cans of condensed milk, and some cockroach-proof glass jars of rice, dhal, curry powder, and nut assortment I liked. I grabbed a handful of them and threw them distractedly into my mouth as I walked around the house, turning some lights on. I finally returned to my unfinished letter.

What I really crave is meat. Red meat. I would give anything for a steak cooked rare with a smudge of black butter gravy like my mother makes, burning the butter just a little to give it that smoky taste! My mouth starts watering when I imagine the accompanying side of lettuce doused with home-made Dijon vinaigrette and a mountain of pommes frites. A stupid, stupid thought for someone living on a vegetarian campus. Fact be told, I'm not doing great as a vegetarian. I'm hungry all the time, and ravenous for macadamias, cashews, peanuts, almonds, which I've been told are rich in protein. I love them all, but unfortunately, they are also full of calories. Noticing my weight gain, Stefan read a few books about dieting and took it upon himself to put a scale on the dining room table ... Yes, you read it right. A scale, to measure what I put on my plate. He wants me to be slim, like a dancer or a model. His pretty French wife. I pretend to go along because it is too much work to argue with him. Of course, he doesn't know about the nuts I eat behind his back. Still, I guess it would be good to lose a few pounds, but if I chose to lose weight, it will me my decision, not his.

Night settled in. My head spun with a crowd of ideas and emotions. Tugged back and forth between feeling independent and feeling betrayed, I was confused. When I'd first moved in this house, I'd enjoyed its uncluttered spaciousness, but now the empty rooms echoed with voiceless questions that clamored angrily in my head. I wanted answers from Stefan. I wanted answers from myself. Why did I seek his approval?

I retrieved the letter I had left on my desk, sat down and grabbed my pen.

So, here I am, intent on not being eaten alive by mosquitoes and sulking about my husband. Marriage is not what I expected I guess, but don't tell Maman. I don't want to worry her. I think Stefan intends to punish me with his silence. I was pretty sure that 'punishment' was a word I had left behind along with some of my childhood's worst memories. Why would Stefan want to hurt me for being myself? For demanding we talk about what's important to me?

I thought he would be happy for me when I told him I had discovered the very thing I knew I could do well, like master an exotic instrument and become a pioneer of Indian music when we returned to France. With my years of violin and choir background, it should have been obvious. Why should he have something else in mind for me?

You've known me a long time, so I have to ask: Do you think I am being unreasonable?

I put the letter aside. Opening my heart to Brigitte always made me feel better. It helped me see more clearly what was happening to me. But my letter-writing mood had passed. It could wait till tomorrow. Meanwhile, it was just as well Stefan was not home. Right now, I hated him for reminding me of my stepfather who had'd way too much to say about what I could or couldn't do as a child and teenager.

With my stepfather, I had won. I had practically threatened to kill him to protect my mother and myself—not that I was proud of it, but I was a survivor. Stefan had no idea how strong and determined I could be.

I stepped onto the verandah and lowered myself, cross-legged, onto the cool tile floor. I drew a deep breath to center myself, like I had been taught in a Hata Yoga class I had joined a few weeks ago. I focused on breathing; inhale, hold for five seconds, exhale… hold… start again. Pull in the prana, the restorative life energy present in the universe, calm my thoughts, defuse the drama.

I seemed to vacillate a lot between conflict and clarity, but deep inside I knew I had to trust myself. For the first time in our relationship, Stefan's opinions were not going to prevail. He needed to remember the Minouche he had met in Paris, a young woman who thought for herself. Someone who sometimes liked to wear funky clothes for style or comfort, because that's what people her age did. Someone who loved to read, and write, and talk, and laugh. And most importantly, someone who did not need to be told what to study. I would show him that, wife or not, Minouche was perfectly capable of choosing what was best for her.

After a while, I got up. I was feeling calmer. I walked to my brightly lit study and sat back at my desk. I opened a new page in my journal. I usually looked forward to that moment, when the day's observations flowed from my pen to put into words snapshots of my new life, but tonight, the silence made the prospect of journaling unbearable.

Encouraged by my stillness, Rishu jumped into my lap, climbed against my chest, and butted his head under my nose. His whiskers were teasing my nostrils. "I love you too," I assured him. He meowed back. Maybe he was talking to me, his unblinking blue eyes staring straight into mine, as he gently pumped my chest with padded paws. It was a great display of affection, but his fish breath was too much to bear. I lowered his body onto my lap and rubbed the short fur behind his ears until he fell asleep.

I had the greatest talking cat in the world, but I missed people talk. I would have given much for a few days back in Paris to see my friends, but that idea turned to stone when I imagined myself knocking on my mother's door. There was no going home for me. Too much nostalgia. I slammed my journal shut and got up, letting a surprised Rishu slide off my lap and land on all fours. He meowed in protest, arched his back, stretched, and looked at me expectantly.

"Sorry," I said. "Ready for a walk?" The sound of my own voice surprised me. It sounded like someone else's voice. Rishu didn't seem to notice.

I slipped on my leather sandals, threw my journal, a pen, a small flashlight and a Pashmina shawl in a canvas bag, opened the front door and went outside. I didn't bother to lock up. The night breeze, heavy with the scent of flowers, was warm on my face. I noticed with relief that the mosquitoes' dusk-feeding frenzy was over.

I headed toward the beach, and Rishu took off in front of me. Sprinting like the diminutive puma he was, he ran ahead and made a big show of climbing one of the trees bordering the road. Lying in wait for me to pass, he jumped ahead of me, in search of another tree to climb. My mood always lifted in Rishu's company for he embodied, all in one, the best a cat and a dog had to offer.

At the sand's edge, I kicked my sandals off and turned around. Rishu had climbed the last tree and lay, stretched out, on a lookout branch. The beach's open sky and sand wasn't his territory. It was seagulls' country, and I knew he would wait here for me until I turned around to go home.

The tide was retreating, leaving festoons of briny algae behind. Overhead, the high black sky was dotted with scintillating stars whose glow shed a soft luminescence on the shoreline. I walked toward the gently lapping waves, enjoying the feel of the cool wet sand that massaged the soles of my feet. The mere presence of sand and sea made me feel whole and I resolved to spend more time on the beach.

Just then, something smooth and springy underfoot brought me to a halt. I jumped back. A fish? A snake? Here on the beach? I pulled the flashlight out of my bag and directed a stream of light over a cluster of milky round objects, about the size of a golf ball. I remembered Stefan telling me how turtles came ashore to lay their eggs and hide them in the sand. It would be a few days before they hatched. Unfortunately, he'd also said, few of the baby turtles would survive. Hungry seagulls, dogs and jackals would devour their share before they made it back into the sea. Coming closer, I crouched next to them. The exposed eggs were soft and sticky to the touch. I covered them with wet sand before moving on down the beach.

Such was life, a struggle between strength and weakness. In earnest I invoked Vishnu, whose avatar had once been a Tortoise, and asked him to protect the baby turtles. I also called on Ganesh, the elephant-headed god, patron of artists and musicians, to give me strength and protection in the days to come.

I was surprised by the comfort those thoughts gave me. What had happened to the reluctant Catholic-bred Parisian I used to be? Maybe Hindu gods were seducing me because they were more colorful and merciful than mine. On this beach, under this sky, it felt natural to talk to them. Just like walking where fishermen and villagers had traveled back and forth for centuries made me feel safe and rooted. Could this sand, this sky, these gods, now be a part of me?

I stopped by a small dune and dropped my bag beside me. Still warm from the day's sun, the dune was inviting so I lowered myself to the ground and backed into it. Above my head, a shooting star trailed brightly and plunged into the jungle on the far side of the bay. I wished Stefan were here with me to witness this celestial show. I wondered if he missed me or even thought about me at all. With a sigh, I pushed back deeper into the dune. Grounded by that earthly embrace, I let myself relax and drift off.

I awoke with a start, surprised and disoriented to find myself on the beach. I hadn't meant to sleep in the open and shivered under my shawl, which was now damp with the night air. I was cold. Looking up, I saw that the stars had stenciled new patterns in the darkest part of the sky over the jungle fringing the beach, but they were losing their twinkling pulse. To the east, a slight discoloration spreading over the still surface of the Indian Ocean was becoming visible.

Knees drawn to my chin, I sat up on top of the dune and watched the sea. Right where water and heaven met, the ink black sky had faded to a dull charcoal grey outlining mountainous clouds. As I watched, the silhouettes of these airborne giants turned blood red. Soon, a sliver of light pushed steadily up and burst through them, splashing a diadem of golden light over a palette of vermilions and pinks, and daylight asserted itself, draining the reds and golds into the thin colors of dawn.

Surrounded by this immense water world, I wondered dreamily if, deep below, mermaids stirred from their own slumber, as diffused spears of light penetrated the green caves they dwelled in. Did they play on the underbelly of tides or follow wisps of aqueous dreams to the silvery surface?

I waited until there was enough light to read by and, reaching into my canvas bag, I pulled out my journal in which I had copied a few lines from the Tao Te Ching. "Empty your mind of all thoughts. Let your heart be at peace."

Below Lao Tzu's two lines, which I had lovingly scripted with a calligraphy pen, I had scribbled the stream of consciousness thoughts and images that had assailed me after hearing the veena for the first time the other day. I re-read them in a low voice. *"The veena song enters my body a note at a time, pulled, stretched, wound inside a drop, a tear, a sigh. It dances in my toes, my body. Thoughtless Sufi ecstasy. Orgasmic urgency. Shapeless images imprinted deep. Colors, darkness, light, singleness, one. Surrender. Open your heart. The veena, a landscape of desires."*

I felt again that first moment of discovery, the magic of it. A chill went up my spine at the recollection of the trance that had ensued. Where were those words coming from? I stared at them again. They rang true, yet it wasn't like anything I had ever written before. Protectively, I closed the book and held it against my chest. Those thoughts were too precious and too private to share with anyone. Pen in hand, I sat in the sand and waited for more lines to channel through as they had before, but nothing came.

The breeze, cool and salty, raised the soft blonde hair on my arms and I hugged myself for warmth. Overhead, seagulls shrieked and glided, beak first into the waves for their morning catch. The purity of the moment reminded me of the time I had sat at the prow of the ship bringing me to India. It had been night then. I recalled the giant moon and the metallic hue of the waves licking the flanks of the ship. All this beauty was mine, then and now.

I suddenly felt a surge of hope. Hope for my marriage, hope for the truth coming out about my not being a dancer, hope for my newfound love of Indian music and the veena. Problems and solutions were a natural cycle, like the rising and waning of the ocean facing me. I knew I had to write a letter to the Foundation, a letter that would make changing my major possible, and knew that I would have to break through Stefan's need for control if we were going to have a marriage I could live with. I wanted a peer relationship. That was worth fighting for.

But how would I fight? Fighting was easy when it sprang from hate, as it had for my stepfather, but how could I fight someone I loved?

The sun kept rising, warming the sand and tangled heaps of algae. Farther down the beach, I spied two lines of wiry fishermen hauling ropes over their shoulders as they walked into the water to float the primitive catamarans between which they would stretch their net.

I experienced a moment of envy for their simple life and needs. They brought back my happy childhood memories of getting up at the crack of dawn for a morning of seafaring in my great-uncle's fishing boat in Brittany. Like these catamarans, it had smelled of brine and fish, and of the tar that coated the coiled riggings.

The warmth of the sun touched my face, and though I didn't wear a watch I knew it was time to prepare for school. I hurried back the way I had come and Rishu, mewing and purring, jumped down from the tree where he had been hiding all night. He rubbed his body against my legs and bolted ahead of me as he resumed his climbing and jumping game.

CHAPTER NINETEEN

GANGAN

I got home in time to give Gangan, our new cook, time to soft boil a couple of eggs and grill a piece of toast on the coal while I took a shower to get rid of the sand on my body, get dressed, eat, and head off to my dance class.

Stefan was still MIA. I was worried. I was restless. I knew my dance class would be demanding but I had no appetite and couldn't swallow. Stefan had been gone five days now, and I hadn't heard a peep from him. I had no idea how to contact him or any of his MU friends and found it hard to concentrate on anything I did.

To kill time, on returning from Kalakshetra, I decided to defrost our mini-refrigerator—a wedding present Viktor had waited to send us until we'd moved into Ranga Villa, six weeks ago, just before Christmas.

Intimidated by the modern appliance, Gangan was watching me and standing by to help. He was the newest addition to our lives and a godsend. When we'd been faced with the task of hiring servants, getting a decent cook had been on top of our list for, not only was I unprepared to cook meals on a sooty coal pit, but cooking here was a full-time job.

It required trips to the village and negotiating the price of the local fruit and vegetables, as the nearest food stores were in Mypalore.

I certainly wouldn't have known where to start to pick out a cook and was grateful to Norma for stepping in. After screening candidates for us, she'd highly recommended Gangan, a retired army cook who had worked for a British couple here on the T.S. campus for a dozen years.

Gangan looked older than he was. He was losing his hair, wore glasses, and his bent neck and narrow shoulders made me think of a bony old bird, but he was only forty, and in good health. On hiring him, we'd met his three teenage daughters and his wife, a short, dusky-skinned woman with a lopsided smile. Spirited in the way villagers often are, she'd joked that her husband was too thin, and made us promise to fatten him up, which had made everybody, but him, laugh. By now, Gangan was family, and though we didn't talk much, he was very dear to me.

I could tell he was startled when he heard Stefan's motor scooter sputter and die as it coasted the last yard of graveled driveway to the front of the house.

"Morning, Gangan. Coffee, please," said Stefan poking his head into the kitchen. He sounded tired. I couldn't tell if he had seen me tucked behind the refrigerator, or if he was just continuing to ignore me.

Rattled by Stefan's abrupt entrance, Gangan stiffened, glanced at me over his shoulder and replied uneasily, "So sorry, sire. After I served the Memsahib this morning there was only this much left." Turning the palm of his worn hand up, he laid his thumb across the second knuckle of his extended forefinger.

"Pour what's left, will you. Black. No sugar." Stefan stepped into the bedroom to drop his travel bag. He reappeared a minute later. "Coffee ready?"

Shifting from foot to foot, Gangan grabbed the bottom of his dhoti and rearranged it around his waist, revealing thin bony legs. I felt for him but didn't want to get involved. Admitting guilt was not easy for him, but he had no choice.

"I… I drank it, sire." He sneaked a glance at me, for courage maybe, and carried on. "Master gone four days," he piped, straightening his back. Was there a hint of defiance in his voice? I silently applauded his bravery. "I didn't know when Master be back. I'll boil water and make some more."

Regaining his assurance, he scuttled to the charcoal stove, shaking his head from side to side as he spoke. "Ten minutes, tops, coffee ready sire." He grabbed the blackened kettle sitting on counter and filled it under the water faucet in the sink.

"Don't bother, I don't really want coffee anyway," said Stefan wearily. "Can I have some water instead?"

"Acha sire, sure thing." Gangan turned away from the sink. Eyes lowered, he drew a glass of water from the filtered water jug sitting on the far corner of the kitchen counter and handed the glass to Stefan. He was kind of muttering under his breath, upset probably at being denied the opportunity to make up for swiping the leftover coffee.

Closing the refrigerator door, I stepped to the middle of the kitchen. "Welcome back."

Stefan did a double take and acted surprised. "Oh! Hi. I didn't see you there."

I had been too distracted by his exchange with Gangan to observe him closely, but now, as I faced him, I saw how he massaged his temples with the tips of his fingers. I also noticed how the bright outside light streaming in the window made him squint and how the white around his irises was bloodshot.

"I need to rest," he said. Apparently, he was coming down with another one of his migraines.

Gangan and I watched as he left the room with cautious steps, as if the simple slap of his feet on the tiled floor reverberated all the way to the top of his skull.

After he was out of sight, Gangan turned to me and nodded nervously to punctuate his words. "Sick very bad for the Master. Bad for him, bad for you and for me," he said, a concerned look in his wise old eyes. "You think the Master need to return to French?"

"That's not going to happen," I said, trying to sound reassuring. "He's just coming down with a migraine. Migraines are painful, but they are not life threatening. The Master has had them before and has medicine to deal with them." I understood that Gangan worried about his job, and it brought up the question for me too. What would I do if Stefan decided to go back? I couldn't imagine giving up all the prospects India had in store for me.

Gangan busied himself over the sink. I could hear him talking to himself, maybe saying a short prayer for Stefan and another for himself. I imagined he might ask Lord Ganesh for a long life, his health, and a steady job so he might care for his family and save enough money to provide dowries for his daughters. I knew he would need it to find them proper husbands.

"You want I finish cleaning the refrigerator?" he asked, pronouncing re-fri-ge-ra-tor with difficulty, but also respect.

"No thanks. I'm almost done." I could tell it was a big deal for him to work in a household that boasted such a modern appliance. Maybe, when the time came for us to leave India, rather than sell the mini-Frigidaire, I would leave it to him, for one of his daughters when she got married. That would make her extremely desirable to her future in-laws, provided, of course, they had electricity.

"What about lunch, Mumm?"

I finished wiping the refrigerator door and closed it. "I'll find something to munch on. You go home."

"And the Master?"

"He won't eat." I knew all Stefan would do was sleep and wait until the migraine was over. He might get sick to his stomach. I'd often heard him heaving and trying to throw up when migraines struck. I wondered if the only reason he had come home was because he had felt the migraine coming on.

Reassured that everything was in order, Gangan tucked the bottom of his dhoti in the waistband of the worn khaki shorts he wore underneath. That wardrobe detail had always intrigued me. It had to be a leftover habit from his days as an army cook. I watched him step into the pantry and retrieve an old burlap bag in which he had stored a couple of over-ripe fruit and a small clay dish of ghee carefully wrapped in wax paper. Cooks had responsibilities, but they also had privileges, and I didn't mind it when Gangan finished the coffee or took home a few small items we wouldn't miss. They would have gone bad anyway. We were paying him fair Indian wages, but still, a rupee was a rupee, and I knew every rupee he saved was one more he could pledge toward the dowries he was duty-bound to raise. Three daughters were a stressful karma for a simple cook.

He retrieved his tall, ancient bicycle where he had left it that morning, leaning against the kitchen's outside wall. Deftly lifting his right leg and dhoti over the saddle, he gave himself a push with his left foot and slowly started to pedal toward his village, weaving a little on the road as he went.

As I was leaving the kitchen with a banana and a small bowl of mango slices, I heard Stefan throw open the medicine cabinet door and fumble impatiently for the bottle of pills I knew was there. I could imagine how the blinding pulse in his head was increasing and how desperate he was to derail this migraine if he could.

Back in France, I had used Stefan's migraines as an argument to convince Viktor, his mentor, to help me with my grant application. I had presented that, if I found a way to join Stefan in India, I would be able to watch over his health. And I would have if Stefan let me. But presently he chose to push me away, and though I knew it wasn't right, I secretly savored his distress as I tiptoed into the bedroom and pulled the drapes closed to darken the room.

He surely wanted relief and sympathy, but what about me? What about the way I felt about my husband walking out after an argument? What about the questions I had about his volatile behavior and the guilt he was so good at triggering in me for wanting to study a subject of my choice? Was he aware of his role in ramping up uncertainty about our future together?

CHAPTER TWENTY

FEB 1960 - THE MIGRAINE

I ate the banana and the cool, juicy, mango slices, and left for my Sanskrit and dance theory classes. I was glad for the distraction. On returning home, two-and-a-half hours later, I was relieved to see that Stefan's scooter had remained in the driveway. He was still home. A shudder of excitement went through me for I was desperate for reconciliation. I knew that if he could catch the migraine in time with the Ergotamine pills the doctor had prescribed for him, he could avoid the whole ordeal. Ignoring the loud cawing of the crows perched in the Tamarind tree facing our villa, I kicked off my sandals at the door and hurried inside.

It was eerily quiet. I checked his study in case he had recovered sufficiently to return to his books, but he wasn't there. I silently entered the bedroom and found him there, in the dark, curled up in a fetal position on his side under the double mosquito net enclosing our twin canvas-cots, for we had never bought the large king size bed I had fantasized about. Modern mattresses had a reputation for being smothering and hot. Without air-conditioning, going native was the smart way to go.

Noiselessly approaching the cot, I was struck by his physical appearance. He was asleep, but the one eyelid I could see was twitching and his breathing sounded ragged. He had to be dreaming, and if so, what about? I had often shared remembered dreams with him, my lover, my mate, but he never reciprocated, which upset me. It made me feel left out, even angry at times. Was I not worthy of his trust? Why the wall? What was he seeing when he dreamt? What kind of secrets was he hanging onto?

I saw the bottles of pills by the bed. I guessed he hadn't caught the migraine in time and sleep had been his only option. A loose strand of hair brushed across my face as the blades of the overhead fan swept away the muggy air along with my disappointment. He was home but he was out of commission. With a sinking feeling, I realized that he would be out for a long while.

I suddenly felt bone-tired, deflated. I had come home psyched up, ready for a discussion, a fight even, if that's what it took to end his unreasonable power play, but, once again, he'd eluded me. I left the bedroom leaving the door open behind me to catch any breeze that might circulate in the house.

This relationship was too much work. I sighed. What he expected of me wasn't who I was. I was no dancer, and no obedient wife.

I didn't want to feel sorry for myself, or for him, and wished for anger, because anger would feel better than depression, but I didn't have enough energy left for it, and whatever expectation I had entertained ten minutes ago slipped off me like shed skin. So much of what I had discovered in India so far was uplifting and inspiring to me. Sadly, it was my relationship with Stefan which was exhausting me.

Barefoot in the silent house, I walked to the wire-mesh screen that separated the room from the jungle and peered outside. I caught sight of my closest neighbor, a large solitary monkey we had identified as a male rhesus and nicknamed Loulou after the nosey concierge of the Parisian hotel where my mom and I lived. Like my old concierge, Loulou spent a lot of time keeping watch on our movements from his perch on the denuded branch of an old baobab that marked the northern edge of our yard. He also spat insults at Rishu whenever our sleek Siamese ventured inside the invisible boundaries of his territory. Loulou must have felt my eyes on him because he abandoned the quest for fleas on his pale belly and stared right back at me, his round eyes suddenly curious and eager for something to happen. I shrugged and silently informed him that nothing much would happen here today.

To get away from the stifling bedroom, I grabbed two pillows from my side of the cots and settled down on the floor mattress in the airy living room. Through the tall windows framing the front door, I watched the sky for answers, or maybe for comfort. Untouched by city lights, it was velvet black, and studded with stars.

The next morning, I got up early, as usual, and was shocked by Stefan's appearance when he walked, fully dressed, into the drafty dining verandah where breakfast was laid out. His eyes were still bloodshot. He looked tired and there was no spring in his steps. Those migraines took a heavy toll on him. Angry as I was about his controlling claims on me, I felt sorry for him.

His lack of greeting was a glaring sign of continued disapproval. Obviously, he was still mad at me for making a decision without consulting him. I was tempted to ignore him too, but my desire for working things out was stronger than my resentment over his lack of support. I made the first move.

"How do you feel this morning?"

"Ugh," he grunted, picking up *The Hindu Times* sitting on the table.

"Can I get you a cup of coffee?"

Stefan glanced toward the kitchen.

Following his glance, I said, "Gangan is out, running an errand for me."

"Coffee then. Black."

Pathetic as it was, I was relieved by his three-word response. I took it as an overture for conversation. "Do you have time to talk before you go to your lectures?" I asked, setting a steaming cup of coffee in front of him.

Stefan looked at me then, but I could feel the distance between us. "Have you come to your senses about not endangering your grant with that music stuff?"

There it was. Nothing had changed. "Is money all you worry about?" I asked. Pent-up grievances swelled through me. "What about the quality of life I require? What about taking a chance and embarking on something I feel is right for me?"

"You're right about my wanting money," he said, between two sips of the bitter brew. "I grew up in war and exile, and I worked hard to get financial security. And now I won't stand by as you throw it all away on a whim." With those words, he put his cup down on the table, retrieved the satchel he had dropped by the door the day before, and walked out of the house.

Working on the assumption that marriage was a relationship in which each person agreed to disagree from time to time, I decided to forgive him. I still thought that, in his heart, he would forgive me my independent thinking. I also made allowance for his health because of yesterday's migraine, even though it was no excuse for manipulating me. We loved each other. Things had to get back to normal.

But they did not. Stefan got better and continued to move about his business as if I were not in the house, and his behavior started to affect me. I found myself getting clumsy, dropping things without reason, slamming doors. Maybe I expected a reaction from him, but I got none. He continued to ignore me.

Panic set in. It was suddenly hard to breathe with the weight of an iron hand clutching simultaneously at my throat and guts. I was ready to face an argument, but his silence was terrifying.

CHAPTER TWENTY-ONE

FEELING BLUE

Lying on my back on the poorly lit cot, I stared, through the mosquito net, at the clock sitting on the dresser across the room. 10 p.m. I felt rather than saw the wide ceiling fan blades, sluggishly slicing the hot air above me. Why did things have to be this way between us? I hurled the book I had been trying to read to the foot of the bed and rubbed my sweaty palms over my damp cotton T-shirt. The relentless heat was driving me crazy.

Outside the bedroom's screen, the tropical night was filled with sounds. I could hear the metallic calls of crickets, the repetitious ribbit of frogs and the occasional shriek of Loulou roaming close by. The foraging and scratching of creatures moving in the jungly space surrounding Ranga Villa, our home, made me restless.

I got out from under the mosquito net and tiptoed to the dark living room. Light was shining under Stefan's study door. Knowing him, he was probably poring over his philosophy manuals. I pushed back the tears building behind my eyelids. Why wasn't he talking to me? This is not how I had imagined my life in India. Not alone under a suffocating net. What sane woman would?

I took a quick cold shower to cool off my body and air out my frustration, all the while reflecting that evenings in Ranga Villa were the worst, not just because they were muggy and filled with bugs, but because they were more lonely than any other time of day. Maybe downtown Madras was animated and entertaining at night, but the campus we lived on was a scholarly retreat dedicated to "seekers". It had no cafés, no restaurants, no stores, no cinemas, and what made it a Garden of Eden by day, made it dead and empty at night. I hated my lonely evenings here, especially when Stefan spent long after-dinner hours locked in his study instead of engaging in conversation with me or simply hanging out or reading by my side, as I imagined married people did. And, of course, I hated those evenings even more when he pointedly deserted me, like he had for the past few days.

It was at night that I forgot all I loved about India, when my mind dug out the negative aspect of it: the poverty, the filth, the leprosy, the human turds dotting the side of roads, the strangeness of a culture where men could walk hand-in-hand but I couldn't hold my husband's arm in public. My days were filled with brightness and learning, but what was I doing sitting alone, night after night in that house?

Back in Paris, evenings were social. They were a second chance to catch the day, a special time to get together after school or work. People were eager to relax in sidewalk cafés for an espresso or a drink. They were people-watchers, also there to be seen. They had shows to go to, followed by dinner in after-hours restaurants, and in my silent house, I ached for my Paris, past and present. Paris, a city of lights and shadows, stone and water. I missed everything about it, the endless defilé of barges sliding under the Seine's many bridges, the paved alleys lined with antique bookstores, the cars parked helter-skelter on the sidewalks, the intellectual stimulation of a new play, and the simple joy of talking to men and women who understood every nuance of every word I uttered.

That's when homesickness became visceral and pounded on my guts. I missed the verticality of Paris, the stacking and density of buildings standing side by side for miles in every direction, the excited pitch of Gallic voices leaking out of doors and windows, the playfulness of the wind on sheer curtains. I missed the clippedy-clop of high heels dancing along the pavement at dawn like hooves, making me wonder who was passing below my half-closed shutters. Was it a hooker or just a girl who, having missed the last metro, had to leg it home, as I had done many times?

Numbed by Stefan's distant behavior, I dreamed of waking up in the safety of my mother's furnished room. I even missed the nosey concierge who lay in wait behind shifty curtains to mine gossip like others mine gold. I missed the wooden staircase she waxed on hands and knees. I missed the broken step that squeaked under the weight of the upstairs grouch and bounced under the jumping of children. I missed the neighbors I used to resent.

Why was it that, unlike me, Stefan was able to stay up at night and sit in his study unmolested by mosquitoes, the same mosquitoes that ate me alive and chased me under a net at sunset?

I got back into bed and dug angrily into the bed covers to retrieve my book, but I was too upset to read. How comfortable could I get sitting on a netted island of damp crumpled sheets, first on my elbows, then on my back. The clock's tick-tock was loud in my ears as I contemplated that maybe Stefan was waiting for me to fall asleep before he came to bed, unless, of course, he planned to sleep in his den. I wondered if he would talk to me tomorrow.

His side of the bed was still warm when I woke up, and I heard the reassuring whoosh of the shower. He was still here. I waited until he was dressed and had gone to his study to quickly rinse off. I'd take a longer shower after my dance class.

Gangan had already made coffee, so I poured myself a cup and knocked on Stefan's half-open door. "Do you need a refill?" I asked, pointing to his empty cup.

Without raising his eyes from the books he was gathering in his satchel, he shook "No" with his head.

"I know you're upset about the choice I'm making, but I won't apologize for it. Surely you can understand." I was doing my very best to engage him and meet his eyes, but when he raised his head, he looked through me and beyond me. I could feel anger constrict my stomach into an iron knot. "I've had all I can take of your silence. How would you like it if you had been ordered to study medicine instead of philosophy? We need to talk."

"No, we don't." With those words, he threw the satchel on his shoulder and walked past me to the front door.

I followed him to the front steps in a daze of humiliation and misery. I watched the way his body leaned to the right to balance the weight of the Lambretta as it started. I ached to go with him, hold on to him, put my arms around the raw cotton of his shirt that was starting to fill up with air and balloon against his back. My mind was reminiscing about that shirt, a shirt I had bought for him in a government store where villagers sold garments made with the cloth they wove on home looms, as Gandhi had taught them.

The scooter gathered speed and I watched the way Stefan's hair, still wet from his shower, stuck to his head like a helmet. Suddenly it became unbearable. Something snapped inside me.

"I hate you!" I yelled after him, surprising myself.

Alone, spent from that one statement, I stood, scared and confused. The harsh morning light reflected by the whitewashed wall of our villa made me squint, as heavy tears blurred my vision and rolled down my cheeks and inside the corner of my mouth tasting like warm seawater.

"I hate you!" I said again, this time under my breath, feeling the bitter shape of the words form in my mouth. Not words I had ever imagined I would yell at him. How could I have? Had I not traveled five thousand miles to be by his side because he was the magician whose touch had changed my life?

"I hate you!" I yelled at the silent jungle surrounding the house before slamming the door hard, so hard that Loulou swung to safety inside the foliage of the big baobab where he lived, and Rishu jumped down from the long dining room table on which he'd been napping.

"I hate him, not you," I told Rishu, reaching down to scratch a spot behind his ears, a gesture that always elicited a purr from him. But he chose to ignore me. He waited by the door, stared at me over his shoulder and mewed, a clear request for me to let him out. Brushing the tears out of my eyes, I complied and watched him slink past me like a puma on the prowl. He stopped at the edge of the top step, and I stared past him to see what, under the tamarind tree, had captured his attention.

It was a mongoose. Its body, covered with fur as smooth and sleek as an otter's, undulated as it walked past the verandah on short stubby legs. From the tip of its small, pointed head lit by beady red eyes, to the end of its long bushy tail, it gave an uncontested feeling of strength and purpose. I watched it dig in the soft dirt with powerful paws and munch on a sticky bean-like fruit from the tree.

I had read that mongooses had no natural enemies, and that, in a fight with a cobra, the odds were on the mongoose's side for being faster and deadlier. Rishu must have known that too, because when, a couple of months back, I'd seen a mongoose, probably the same one, find its way through the cat door and into the kitchen, Rishu had jumped on top of the water cooler and watched it steal his food without interfering. I pondered where the mongoose's sense of security came from? Right now, it probably had our scent and knew it was being observed, yet it was neither afraid, nor distracted.

A squirrel caught sight of it and squealed a warning to its youngs as it ran back and forth on a branch overlooking the scene. Unperturbed, the mongoose unearthed some shapeless thing, some larva or grub, and devoured it, after which it set out to clean its nose and shiny whiskers with short strokes from diminutive front paws. Its toilette over, it stretched and moved on with an indifferent glance toward the house.

In spite of my heavy heart, I decided it was an auspicious sign. Kipling's *Rikki-Tikki-Tavi* had visited my garden and reminded me to be strong, independent, and resourceful. I had better dry my tears and get ready to win the next confrontation with Stefan. Meanwhile, I had classes to attend. I quickly slipped into my dance practice outfit, mounted my bicycle, and pedaled furiously to Kalakshetra to catch my nine o'clock dance session.

"Lunch ready," called Gangan from the doorway when I returned two hours later. I was always amused by the way he said that, straightening his stooped body and throwing his head back for the announcement like a soldier sounding the morning bugle.

Behind his cloudy glasses, his eyes looked around the room, as if searching for Stefan. He lifted the corner of his dhoti to clean his glasses, revealing leathery thin legs planted in thickly callused feet. As it dawned on him that Stefan wouldn't be present for lunch he turned to me, his voice full of concern. "Master alright?" he asked. "No sick?" When I didn't answer he continued. "Sore throat maybe? Don't speak to Memsahib. Don't speak to me either."

I wondered how much Gangan had figured out. During my stay in the T.S. guesthouse, I'd observed that servants always seemed to know more than met the eye.

"He's fine," I lied with an assurance I didn't feel. "Doing an experiment. Some research for his professor."

Gangan looked at me blankly.

"Not talking, you know. Like a Saddhu. A holy man. He promised not to talk for a few days." It sounded so good I almost wanted to believe it.

Gangan shook his head, and I could see that it made sense to him. He had surely heard of yogis who made vows of silence for years, for life even. But then, he knew Stefan was no yogi, and he must have heard me yelling after him, so he would know something was the matter with us.

"Not too long I hope, Master no talking?" he said finally.

"Not too long," I confirmed, getting up and following him to the verandah where lunch had been laid out.

That verandah had originally been an outdoor terrace, but, like the bedroom, we had transformed it into an extra room by fencing it with a screen mesh to keep out our furry and scaly neighbors. As I played with the food on my plate, some boiled potatoes, sticky okra which Gangan referred to as *ladyfingers*, and something white and starchy I didn't recognize, I wished anew that, instead of the British army, Gangan had spent some years working for the French or Portuguese colonists who still occupied small territories in South India. His cooking might have been more to my liking.

But food wasn't the issue. The issue was Stefan's inflexibility over my decision to change the course of my studies. What was I to do? Go over his head by writing a letter to the Paderewski Foundation to get them to approve my change of direction? It was risky, and Stefan would be furious, but I couldn't think of another way to go. I hadn't found the words to convince him that my plan was sound, but if the foundation approved it, his concerns would be addressed, and he would have to accept it.

So, I sat down in my small study with pencil and paper and started on a draft which I would type when I was satisfied.

CHAPTER TWENTY-TWO

CONFRONTATION

It had been twelve days since Stefan had last spoken to me. Late that afternoon, when I heard Stefan's scooter coast into the driveway, I ignored the commotion his return caused, as he let the front door slam, kicked off his sandals, and dropped his book-heavy bag on the tiled living room floor.

For the past hour, I had been poring over my Sanskrit lesson, tracing the geometrical shapes of its ancient alphabet, and admiring the way most letters fitted into squares. I was surprised when, a few minutes later, I caught Stefan's reflection in the small mirror sitting on my desk. Lingering by the door of my study, he was watching me.

Despite the ceiling fan, it was hot in my study, and I became self-conscious, as if in the presence of a stranger. My face and throat were covered with a light sheen of sweat and the thin turquoise cotton sari I was wearing was damp around my waist. Perspiration tickled the back of my neck under my loosely braided hair, and the fresh garland of jasmine I had woven into it before my dance class this morning had to be wilted by now. Still, their pleasing smell was strong, and I wondered if it was that fragrance that had attracted Stefan to walk in, barefoot and silent behind my chair, as if to kiss my neck like he used to when we first moved into that house.

Though I felt a desperate need to make things right between us, I had a lot of questions on my mind. He had to be aware of the aggravation his objections to my new-found interest in music were inflicting on me and know that his rebuff and his silence were harsh and cruel. But I could also see how silence worked for him. Even in Paris, I could remember times when he'd used the power of silence knowing the distance and immunity it gave him. It afforded him protection when he felt tired, fragile, or unsure of himself, which might be more often than I suspected.

He had, of course, had a lot to contend with in the past few months. There were the many demands of married life added to the frustration of getting no closer to answers in his spiritual search, and to top it all, our financial security endangered by my enthusiasm for choosing a new study path. But wait… What was I doing? Why was I conjuring up excuses for his unforgivable behavior? It was high time to sit him down for a serious talk.

When I turned around, I quickly realized that he hadn't come to bury his face in my hair to share in the comfort of giving and receiving love, for his aqua-colored eyes were distant and cold. Before he could explain his purpose in visiting my study, I went on the attack.

"Did you come here to tell me you'll support my new study plan?"

He took a step back.

To my surprise, I felt oddly calm. Earlier, I had feared a confrontation, but now that I no longer had a choice, I found that the fear was gone. I was no longer worried about consequences. I would have preferred to break his silence more gently, but if provocation was what it took, I was ready for it. The only important thing was to melt down the wall of ice that had grown between us, making me, and maybe him too, miserable.

Stefan looked suspended, as if he'd been about to say something, but couldn't find the words. I took it as a cue and stood up. "We have to talk. Either that, or I move out."

A look of incredulity crossed his face. "Move out? Where? You're my wife! You can't do that!"

I sneered. "Well, well! It looks like you've found your tongue. I guess we are making progress. I was starting to wonder if the prospect of destroying our relationship meant anything to you."

Stefan shook his head. He looked bewildered, and pale in spite of his bronze tan. "What are you talking about? Of course, our relationship means something to me."

I kept my voice tight. Seeing him squirm was new and fed my assertiveness. "Would you call our marriage a relationship, or is it just a co-habitation? I have been dying to ask you. Why did you encourage me to come to India if you're not interested in having a normal life, you know, a life involving communication, affection and sex?"

I was as surprised as he seemed to be by the way words organized themselves and flowed out of my mouth. Stefan advanced into the room and grabbed my arm. "Look, I am sorry for my withdrawal. It was not entirely aimed at you. It started as an exercise in silence that Professor Mahadevan asked us to attempt to see how long we could last without succumbing to the chatter and useless talk that clutters our mind. It felt good. Liberating. More like a retreat for me. It allowed me to sort out my feelings and my thoughts. For months now, I have been craving some time of my own..."

I interrupted him. "You could have told me. I would have given you all the space you craved. Why didn't you speak up? Tell me about your professor's experiment?"

I could see by the look on his face that he had not suspected how serious things had become between us. How could he? I had never really stood up to him until now. I watched as his shoulders sagged and a look of exhaustion crossed his face.

"I don't know," he murmured. "There are so many things I feel, or fail to grasp, or can't explain."

I again suppressed the wave of sympathy creeping in on me. He had just been sick, and part of me wanted to give him a break, but the other side, the new side of me, incited me to push on.

"We've been together for how long? Almost two years, and I feel like I still don't know you. Who are you? You know a great deal about me, but I know almost nothing about you." I snorted. "You made sure of that with your private attitude. Why are you so secretive about your past?"

He shifted uneasily under the attack, raised both hands, palms facing out as a shield, and stammered, "I... don't... know."

"Do you have something to hide?"

"Only from myself. If you had any idea about the dreams and memories still haunting me, you would understand."

A bead of sweat rolled along his nose. He wiped it off with his fist.

Hands on hips like the proverbial fishmonger's wife, I was the one in control for now but, although it was a powerful feeling, being so adversarial felt wretched, quite the opposite of what I had dreamed our relationship to be. I stood stiffly next to my desk and watched him dry his face with the tail of his un-tucked shirt.

"It's so hot in here," he said. "If you want to talk, can we at least go to the beach where it's cool?"

It sounded like a peace offering, and as I stood weighing his words, I suddenly felt itchy and irritated by the muggy heat. Maybe we had gone as far as we could in that first round. It was more than we had communicated in a long time, and an evening stroll on the beach sounded good.

"Let's do it."

I followed Stefan to the front door and found my sandals on the porch where I usually left them. As if guessing our intention, Rishu was out the door in a flash. He ran a few yards and turned around to wait for us, ears flat against his head, whiskers quivering in the cooling outdoor breeze.

Stefan led the way down an overgrown path winding through the dense tropical vegetation. It was narrower than the trail I usually took to the beach. Giant rhododendrons thrust their smooth oily leaves against the length of my sari, slowing my progress, and sap-heavy flowers brushed against my face.

It was only a fifteen-minute walk, and this was a friendly jungle kept under control by local gardeners, but I was nervous. The thought of snakes, and whatever might forage across the mulchy path we followed, made me nervous. Though I would have liked to stay mad at Stefan, I moved closer to him. His presence made me feel safer.

Rishu dashed ahead of us, his silver coat fluffed like a mane around his neck and shoulders, his dark tail, long and thick, trailing behind him. When we reached the first dune, he stopped to jump and claw his way up a gnarled tree trunk.

"Let's not forget to come back this way," said Stefan. "Remember the time I forgot him, and he stayed in a tree all night?"

I hadn't forgotten. I wondered if Rishu had considered Stefan might never come back, as I had when, on a tense winter night in Paris, Stefan had announced he was leaving for India. I was so in love and so scared to lose him.

We took our sandals off and placed them under Rishu's tree. I watched as Stefan stooped to arrange a few pieces of driftwood to mark the entrance to the path we had emerged from.

In a way, Rishu was his cat more than mine. Stefan had spent hours teasing him, training him to jump higher and higher to fend off fake attacks. Rishu had grown strong playing war games and Stefan had scars to prove it. I found it strange that Stefan knew how to show his love to a cat but often failed when it came to his family or me.

Under our feet, the sandy dune was warm from the day's sun. Farther down, a vast expanse of wet sand told us the tide had retreated as far as it would go for the night. The breeze picked up, raising the hair on my arms. It smelled of salt and algae. Releasing a barrette, I let my hair down and ran my fingers through it to allow sweat to dry from my scalp.

To our right, the jungle rose like a wall. I heard a loud rustling sound and looked back but saw nothing. Leaving the dunes behind us, we strode barefoot to the water's edge and waded in the shallows. Undulating ripples licked our feet and legs and cooled the stored heat in our bodies. There was something timeless about the darkening water. The near silence was soft and velvety as was the late afternoon air, and neither Stefan, nor I, wanted to disturb the moment. We walked side by side for a long time, wet sand sinking under our toes and heels. It was ironic that having clamored for communication for so long, I now didn't care for words.

Once in a while, his arm brushed mine and I couldn't help but acknowledge with longing the electric thrill of his touch. It reminded me of the happy moments we had spent when our relationship was new, the touching, the dreaming, the breathless anticipation of walking to his bachelor's pad at a time when all the streets of Paris led to his bed.

We'd been walking for a while in the golden glow of the lowering sun, when the strong smell of drying fish gave away the fishing village before we reached it. Resting several hundred feet apart, the two catamarans I had watched the other morning had been pulled up to dry sand. Armed with hooks and twine, the fishermen were checking the net stretched between them. But for their loincloths, the men were naked, their dark skin grayed by the brine that covered it. They were examining the net for rips and tears, reinforcing a knot here, replacing a floater there. They would be ready before dawn, with hundreds of yards of that heavy net coiled and distributed evenly between the two catamarans. They'd wait for the rising tide to lift them off the sand and out to sea, where each crew would drop its half of the net overboard and row apart to stretch it between them.

I'd often seen them return in the morning, beaching the catamarans on the sand as the whole village, old men, women and children ran excitedly into the surf to help pull the unwieldy net writhing with silvery life.

We sat on a lonely rock and watched for a while, awed by the task these villagers accomplished day after day with their simple tools.

"They know how to feed a whole village," mused Stefan. "My father was a good provider too. When we were in Siberia, he was a better hunter than the other prisoners."

"Why is that?" I asked, thrilled by that opening into his childhood.

"Because he'd done it so often in Poland, in the forest where we lived."

"You lived in a forest?"

He nodded. "My father was a forest warden, a civil servant," he explained. "It was a good job. He owned a house in town and had built a log cabin in the forest.

"So, what happened to your homes when the Russians came?"

Stefan shut his eyes tight. His chin dropped to his chest for a few long seconds. When he lifted his head, his eyes were haunted. "I don't like to speak about this with anyone, except for my brother who was there with me. In fact, I've spent most of my adult life trying to forget it. It's as if I've buried it far away in my mind."

"Maybe talking about it would be good," I said. "Can you remember anything at all?"

"All I remember is that one day, on coming home from playing in the forest, my brother Mietek and I saw a red star nailed to our log cabin door. There was some kind of notice under the star. It was signed with a red sickle. I was only four at the time and couldn't read what it said, but I remember liking the star. We were about to enter the house when a thundering crash made us jump back. There was our father, swinging a short-handled axe. He was destroying everything but the walls inside the cabin."

"My God! Why was he doing that?"

"Mietek and I had no idea. We were terrified. We watched from outside, half hidden behind a broken window. We couldn't under-stand. Our father was raving. "No God-damned Russians will sit at MY table or make love in MY bed." Was this the same calm and loving father who, a month ago, had brought home to us a wolf cub he'd rescued? From our hiding place, we looked around for the pup, but it was nowhere to be seen."

Stefan's eyes were open, but I don't think he saw where we were. He was back in that cabin on that heart-wrenching day. I took his hand, but he didn't respond. "What about your mother?" I asked. "Didn't she try to stop him?"

"She was crying in the middle of the wreckage. Praying. Whispering a litany of grievances to a god who had forsaken her. But her hands were busy stuffing things into the lining of our thick winter coats." He paused. "She probably would have joined him in the rampage if Father hadn't instructed her to hide our most precious belongings—photos, documents, jewelry and money. He knew we could use them later to barter and trade." He paused to look at me in the diminishing light. "It's weird how memory works. I've forgotten so many things, but I can still see her stitching the lining of the coats shut with waxed button thread."

"Did your father ever calm down?"

"Not for a while. His axe and wrathful words bounced around the wrecked rooms. But when he attacked the steps leading to the cabin's second floor, my mother barred the way with her body. I was horrified. 'Not the stairs,' she commanded our father. 'And not the walls! You read what the notice said. The soldiers will shoot you if you bring the house down. What will become of me, then? What of your sons?'"

"How brave of her."

"That did it. He threw down the axe and called Mietek and me. That's when we found out our family had been ordered to go to the train station. We were being deported by the Russian soldiers who had come to our town. 'You're going to help me,' he said. 'There is work to be done before we leave.'"

"So, the Russians didn't march you to the station? You went there on your own?"

"We did. But before we left, my father built a fire and together we burned papers, books, letters, and clothes. All the things we couldn't take along. And he slashed the deep sofa piled high with the colorful cushions my mother had spent hours embroidering. I can still hear Mietek and I cheering as a million goose feathers danced in the sunlight pouring through the shattered windows."

Shuddering with mental exhaustion, Stefan took a couple of long breaths, and I gave him time to get back to the present. After a while I gently asked, "How much stuff were you allowed to take?"

"Just one suitcase."

"And you walked to the train?"

"Yes. We had a horse carriage and a mare, but as we were about to get underway, our father sent us ahead down the road. He walked back to the stable. We heard a gunshot. When he rejoined us, his face was wet with tears. We asked no questions. We knew."

"Why did he do that?"

"He knew the soldiers would requisition her for the army. She would have been starved and abused, eventually butchered for food."

He stopped again and swallowed hard. I knew how hard reminiscing was for him and told myself to be patient. I was determined to learn as much as I could but getting that painful story out of him was like pulling teeth. "What happened next?"

"We walked to the station. It wasn't very far, maybe a mile or so. When we arrived, we were marched into a wagon, like cattle. I started crying when soldiers banged the heavy iron doors shut. The rattle of chains and locks could be heard through the walls. When Mietek asked our father where we were going, 'To Siberia,' he answered. He'd sworn to never lie to us."

So now I knew the nightmarish event Stefan had lived through as a child. I fought the tears obscuring my sight. I couldn't begin to imagine how completely Stefan's life had changed in one day. Because of my stepfather's drinking, my mother and I had suffered abuse in the past, but nothing like this. Maybe Stefan's nightmarish memories explained his migraines. Maybe they also explained his need to control his environment.

Stefan stood up, stretched, and pulled in a few long breaths of the salty night air. He offered me his hand to get up and proposed we retrace our steps.

Clad in the thin cotton sari I had worn during the day, I was cold. Whether it was the mention of Siberia or the night air currents cooling the beach, I shivered. But I feared he might stop talking if we went home. Pointing to the gooseflesh on my arms I suggested we warm up for a while in the shelter of some nearby dunes and he agreed.

I knew that what we had come here to discuss were the problems of our relationship, but it now looked like it would have to wait. He'd never before been so candid about his past and I wanted to hear all he was willing to share and find out where that ill-fated train had taken them. But I was afraid to sound callous. Hesitantly I asked, "Do you remember Siberia?"

"I remember the sky there. Impossibly high and cold. In the summer, daylight stayed on for weeks at a time, but winter was ghastly. When the long night finally came, some of the boys, older than my brother and me but too young to go to the mines, made up stories to scare us. Tales about lurking white tigers and werewolves. Fortunately, because Mietek and I were only a year apart, we were not separated when we were sent to the Stalinist schools."

Twilight was falling fast now. "What were they like, the schools?" I asked, as we backed into the still-warm sand.

Lulled by the semi-darkness, Stefan started to talk again. "The schools? What do you think? Schools were there to brainwash us," he said. "There was much bullying going on. My brother fought a lot to protect me. He was bigger than me and looked tough, but we both were scared. We missed our parents."

"Where were they?"

"They lived a few miles away in a bleak settlement and worked in the salt mines; at least, I think they did. They still won't talk about those days, but I remember hearing that the ones who got sent to the mines were the lucky ones."

Stefan lifted himself on one elbow and, absent-mindedly, let a handful of sand slip through his fingers. He had elegant hands with long slender fingers and delicate wrists. Observing him in the soft darkness, I felt sure he wouldn't have survived the mines.

I dug my toes into the sand to keep them warm, and asked, "Were you allowed to see them?"

"Only on special holidays. That's when the men were given time out to hunt and fish to supplement the food rations. They had no guns of course, but my father knew how to set traps."

"So, how long were you there?"

"I'm not sure, three or four years."

"You don't have to answer if it's too painful," I said, "I'm grateful for all you've already shared, but your story is so extraordinary. I'd like to hear more, if you can stand it."

I let the silence settle between us for a moment, before saying gently, "You're here now, so how did your family get out of there."

"It may sound crazy, but one day they simply released the Poles from the labor camps. Officers came and exhorted the men to join the Russian army to fight the Germans."

"Hadn't the Germans been their allies?"

"They had, but that was before Hitler turned on Russia and attempted to finish what Napoleon had failed to do," said Stefan.

"To conquer Russia?" Summoning recall from past history classes, I knew it had been an arrogant plan for Napoleon, and apparently, Hitler had learned nothing from our short emperor's mistake.

"Yes. When the Russians realized they might be defeated by the Germans, they switched sides and joined the allies. At that point, the same people who had enslaved us started calling us 'brothers' and urged us to enlist to defend 'the Motherland' against the 'Teutons,' our common invaders."

"But the Poles didn't buy into that, surely?"

"No and yes! They didn't want to join the Russians, but they wanted Poland back from the Germans. So they swore to fight on the Western Front on condition their families be allowed to leave with them."

"And the Russians agreed?"

"They were losing the war and needed soldiers desperately, so they agreed. Anyway, Poland was no longer the enemy. Germany was. Within days, we left Krasnoyarsk by train."

"Krasno... what?"

"Krasnoyarsk, in eastern Siberia. But soon the trains were requisitioned for the army, and they put us on trucks heading South. Then the trucks ran out of gas, and by the time we reached Kazakhstan, it was pretty much every man for himself. We stuck together as much as we could, thousands of Poles riding, walking and floating down canals in abandoned barges. A long exodus, a nation in motion." He stopped talking, eyes fixed on a faraway point where the sea met the sky.

I had to keep him talking. Who knew when he would open up again? "What else do you recall about those times?"

"We were kids, and however rugged the trek was, traveling with our parents was more fun than the military school we had left behind. We didn't understand that our parents were starving themselves in order to feed us. People we knew and loved, relatives and neighbors, fell behind and disappeared. There was nothing the surviving parents could do except take in the orphans and keep moving. Every week our stream of refugees grew smaller. Looking back, I know that it could have been us left behind, but thanks to my father's resourcefulness, our family made it."

"What did you do all day long?"

"We walked. Sometimes we rode horses, mules, even camels. Going south, in places like Uzbekistan and Tajikistan, we met tribal people and joined their caravans. We stole food when we could. My brother and I were especially fond of onions. We prayed a lot. Our parents made us. When we were hungry, we sang patriotic Polish songs at the top of our lungs. And then, one day, we came upon the Indian Ocean. We had arrived in Karachi. I had never seen the sea before. It was an amazing sight."

"What was the city like in those days?"

"I'd nothing to compare it with, but it probably resembled Old Bombay. A port city filled with friendly Hindu people.

Far off, beyond the sandy beach, a giant moon slowly emerged from the darkness in which the ocean met the horizon. As it rose, splashing tongues of silver over the revealed waves, it gradually shrank and, ever modest, proceeded on its journey toward the stars.

I was drained. Speechless. My mind was a whirlwind of images as I got up from our sandy cocoon and helped Stefan to his feet. Without consulting each other, we walked silently back to our point of entry to the beach and retrieved our sandals.

On hearing us, Rishu climbed down from his tree, head-first like a lizard. His black lips were pulled back, revealing the tip of a small red tongue framed by two impressive fangs. He was the living image of a mini saber-tooth tiger. Rishu, our fearless protector against the jungle's dangers.

CHAPTER TWENTY-THREE

GROWING STRONG

The February weather was mild and dry but, from day to day as I walked or cycled back and forth to school, I could feel the sun getting warmer and warmer on my back. According to Norma, the last two months had been temperate this year, somewhere in the seventies, which was unusually cool for Madras. I wasn't looking forward to May, when the temperature was expected to rise well above 90° F. By then, hopefully, we would have found a second-hand scooter for me.

Meanwhile, I was experimenting with the local ways to cool down our house. My favorite, which I was doing now, was to pour a bucket of cold water on the porous living room tiles. The evaporating water always brought the temperature down by several degrees.

As I put away the bucket and pulled the shutters half closed on the side of the house basking in full sun, I reflected that it had already been a week since Stefan had opened up long enough to share some of his memories about his years in Siberia, but we still hadn't reached an agreement on my fervent wish to study the veena. Nothing more had been offered to justify or explain his adamant convictions that so strained our relationship. I had started drafting a letter to the Paderewski Foundation, but felt unsure, not only of my English grammar, but also of the format my request to them should observe. I had no experience in that type of negotiation and was hoping to enlist Stefan to help me, if only I could make him understand my plight and my plan. Unfortunately, his migraine had derailed his reading for a mid-term exam, and, in order to catch up, he only left his study to eat and sleep.

The sudden outpouring of the hardship he'd endured as a child threw some light on his need for stability and control, but it didn't change the fact that he'd skillfully avoided discussing the issues I was bringing up. Had anything actually changed between us?

Maybe what had changed was my trust in his ability to love me for the person I was. I had put enough faith in him to travel 8000 km just to be with him. I had done it blindly, eager to share his world, sure he could never hurt me. But now, as I looked at him, I wondered.

I let out a long sigh. It looked like the honeymoon was over, but I wasn't going to give up who I was in order to be his wife. Daily life was bound to cause a few nicks and dents in a marriage, but who was he to decide what I could or couldn't do? I so wanted to immerse myself in the music that made me feel part of an India I wanted to belong to. If it fell on me to forge ahead, so be it. With or without Stefan, I had to get things moving.

I decided to call on Rao, the veena master who had awakened my passion for that instrument, but rather than calling him on the phone, where my French accent might throw him off, I decided on a short letter. Not only had the British left behind a great railways network and established an efficient postal system, they had also left the English language, a potent cultural bridge. Full of determination, I went to the T.S. post office and, ignoring the consequences my actions might cause on the home front, mailed my letter to the guru fate had thrown in my path. In it I mentioned that, being out of town on business, my husband was unable to accompany me, and expressed my impatience to discuss taking veena lessons from him. I added that, unless I heard back from him, I would visit him five days hence at two in the afternoon.

I was anxious and kept my fingers crossed that nothing untoward would derail my hopes. But the next five days passed without push-back, so, on the appointed date, I walked to the campus's exit gate and took a rickshaw to his house. I soon realized that it wasn't very far, and I could have bicycled there, but then I would have arrived all sweaty, providing I didn't get lost. The driver pointed to Rao's house at the end of a row of bungalows adjacent to the Mylapore district. As I was expected to do, I bargained for the fare, and the rickshaw-wallah left, satisfied with the tip I had given him. I had been warned that drivers routinely overcharged foreigners, but I was getting better at the game. I walked the last fifty yards to the house, gathering a crowd of children as I went.

Like the neighboring structures, the house was low and square and had a bare front yard enclosed by a short white wall. There was an outside staircase to a flat roof. Looking up, I saw, stretched across it, a bright purple and orange sari flapping like a flag in the morning breeze. I was sure there would also be sleeping cots there. At night, roofs were usually cooler than houses.

Rao came to the gate to welcome me. The telling white thread peeking under his collarless shirt reminded me that he was a Brahmin. Knowing that, I was struck by the gentle tone of his voice as he chided the children into dispersing. It was quite different from the overbearing tone of the Brahmins I had encountered until now.

When I'd met him, he'd been sitting on a stage behind his instru-ment. I could see now that he was thin, taller than me, and wore his dhoti differently from the men living in Madras, for it was wrapped around his legs and looked more like a pantaloon than a dhoti, which is worn like a sarong. His hair, though short, was wavy, another detail that set him apart from most Madrasi Brahmins I had met. From what I could guess, he was appealing to the children's better selves to leave me in peace, and most of them dispersed without fuss, though a few stood their ground, avoiding his eyes as they dug their splayed toes into the red dust.

Holding the door open for me, Rao ushered me into the house. It was cool and dark inside, and my eyes quickly adjusted. Straight ahead of me, an alcove in the whitewashed wall was filled with a garish image of the goddess Saraswati playing her divine veena. The image was set in a thin gilded frame and garlanded with a fresh string of flowers. A bowl filled with uncooked rice had been placed under the picture and incense sticks, stuck into the rice, were slowly burning. They added their fragrant wisps of smoke to that of a brass oil lamp that threw a dancing shadow on the wall behind it.

Through a door to my right, I got a glimpse of a woman squatting in front of a large stone mortar. She was grinding something I couldn't see, switching the pestle from hand to hand with practiced ease as it traveled against the side of the stone bowl.

Rao gestured to her to join us. "My wife, Savitri," he said.

She came forward, brushing streaks of pearlescent flour dust from the end of her sari, which she tucked into her waistband without self-consciousness. She had a warm cinnamon complexion pitted by what must have been smallpox, but her large eyes, made bigger still by the kohl she used, and her winning smile, made one forget about her skin. She brought her hands together in the now familiar "Namaste" greeting.

"She does not speak English. That makes her a little shy," said Rao. Turning to her he spoke in a dialect that didn't sound like Tamil, the local language in Madras. She nodded and returned to her task in the kitchen.

When he turned back to me, he must have read the question on my face. "I was speaking Telegu, our mother tongue, as we are both from Andhra Pradesh, an Indian state north of Madras," he explained. "You will need to study it if you pursue your interest in music. The lyrics of most classical songs are written in Telegu."

He invited me to sit on a thin floor mattress covered with a colorful bedspread, but my eyes were on the opposite wall where two polished veenas rested on a bamboo mat, their stylized dragon heads catching the light angling down from a small window, high in the wall.

"May I touch them?" I said, pointing to the instruments.

"You may touch this one," he said pointing to the smaller of the two. "The other one is mine, and only I commune with it."

Settling down on a mat across from me, he sat erect, cross-legged with his back against the wall. He adjusted his dhoti across his knees and pulled both feet under him, soles tucked away.

I kneeled behind the veena he had pointed to, and he watched as I reverently touched its strings and the brass frets under them. I caressed its wooden neck, the curve of its bulbous resonating body, and let my fingers trace the intricate inlaid bone decorations adorning the top of it.

"So, you are serious about studying the veena?" he asked, absently massaging a large callus on his ankle bone.

"I am."

"Foreigners who come here do not usually have what it takes. They glean what they can within a few weeks and go back home thinking they have mastered our music." He watched my face closely. "We believe that it requires at least seven years to scratch the surface of any musical discipline. Do you have that kind of patience?"

Did I? I hesitated. "I think I do," I said.

"But you are not a musician, are you? I am trying to understand why you want to study our music."

I took in a deep breath and held it for several seconds. "The truth is… I don't know. I really don't, except that after I heard you play, I just *knew* this is what I was supposed to do, what I needed to do in India. Not the dancing."

"So, you are a dancer?"

"Oh, no. Not a dancer. Just a hopeless dance student."

"I see. How did that come about?" asked Rao.

"My husband's idea. He'd love for me to be a dancer."

"I see. And?"

"And it's not happening. I never trained as a dancer before, and I'm afraid it's too late."

"What makes you think it will be any different with our music?"

"Oh! I have studied music in France. Violin as a child, solfeggio and voice in school, and I sang in an award-winning choir."

"I see. What about your husband? Does he approve of your interest in studying the veena?"

I took a second to answer. I didn't want to start this relationship with a lie. "No. Not entirely. Not yet. But he'll come around when he sees I am committed to it."

He nodded thoughtfully before continuing. "You know that unless he approves of your choice, I will not be able to teach you. This is not Paris or London. It would be unthinkable for me to teach you against your husband's wishes."

His words sank into me like shards of glass. I shuddered at the thought of the power this country was giving to the man I had married. My mother had made sure to raise me as an independent entity, and now this. It was strange to consider the threat to my fundamental right to self-determination. I bit the inside of my mouth and crossed my fingers under the edge of the sari I wore.

Rao was watching me go through my changes. Maybe he felt, more than understood, what was going through my mind.

"I do hope your husband comes around and supports your desire to study the veena, but there is more to it. if I decide to teach you, you will need to devote several hours a day to practice. Do you have that kind of stamina?"

"Absolutely. Yes. I can't wait to get started."

He smiled at my enthusiasm.

"We still have a lot to talk about." He turned toward the kitchen and called out, "Savitri, *garam chai!"*

From the kitchen she said, "Hot tea," for my benefit. She knew that much English. I knew that 'garam chai' meant 'hot tea' in Hindi, and marveled at the many languages Indians used. Living in Madras, Rao knew Tamil, Hindi, English, and probably more.

As we drank a cup of strong black tea loaded with sugar and milk the way south Indians serve it and nibbled on cardamon-scented sweets Savitri had made, a plan emerged. Pending Stefan's approval, Rao would come to our house four times a week for an hour. And he would loan me a veena until we found a suitable instrument for me. He would teach me the veena and the fundamentals of music theory to prepare me to take the November entrance exam to the Central College of Karnatic Music, a government institution equivalent to any western music conservatorium. By becoming a full-time student there, I would satisfy the grant's review board and Stefan's concerns would be met.

It was a good plan that should convince Stefan to support my change of direction. But would that be enough time for me to get ready to pass the music college exam?

As if reading my mind, Rao looked at me questioningly. "You are still a student at Kalakshetra, are you not? How do you plan to find time for two demanding schedules?"

"I don't know how, but I will be ready. I swear I will make it work." I laid my hand on the veena closest to me, seeking a connection and a blessing from it. "If my husband agrees, when can we start?"

"Soon," he said, with a wag of his head. "Eight months is a very short time to acquaint yourself with a veena."

I found it easy to talk with Rao. The unadorned directness with which he spoke reminded me of Krishnamurti, the Indian philosopher whose talks I had attended the previous month. So I wasn't surprised when he mentioned that he was a regular at Krishnamurti's lectures and was often commissioned to play for him when the illustrious lecturer was in town. It was a nice piece of serendipity that made me like Rao even more.

From time to time, Savitri padded discretely around us, refilling our cups and the platter of delicate bite-size deep-fried sweets that seemed to melt in my mouth and leave me wanting more.

When it was time to leave, Rao retrieved a few coins from a jar he kept by the door and went outside. Through the open door, I saw him recruit the oldest of the children playing on the street and direct him to go fetch a rickshaw for me.

As I drove back home, I was exhilarated at having recovered control of some part of my life. I was surprised at how simple it had been. I couldn't blame Stefan for all that was wrong between us. Ever since I'd met him, I had allowed him to make most decisions for me because it was easy.

Regaining some autonomy was a worthwhile battle and I felt empowered by it. Armed with the plan Rao and I had devised and the information about the CCKM—*Central College of Karnatic Music*, as it was known locally—I would be able to justify my new academic goals and convince Stefan to help me write a strong letter to the Foundation. If all went according to plan, I was hopeful that he and I would enter a new era in our relationship.

CHAPTER TWENTY-FOUR

MAR 1960 - LATE NIGHT RUMINATION

On my way back from visiting Rao, I had been thrilled to get a message from Nellie Caron, the French musicologist I had been introduced to a month ago at the veena concert. She was back from Thailand where she had given a series of lectures and wanted to know if our invitation to stay with us still held. We didn't have a dedicated guest room, but she didn't care. She was tired of hotels and looked forward to our company, however modest our accommodation. I was excited at the idea of having a guest. I'd never lived in a place big enough to have one. So I sent Gangan to borrow an extra charpoy, some extra bedding and a mosquito net from the T.S. warehouse, and made a bed for her in my study to give her privacy.

There had been so much tension between Stefan and me in the past few weeks that I was grateful for a visitor, and a French one at that.

Nellie was middle-aged and rather plain, but her quick wit and encyclopedic knowledge made her a pleasure to talk with, and I'd been amused to observe how Stefan's moodiness had evaporated in the company of our new friend.

She was an expert on Indian music. She knew Rao well and had published papers about him in France and in the Ethnomusicology review of an American university. I'd enlisted her help in convincing Stefan of the worthiness of my goal, and I think she was slowly bringing him around, for she had a lot to say about ethnomusicology, a new word for me, which she explained as the merging of anthropology and musicology. According to her, ethnomusicologists were the true ambassadors of goodwill beyond nations, and she made a point of assuring Stefan that, should I thrive in my veena studies and graduate from the CCKM—*Central College of Karnatic Music*—she would recommend me for a teaching post at the CEMO—*Centre d'Etudes de Musique Orientale*—in Paris. Stefan had been quite impressed by her endorsement. It would be quite a notch up in my social status and would mean the world to Maman.

Beyond being excited by Nellie's support for my new objective, I was enjoying her visit, for it had restored some kind of normality into our lives. Between sightseeing locally and taking her to visit a few architectural landmarks out of town, there had been no time for Stefan and me to argue about anything, and Stefan now appeared ready to help me compose a letter that outlined the plan I had discussed with Rao. I had started that letter in earnest a while ago, but my English was so rudimentary that I'd been obliged to ask for his help.

Speaking French, dreaming about mastering the veena and becoming a goodwill ambassador, and chatting about home with Nellie had been enjoyable, but she was due in Sri Lanka for an international conference the next weekend. Although I missed her company, I was happy to get my study back to focus on my classes.

I glanced at the clock on my desk and noticed that it was one in the morning. Except for the muted hooting of an owl and the occasional scratching and rustling of nocturnal rodents outside my study window, silence permeated the airless night.

For once, Stefan had gone to bed early and was asleep. I had stayed up to review how many dance theory and Sanskrit lessons I had missed during Nellie's two-day visit, but enough was enough. I yawned, closed my notebook, and smoothed Rishu's short silvery coat as he curled on my lap. I was flattered he'd chosen to keep me company tonight, for I knew night was his favorite time to hunt. Static electricity crackled under my fingers as I pinched one perfect charcoal gray ear. Without waking up, he stirred when I gently put him down on a padded guest chair, but that didn't last long. He woke up, rounded his back, extended his front legs, and pushed back on his powerful thighs. Playtime? He jumped on my desk and padded on piles of papers and books, swishing his powerful tail, and whipping a picture frame off balance.

I caught the small frame in one hand and prodded Rishu off the desk. I set the photo down, and Stefania, Stefan's mother, peered at me out of pale opal eyes, which I knew expected so much of her son. She was beautiful without makeup or enhancement and had sent me that framed image of herself to consolidate our mother-in-law/daughter bond. She hoped that her photo would remind me to send her frequent news about Stefan, who seldom wrote home.

I locked eyes with her and felt moved at the thought of all she had endured. In spite of it all, or maybe because of it, she was the one who had instilled a sense of purpose in her son. On the way back from the beach the other night, he'd told me, half shyly and half defiantly, that he had grown up listening to her account of how, when she was pregnant with him, she had been visited by an angel who had announced in no uncertain terms that her son had a special destiny.

Little did she know that he didn't believe in angels, or the Catholic Church, or even in God—at least not the way she did. Nor did he believe it was his destiny to restore Poland to its previous glory, as she

214

occasionally fantasized out loud. But maybe that angel had brought him here, to India, to search for a path to an enlightenment that hid under many names in various sects and religions. Nirvana. Self-realization. Escape from the wheel of life.

For over a year now, he had been studying sacred Hindu scriptures, visiting ashrams, questioning gurus, and toning his physical body with Hata Yoga. But from his own account, nothing he did held answers for him.

I often felt his disillusion. Where was the illumination that supposedly lay in wait for him? Did it really exist, or was it all Hindu myths and stories? I sensed his frustration at still being ordinarily human. Why else did he succumb to the dreadful migraines that drove him to bed?

And to top it all, there was me. Minouche. Marrying me had probably seemed like a good idea at the time, though I was no longer sure Stefan had wanted to get married at all. Maybe it had been the idea of the friends he'd stayed with while waiting for my ship to arrive in Bombay. What if Maurice and Hiribai had reached vicariously through Stefan and me for the romance they had been denied when Maurice, the poor Polish engineer, had fallen in love with Hiribai, the rich Parsi heiress? The difference in their social status may have prevented their marriage, but maybe not their thrill at playing matchmakers. I couldn't really be mad at them. Their intervention had given me status in India, and more security than I had known my whole life.

I picked up our wedding photograph and traced Stefan's handsome face with my fingers. He and I had enjoyed a good thing in Paris. He loved me then, and must have loved me when I showed up in India for no other reason than to be with him. But why marry me? Maybe it was because dating didn't exist in a country where a man couldn't take a girl to the movies, lest her whole family tagged along. I guess he'd had time to figure out that there would be no sex without a ring. So, I could see how marrying me offered physical rewards, plus the convenience and comfort of living together. But he'd been badly prepared for the demands of a fulltime relationship. As frustrating as it was for me, it must be exhausting for him, considering his need for control and my newly discovered assertiveness. No wonder he had needed time out from all that married stuff and taken a few days away from me. And it was no good trying to discuss it with him. It only made him angry. Angry at himself, and guilty too, which made it worse, and was no way to reach enlightenment.

I wasn't proud of my own outbursts and knew I may not have handled our conflict over music well. But why couldn't he see that it was up to me to decide what career I wanted to pursue? I didn't know how he envisioned his own prospects. Would he teach? Write? Lecture? Whatever it was, I certainly wasn't telling him what to choose.

The window was open, and I took in a long breath. The air was scented with jasmine and the bitter-sweet smell of the sticky pod-like fruit that hung on the tamarind tree shading the house. I breathed in again. My mind was jumping all over the place and I wondered if Stefan thought of my stubborn streak as a quality or a flaw. My resistance to his wishes must have taken him by surprise, but there was nothing wrong about a woman being strong. It had kept his mother and mine alive.

I got up and stretched, raising both arms before bending forward and letting my head and torso hang for a full minute until I could touch my toes. Satisfied, I straightened up and slowly twisted my back to the left, then to the right, to limber up. It was too hot to do anything more, and I was tired. So, I promised myself to spend more time doing yoga in the morning as it helped me with the dancing, which I would have to continue suffering through, until I was able to join the CCKM as a full-time student.

With that in mind, and encouraged by Nellie, I'd arranged for Stefan and Rao to meet formally over tea at our house on Saturday. It was circled in red on my calendar and a lot hung on that date. Things would definitely be easier if Stefan and Rao became friends. For if they got along, I would be able to start private veena lessons with Rao, regardless of the Foundation's response to the letter Stefan had finally promised to write with me. Kalakshetra would be closed for holidays in July. If my projected studying for the college exam permitted, maybe Stefan and I could plan a short trip. It would be so nice to forget about our studies and have fun doing things together as we did in Paris. There was so much I wanted to see. I turned off the light and the ceiling fan and left the window of my study open. The screen would prevent unwanted furry or scaly visitors. Next, I firmly closed my door, aware that in the past, Rishu had deposited gifts from his night hunting under my desk. Time to sleep. Tomorrow was another day.

CHAPTER TWENTY-FIVE

JUBILATION

As I waited nervously for Stefan and Rao to meet, Stefan became more open to discussing my desire to switch my studies to music. Nellie's promise to help me get a teaching post in Paris if I graduated from the CCKM had given an academic twist to my intention to study the veena, and her explanations about ethnomusicology had impressed him. It seemed that, if he couldn't have a dancer for a wife, he would settle for an ethnomusicologist, who stood to be, as Nellie had explained it, an ambassador of goodwill between nations.

Stefan had grasped the political aspect of that definition and knowing that the Paderewski Foundation was keen on good will and ambassadorship, he fully intended to spin it in our letter.

I was thrilled when the meeting I had arranged between him and Rao turned out to be a success, in part because they both were great admirers and followers of Krishnamurti, but also because Rao did a much better job than me in presenting to Stefan a solid and affordable study plan that would prepare me to take the entrance exam to the music college.

As I watched my husband and my to-be guru discuss my fate, I was amused to notice the similarities in them. Both young, and idealistic, one blue-eyed, blond descendant of the warring Celts and Goths that had raided central Europe for centuries, the other dark and fluid, the silent inheritor of a three-thousand-year-old musical tradition. Stefan, dreaming of nirvana achieved through knowledge and books; Rao, dreaming of it inside the pure sound of his instrument.

When, at last, an agreement was struck and, in accordance with Rao's suggestion, March 21st, was chosen as an auspicious date for my first veena lesson. I was ecstatic. As planned, he would loan me an instrument until he found a suitable one for me to buy. And he would come to our house three times a week, which was convenient as I still didn't have a scooter. Meanwhile, I would continue all my classes at Kalakshetra until I became a full-time student at the CCKM. Considering that I was expected to practice the veena at least two hours a day, I would be very busy, but I was jubilant.

The next step would be to send that long delayed letter to our grantors, explaining my reasons for switching my major to music and asking for their blessings.

Maybe it was because we had been thinking so much about them that a letter from one of the Paderewski Foundation's officers arrived, informing us that he was on his way to New Delhi and would make a stop in Madras to meet us on March 15th, seeing as no Foundation member had ever met either of us in person.

I sounded like pure serendipity and Stefan was pleased. That would save him writing the letter we'd been working on, and, in true Stefan fashion, he was very sure he could impress that person. He was, after all, the golden boy of the Polish intelligentsia in Paris, but I was terrified. There was always a chance that they would discover I had lied on my grant application. Sending a lie in the mail was quite different from a face-to-face interview with one of them. Stefan wasn't worried.

"No reason to fret," he said. "They're probably just planning a photo op for their stockholders, you know, to show them where the money is going before they do a fundraiser. That's the way these organizations work. Do you know how little your monthly hundred-dollar stipend means to them? For us, here, it's a lot. For them it's a small drop in a very large bucket."

Still, I worried. "What if he talks to me in Polish and I don't understand him? Your parents made an effort to understand me when I met them, but my vocabulary is limited."

"He may speak to you in Polish, but if he read your file, which he probably did, he knows that you grew up in France. So, he knows that you never knew your Polish grandfather who had abandoned your grandma before your mother was born. It's a perfect cover story."

"True, but still…"

"Look. Why don't you get your teach-yourself-Polish Berlitz book out and practice a few easy welcoming sentences? That will be enough to impress him, and show him that, at heart, you're a Polish patriot."

And that was that.

Stefan had been right about the purpose of the Foundation's envoy. He had brought a photographer along and asked to take photos of the classes at Kalakshetra, which we did. But the best news of all was that, after listening to my proposed new study plan, he gave it his unreserved approval. Ethnomusicology was a new field, and the Foundation would be proud to add it to its roster of academic grants. He had the photographer take several shots of me sitting with Rao and our veenas. It was so easy; it was almost anticlimactic. And to think Stefan and I had fought and sweated so much over that issue.

He also told us that a new grantee from Hungary was on his way to Madras. He hoped we would extend our welcome to him and help him get settled.

CHAPTER TWENTY-SIX

APR 1960 - SA RI GA MA

Madras, April 7, 1960

Ma petite maman adorée,
Adored mother? Why was I using such rococo language to talk to my mother? Was it, maybe, to make up for the fact that I had deserted her in Paris? I changed it to: *Maman Chérie.*

My fingers rested on the typewriter keys, but I was stuck. I wanted to tell her about my veena lessons but didn't know how to explain Indian music concisely and clearly to her.

I'll never forget the quarter-size violin I found under the tree one Christmas morning, and how you arranged for music lessons. Thanks to you, I could read music by the time I turned five. I have vivid memories of how sore my neck and shoulder were from holding my small violin, and how we both grimaced at the scratchy sounds escaping my inexperienced bow. Do re mi fa sol la ti do… Practicing the scales, back and forth, and you helping me decipher the partitions of children's songs to develop my music reading.

Eventually, I tamed the cat-gut bow and was able to work on simplified arrangements of the masters: Mozart, Bach, Vivaldi. I wasn't a child prodigy, but I held my own and enjoyed my teacher and his lessons. He was encouraging Maman to enroll me in a music school, but all that changed when, to give me a normal home and a father, she got married. There was no love between my stepfather and me, but I clearly remember how, trying to get my affection, he brought a puppy home for me. It was a smallish but handsome dog, part mutt, part Pomeranian. As most kids my age would be—I was eight—I was entranced by my new companion and named him *Bijou*, for jewel.

I fed him, brushed him, walked him, ran him, and put glorious bows in his fur. Maman loved him too. He was a perfect puppy except for one thing. Whenever I brought my violin out of its case and started practicing, he howled. The neighbors' complaints quickly put a damper on my playing.

But I shouldn't have worried about that, because shortly thereafter, the one Maman had trusted to complete our small family pawned my dainty violin to go to the races. I didn't want to remind her that our troubles had started with her marrying that man, but she knew. She'd said it many times herself.

Thanks to her though, everything I had learned on the violin helped me when I was selected for the choir in middle school. Do re mi fa sol la ti do. Reading music made it easy for me, compared to those of my schoolmates who had never learned to play an instrument.

I returned to the typewriter.

I have now been studying with Rao, my new music teacher, for four weeks, and the first thing I've learned about Indian music is that it isn't written down. There will be no pages of staves, no music scores. There is a solfeggio that I'm learning orally, but the notes go by other names. Goodbye, do re mi...

Enter "sa ri ga ma pa da ni sa" which opens the door to India's love affair with mathematics. Just imagine. In Indian music theory, a seven-note scale can be combined in sixty-four different ways because musicians here are trained to hear sixty-four distinct notes in a scale. That said, there are hundreds of scale combinations, and because each combination conveys a unique feeling of time, color, and mood, each is known as a 'raga,' and is granted its own name, like 'Mohanan' the charming one, or 'Bhairavi' the devotional one.

But that's not all. Where ragas give us melody, 'tala' gives us the rhythmic patterns inside each tune. And there are lots of different tala signatures. I was already aware of tala in my dance class. The triple time footwork my dance teacher beats on a woodblock is an illustration of tala. Now I must study tala within the veena exercises Rao, my private instructor, is teaching me.

It's fascinating, but so complex that I'm grateful Rao, my teacher, only feeds me little pieces of information at a time. He gives me enough space to repeat and memorize them, as the written notes I scribble remain too vague to nail the exact nature of a raga or tala.

Rao and I have been looking for a suitable instrument for me, but the good ones are hard to find. So, for the time being, I'm using one of his, a sweet-sounding, but heavy instrument. Sitting in lotus position under the weight of that veena when I practice is hard on my knees, and I dream of the day when the various parts of my body will stop aching, so I may enter the music free of distracting pain, especially on the fingertips that commune with the veena strings.

I looked at the tips of the index and forefinger of my left hand, the ones that came into contact with the metallic strings of the veena and decided I wouldn't try to explain that part to Maman. She would be horrified to hear that my fingertips had blistered and bled when I'd first pulled on those strings to find the right notes. But it was better now.

Eventually, the soft flesh of my fingertips would grow callus grooves. It had been challenging, but I'd gritted my teeth and pushed through the pain because, without them, I would never find the voice of the veena. Funny how its divine sound was born under thick, ugly skin.

Once again, as for the dancing, I reflected that I was faced with learning an Indian discipline from zero, as a child would, for I had no prior experience of them. But my heart was so strongly determined to master the veena that Rao couldn't help but be impressed with my progress.

I heard a knock on the screen door and got up to let Lycette in. My letter would have to wait. It had been a long time since Lycette had stopped by the house, and I was thrilled to see her. She had come with Ranjani, one of the dancers in her advanced class. "I have a favor to ask you," she said, dropping on a floor pillow and pointing to Ranjani to do the same.

"Before you ask," I said to my two sweaty guests who appeared to have come straight from a dance class, "water or lemonade?"

"Water, please," they answered in unison.

I went to the kitchen and instructed Gangan to bring a pitcher of ice water and three glasses. When I returned, I sat on the floor mattress that served as a sofa and pushed one of the remaining floor pillows against the wall to support my back, sore after a long seance of veena practice. "What's going on?"

"I just volunteered to help Sharada choreograph a dance rendition of the Ramayana," said Lycette. "You've read it, haven't you?"

I snickered. "They'd probably kick me out of Kalakshetra if I hadn't." The Ramayana was the most famous Hindu epic, and my teachers had been very keen on my reading it.

Lycette rolled her eyes. "Right. Well, I was wondering if you might volunteer some time to help with painting decors, you know, back-stage stuff."

My eyes flew wide open. Me? Volunteer for a theater production at Kalakshetra? I was so excited I hardly could believe my ears, but then reality struck. Would that leave me enough time to practice the veena? "I really, really would love to, but I need to know how many hours it would require of me?"

"I know," said Lycette. "Veena is your priority. I'm sure a couple of hours a week for the next month would be enough"

"Does Sharada know you were going to ask me?"

"She suggested it," said Lycette.

"Maybe I could swap some dance classes for production work?"

"I believe that Parvati, your dance instructor, isn't quite as demanding as she was when you first joined. Having lowered her expectations about dancing, she now has a better understanding of who you are and understands your interest in theater."

I laughed. "That's a nice way to put it."

"Anyway, we would really like having you work on this project with us," said Ranjani, in a shy voice, as I poured water from the pitcher and passed the glasses around.

"I'd love to. It's perfect in fact. Helping backstage will allow me to learn how Indian plays are produced, which is something I wanted to study from the start."

"So, that's settled. I'll let Sharada and Parvati know," said Lycette, grinning with satisfaction. She took a big swallow of water and looked at me inquiringly. "How is Stefan? Still giving you grief about studying with Rao?"

"No, quite the contrary. No grief since I got the green light from the Paderewski Foundation. I also think he's found a kindred spirit in Rao, which helped a lot. They can discuss Krishnamurti's lectures for hours."

"Thank God for that," said Lycette. "What about you? What do you think of Rao? You've been working with him for a while, haven't you?"

"Four weeks now. It's funny, but from what I can tell, and it's just my opinion," I added, nodding at Ranjani, "Rao isn't a typical Brahmin. His Andhra Pradesh roots appear to have made him more open to outsiders and outside influences."

"It's possible," said Ranjani in a conciliatory tone of voice, which was kind of her as I knew her father to be a prominent local Brahmin. "People from Andhra Pradesh have a reputation for being poets, and dreamers. So maybe it is his nature."

"Whatever it is, I'm very fond of him, and feel lucky he's agreed to teach me."

"What about your dance classes? I hardly ever see you at Kalakshetra," said Lycette. "How is that going?"

"I had a talk with Sharada and Geeta earlier this month and they agreed to modify my dance and Sanskrit class schedules so I may spend more time on the veena. If Sharada agrees to trade a few more classes for the Ramayana production, it will be perfect."

And it was, I thought, sitting in my house with my friends. Spacing the dance classes, focusing on the veena, and about to get involved in a stage production of the Ramayana. I had a lot to be grateful for.

CHAPTER TWENTY-SEVEN

JUN 1960 - FIRST MONSOON

I had slept badly, and it was no surprise, on waking up at dawn, to find out that it was already hot and muggy. After allowing myself the luxury of a ten-minute reprieve, I turned off the snooze alarm, got out of bed and jumped in the shower to get ready for my 8 a.m. dance class. Stefan was gone for an April term-end exam. It used to bother me to not find him next to me when I awoke, but in the last few months I had gotten used to his early MU schedule. Indians were definitely early risers.

I walked to the kitchen where Gangan greeted me with a thermos of Madrasi coffee he had brought from the village. He poured some in my favorite cup and the pungent aroma filled the room. That concoction was a local treat which I had seen the villagers prepare by bringing large quantities of coffee grounds and water to a boil, which they then whipped and frothed with sugar and milk. Gangan still made regular drip coffee for us, but I always looked forward to him bringing that special coffee back when he went early to the market. It was a deliciously Indian way to start the day.

I still missed Nellie. She'd been no more than an acquaintance when she had accepted my invitation to stay with us last month, but she'd grown on me very quickly. I had been especially thrilled when, using her VIP status, she had arranged for us to receive a grand tour of the music college. I'd been impressed by the building itself, a sprawling mansion a rich patron had donated to the Madras government to open a school dedicated solely to Karnatic music, the specific music style of South India. It was a sunny place whose large rooms, now converted into individual classrooms, had a splendid view on the Adyar river. And across the river, linked by a city bridge, I was thrilled to discover the tall Theosophical Society headquarters building. That meant I wouldn't have far to go to attend classes.

Things were finally on the move for me. With the dancing on the back burner and my private veena classes with Rao lined up, I was happy and felt reasonably in control of my life. Volunteering for the production of the Ramayana was more fun than work and was less demanding than I'd feared.

Holding the warm cup of coffee in my hand, I sank into a caned armchair and stared out at the familiar jungle surrounding our bungalow. The thorny bougainvillea's facing me were dusty and limp with drought. The morning air was still. Overhead the leaded sky weighed upon me and made it hard to breathe. What I would have given for a crisp Parisian morning, when chilled northern winds rushed down our large stone avenues.

Little by little, the morning light grew into a blinding glare, but still I saw no sun. Perspiration rolled freely down my torso and gathered in the hot crease of my thighs. Hoping for a hint of breeze, I pushed open the screen-door and walked into the garden.

I saw Rishu at once, crawling in the dry grass, silent and watchful. Beyond him, I noticed what looked like a stump slowly hovering left and right. With a shock, I realized it was a cobra, its hooded head even with the tall grass. I could imagine its long body coiled and ready to strike.

Like in a dream where colorless words are yelled but never heard, I felt myself crying out Rishu's name, but he ignored me. In a rush of panic, I stumbled and dropped my cup, which caused Rishu to jump back like a spring. Six feet away, the cobra held its attack pose for a few more seconds before uncoiling and slithering away, invisible inside the rustling grass.

Rishu meowed in protest and looked at me, as if disgusted by my interference, but to my relief he gave up his stalking and stretched lazily on the verandah's tiled floor. Now that the alert was over, anger swelled in me. I yelled at him, "Stupid cat! Hunting a cobra, are you?" I was more than a little scared. A cobra, so close to the house! Alerted by my outburst, Gangan came outside. Seeing my cup on the ground, he bent cautiously to pick it up. Luckily—for it was the one with a picture of the Sorbonne Brigitte had sent me—it hadn't broken. I was weak at the knees when Gangan and I walked back inside the house, and I told him what had happened.

"It's alright, sire." For some reason, "madam" and "sire" appeared to be interchangeable in his vocabulary, "You saw with your eyes. Cobra gone, no more trouble."

He washed and refilled my cup from the thermos bottle holding the rest of the good coffee.

"Cobra not bad, cobra good."

With his back to me, he surreptitiously raised his joined hands to his forehead in silent worship. Turning around he explained patiently, as if talking to a child, "Cobra God, good God, just taking care of his business."

And what business might that be, I wondered, still in shock? Kill my cat, slither into the house and sleep under my bed? I bit my tongue, for Gangan was a Hindu and he believed in what he was saying. In any case, I didn't want to upset him. To be truthful, I even liked his cobra theory. I had heard there were cobras around, but I never quite believed it. Why would I, when barefooted gardeners and servants shuffled back and forth through the grass between the bungalows? But then I recalled the morning when Sujita, one of my Indian classmates, had pointed to a small plate of milk placed under a tree bordering the path to Kalakshetra. "A gift to the cobra that lives there," she had explained, "to protect the children walking past."

Of course, there had been a famous incident at the house of Umadevi, the eccentric old Polish woman who lived by herself near the pond. She was the only one I had befriended among the older theosophists after arriving in Madras.

As the story went, a nest of cobras that had lived for years in the thatched roof of her lodging had somehow been knocked down by the wind and had fallen on top of her mosquito net during her midday nap. When asked, Umadevi simply answered that she had quietly waited for the cobras to find their way down and out of her house. Always eager for miracles, the villagers, whose god Shiva wore a cobra coiled around his neck, had quickly spread a rumor that she was blessed. They still left offerings on her doorstep.

I couldn't wait to write to Brigitte about this latest incident. It was one more thing I would have to admonish her not to mention to Maman. I was afraid she would die of fright if she heard about it.

With all the excitement, I hadn't paid much attention to the morning light. It had dimmed to a murky lead color. Streaming from the northeast, billowing black clouds rolled across the lowered sky like balloons searching for a place to land. Every living thing stood poised, waiting.

Suddenly, long jagged streaks of lightning tore the clouds' pregnant underbellies. Before the rumble of thunder had even died away, I watched water break free from them and pound the trees, making small craters in the earth with an explosive force I had never experienced. The air smelled of ozone, upturned earth, and crushed flowers.

The July monsoon I had heard so much about was arriving early. Having reached Madras the first week of August last year, I had missed most of that year's short monsoon season. So short apparently, that, according to Norma's husband, who knew about these things, last year's rice crops had suffered from a shortage of rain.

And now, looking outside the open door, I wondered how I would get to my morning classes if the rain kept up, which I was pretty sure it would. Would there be flooding? Would Stefan be able to drive his scooter back from the University?

After months of sweating and baking in the heat, my exposed skin was chilled. In no time, wetness slipped through every gap of the house and made the walls and the tiled floor damp. Part of me felt a little scared by the violent drumming of that rain, but part of me wanted to run back outside with arms outstretched to drink the fat drops rolling off the roof, the branches and the leaves.

Stuck without car or telephone, I turned to Gangan who, right now, was the ultimate authority on Indian weather. "Do you think classes will be cancelled? Will they close the school?" I was hoping they would.

Nonplussed, he looked at me. "It is just monsoon. Everything go normal. Madam got umbrella?"

I didn't.

"Madam needs umbrella, most necessary. I go borrow one for today."

I watched as he straddled his old bicycle, handlebar in one hand, his worn cotton dhoti and beat-up umbrella in the other, pedaling in the rain with unconcerned ease. He came back ten minutes later and handed me a brand-new umbrella he had borrowed from the campus office. They must have had a bunch of them waiting for such an occasion. I went out to the covered porch and unfurled the beast. It was deep and black with a wide span and a polished wooden handle. It looked big enough for three people. Gangan looked at me approvingly.

"Now you okay. Walk in rain no problem. Most perfect for you," he said.

I looked wistfully at my bicycle sheltered under the porch. Earlier it had been a great relief to bicycle rather than walk to class, but I wasn't ready to ride in a sari with an umbrella big enough to pass as a parachute. So, walk I would. I still longed to have my own scooter, but for once, Stefan and I agreed that, unless we found a really great deal on a scooter, we would save our money to travel.

Half an hour later, dressed in a dhavani and my oldest leather sandals, I convinced Gangan that porridge was out of the question and munched on a piece of toast and a mango before stepping onto the road. By now, the rain had acquired a steady rhythm, a rhythm I would get to know very well, as it would pervade everything I did for the next two months. The monsoon had just started, and I already felt like it had been here forever.

As more umbrellas joined mine on the road, I fantasized that anyone looking at us from above would see us as an overnight sprouting of tall black mushrooms. Leaving the T.S. campus behind, I reached the street, where nobody seemed shy about showing a little skin, as saris and dhotis were hiked up to avoid the splash of rickshaws and taxis swerving around.

I found myself smiling under our black ceiling. Revived by the electricity palpable in the air, uplifted by my first monsoon, I was at one with the crowd.

After a fortnight of steady rain, a layer of mold resembling short grey moss was growing freely on every piece of leather to be found in the house. Our sandals and shoes were the first target, and suitcases and bags followed. The delicate Parisian purse I saved for special occasions hadn't been spared. Every surface felt damp to the touch. Bottles, plates, walls, towels and clothes, even my books felt changed by the ambient humidity. And there was nothing I could do about it until the monsoon abated.

Day by day, the excitement and relief brought by the rain disappeared, replaced by a longing for change.

Our recent confrontation had changed Stefan for the better. Maybe the fact that the Paderewski Foundation had approved my new study plan had something to do with it. He had also observed a few of the veena lessons I was taking at home, four days a week, with Rao, and seemed to be getting used to the idea that his wife was a musician rather than a dancer. We were making love again, and in spite of the oppressive rain, he seemed happier and lighter than before. He was making a visible effort to be more social, taking me to town once in a while for a protein-rich Tandoori chicken followed by a movie. He'd even suggested we invite several French-speaking students from Mauritius we'd just met for dinner. He thought that, at the same time, we should invite the freshly arrived Hungarian student, also on a Paderewski grant.

So, things were on the up and up under our roof. Stefan was coming around. I now had a solid study plan and four more months to continue preparing for the college entrance exam, and Stefan had his eyes on a small scooter that would allow me to go to Rao or downtown without waiting for him or taking rickshaws. Life was looking good.

CHAPTER TWENTY-EIGHT

NOV 1960 -
FIRST DAY AT THE CCKM

November 23, 1960. I circled today's date on the Saraswati calendar hanging on my living room wall. It was my first day of school at the CCKM, but it was more than that for me. Sixteen months to this day, I had disembarked from the Messageries Maritimes ocean liner in Bombay with a heart full of love and a head full of dreams. Dancing or theater? I didn't have a very clear plan, but I had faith that India would provide whatever it was I needed to elevate my station in life. I had tried and failed at becoming a dancer, but leaning on the certitude that I was in the right place at the right time, I had spent the last five months preparing relentlessly for the November 7 entrance exam of the music college.

Miraculously, I'd passed it. I was elated and exhausted all at the same time. To prepare me for it, especially the oral exam that covered a lot of obscure music history, Rao had relentlessly quizzed me and conducted mock interviews. I was grateful for his help and dedication and knew that I could never have handled that exam without him. It had been nerve-wracking, and I nearly got sick to my stomach when the only woman on the board of examiners asked me to play one of the required veena compositions. Fortunately, it was a piece Rao had spent a lot of time teaching me, and after a moment of hesitation, I was able to play it satisfactorily.

But it was all behind me now, and on this bright November morning, I rode my newly acquired scooter to the CCKM and arrived before eight, fresh and groomed for my first day of school.

The CCKM occupied a huge, dazzling white, one-story building sprawling along the bank of the Adyar estuary. I had heard from Norma that the building had been reclaimed from the Indian government in 1947, after a wealthy British shipping company had closed shop and gone home. The large grounds surrounding it were planted with a variety of fruit trees and flowering bushes that provided shade. I parked under a tree inside the school gates and breathed in the salty breeze flowing from the estuary. It was lovely, loaded with the mixed scents of flowers and tides.

I entered the building looking for the classrooms, but an attendant directed me to the auditorium. In good English, he explained to me that the astrologer who had chosen this auspicious date to reopen the school was to perform a religious service, a puja as it was called, that involved praying and chanting. Somewhat in awe of standing in the famed institution, I joined the gathered students and the music teachers, Brahmins, mostly, some of which, Rao had told me, were well-known career musicians.

We all sat down on the bare floor, the girls to one side, the boys to the other. Tall and erect, the teachers throned in the front rows with their backs to us. My eyes drifted to the walls where pictures of musicians competed with an image of Gandhi, who himself competed with the many gods of the Hindu pantheon.

The priest performing the puja was facing a wide alcove scooped in the wall. Flower garlands smothered a large framed poster of the Goddess Saraswati playing the veena and, under it, numerous sticks of incense planted in rice bowls, and two decorative peacock-shaped oil lamps, put out tendrils of temple-smelling smoke.

As my attention drifted to my classmates-to-be, it struck me that I was the only white student. From what I could see, teenage girls appeared to make up seventy percent of the student body. The last thirty percent were young men, including a shy-looking Indian youth wearing a Catholic priest's collar. A novice? His presence puzzled me. I had heard about the work of missionaries to recruit "Rice Christians" and wondered if learning South Indian music to ingratiate themselves with the Hindu population was part of their strategy. I had always thought that Mass was much the same anywhere in the world, and though I tried to imagine church hymns and liturgy sung Indian-style, I couldn't quite get a sense of it.

The corpulent, bare-chested Brahmin performing the puja ended it with two prayers in which the students joined in. I figured I'd heard them in Kalakshetra, because they sounded familiar. One was to the Goddess Saraswati, the other to Ganesh, the elephant-headed god, who, remarkably, was the patron of artists and… thieves. You had to appreciate a religion that made room for thieves, at least to the extent of allowing them a patron.

Then, as if responding to a mysterious signal, everyone got up. I was more than happy to rise from the floor and stretch my legs. Eager to get to my class, I was looking for direction when the girl next to me touched my arm and whispered, "Wait." An attendant was passing around a leaflet printed in Tamil, in Hindi—India's official language—and in English, the second official language. On it were the words to the Indian National Anthem penned by Rabindranath Tagore, the famous Bengali poet and nationalist I had read about.

The students began to sing. The Hindi lyrics followed a simple, almost folksy melody. The English translation I held in my hand spoke of valleys and streams and snow-capped mountains. It was a soothing and elating anthem, and I was quite seduced by the lyrical and spiritual message of Tagore's poem when, after the song ended, the principal called my name and asked if I would sing the national anthem from my country. I guess it was his way to introduce me, a French person, to the other students. It was embarrassing to be singled out, especially because I had never sung La Marseillaise solo, and in public, but I didn't have a choice. I put my heart into it, aiming to stir some enthusiasm and patriotic feelings into the tune, the way I remembered it.

"And what do the words say?" asked the principal when it was over.

Having never given much thought to the literal meaning of that anthem, I was mortified to do so now. La Marseillaise was nothing like Tagore's poem extolling the many landscapes of India from the Himalayas to the seas. It had been written in 1792 after France declared war against Austria and was originally titled, "War Song for the Rhine Army." It was a revolutionary song, loaded with battle cries, and thirst for the enemy's blood. I couldn't possibly allow my new classmates and teachers to think of the French, and me, that way.

Rather than translating, I fudged by explaining that the anthem reflected a time when France had been invaded and was rallying for battle. Fortunately for me, my audience soon lost interest, and we were all excused and sent to our first class.

I had been assigned to an instructor named Sri Prakash and, after getting direction, I stepped expectantly into the room where veena was taught. In a conscious effort to blend in, for I so wanted to be accepted and make friends, I had avoided wearing the silk sari Norma had offered me, fearing it might appear pretentious. I had, instead, chosen a royal blue cotton sari whose dark red border matched a blouse cut with a modest neckline. My hair was combed back into a French roll, my eyes lined with kohl, my wrists jiggling with seven glass bangles, one for each day of the week, as was the custom. The floor of this room was covered with a grass mat. On sitting down behind one of the veenas provided by the college, I carefully tucked my feet under my sari to avoid presenting their soles to the pundit facing me, which would have been an unforgivable faux pas. This was my big day.

Sri Prakash sat with his back against a large floor-to-ceiling window overlooking the wide estuary of the Adyar River. It gave him the advantage of seeing our faces clearly, while keeping us half-blinded by the morning sun.

He was a big man, tall for a South Indian native. His most remarkable feature was his massive head; his high forehead merged with the shaved front half of his skull, while a mess of reddish-grey tousled hair erupted like a mane on the back of it. The sunlight reflected from the river built a bigger-than-life aura around him.

His glance fell upon me. It was cold and made me feel small. It also made me uncomfortable because his eyes were not quite lined up. One of them looked straight at me while the other appeared to look over my left shoulder. Out of respect, for he was the teacher, I dropped my eyes down and stared at the mat. For a moment, I didn't dare to look up again. When I did, he was addressing the class in Tamil. He must have known I didn't understand, but he never apologized or translated for me. I would, of course, have appreciated any kind of acknowledgement, but who was I to tell him how to run his class. I'd just have to find out what he'd said later.

Prakash played a short and lively piece and we listened. His music was powerful. His fingers plucked the strings with a fierce vigor that felt very different from the romantic voicing Rao got out of his instrument. Sri Prakash's energy resembled his person, large and thunderous.

He stopped playing, worked his tongue around the remnant of a leafy chew he had kept hidden in one cheek, and spit it out into a half coconut shell resting on the floor by his side.

There were ten of us, a boy and nine girls, arranged into a half circle around him. He turned to the boy, who was sitting closest to him on his left, and again, addressed him in Tamil. The boy nodded and played back a correct, though paler, version of the piece he had just been shown. Prakash snorted his disappointment and pointed at the next student, a girl, with his chin. He grunted an encouragement to go ahead but she was nervous and failed to complete the song section. He commented, again in Tamil, and moved on to the next girl, and the next. Was he using Tamil on purpose, to exclude me? I hadn't been warned Tamil was a required language in the veena class. Moreover, I was sure he spoke English. All educated people in Madras did. The girls in my class all spoke English, for God's sake!

I was the next-to-last student sitting to his right, and by now I had figured out how the song went. It was a song Rao had anticipated I needed to know. I was looking forward to playing it for Prakash, but skipping me, he spoke directly to the girl next to me. I expected he would ask me to play the next time around, but the class went on for a whole hour, and Prakash continued to pretend I wasn't there.

I was confused and hurt. Why was he ignoring me? On the other hand, while it was maddening to be left out, it was also a relief. Prakash was so fierce, it was hard not to be cowed in his presence, and my desire to speak up soon petered out. Then another thought struck me. This being the first day, could it be he thought I wouldn't be ready to play and wanted to save me the embarrassment?

This wasn't the welcoming class I had anticipated. I oscillated between consternation and frustration. On top of everything, my legs were falling asleep under me, but stretching them in front of me to bring back circulation in my tortured knees and ankles was unthinkable. I missed the small pillows I used at home to ease the pain.

The end of the class didn't come soon enough for me.

"Aie! Are you alright?" asked one of the girls gathering her books.

"I'm fine, thank you," I lied, leaning on the wall until my legs could support me.

"I am sorry he was rude to you. He is, what do you call it? A bully," she whispered behind her hand as she waited for me in the door. "But do not worry. The other teachers are not like him. What is your name?"

"Minouche."

"Meenouche. It is a nice name," she said, repeating it in a sing-song voice. "I am Padma."

"Can you tell me what he said in Tamil?" I asked, reaching for a pen and the brand-new notebook I had chosen for this class.

"Yes. Of course," she said, eager to be helpful. "I will tell you while we eat our lunch. But right now, you better step outside to stretch your legs before the next class."

"Is it that obvious?"

We both started laughing.

It had been a stressful morning, but I had made my first friend in that school.

CHAPTER TWENTY-NINE

FEB 1961 - SRI PRAKASH

Days turned into weeks, and weeks into months as I settled into my new routine at the CCKM. The choreographed Kalakshetra production of the Ramayana had been a big success in December, and I had even received credit for my work as a volunteer. My dancing routine had lightened up considerably, and Sharada was looking into finding a proper dance tutor who would come to our house and continue my training at a slower pace.

The first of the year had arrived and gone without a splash, as Stefan refused to celebrate the holidays, which he considered arbitrary, therefore stupid. It had saddened me to see the end of year slip by without a *Joyeux Noel* or *Jour de l'An* celebration, and the traditional gift exchange it occasioned. But my new Indian friends and classmates had banished my regrets by inviting me to participate in their frequent Hindu festivals. The stories of Père Noël dropping into chimneys were nice enough, but how could they compare to the chaotic processions of caparisoned, slow-moving elephants, pulling or pushing tall, ornate wooden chariots carrying Hindu deities buried under hundreds of flower garlands as they made their way to the temples? Not only was it a moving display of faith that resonated in my heart, but it was also a great opportunity to photograph the delirious devotees, the musicians fronting the processions, and the colorful villagers and gypsies who'd come to town for the festival. In the end, Noël and New Year made little sense here, and receded gently into my memories of yesteryears. I was here now and was in love with India and its festivals, big or small, long or short, pulling at my heart strings all year long.

The only person I couldn't figure out was Prakash, my veena instructor. Every day, for the past three months, I waited for a miracle as I sat in class and tuned my veena. Today Prakash would talk to me. He would ask me to play back the last lesson and be pleased to hear that I had been resourceful and found ways to get the information he denied me by speaking Tamil in the class. He would smile and say my name.

But every day was another disappointment. Another burn, as the same scenario repeated itself. The male student appeared to be Prakash's favorite. Prakash spent more time correcting him and encouraging him, grunting his approval when the boy, Muthu, came close to emulating the songs he was teaching us. Muthu was obviously talented, and Prakash took the time to show him variations, and demonstrate difficult fingering.

He didn't spend as much time with the rest of us, even though, in my modest opinion, some of them, Padma among them, demonstrated the same scholarship as Muthu.

Now that Padma and I were friends, and that she trusted me to keep secrets, she would rant and rave about it. Her large almond-shaped eyes bordered with kohl would shine with frustration, and her lovely oval face distorted by anger would turn a darker caramel shade as blood rushed to it. "He thinks we are only taking music as a means to find a better husband, you know. Our parents think the same. For them, learning music is just an additional asset to be added to our dowry, same as dancing."

"How does that make you feel?"

She shook her head violently, and her long jet-black hair fell in front of her face like a curtain. "I hate it. As long as I can remember, I wanted to be a performer, and I pray that my parents will respect my wish and not marry me off before I can complete my studies. What if the husband they choose forbids me to play the veena? It has happened to other girls I know."

I nodded my understanding. She knew I couldn't do anything about Prakash or her parents' beliefs, and we settled into a thought-filled silence. After a while, I asked. "And what about Muthu?"

She grimaced and let out a frustrated sigh. "I think Prakash is grooming him to be his disciple. In India, all outstanding musicians want a disciple to uphold their style and repertoire."

She reached forward and laid her hand on my arm. "What about you? What are you going to do? Are you going to report Prakash to the principal?"

Mulling over that question, I scratched a mosquito bite on my ankle. "I don't know. If Prakash found out I snitched on him, he could kick me out of the class?"

She bit the inside of her cheek. "He cannot do that. He is a teacher. His duty is to teach you."

I hoped she was right, and I thanked the gods for her and for Rao, who both helped me keep up with Prakash's daily workload.

Fortunately, some of the other instructors were friendly, and I looked forward to the vocal lessons. Compared to Sri Prakash, Keeran Villupillai, KV for short, was young, handsome, and very charismatic, and my stomach fluttered when he turned his luminous grey eyes on me. My voice wasn't very strong, but I had perfect pitch, which he had openly praised me for in the last three months, as we practiced vocalizing different ragas, in various talas, or time signatures. He was kind and steady, and slowly guided us into the complex world of *ragamalika*, the garland of ragas, meant to familiarize us with the many shades a single note can take in the classical repertoire we were studying. I adored his classes and had a little bit of a crush on him.

Aside from my veena and singing lessons, I also took drumming three times a week. My teacher, M. Ayer, was old and solid, like the *mridangam* he taught. Sitting on a mat behind his drum, he resembled a compact pyramid. The shaved front of his skull was dotted with brown age spots, while the back featured a thin, white shock of hair tied in a Brahmin knot. His brown and lined face matched the color of the leather heads of his two-headed drum.

I liked him a lot too. Because I was a complete beginner, and a girl—no other girls were taking drumming—he taught me separately and was endlessly patient as I stumbled through the complicated combinations of fingerings and rhythms. I had heard that he still played with prominent performers, and was curious to know why, now in his 80s, he'd accepted this job as a *mridangam* instructor. But I couldn't ask him because the only English words he knew were the numbers he counted on his fingers before clapping his hands to demonstrate drumming patterns.

I wasn't worried about the music theory class. Though it was taught in Tamil, the attending professor spoke some English and was eager to direct me to a few rare books published in English. Plus, I had Rao to talk to.

Except for Prakash, my impression was that all the instructors in the college supported and encouraged me. Padma had even told me that it was rumored they hoped I might become a spokesperson for Karnatic Music when I returned to France.

CHAPTER THIRTY

MAY 1961 - ANUP'S TALE

As May ended, the pre-monsoon weather in Madras turned muggy, muggier, and muggiest. Last year's June monsoon had come early and surprised us with a huge storm, but this year was just miserably sweltering.

Looking for something light and cold to eat, I went into the kitchen and stuck my head inside the door of our small refrigerator. On the top shelf I found a mango, a fresh coconut Gangan had already cracked open, and a left-over slice of jackfruit. I fixed myself a plate, grabbed a napkin, and sat on the tiled floor next to my veena to eat, but even the floor radiated heat, so I decided to walk to the beach before the airless space of our small villa smothered my every thought and turned my limbs into sludge.

I looked for Rishu, but he was nowhere to be seen. Nowadays, he often chose to nap at Norma and Anup's, my cat-loving neighbors. As their house sat right on the beach, a few hundred yards north of the path I was taking, I made a mental note to call on them to check on Rishu on my way back.

As soon as I reached the sandy rise demarcating the beach, the moist ocean breeze brushed my face. At first, the dewy air stream was comforting. It conjured up memories of my mother's cool hands when, as a child, I came down with fever. But after a moment, it enveloped my overheated skin and clothes like a cold shroud, and I almost found myself wishing for a shawl or a blanket. I hurried to my favorite sand dune and sank into it. My face and arms were still chilled, but the wall of sand was warm on my back.

Not exactly lonely, but alone nonetheless, I wished Stefan and I could spend more time together, to enjoy the beach and the swimming and the talking that usually accompanied our treks in the sand, but he had again left early to attend a lecture.

As the breeze flipped my hair and blew sand around me, I shut my eyes and pondered the series of moments that had propelled me to where I was now.

As, frame by frame, images of my past scrolled behind my closed eyelids, I saw my mother's smooth and youthful face, and recalled the many afternoons she brought me, a toddler, to the Luxembourg Gardens to play in sandboxes and ride the merry-go-round. As a teenager, I remember watching her face, gaunt and haunted, and her bruised neck hidden behind a scarf as we escaped the darkness of her ruined marriage. I saw myself, later, basking in the city lights of a Paris I thought I would never leave, and felt again the exuberant power of a first love tearing me away from it, and sending me across several seas in search of my lover's embrace. I relived my first hour in Bombay and my sense of wonder at the mysteries of an India whose gift to me was still untapped.

But today, reflecting on Stefan's penchant toward controlling most aspects of our joint lives, and in spite of the effort he seemed to be making to change, I wasn't sure my marriage would work. Still, I gave thanks to him, for without him I may never have found my way to this country that filled my heart with awe and learning.

Lost in thoughts, I was listening to the whoosh and flop of the breaking waves when the sound of cloth flapping like a mad sail caught my attention. I opened my eyes and was surprised to find Norma and Anup smiling at me. I loved Norma. She was the middle-aged American expat who had helped me when I'd first arrived. She'd introduced me to my future classmates and dance teachers at the reception given in our honor. Though her husband was the brother of the T.S. president, he bore no resemblance to him. Where the president looked like a scholar, slim and slightly hunched from years of studies in books, Anup was tall and strong like an Indian Zeus. Like Norma, his hair was long and white, but while hers was braided Indian-style, his was wildly flapping in the wind. Behind them, gulls veered and grazed the foamy tips of mounting waves with extended wings.

Under attack by the increasing wind, Norma's sari threatened to unwrap itself and fly away, and her long heavy braid whipped wickedly at her face. She playfully kicked my foot. "Catching a nap?"

"No. Just daydreaming. Meditating maybe, I'm not sure."

"You'd better come with us," said Anup, peering thoughtfully at the dark clouds amassing on the horizon. "I think a storm is coming, and I am seldom wrong."

I lifted my eyes to the sky. "Do you think it's the monsoon?"

Anup turned into the wind and started to walk. "Could be. But storms also happen."

Norma offered me her hand and pulled me to my feet, and I shook the sand off me as we started walking toward their house. On reaching it, we settled into the living room, which was the largest room in the house. After fighting the roar of rising winds outside, the silence was deafening. I sank into a heap of fluffy pillows atop a low bed set against the wall. There were no photos or paintings on the white-washed walls, but who would need them, with a floor to ceiling window facing the sea?

Norma may have been American, but her home was Indian. The furnishings were spartan. A low table, a few leather poufs, and a reading lamp next to a deep leather armchair, which, to my consternation and embarrassment, appeared to have been clawed and defaced by its occupant, my very own Rishu, who yawned, stretched, and continued to ignore me.

My friend's choice of leather furniture had surprised me on a previous visit, but Norma had told me that the hides from cows that died of natural causes were not deemed offensive to Hindus.

The featured piece of furniture in that room was a large state-of-the-art radio, with round dials and a pull-out shelf on which sat a record player. Under it, several short shelves bulged under the weight of music albums.

Anup went over to the turntable, picked a record, and carefully set the needle on the disc. Male Indian voices spiraled forth, gliding and overlapping, stretching bits of graceful melodies that ended in sprightly curlicues. Instrumental music was easier to listen to than vocalization, but I would need to familiarize myself with all musical forms, and I suspected that it was why Anup, who had appointed himself my music advisor, had chosen that particular record. I had an open invitation to listen to his music collection, which was a godsend, since I didn't have a record player of my own, let alone a lifelong collection of classical Indian music LPs.

He lifted Rishu with both hands and poured him gently on a large floor pillow before settling into the armchair. "The Daggar Brothers," he said, pointing to the record. "Hindustani singers, famous in Hyderabad." He went on to explain to me the difference between the different styles of vocal music.

Norma inquired if we wanted tea and walked to the kitchen to prepare it. I took that opportunity to ask Anup a question that had been on my mind since joining the CCKM six months ago, a question I hadn't dared ask for fear of being disrespectful.

Eyes closed, Anup was enjoying the record he had put on. I cleared my throat to get his attention. "What do you know about Sri Prakash, the veena teacher at the CCKM?"

He slowly opened his eyes and turned to the record player to lower the music. He seemed to be debating his answer. "Some good things, and some bad things," he finally said.

Intrigued by his answer, I moved forward to sit up straight on the edge of my pillow. "Like what?"

He took his time to search for the right words. "Like there are things that have nothing to do with you, personally, but they may affect you all the same," he said in a low voice.

I bent forward to hear him better. "What do you mean?"

Biting on his lower lip, he turned off the music altogether. "I am not sure I should talk about it, but maybe it would be better if you knew."

By now I was sitting on hot coals. "If I knew what? I am just curious about Prakash's method of teaching."

"Precisely. You may run into a difficult situation with him," he said.

Norma walked in with three empty cups and a small jar of honey, which she set on the low table.

I waited for Anup to continue.

Anup threw a worried glance at Norma, and waited until she'd left the room. "He has probably been hard on you," he said.

I felt like jumping up from my pillow. "It's not that he's hard on me," I said. "He just ignores me, and I don't know why."

Anup nodded. "That is because you're a foreigner, and he hates foreigners. Especially British people."

Unable to sit any longer, I stood up and cried out. "But I am French! Not British."

Anup shrugged tiredly. "I know, I know, but to him, all foreigners

249

are devils."

Now, maybe, we were getting somewhere. "What happened to make him that way?" I asked.

"It is a long story." He removed his thick-lens glasses, which he cleaned with the long white scarf he wore around his neck. He cleared his throat. "In 1947, a few months before India's independence, Sri Prakash was a happy man. He was a respected musician, had received many awards and was blessed with a loving wife, a son, and a precious daughter. But his good fortune came to an end abruptly when his daughter was disgraced. She was only thirteen at the time, very beautiful and a promising dancer here, at Kalakshetra. She had gone back to school in the afternoon to rehearse some choreography that was being staged with the students. When dinnertime came and she hadn't returned, her brother went looking for her and found her unconscious and bleeding in a mango grove. It turned out that she had been beaten, raped, and left to die in that grove. The doctor who was called was able to save her life, but the child was so traumatized, she was never quite right after that."

"Oh my God!" I cried, covering my mouth with joined hands.

"You're not telling Minouche that horrible old story, are you?" asked Norma, frowning, as she walked back in the room with a steaming teapot.

"Better she finds out now why old Narasimha is giving her a hard time in his class," said Anup, looking at Norma.

"Narasimha?" I said. "I thought his name was Prakash?"

"Narasimha is a nickname his students gave him," said Norma. "It refers to the fourth incarnation of Lord Vishnu, when he appears to mankind in a half-lion and half-human incarnation."

"The name suits him," said Anup with a conspiratorial smile. "He has a big head and a mane. He looks fierce."

The thought of a child being raped was burning a hole in my heart. "Who would do that to a child?" I asked, holding back tears. "Were the rapists ever apprehended and punished?"

Anup shrugged. "No. The local police did trace the rape to three drunken British soldiers stationed in Madras. But as you might expect, the British Government did not want the publicity of a rape trial just as India's independence was brewing. You have to imagine the chaos, the mixed political signals. All was in turmoil and no judge would touch the case. The troops just got moved around, and justice was never served."

"The poor girl..."

"Yes, the poor girl." Anup got up and walked to the window. The sky that had been blue an hour ago was roiling with threatening black clouds intermittently illuminated by jagged lightning striking the waves. The thunder and dramatic sky seemed to enhance the suspense of Anup's account. I peeked at the watch on Anup's brown and bony wrist. It was only three in the afternoon, but it felt like night.

Returning to his armchair, Anup continued. "You see, rape was considered shameful for the family, and as much as he wanted to petition for justice for his daughter, Prakash's hands were tied by his Brahminic pride, and to his status as a prominent musician in Madras." He bent forward and lifted the steaming cup Norma had poured and placed on a saucer on the console next to him. He took a sip and held it against his chest with both hands.

I had heard how widows and disgraced women were sometimes burned alive. I shuddered at the thought. "What happened to the girl? Did she commit *sati*?" I asked, fearing the worst.

After a long sigh, Anup continued. "Thankfully, the British put an end to that. Most of the time anyway. But tradition and prejudice turned Prakash's daughter into an object of shame who could never marry, never even go out in public. He's been hiding her for the past... how long has it been, Norma? Fifteen or sixteen years?"

"Fourteen, I think. Maybe it would have been better for her if she had died," said Norma quietly.

251

"This is all so, so sad!" I said, stunned at the thought of that young girl hidden away by her family for a decade and-a-half.

And then it hit me. What had happened to her was ominous, but, as upset as I was about her fate, I couldn't help resenting the injustice of the situation I had inherited. "There has to be thousands of music teachers in South India, and I just happened to end up in the class of a man who hates foreigners. What are the odds of that?" I asked Anup.

Just then, a violent thunderclap shook the house, and as I raised my eyes to the churning sky and caught sight of the crested waves besieging the beach, I felt guilty of my self-serving thoughts. "What's that girl's name," I asked. I wanted to keep her in my heart.

"Her name was, sorry, *is* Laila," said Norma over her shoulder, as she left the room to warm up the tea kettle that had grown cold.

Anup bent over to pet Rishu who slept peacefully at his feet. "Well, now you know," he said. "If Prakash gives you trouble, it is probably not because of your ability as a student."

"He can still fail me," I said, feeling the weight of my carefully planned study program waver under me. "And if he does, I will lose my grant. What about the School Principal? He must be aware of Prakash's mind-set. Can I count on him to make sure Prakash behaves fairly with me?"

Anup turned to me. "I cannot talk for the principal, and as far as Prakash is concerned, you will have to find your own way to his heart. Maybe it is time for him to get over his anger. Maybe you can help change his mind about foreign devils. After all, as you say, you are French, and a smart lady. I do not think they have ever had a foreign student at the CCKM. You are the first, let alone a woman."

After that, we drank our tea in silence, and I mulled over what I had just learned. Anup's revelations had shaken me. Though those events belonged to the past, I was worried about the two years to come. Part of me was scared, but, looking back to all the difficulties I had already surmounted to get here, I had to believe my luck would prevail. I wondered what Stefan would think about all this.

I looked outside and saw that Anup had been right about the amplitude of that storm. The sky was getting darker by the minute, and the wind coughed sand and whistled around me as I opened the door to leave their house. To my surprise, Rishu sneaked between my feet when I stepped out and sprinted home without waiting for me.

CHAPTER THIRTY-ONE

JUN 1961 - LETTER TO BRIGITTE

The furious storm I had witnessed at Anup's and Norma's beach house had indeed heralded the monsoon. It had now rained non-stop for nearly two weeks. The surrounding road and villages were flooded, and I had given up trying to drive my scooter to town. One thing I was learning was that living in India required an immense amount of patience.

Along with most surrounding schools, the CCKM had chosen to close until the road conditions improved, leaving me time to write a long-overdue letter to my best friend.

Sunday, June 11, 1961

My dearest Brigitte,
It's been a long time since I last wrote to you. Be assured that I haven't forgotten you. It's just that for the past six months my life has been centered around my veena training. I'd assumed that passing the music college entrance exam would be the toughest obstacle, but now that

I'm in, I still feel that I don't belong. The veena instructor I have been assigned to doesn't like me. He ignores me. Pretends I'm not in the class. It's so frustrating, I want to scream. As a result, and in order to keep up with the college curriculum, I had to increase the number of private veena classes I take with Rao, the musician I told you about in an earlier letter. I wish he taught at the CCKM, but no such luck as the college is funded by the state and staffed with famous local musicians. Without any support from the instructor, I'm working hard to master the first-year course, but the pressure to measure up is intense.

I got up and went to the kitchen looking for something to drink. In our mini refrigerator I found some leftover Madrasi coffee Gangan had bought for me in the village that morning. It was one of my favorite drinks. I poured it into a cup and carried it back to my study. It was sweet and delicious, and even cold, it smelled of lightly burnt caramel. As I sat back down at my desk I thought about what I had learned from Anup the other day. I was of two minds about talking to Stefan about it. For one thing, I didn't want to bring up my difficulties in Prakash's class. That would undoubtedly cause him to lecture me about the choice I had made when joining the CCKM. I would first find out what Lycette and Sharada knew about Laila. They were my source for anything having to do with India as a whole, and Madras in particular.

I reread the beginning of my letter and picked-up the thread.

If studying violin was tough when I was a child, I can assure you that it's nothing compared to sitting cross-legged on the floor for an hour or two at a time. Even when I rearrange the pillows placed under my ankles and knees, I have to push through the pain and the numbness on a daily basis. I used to find it strange that Indians sat comfortably on the ground for hours, but then, they grew up without chairs. Now that I've joined the music college, my dancing schedule has tapered off to two classes a week with a tutor who comes to our house.

The only good thing about the continued dance classes is that I have lost ten pounds in the last year. I like being slimmer, but I still drool at the thought of tender steaks grilled medium rare with Grey Poupon mustard, and long golden pommes frites. As I told you earlier, I'm a devious vegetarian and smuggle fish and meat into my diet when I go to town. There are so many local dishes to enjoy: spicy lamb Kebabs and curries, crispy papadams and naans, Masala dosais, mango chutneys and pickles, and my favorite... tandoori chicken! There are also excellent Chinese restaurants. I wish you were here to enjoy all of these with me.

I know you wonder about Stefan and me. To tell you the truth, I feel quite disjointed at times, seeing as how uneventful my married life is, compared to what it could be if Stefan spent less time with his books and more time with me. More than ever, we lead parallel lives. His and my studies. His and my schedule. His and my goals. What can I say? That a long time ago you told me so?

If you promise not to tell—but who cares what people may think of me in France—I have a crush on my vocal teacher. I can't quite explain it, but something about him fascinates me. Maybe it's because he does pay attention to me and because someone had to fill up that spot in my life. But don't worry... it's all a fantasy and daydreams.

All in all, and in spite of my sore knees, ankles and butt, and that dissenting veena instructor, I'm in love with India. You should see how India pours color onto the saris of the poorest villagers. And how the dark green of the date and coconut palms contrast with the tender green of new rice fields. All of this under a perpetually blue sky, except, of course, now, because the monsoon is on and everything around me is turning moldy and damp.

Which reminds me, did I tell you that we bought a second scooter for me? When I go out, I am now free from embarrassing sweat stains, bicycle grease and ugly rips at the bottom of my saris. And we can take short trips. Last month, Stefan and I drove our scooters out of town to photograph a nearby temple carved out of one giant sandstone rock. Rao, who teaches me veena privately, came along and rode with Stefan. His wife rode with me. At first, I was nervous to have a passenger, but she's a small thing and driving with her was easy enough, and every-thing went well. We traveled through some blood-red canyons, and I felt as if I'd stepped onto another planet. I so wish you could have seen it. So, if you ever decide to come and visit, just think of all the escapades you and I will take.

India is full of surprises and I'd love to show you every one of them. Do you know that mangoes and bananas come in green, red, and purple? They even come in blue. I'd never seen anything like it in Paris. We also have pomegranates and, of course, coconuts, but the most amazing of them all is the sweet and juicy jackfruit, the largest tree-borne fruit in the world, that can weigh as much as 30 kg. Enough to feed a small village.

Sadly, you won't find Indian spices in my kitchen because old Gangan, my cook, is a sweet man, but twenty years in the British army have ruined him for me. He can't prepare Indian dishes and his other recipes are so bland, they wouldn't pass muster with rabbits. Why keep him as a cook then? I don't know. I like him. He is sensitive and discreet. More than once, when Stefan was away, he turned out to be the only company I had. And our cat loves him, because, in spite of the strict vegetarian rules on our campus, he brings fish from the village to feed him.

So, disjointed or not, life goes on. For my twenty-first birthday next month, I asked Stefan to take me to Pondicherry, a small French enclave, three hours south of Madras. I'm quite intrigued with it, as the people there still speak French, and they have a thriving French school. But Stefan has shown no interest in fulfilling my wish. He often says that birthdays and holidays were just created for commerce, and he is loath to celebrate them.

Not what I expected of marriage. But then, who knows what that should be like. Maman's marriage was hardly a role model, and the Indian couples I know live in large joint families with different cultural norms and taboos. How can I hope to understand my relationship to Stefan by comparing it to an arranged marriage? I just do the best I can to stay sane by focusing on my own projects.

Since joining the music college I miss Sharada who teaches dancing at Kalakshetra. She's the closest Indian friend I have. I also miss seeing more of Lycette, something you'll probably find hard to believe after all the drama her mere existence put me through, back in Paris. But she's smart and funny. We laugh a lot and I'm sure you'd like her. We've become quite close, and Stefan is uncomfortable with our friendship. He must wonder what she's told me about his crush on her before I came. But she's too good a friend to ever bring that up.

How are things in Paris? I'd love to hear about the old gang. Jean-Pierre? André? And what about you? Are you still seeing N'mamba? How is your thesis coming along?

Don't be as lazy as me. Write.

Baisers,

Minouche

CHAPTER THIRTY-TWO

JUL 1961 - CHARLES

I woke up to a sunny Sunday morning. The monsoon was long gone and the house bathed in silence. I listened to the chittering of the birds outside and relaxed. No human sounds. I knew Stefan had left early for an extra-curricular meeting with his mentor at the university, and Gangan had gone to the village to find some fish which he regularly smuggled back into the T.S. for Rishu. While there, I knew he would be looking for some vegetables, maybe some large eggplants if he were lucky, that he might slice up and fry to serve with rice pillai, one of the few Indian dishes he knew how to cook. I hoped he wouldn't return with okra, which he referred to as "Lady Fingers". I didn't care at all for these slimy, hairy, things. Our limited choice of leafy greens wasn't Gangan's fault. The presence of local veges was limited, and their quality poor, because Indians didn't consume them as we did. We liked them steamed, or gently sautéd with butter, salt, and pepper. They curried, fried, and pickled them. Indian growers were not to blame either. It was the soil that had been depleted for centuries, without the help of enriching manure and the alternate planting cycles our farmers had practiced for generations.

It was going on 9 a.m., and already getting hot. The gardener had come and gone. He always came at dawn, in the coolest time of day, and the washing woman wasn't due until this afternoon, so, taking advantage of that quiet, alone moment, I decided to take a shower.

I leisurely soaped myself under the tepid water, washed and rinsed my hair and turned off the shower. I grabbed my favorite towel off the rack, wrapped myself in it and was reaching for the smaller towel I needed to dry my hair when the bathroom door burst open.

"Ooops, sorry, didn't know you were in there."

I repressed my surprise but not my anger as I stared the intruder down. "You should have. This is my house."

In his middle-twenties, short and rotund with bristly copper hair and small dark eyes looking out of a pink and pudgy face, Charles was planted there and didn't show sign of leaving any time soon. Not without what he had come for, anyway.

"May I borrow your shampoo? I just ran out."

Charles was the Hungarian student the Paderewski Foundation had recently inserted into our lives. I found nothing to like about him but, at first, I'd done my best to be polite when, using us as a reference, he moved into a small bungalow adjacent to our house. It was a two-room place used as a servants' quarters for whoever lived in Ranga Villa before us. It hadn't taken long for Stefan, the Pole, and Charles, the Hungarian, to become tight friends. Hailing Russia as a common enemy, they enjoyed lengthy political discussions that held no interest for me.

I pulled the towel protectively around my body. "Will you please get out!" I said, between clenched teeth.

Ignoring my obvious annoyance, Charles held out his hand. "Shampoo?"

I wanted to throw it in his face, but held back. No need to escalate the incident. "In a minute," I said, pointing to the door.

"But…" He backed into it and stumbled out.

Holding the towel tight around my body, I slammed the door shut and pushed the lock I'd had Stefan install for privacy, even though Gangan and our laundrywoman, who occasionally relied on the high pressure tap the bathroom offered, were keenly aware of not disturbing us when we bathed.

I finished drying myself, combed my hair, and cursed when I realized that the clothes I had laid out earlier were in the bedroom. I cautiously opened the door and peered into the room. Empty. I dressed quickly and joined Charles who was now sitting at our dining table in the verandah, munching on some of the fruit and nuts we kept in a bowl. I snatched the bowl and set it away from him.

"Let's get a few things straight," I said, standing across from him. Having never before been in this situation, I was feeling amped-up and fed on my irritation to say what needed to be said.

"Being Stefan's friend doesn't give you the right to come and go in our house as though you lived here."

"I know, sorry," he sighed, his foot tapping some obscure rhythm on the tiled floor.

I could see that he didn't care, but I pushed on. I had to get through to him. "This is my home, and regardless of your friendship with Stefan, I expect you to respect our privacy. Especially *my* privacy."

"Yes, of course," he said, his small eyes vacantly scanning the kitchen counter visible behind my head.

"Do you?"

"Yes. Can I have the shampoo, please?" he said, stressing the word "please". "I'm going to be late for my date. Which makes me think," he rolled his eyes, and bit his upper lip like a repentant child. "If you're not going out this morning, do you think I could borrow your scooter?"

"The answer is no. N.O. You cannot borrow my scooter. As a matter of fact, you cannot borrow anything." Ignoring Charles' mumbled curse in Hungarian, I got up, walked to the open kitchen door and spoke to Gangan who had just returned from his errands in the village.

"Gangan, can you please get the used shampoo bottle out of the shower and bring it to me?"

"Acha, Mum." I couldn't help smiling at old Gangan. He'd finally stopped calling me "Sire."

He came back a minute later with the wet and half-empty shampoo bottle.

I extended the bottle to Charles. "I don't want it back. Keep it. But this is the last thing you can bum off me. And remember, from now on, you come over on invitation only."

Grinning, he snatched the bottle away and dashed out the door without as much as a nod of thanks.

After Charles left, I sat down and attempted to meditate for a while, but my heart was still beating fast from the confrontation. My mind was restless, and I couldn't face the idea of sitting still to study as I'd planned. I worried that Stefan might not approve of my remonstrances to his friend. Hopefully, Charles' intrusion on my shower would help convince him to set some boundaries.

Outside our verandah, chipmunks were foraging under the tamarind tree, and Loulou, our rogue monkey neighbor, watched me from his perch on the tall Himalayan oak tree a gardener must have planted in the T.S. forty years ago. As I sat listening to the wind rustling through its branches, my mind slowed down enough to contemplate my situation at the music college. Anup had spoken about Prakash's ongoing vendetta with foreigners after his daughter had been harmed by some British soldiers. I wished there were more of us, foreign students at the school, but I was the only one. Maybe that was why I was taking the brunt of his disgruntlement. I hated the sense of rejection I got from him, but, so far, with my classmates' help, I had been able to grasp the essentials of each class, to be reviewed with Rao later.

Apart from Prakash, I very much enjoyed the college and looked forward to each new lesson, especially the daily singing class. I had discovered that our vocal instructor, Keeran Villupillai, known as KV, was a widower whose wife had died giving birth to their third child. He was young and vibrant, and sometimes I sat mesmerized as he held a perfect note, or demonstrated a particularly lyrical music passage. If, by chance, his eyes caught mine, my whole body would heat up, and my breath became ragged with a strange longing. I enjoyed that feeling. It was but innocent enough. Pure. A wordless contact, which left me daydreaming of exotic romance.

I sighed, remembering how I used to fantasize after Stefan left for India. I would daydream about him too, imagine about how I'd surprise him by finding a way to go to India, even though he didn't think I would, or could. But I had succeeded, and he was the one who had surprised me by marrying me. Nowadays, I wished Stefan would enjoy spending more time with me, sharing the things that I liked, like driving into town for fun and exploration, or take a long walk on the beach after a swim. I knew he liked Indian music, but recently he'd declined going to any of the concerts I attended. He had become too serious and seemed consumed by his studies, as if the whole weight of Hinduism rested on his shoulders.

At school, I resented Prakash but understood that by ignoring me and isolating me he satisfied his anger. Fortunately, I had classmates who were friendly, although not close enough to confide in. I had sweet Sharada, my go-to on Indian culture, and Lycette, my world-traveled friend who reminded me a lot of Brigitte. Truly, I was blessed, and in awe of my good fortune at having received the grant and being admitted to the music college, thus getting a shot at changing my life for the better. I had much to be grateful for.

The only thing I couldn't get enough of was the daily companionship and loving attention of the man who had stolen my heart.

CHAPTER THIRTY-THREE

THE GLASS

Stefan had gone to the University, leaving me free to meet Lycette for lunch in a downtown restaurant that my ex-neighbor, the Aussie, who wasn't a vegetarian, had recommended. She had taken a cab and was already there when I arrived.

"Still fantasizing about your vocal teacher?" she asked, with a mischievous grin.

I shrugged. "No harm in daydreaming, is there?"

"No harm at all," smiled Lycette. "So, what's been going on since I last saw you?"

I waited a bit for effect, and then told her. "I invited KV to our house. I was curious to know him as a person, talk with him, like I talk with Rao, one-on-one, away from Stefan and from the school."

"And he came?" said Lycette, her eyes widening in surprise.

"He did."

"I can hardly believe it. How was his English?"

"It was good enough to inquire politely about my husband's where-abouts. He was surprised to hear Stefan was out. Apparently, it wasn't proper for us to be alone, but I fudged. I said Stefan was expected back soon, which of course wasn't true. Anyway, I let him know our cook, Gangan, was in the house."

"Does a cook count as a chaperone?"

"I don't know."

"So, what happened?" said Lycette, signaling to the waiter who had come to our table to go away.

"I offered him something to drink. He asked for a glass of water."

"And?"

"I went to the kitchen where Gangan handed me a tray with a tall glass of iced water, but instead of picking up the tray, I took the glass to the living room, and…" I stopped to take a bite of the plain but warm naan bread a waiter had just brought to the table.

"…and then what? You're driving me crazy with suspense," said Lycette, leaning over the table to catch my every word.

"Stop interrupting! As I was offering him the glass—I was nervous, probably shaking a little—my fingers brushed his..."

"Oh! No!" Covering her mouth with her hand, Lycette cried out, as though the outcome was clear to her.

"As I was saying, my fingers brushed his hand. It was not intentional, well, not entirely," I blurted, unwilling to explain what had possessed me to do it.

"I know you've been fantasizing about him, but what could you hope for? You know he's a Brahmin!"

"So what? I was feeling reckless, hoping for something, anything. A glimpse of connection."

She stared at me, disapproval written all over her face. "Tell me what happened."

"What happened is that our fingers touched, causing my heart to nearly burst out of my chest, and then the glass crashed to the floor. When I looked up at him, I realized that he had intentionally dropped

266

the glass and stepped back."

She groaned. "What part of 'he's a Brahmin' don't you understand? Of course, he would drop the glass. You're a foreigner. Impure. That reaction was bred into him. He didn't even have to think about it." She paused before asking, gently this time, "So what happened after that?"

She patted my arm to bring me back to the conversation. I could see she was trying to make up for her righteous outburst.

"I guess Gangan heard the crash. He came out of the kitchen, mumbling in Tamil something I didn't understand."

"I suppose that put an end to KV's visit?"

"Yes. He mumbled something, turned around and left. He never apologized. You can imagine how stunned and embarrassed I was. I think Gangan was upset too. In his own way he tried to comfort me. 'He Brahmin, won't take from you.' Did everyone, even my cook, have it figured out but me?"

"Don't feel bad. These things happen. I got thrown out of a Brahmins' restaurant once for trespassing into their kitchen." She shook her head and pretended to examine her nails for a few seconds. I was grateful for her silence.

"I got another insight out of this encounter," I said, after a few seconds had passed. "Pink—you know that's how the locals think of us—well pink isn't beautiful in Madras."

"Well, I am inclined to agree with them," said Lycette. "Of course, I'm not talking about you or me, but pink is probably the adjective they slap on the die-hard British ex-pats still hanging out at their old Country Club, as if they had any business there."

I looked at the far wall of the restaurant where framed and garlanded portraits of S. Radhakrishnan, India's new president, and Jawaharla Nehru, his prime minister, hung. They now were in charge of this huge emerging and divided republic. "I know so little about India. Before coming here, I spent most of my time reading about music and dancing.

I should have paid more attention to history and politics, but it wasn't something I was curious about."

"You could always brush up on The East India Company whose actions set the stage for the British Raj," said Lycette, her face more serious than I had ever seen it. "It's true that Indians, rich and poor, were subjected to a lot of humiliation, injustice and abuse for three hundred years, but, to be honest, none of the other colonial powers–French, Belgian or Dutch–were any better."

"I get that, and you are right. And I'm sorry I created that incident" I paused and broke another piece of naan. "I guess I just wanted some attention. I get little of that with Stefan nowadays." I brought it to my mouth and took a bite. "I have such a strong desire to belong, but some days I think I'm invisible. Look at the way Prakash treats me."

She shrugged. "I think you exaggerate. Most Indians we know are actually quite nice to you. And definitely nicer than they would be if you were British." She motioned for the waiter hovering around our table to approach. "Let's order before they throw us out," she said, though we both knew they would never do that. "You can tell me the rest of the story as we eat."

As we waited for a free waiter, I took a better look around. It was not a five-star restaurant, but it was bright and clean with more framed posters of gold-laden gods and goddesses looking benevolently over us. I had been told this place was family-owned and I observed an old woman, maybe the grandmother, watching us from the kitchen door. The twelve or so tables filling the space were busy with hungry patrons from all walks of life, some in suits, and some in dhotis. Inside the door, on a small, raised platform where an old cash register stood like a work of art, the owner, a good-looking man in his forties wearing a thick gold chain around his neck, bossed the two waiters and chitchatted with the patrons.

It was warm inside, but in spite of the heat, I enjoyed the lack of A/C that would have killed the smell of the food surrounding us. The delicious aroma of saffron, cumin and coriander wafted from the tables around us, and the muted song of pots and pans coming from the kitchen added their color to the conversations floating around. I was glad we had eluded the T.S. and come here to indulge our craving for meat.

We ordered a half tandoori chicken each, with garlic naans, and mango pickles. We also asked for a side of curried potatoes, even though we probably wouldn't be hungry enough to eat them after enjoying our protein loaded chicken.

Having ordered, Lycette picked up the conversation where we had left it. "So, what about KV? You're still in his class? Everything all right after that fiasco?"

"Yes, and no."

Putting down the frosted glass of lhassi, a minty yogurt drink the waiter had brought her, Lycette asked, "What do you mean by "yes, and no?"

I waved to the waiter to bring me one of these too. "KV asked me to stay after class last Monday. I thought he might want to apologize."

"Did he?"

"Uh-uh, but he did tell me, in his charming broken English, that he needed some pictures taken. I see now that it was probably why he had accepted my invitation to come to our house in the first place."

"At least he seems to understand you never meant to offend him."

"You mean... to pollute his holier-than-the-rest-of-us self?"

She dismissed my sarcasm with a toss of her hand. "Forget that. What happened is that he must have heard about your photographic skills. What does he need photos for?"

"Are you ready?" I said, enjoying the suspense before I dropped the bomb. "His wedding. He's getting remarried."

"Remarried! Well, that makes sense. He's been widowed for two years. His children need a mother, and he needs a woman."

"I guess. The big surprise is that he's getting married to Lakshmi, his star student."

"Aie, aie aie! That's a fantasy killer for sure! Do you know her?"

"Yes. She's in my class. Her name is Lakshmi, and she's of course from a Brahmin family. Beautiful, talented, and about twenty years younger than him. And she adores him, as do the rest of his students, including me."

The waiter brought fresh naans to the table and we started picking at them. They were too hot to eat, but we were starving.

"So, are you going to do it?"

"What?"

"Take pictures at his wedding?"

I rolled my eyes. "What do you think?"

She looked at me, unsure of what I meant.

"I will, of course. Fantasy time is over." I took a long sip of my lhassi. "He was all smiles after I agreed. Very pleased. My new best friend! He is sending us a wedding invitation."

"That's quite an opportunity! Think, Minouche! You just got carte blanche at a Brahmin's wedding. It's a great privilege."

"I know, I know," I said with a sigh. "Anything for the sake of ethnomusicology."

"How come you waited a week to tell me all this?"

"I was waiting for the right time. I'm still embarrassed by what happened."

Finally, the pink and steamy tandoori chicken arrived on a platter of saffron rice, along with small bowls of chutney. Happy to leave the account of my ill-fated infatuation behind me, I descended on the chicken like a hungry crow.

"This is delicious, the best I've had in a long time," I said, biting into a plump, juicy leg.

Lycette smelled and examined the pink chicken thigh sitting on her plate. "It's okay, but not the best," she said. "The color is not quite right. Do you know that they have to marinate it overnight with spices and dye to get that color?"

"Do they really?"

"In my opinion, the Moti Mahal, in New Delhi, makes the world's best tandoori. They also roast the most delicious garlic naans! Oh, I would fly there for lunch if I could."

"Is that what you did when you were Madame the Consul of Uruguay?" It was hard not to tease her about some aspects of her past life.

"I lived there, so, no flying necessary. But using my husband's consular title always got us a reservation and a good table," she said, with a wink.

"How could you give all that up, a driver, jet set friends, first class everything, a personal dresser and maid?"

"But Minouche! He was a gangster! And I was turning into a puppet. His puppet. I got pretty good at playing the part of a diplomat's wife, but that's not who I am." She sat straighter and threw her head back. "I'm a dancer."

"What about him?"

"The diplomatic pouch was too much of a temptation for him. The fancy Rolex watches he smuggled, along with uncut diamonds and heavily taxed items like cameras and such, were the last straw. I got away fast. Packed one suitcase and came down here. A good thing too. I had gone soft and had to get back in shape. Being a dancer is hard work."

"No kidding. Indian dancing sure fooled me. Such a blend of glamour and spirituality. At first it made me feel special, like I was a vestal and belonged to a tradition going back thousands of years--"

"-- Classical Indian Music belongs to that same tradition,"

interrupted Lycette.

"True. You can have the glamour. I'll stick to music. All I got from dancing was stamping the ground till my heels bled, and my knees cried for relief."

"That's what happens when you start. And then the bleeding stops; in time the pain gets less noticeable and you're able to buckle down and train for real. If you're lucky, you become dance itself. All great dancers –Nijinsky, Nureyev, Margot Fonteyn, Martha Graham–were forged by fire on that anvil. I endure the pain because I want the feeling of freedom that lies on the other side of it."

Leaning forward over the table, Lycette pointed at my left hand. "You too are paying your dues. Look at your fingertips. The thick calluses and deep grooves that still bleed when you play too long. They tell your story. When people in this town look at you, they not only know you're a musician, they know you're a veena player."

I looked at my fingers. I saw short nails underlined by grooves made black by my veena's metal strings; not beautiful hands in the way most people think of beauty, but strong, smart, intelligent hands that could coax and pull melodies out of strings. I loved my muscular fingers and small, squarish hands. It occurred to me that they were a truer portrait of me than my face would ever be.

"So, okay. You're a dancer and I'm a musician," I declared, cleaning my plate with the last piece of naan before rinsing my right hand, stained by the tandoori dye, in the lemon-scented water-bowl the waiter had discretely brought to the table while we talked. "Shall we celebrate with dessert?" said Lycette, eyeing a tray of sweets the owner was showing patrons at another table. She got his attention and ordered lychees. I hated these sweet syrupy fruits and settled for mango ice cream.

"What about that tragic rape story Anup told you about Prakash's daughter?" she asked, her lychee-filled spoon suspended in mid-air. "Did you find anything new?"

"Not a thing."

"So now what?"

"I need time to look into it," I sighed. "The extra classes I arranged with Rao have kept me busy."

We ordered coffee. The owner returned to our table with two cups, a pot of coffee and a smaller container of cream. "Special for you," he said. He proceeded to prepare it like the elegant steward had once done on my first train trip to Madras, by first pouring the coffee in the cup, stirring sugar in it and trickling the heavy cream onto the back of a spoon, to let it swirl and float atop the bitter brew.

It was a great show, but it no longer impressed me, which made me wonder. Was I getting jaded? What would it be like to be on my own when I went home, without servants or attentive waiters? India was subtly altering my expectations and I'd better watch out. I didn't want to turn into a snotty brat.

Lycette finished her coffee and asked the waiter for more. "This place is okay, but I heard about a new tandoori restaurant modeled after the famous Moti Mahal in New Delhi. We should go there next time we go on a protein run."

"That would be fun. What is it called?"

"Moti Moti."

"Deal."

She put her coffee cup down and reached for the small dish of aromatic cumin seeds the owner had placed on our table to freshen our breath after our meal. "I meant to tell you, Sharada heard about an old woman, a witch and a healer. They say she's psychic. We want to meet her. Feel like joining us?"

"Sure! I'd love to. I've never met a witch. Do you think I could take photos, or maybe film the encounter? We just bought a second-hand super 8 camera."

"That would need to be arranged in advance. For now, let's just pay her a visit." She pointed to her right heel under the table. "I have an old Achilles tendon injury that flares up once in a while. Let's see if she can heal that."

CHAPTER THIRTY-FOUR

THE WITCH

A week-and-a-half later, after Sharada had made the proper arrangement, we set out to visit the old woman reputed to be a witch as well as a healer, in hopes she could relieve Lycette's old foot injury. The three of us took a rickshaw to her house, in a part of town that stretched north of the harbor. It was part slum, but also part bazaar, with its myriad store fronts advertising cigarettes, canned foods and tax-free electronics from Hong Kong, probably bartered by sailors touching port. The streets were vibrant with hole-in-the-wall businesses offering indoor/outdoor barbers, saucy prostitutes of both sexes, self-proclaimed dentists and doctors to the poor, herbalists, healers, palm readers and blackmarketers.

Lycette pointed to a man sanding what looked like long wooden boxes. "Is that a coffin maker?"

"Where?" I was as surprised as she was.

"There, the store with the large cross in the window."

"No coffin for me, thank you," said Sharada. "I'll take a funeral pyre anytime."

"I guess they provide for the Christian community," said Lycette. "What about the Muslims? Do they get buried too?"

"I don't know much about them," said Sharada.

The rickshaw driver, who must have understood more English than he pretended, turned his head and spoke over his shoulder.

"Muslims die, get washed first, then wrapped in Kafan, white burial-shroud cloth, and get buried fast fast, in own Muslim cemetery. No coffin."

He turned his attention back to driving just in time to swing the rickshaw around a cow that had wandered into the middle of the narrow street.

Though we got jostled against each other on the slippery vinyl seat, we were none the worst for the scare. Lycette was the first to recover.

"Nothing to fear, ladies. Just another Madrasi driver!" she said tartly. The driver didn't respond to her taunt.

Eventually, the rickshaw pulled alongside a small building. It was more than a hut, but not quite a house. The low wall surrounding the structure had created an inside courtyard in which a peacock strutted freely, his long iridescent tail feathers trailing after him. Outside the wall, a few children looked in, attracted but wary, for peacocks were well known for their mean disposition.

Sharada went in first to seek an audience. She soon returned to the door and waved us in. It took a minute for my eyes to adjust to the dim interior.

The woman we had come to see sat on a ropy, raised charpoy. I could see why people thought of her as a witch, for she was ancient and grizzled, her skin the color of burnt chestnuts. Waist-long, metal-grey hair fell upon her shoulders like a veil. Her open eyes, covered with a milky cataract veil, were sightless, and dried tears had crystallized in the crevices of her skeletal face. Her thin arms, fragile as birds' bones, were free of the white sari hanging on her wasted body. The thought

276

crossed my mind that she indeed should remain indoors, for it looked as though the least gust of wind might pick her up and toss her up into a tree, where she might well belong.

Sharada spoke softly to her, and the old woman bid Lycette approach and place her foot on a tall, upturned clay pot sitting in front of her. Mumbling a string of incomprehensible words, the healer placed one hand above the offered foot, careful not to touch it. She then reached under her sari for a pouch out of which she extracted a pinch of powder that she placed in her palm and blew over the injured heel Lycette had told me about.

"Acha," she said, nodding, which we understood to mean that she was done. She pulled her hands back and laid them carefully in her lap.

Lycette stood back, stretching her ankle back and forth, a surprised look on her face. I couldn't wait to ask if the pain was really gone.

I knew the witch couldn't see, yet I had the impression she was looking straight at me. Suddenly she rattled a long string of Tamil words in Sharada's direction, and simultaneously gestured for me to come closer. I approached the charpoy with apprehension. "It's okay," said Sharada. "She guessed you are a foreigner and is curious to "see" your face."

Sharada directed me to kneel on the floor in front of the witch. I complied, filled with apprehension. I could hear my heart thud loudly in my chest, and my throat felt scratchy and dry. The old woman extended her arms and hands in my direction without ever touching me. I felt heat radiating from her dry palms that were the faded color of dried-out rose petals. A soothing wave of energy relaxed my neck and shoulders as she continued her examination. She kept a running commentary to herself, and her words washed over me like music. I floated away. Mesmerized.

After she stopped, it took me a second to orient myself and straighten up. I turned to Sharada. "What did she say?"

"She says that you are back. She says she sees you far away, across the seas, alone, but not alone. She says you must learn all over again what you once knew. She sees many famous people around you, but not you. She says that you must find the girl wearing green."

CHAPTER THIRTY-FIVE

AUG 1961 - THE INDIAN BRIDE

Because the wedding I had been hired to photograph had been scheduled in the middle of the college summer vacation, Stefan and I were forced to postpone our travel plans to northern India. Duly calculated by both families' astrologers, the most auspicious date for that union turned out to be August 17.

One day before the big event, I arrived early at the home of the bride-to-be and parked my scooter in the shade of a banyan tree overhanging the white-washed building. Visiting Lakshmi today wasn't part of my assignment. It was my idea to take pictures of the bride being prepared for her wedding. Because of import taxes, film and recording tapes were expensive in India, but I hadn't asked for any money, and none was offered. However, an agreement had been struck with KV. In exchange for photographing tomorrow's wedding and recording the evening concert as a favor, I would be allowed to keep a copy of the photos and recordings we made. It was an excellent deal, serving my purpose to gather all the material I could about Indian life.

The front of the house was deserted. There were no men in sight, which made sense. Getting the bride ready was the women's task, one I hoped to catch on film. The front door was open a crack, so I removed my sandals and walked into the parlor where I ran into Lakshmi's mother. With a lot of hand-gesturing, nodding, and a blend of English and Tamil words, she welcomed me and managed to convey that her husband and sons had been sent away to her brother-in-law's house.

We crossed a large outdoor courtyard. It was bordered on all sides by low buildings and led to the back of the house. A finely carved wooden screen, like some I had seen in upscale Kashmiri shops, hid the entrance to her large living room. I stepped around it and was met by a buzz of female energy as palpable as a swarm of bees. Still blinded by the outdoor glare, I couldn't make out who was there, but detected at once the familiar smell of the coconut oil South Indian women use to gloss their hair, combined with the sweet fragrance of jasmine. As my eyes adjusted, a dozen women turned away from the lavish jewelry they had been admiring to stare at me. I could read the surprise on their faces. I was, after all, the only foreigner in that room. I joined my hands in greeting, unslung my camera bag and placed it gently on the floor.

"Minouche, over here," called Lakshmi. She switched to Tamil to introduce me to her entourage. She wore no make-up, yet looked so beautiful that it took my breath away. I could feel her pride and excitement. It crackled around her like electricity. Her oval face, already fair by South Indian standards, was being rubbed with a saffron paste that gave it a golden glow. I had always thought of her as a talented and unassuming schoolmate, but today, the inner fire burning inside her almond-shaped and kohl-lined eyes startled me, for she was no longer the passive friend I had come to know. Tomorrow was her day, and she was free at last to reveal a passionate side I had never suspected. Her self-confidence sent a chill of guilt up my spine, and I felt my cheeks heat up as I recalled my erotic fantasies about her soon-to-be husband.

She sat on the floor in her petticoat. Her lustrous hair, freed from the single braid that usually restrained it, cascaded over her shoulders and back, all the way to the floor. She held her hands and feet extended to a couple of henna artists, two wizened widows whose white cotton saris, as plain as the white-washed walls, contrasted with the vivid saris of their female entourage. Undisturbed by the hubbub, the two artists were concentrating on their intricate designs.

Lakshmi stretched her back against the wall she was leaning on, and invited me to sit near her. "Minouche. Sit down. Keep me company while they paint the henna designs on me."

As fascinating as that was, I had other plans for this visit. I pulled my camera out of its bag and showed it to her. "I prefer to stand. I'd love to take photos showing how you're being prepared for your wedding. Is it alright with you?"

"I do not mind. But do not take any naughty shots of me," she said with a surprisingly sexy twinkle in her eyes. "And be sure to make me look beautiful. You promise?"

"I promise."

I raised the viewfinder to my eye and looked through the lens. The light filtered by the shaded windows was soft and lit the scene in a magical way. Around me, the women showed each other the formal saris they would be wearing the next day for the actual ceremony, and their musical Tamil chitchat filled the room. I reached for my light meter and stopped hearing them.

An opulent red silk sari, the richest I had ever laid eyes upon, lay on a table for all to admire. The whole length of it, all six yards, was embroidered with a gold paisley motif and a solid gold border. As the light fell on it, the twenty-two-carat jewelry displayed next to it was splashed with shades of crimson. It was strange to think of a bride wearing red, but in India, blood red was the color of fertility.

I was drawn into the moment of this young woman's life. She had been my classmate, just one more girl in the class, pretty, but not enchanting as she was now. Tomorrow, thanks to the matchmaking efforts of several astrologers, her parents and a go-between, she would be united for life to a handsome and talented widower. In an instant she would become a wife and the mother of his three young children. Looking at her through the lens, I searched for wariness or concern, but only saw the radiant happiness of a girl who had met her expectations. She had been KV's best student and must have been in love with him and his music from the start. I felt a pang of jealousy. Here she was, the perfect Indian bride. Had he desired her silently? Had he been singing to her in our class? Not to his long dead guru as he would have us believe? And not to me, when I thought he might, when my skin tingled with longing, and my heartbeat threatened to crash under the spell of his voice?

It was totally absurd, but half of me rejoiced about her good fortune while the other half resented it, knowing that tomorrow she would become his Shakti, his inspiration, his source of energy and power. In comparison, my marriage felt empty.

As I took picture after picture, admiring Lakshmi and the women around her, enduring, nurturing and solid, the absurdity of my fantasies about KV finally hit me. How could I have been so ignorant, shallow and selfish?

"You look so serious. What are you thinking about?" asked Lakshmi, blowing on her fingers to make the henna paste dry faster.

I hadn't been aware it showed. "I'm thinking about my life!" I answered truthfully.

Looking at me with her doe eyes, Lakshmi insisted, "What about it?"

"You and your family make me feel like I've stepped into the real heart of India," I said. What I didn't say was that my brain was reaching out for an explanation to the sense of déjà vu I was experiencing in that house. The crimson sari, the gold, the henna, the lustrous hair cascading down one's back. Could the old witch have seen beyond my present life? I paused and added as sincerely as I could, "I'm happy for you, and grateful for your letting me share this day with you."

Lakshmi gave me a dazzling smile. "I am the lucky one to have you as a friend." She patted the stone floor next to her. "Will you sit with me for a little while? Tell me about France. Maybe I will go there with my husband someday, on a concert tour. Do you know that Prakash was invited to go to Berlin four years ago?"

"Did he go?"

"Of course not. He made a big show of refusing the invitation by burning it and throwing the ashes in the Adyar river. He stated publicly that he was not about to accept anything from ignorant westerners who could never appreciate the depth of our oldest musical tradition."

We chatted about the irascible Prakash for a while, and I almost asked her if she knew anything about his daughter, but realized that Layla's tragedy would have happened way before her time. In the end I held my tongue. I didn't want to cast rain on her happy day.

I spent the rest of the day with them. For lunch, Lakshmi's mother had servants bring trays of masala dosais filled with spiced potatoes, onions and green chutney. She also brought idlis, one of my favorite south Indian dishes, made by steaming a fermented combination of rice and lentils, best smothered in freshly churned buttermilk, lime and mango pickles. On a separate tray were small bowls of vegetable curry and rice, as well as cups of spicy rasam broth.

Lakshmi, who waited stoically for the henna applications to dry, ignored the food. Her mother and friends offered to feed her, but she refused. She may have been too nervous to eat, or afraid to destroy hours of henna artistry. Or maybe she was fasting on the eve of her momentous day. Maybe her mother's offer to feed her was only part of tradition. Since coming to India I had discovered that fasting was a prelude to many of their rituals. As I ate with the women, she distracted herself by humming passages of her favorite ragas. Perversely, I wondered for an instant if those were also KV's favorite ragas.

I delayed the moment to leave. I didn't want to go. For the past few hours I'd felt part of this family and I wanted to lie on the floor and sleep right there with the others. I longed to belong in this home enriched by two thousand years of Hindu tradition. But they didn't ask me to stay. They knew I had a home and family of my own. What they didn't know, was how bittersweet both were for me, and how I missed the nurturing companionship of women, my mother, my girlfriends.

But the night fell. I had no more excuse to stay, and I reluctantly went home. It had been an incredible day. Spending this special time with Lakshmi's family had been familiar in some ways and left me wishing I'd been born here. Was it possible that I'd actually lived here before? In some other life? In another time?

CHAPTER THIRTY-SIX

THE WEDDING

The next day, Stefan and I got up at dawn and packed our camera bags, making sure we had enough color film to capture the whole ceremony. Separately, we packed twelve alkaline D batteries, two microphones and three reels of tape, along with the new tape recorder that Viktor, Stefan's godfather and mentor, had sent us tax-exempt—saving us a ton of money—with the help of a Paderewski scholar passing through Madras. It was a Nagra, a professional machine which film people used on location, and Stefan was quite excited about it. The upcoming concert would give him the perfect opportunity to try it out.

"You stayed at Lakshmi's pretty late last night," said Stefan, a little too casually as he secured the equipment case to his scooter with bungee cords.

"Just prepping the assignment," I said, unable, or possibly unwilling, to explain to Stefan my strong feelings of belonging among the women preparing Lakshmi for her wedding. The sense of déjà-vu I'd experienced had felt normal to me, and, at the same time, unsettling. Looking at the wedding as an assignment was easier.

When we arrived at Lakshmi's house, an early-rising crowd of relatives and friends had already arrived and were milling around. I had heard that weddings in India often lasted for a week, and could involve hundreds of people, including caterers, dancers and musicians. But with only a hundred guests or so, this wedding appeared low-key, and, as far as I knew, having only been retained for the day, the celebration would end after the concert tonight. Maybe because it was KV's second marriage, most of the pomp and extravaganza had been left out, to focus on the religious ceremony.

The chatter was festive and friendly but, through the lens, I was amused to capture the sight of women eyeing each other critically, comparing saris and itemizing each other's jewelry. Remembering the witch soothsaying, I looked around for a green sari, but there were none. Blues and yellows, purples and golds, filled the courtyard like exotic flowers. The men were impressive in their starched white kurtas, their gold-trimmed scarves folded formally and thrown across one shoulder. Most wore the long white dhoti favored in this part of the country.

Lakshmi's father gave Stefan a key to a closet where the Nagra would be safe until it was time to set it up for the concert. Stefan thanked him and pulled his super 8mm film camera out of the bag. After making sure it was loaded, he signaled to me that he would stand outside to watch for the groom's arrival.

In the central courtyard, where giant floor mats had been spread to cover the ground wall-to-wall between the interior buildings, a low platform had been erected under a colorful tent. Bare-chested Brahmins had already lit a ritual wood fire inside a deep stone vessel. Cross-legged on the bare wooden floor, they performed a purifying puja, or service, to enhance the propitiousness of the moment. The whole area was strewn with rose petals, and two servants appeared bearing large brass dishes filled with yellow bananas, green and purple plantains, whole coconuts, lemons and mangoes, as well as a bowl of shiny white rice, which they set down, for later, under the edge of the stage.

The flames' reflection twisted and danced on the brass peacock-shaped oil lamps, and on the water urns and bowls, and I was trying to capture those ephemeral images when Vasanta, one of Lakshmi's younger sisters, rushed to my side.

"Hurry, Minouche. Come with me. The bridegroom is arriving," she said.

I followed her and saw a pageant of men streaming down the street. Two fat Brahmins led the procession. They were playing *nadaswarams*, a loud and shrill black oboe-like wind instrument whose sinuous voice reminded me of the snake charmer's music I had heard in front of a tourist hotel in downtown Madras. I stared, fascinated, as the air trapped inside their mouths stretched their cheeks into moving bubbles. Behind them, a drummer punctuated the march on a two-headed drum secured with a strap around his shoulders. The music was joyous and loud, and people lined the street and gawked at the advancing group. Gleeful children ran alongside the cortege, and Stefan walked among them, mini-camera in hand, his cheeks flushed with excitement. I started taking pictures of the procession. The air smelled of the dust, sweat and excitement generated by the marching band, and I strained to find KV among the men, but he was nowhere to be seen.

"In the old days," said Vasanta, "the bridegroom and his friends would arrive on horses and kidnap the bride. Or at least, pretend to. But those days are over," she added, with a regretful glance at the merry men. "It was so romantic."

I agreed distractedly with her, for I had just discovered KV surrounded by a gaggle of men posturing loudly with warlike gestures. My breath caught at the sight of him. Had I really allowed myself to imagine I might be the first to thaw KV's widowed celibacy? It had been two years since my wedding night in Bombay, and the chemistry Stefan and I had shared under the slate roof of the old Parisian mansard where he lived, had briefly flared upon my arrival. But it had faded. Sex without playful foreplay and desire was no longer romantic. It was what it was. Rare, and rushed. So, who was to blame if I had allowed myself to fantasize about another man? Maybe there had been too many loveless nights spent waiting for Stefan to put down his books to join me in bed. Or come home.

I took refuge behind the camera that hid a tear Stefan's remoteness had brought to my eyes, and focused on the job at hand.

KV wore creamy white silk garments that hung heavily on his slim body. His light-skinned face looked flushed and excited as he pushed his hair back and wiped his hand on his scarf. I focused on his head and zoomed to get a shot of his profile, the little curl that always fell over his left eye, the tinge of grey visible along his ear. I took a few shots and turned away resolutely. No more lingering regrets. I was here to document his wedding as an anthropologist and musicologist would, which was as good a definition as I could give to anyone asking me what ethnomusicology was.

I followed the procession to the inner courtyard where Stefan was now filming.

After an exuberant entrance, KV's companions settled down and escorted him to the side of the platform where the rite would be performed. I saw him remove his shirt and rearrange the white thread lying across his chest, the thread that identified him as a Brahmin. He carefully folded the white scarf he had been wearing into a narrow band and threw it over his left shoulder. Eyes fixed to the ground, he stepped onto the platform, walked past the ceremonial fire, bowed to the attending priests, his hands folded with palms touching in a respectful Namaste greeting, and sat on a mat. The attending priests smeared his forehead with ashes from a ceremonial bowl. They allowed family members and well-wishers to come up and place garlands around his neck. His chest was soon covered with flowers.

As Lakshmi entered the courtyard, hidden from head to toe inside her blood-red sari, silence fell on the gathering. I could hear the clickedy-click of her toe rings on the bare platform floor, like a heartbeat, as she approached her husband-to-be, and sat by him.

Even though he had seen her face in his class for the past three years, her head, today, was covered and her features hidden. I moved closer, hoping to catch her attention, but she never lifted her eyes, which remained fixed on the ground in the shy and demure posture expected of a bride. Then, she too was decked with flower garlands and, as I framed their bodies in the viewfinder of my camera, I realized they both looked like the deities I had seen in temples.

Stefan, who had disappeared for a while, signaled to me that he had put the 8mm camera away. "Ran out of film," he mouthed from the other side of the courtyard. He was now holding our second-best camera, a Leika, and indicated that he would be taking photos from the other side of the ceremony.

Just then, the Brahmins' chanting of Sanskrit verses increased in volume in a kind of hypnotic rhythm, and the head priest handed KV a long black and gold beaded necklace with a gold pendant, which KV tied around the bride's neck.

"The *mangalsutra*," whispered Vasanta, standing by my side. "It is most important in our tradition."

"How so?" I asked, zooming in on the necklace.

"Each bead is auspicious and has divine power. It signifies protection from evil."

I saw KV reaching for the necklace with one hand, and offering his free hand to pull Lakshmi to her feet. He then gently walked her seven times around the ritual fire, without ever releasing his hold on the black and gold beads adorning her neck.

Nodding wisely, Vasanta said, "My sister can never take it off."

"Even when bathing?"

"Even when bathing."

A murmur of approbation and cheers rose among the guests. Some applause even suggested it was the end of the ceremony, but the couple sat down again, and the chanting continued. When the bridegroom and bride finally stood up and came down from the platform they'd been sitting on, they were showered with a rain of rice.

"For wealth and fertility," said Vasanta, as she joined her family and friends in the joyous ritual. I suddenly recalled how Miss Petit's servants had also thrown rice at Stefan and me after the notary public had declared us husband and wife. A well-wishing gesture I hadn't understood at the time. I wondered if they also did that in France, but, having never attended a wedding there, I had no idea. It was strange that my mother and I had never been invited to one. Had we really been so isolated? Forgotten by family and friends because my stepfather was a drunk?

Out of the corner of my eye I saw the guests, heading toward a room whose floor was covered with long narrow mats so food could be served on banana leaves. I was starving and motioned for Stefan to join me. As I sat comfortably on the mat, covering my feet under the edge of my sari, I chuckled. "Remember the short dress I was wearing at the reception Kalakshetra gave for us when I arrived in Madras? What a nightmare it was to keep my legs and feet covered."

"And a good thing too, that Sharada rescued you with a shawl," said Stefan, grimacing at the embarrassing memory.

A commotion at the entrance to the room caught my attention. I turned around and was surprised to see the music college staff, led by Prakash, entering the room. All six feet of him looked regal in a starched dhoti and kurta, with a long white and gold scarf thrown over his shoulder. More than ever, he looked like *Narasimha*, the lion-headed God, with his mad hair foaming out like an aura around his large skull. He was laughing at something one of his friends had said. Truth be told, I had never seen Prakash laugh or even smile. He caught me looking at him and returned my stare. To this day, he hadn't looked at me straight on in class, and now, I found myself under the scrutiny of his misaligned and slightly globulous eyes pointing in different directions. One pointing right at me, the other over my left shoulder. Afraid to betray the discomfort his stare and physical presence imposed on me, I turned to Stefan who had watched the exchange. Leaning against me, he whispered in my ear, "Reminds me of car headlights in need of an alignment." Suppressing a giggle, I elbowed him in the chest. Making fun of Prakash in public was a really bad idea.

After eating our fill of a delicious jackfruit curry and a dozen more tasty south Indian dishes, cooked and served out of a vegetarian brahmin kitchen, we skipped the varied array of rich sweets laid out on a festively decorated table, and retreated to the courtyard to breathe fresh air and shake off our food-induced stupor. It was only three in the afternoon, and the concert wouldn't start until six, when it got cooler, but now that many of the guests had disappeared inside the house, or departed, it was a good time to set up.

Stefan got the Nagra out of the closet where he had stashed our equipment and we asked permission to save a spot in front of the makeshift stage where the marriage had been conducted. Meanwhile, the vessel holding the fire had been moved out of the way, the floor swept of rice and flower petals, and lights had been added to the flower garlands lining the edge of the stage and the canvas roof that would protect it from evening dew. At the back of the stage, an oversized poster of Tyagaraja, the musician-saint revered by all artists, was encased by flower garlands lit by thick braids of small colored lights.

We now had to find a spot where the microphones would be protected from the wind and the chatting of the audience. But as we didn't yet know how many musicians would perform, and where they would sit, positioning the two microphones we owned would have to be done when they came onstage.

Stefan, who didn't trust anyone to keep the Nagra safe, chose to bring out a book and read in the shade of the colorful awning covering the platform. I left to reload my cameras with color film, after which I retreated to the women's pavilion where I had met Lakshmi the day before, but she wasn't there. She had probably retreated with her husband for a short rest, or an intimate moment, before tonight's concert. I sat down against the wall and closed my eyes, hoping for a cat nap, but sleep didn't come.

With a sharp pang, I thought back about my own hasty wedding to Stefan four days after disembarking from the passenger liner that had brought me to Bombay. I had been wearing a plain white cotton dress sewn in a day by a bazaar tailor, a pair of cheap white shoes, and a square yard of veil to pin on my head. White on white on white... the ultimate colorless shade which, in India, was a statement of widowhood. It had all been so bare, with only a notary public, our hosts pushing seventy, a cook, a child and a few servants. The notary had collected a few signatures on a marriage certificate, and lunch had been served. Afterward, everyone had retreated for a nap. Except for Stefan and I, too hot and too nervous to lie down together.

Suddenly I wished my wedding dress had been a vibrant red, like Lakshmi's sari. At the time, it had all felt like an adventure, but I could see now that I had been cheated of the preparations, the fun, the good wishes and participation of all the people who loved me. My eyes filled with tears. Would a more elaborate ceremony have generated more romance? It certainly would have left better memories.

I came to as Lakshmi's mother touched my hand. "Your husband... looking for you."

I jumped up and rejoined Stefan near the stage. I was surprised to see that the courtyard was now filled with guests patiently sitting on the giant floor mats. Women and children to the left, and men to the right, as was the custom at concerts. The women's shimmering silk saris caressed by the setting sun made me think of a colorful mosaic. Somewhere in the back of my mind, it all looked so familiar. More people were standing in the back. I guessed that those who hadn't been invited to the ceremony had been invited to the concert.

And now the musicians arrived, greeted by the spectators as they walked through the crowd and settled on the low platform. KV was center stage, and Stefan quickly angled a microphone in front of him. The *mridamgam* player sat to his right. He was applying a wet paste to the bottom head of the drum sitting on his lap, and hitting its rim to check its pitch. A violin player sitting to KV's left was tuning his violin and moved back a little to make room for Prakash and his large veena. Behind KV, one of his students was strumming a *tambura*, the continuous harmonic drone to which all the instruments were being tuned.

The concert started with a short prayer followed by an animated piece meant to warm up the musicians. It was followed by a devotional song I recognized as one of Tyagaraja's popular compositions. Soon after that came the *pièce de résistance,* the long improvisational *alap,* during which KV's luminous voice demonstrated his mastery of the melody and time signature, after which, each of his accompanists took turn improvising their own versions of the song.

I had attended many concerts, but the smaller setting and intimacy of this performance brought a sense of exultation into my heart, as I aimed my lens at these five local artists who brought to life the spirit of Carnatic music, which today was still a living musical tradition and an essential cultural aspect of South India.

After a while, having taken a whole roll of photos of the same five people, alone and in various group combinations, I put my camera down and settled happily as a listener as one by one the singer, the violin, the veena and the drums embarked on their solos. The noise around me disappeared, as did the mosquitoes who had discovered us, as did the crushing weight of my ankle bones inside my skin. This music was so much larger than me, than the world I knew. Content to just *be,* I closed my eyes and let South India's voice fill my body and my heart.

CHAPTER THIRTY-SEVEN

POST WEDDING BLUES

It had been a week since KV and Padma's wedding and, after the lesson with my dance tutor who now came to Ranga Villa twice a week for a one-hour class, I was lazing around the house, feeling the afterglow of sex for the first time in a long time. Stefan had been surprisingly attentive for the past few days, taking time out to sit with me and talk about future trips he wanted us to take. I wondered if, like me, that wedding had triggered in him an emotional need to connect, but it was hard for me to feel secure in a relationship with a husband who took off rather than discuss important issues, and often seemed to prefer books to my company.

Midday sunlight poured through the verandah's screen and splashed the room with shards of light that hurt my eyes and bounced off the whitewashed walls. Rishu, who had opted to lie on the floor instead of a pillow, turned on his back and stretched to his full length to catch the slightest hint of breeze on the short fur of his belly. I thought about sweeping a few buckets of water on the porous floor tiles to bring the temperature down several degrees, but decided it was not worth the trouble. I put down the book I had been reading, and gazed outside, searching for my four-legged neighbors, the mongoose, the squirrels, and Loulou.

In spite of Stefan's renewed attentiveness, I had a lot on my mind but couldn't write home about it. I couldn't let my mother know I had some misgivings about married life. She'd sacrificed too much to keep me in school and had shared my dream of rejoining Stefan in India. I knew my assumed bliss buoyed her life and I couldn't stand the thought of destroying her bubble of happiness.

The one person I longed to confide in was Brigitte, but she wasn't known for her discretion. She hadn't approved of my leaving Paris, had even been a little jealous of me at the time, the way best friends some-times are. I suspected she might even take pleasure in leaking the bad news to our shared acquaintances, which would eventually get back to my mom. I was stuck with keeping my feelings to myself.

Fortunately, there was Lycette, who had promised to come over after class. How strange that I had thought of her as my rival before coming to Madras, and now, I couldn't think of a better friend. I went to the kitchen to ask Gangan to brew a fresh pot of coffee and went outside.

Armed with a native hand-held scythe, the T.S. gardener had recently chopped the dry grass and low bushes surrounding our house, and the outdoor air smelled of dust and sap. I walked to my favorite tree, the giant tamarind fronting the house. I knew that a chameleon I had baptized Leon, hid in its lowest branch, and it was both a challenge and a game to discover it, frozen, camouflaged among the leaves, big bulging eyes unblinking, waiting to lash an impossibly long tongue at unsuspecting insects. Crows circled the top of the tree, hunting for small rodents that fed on the long, sticky beans hanging between the leaves. But Leon was nowhere to be seen. After a few minutes I saw Lycette riding her bicycle to the house, a beat-up black and red Schwinn with a front basket filled with books, and an empty luggage-rack wrapped with a frayed jumping rope in the back.

The sight of her on that rusty old bike made me smile. "Bonjour! I'm happy you came." I gave her a kiss on both cheeks and we walked into the living room, a large space I kept scarcely furnished to host my private dance and veena lessons. "Gangan is making coffee."

"Whooo! I'm beat. It was a tough class. Can I have water first?" Her dance outfit was drenched in sweat.

Gangan must have been listening, because he hurried in with a pitcher and two glasses. I think he liked Lycette. She thanked him and guzzled down a whole glass of water.

"Want a pillow?"

"You don't want me to. I'm too wet." She brushed a stray strand of hair from her face and lowered herself, cross-legged, on the bare floor.

I pulled a thin cushion under my ankles and sat on the floor across from her.

"So, tell me about the wedding? How was it?" she asked.

I described the highlights of the ceremony for her, and tried to explain how the complex ritual had impressed me, but also left me feeling sort of cheated. "The loud music announcing the bridegroom's arrival, the mysterious Hindu chanting in Sanskrit to call on the gods and goddesses to bless that union, and the large and colorful gathering of family and friends was very impressive. I felt in my bones the excitement and anticipation passing between Lakshmi and KV when he took her hand and led her seven times around the fire. Compared to that, my rushed Bombay wedding was incredibly plain. Kind of washed out."

"Don't say that. I saw the pictures that were taken that day. You looked happy."

"Of course, I was happy. I had realized my dream of being reunited with Stefan. Having never before attended a wedding, I didn't know what it could have been like."

Lycette stared at me and shook her head. "Weird."

"I know it's weird, but when I think back to the way our marriage was expedited, I wonder why Stefan bothered to get married at all. Did he, by any chance, do it because he needed a French passport?"

"There are easier ways to get a passport," said Lycette. "He could buy a forged one on the blackmarket. Stealing one wouldn't work, but, considering how charming and handsome he is, he might seduce the right embassy clerk…" She cracked up, and I couldn't help but join her. She had a way of deflecting my worst scenarios, and making me laugh in spite of myself.

"Stop," I protested, after catching my breath. "You've made your point, but my registration with the French consulate is definitely facilitating the renewal of his travel papers. As a matter of fact, his application for a French passport is being processed right now."

"I don't think Stefan is that devious," she said, "and you can't begrudge him wanting to legalize his status. Can you imagine what it's been like for him, living in exile after the Poland he was born into was swallowed by the USSR. The Poles who stayed became Russians. Those who emigrated were left with no country to call their own, and consequently, no passport."

"I know. And without passport, he's a nobody."

"Or worse, a suspicious shadow in all the places he passed through, including France." Lycette knitted her eyebrows, as she did when something stirred at her heart.

I shook my head to dislodge the crazy thoughts that had dug their talons into my brain over the past weeks. "You are right," I sighed. "Still, there are days when I fear Stefan regrets his decision. We've only been married one year but it seems that some of it has been a burden for him. On the other hand, he made India a reality for me. For which I can only be grateful."

"And you should. Instead of worrying about what Stefan thinks or doesn't think, you should count your blessings. Look, you have a house, a grant, a clear study goal, a husband who cares for you at least 90% of the time, so give him a break for the last 10%. You have tutors, gardeners, a cook. Unlike me, you have someone to daydream about, and you even have the greatest Siamese cat in Madras," she rubbed Rishu's offered belly. "So, tell me. Who is the lucky one? I have a soon-to-be ex-husband who will be charged for fraud, expelled from the diplomatic corps and will make sure I get no alimony… but," she gave me a brilliant smile, "I don't care. I now am 100% free to focus on dancing, which to me, is the most important thing."

Feeling a little bit silly about my earlier, misguided whining, I poured the coffee into our cups and asked, "Will you at least have money for tuitions, food and lodging?"

"Not to worry. I still have jewelry I can sell."

"I guess you're right. I shouldn't complain."

She stopped talking, straightened her back and stretched her arms above her head just as Gangan walked in and set the tray with coffee, sugar, milk and cups in front of us on the floor. He returned to the kitchen to fetch the leftover pastries Norma had given me the previous day after hosting a formal tea for some English ladies.

I liked my coffee black. Lycette stirred a dollop of milk into her cup and reached for a cookie which she dipped into the dark brew. Graciously, she changed the subject and asked, "How come you're not in school?"

"A complicated astral conjunction prompted the school's astrologers to declare a three-day holiday," I said, biting into a crumbly scone.

"Good for you. I wish Kalakshetra's astrologers had read the same conjunction in the stars. Anyway, what's going on with the newly married?"

"KV is out till next week. I miss his class and look forward to his return."

"And… no more fantasies I hope?" she said, with a hint of a smile.

"None. Cross my heart!" I laughed. "But he's still the best vocal teacher they have, and I'll need all the help I can get to pass the year-end exams."

"What about Lakshmi? Do you think she'll be back in school?"

"I wonder. Maybe she'll have to settle into her new role of wife and mother. Kind of a shame really. She is a promising artist."

We chit-chatted for a while longer, but it was obvious the wet clothes drying on Lycette's body were making her itch. I knew she was dying to get into the shower, so we got up and I saw her to her bicycle outside.

On the way back in, I tried to raise Rishu from his nap with a playful jab of my big toe on his soft belly, but he refused to acknowledge me.

I curled up into a comfortable cane chair and did my best to clear my head of all my fanciful scenarios. Surely life was simpler than I imagined. As I lay there, almost asleep, I reviewed the list of blessings Lycette had enumerated and felt silly. She was of course right. I had so much to be grateful for. In Madras she had none of the things I had, no house, no servants, no husband, not even a boyfriend. All she had was her dancing. She didn't even seem to have time for girlfriends, except for Sharada and me, which gave me an idea. Stefan had told me that the main theater in Madras was playing Ben Hur, an American film with a great cast and an amazing chariot race. Maybe I could talk him into inviting Lycette and Sharada to go to the movies with us.

CHAPTER THIRTY-EIGHT

SEPT 1961 - THE GARDEN

Expats always said that September in Madras was the best time of the year, and they might be right because this morning felt a little like April in Paris, mild and temperate with flowers blooming on every bush and tree in sight. I gathered my notebooks and covered my veena with a handwoven Kashmiri shawl Stefan had bought for me. I had picked up that habit from Rao, not because of the dust, or the cat's curiosity, but out of respect for the instrument and the music attached to it. I quite liked that routine. It meant that Rao's lesson, or the practicing he had suggested, was over, and I was free to plunge into some exciting novel, with the help of my English-French dictionary.

I sat down in my favorite cane armchair in the shaded verandah with an English novel and my French-English dictionary, which I was using less and less as my English skills got better. There was a knock on the screen door.

"Ola! Anybody home?"

It was Lycette, showing up unannounced. Excited to see her, I jumped up and let her in. I noticed a new lilt in her voice and brought my hand to my mouth to hide my grin. "Hey! You're back and your accent is back too. I bet you were talking to your folks in Argentina."

She shrugged. "I pick up my old accent when I speak Spanish with them, but don't worry, it will be gone in an hour."

"I shouldn't make fun of you," I said, contrite. "I'm a mess of accents."

"You certainly are, *querida*. Who else in Madras spikes the queen's language with French and pidgin?" She bobbed her head like a silly celluloid doll. Lycette could always make me laugh, and today was no exception. When I could breathe again, I enquired: "How are your Mom and Dad?"

We spent the next hour catching up. She was brimming with news about her friends and family, especially about her younger brother who had been hurt in a roundup of the cattle they maintained on the ranch where they still lived. Fortunately, he was healing well.

We both were enjoying the end of a semester break and, knowing that Stefan was at the University and that she and I wouldn't have much free time once our respective schools reopened, we decided to ride into town on our own, and go to Moti Moti, the new Tandoori restaurant she had told me about a while back. In theory, our vegetarian diet should have been ideal for anyone living in a tropical climate, but we both had noticed we had more energy after a protein-rich meal. On the way, we stopped at Higginbotham's, on Mount Road, so I could buy a few more novels. With Stefan engrossed in his studies at night, reading had become my main entertainment.

By the time we reached Moti Moti, we were famished. Remembering Lycette, the owner, a bearded, turbaned Sikh dressed all in white in a starched linen suit, rushed to greet us. He offered us a table in the middle of the floor, but Lycette pointed to the back wall where a few tables were discretely separated from the main room by a tall wooden screen artfully perforated with geometrical designs. I wondered if, in the old days, such a screen would have allowed the women of a harem to spy into the audience rooms they were not allowed into. In this restaurant, its presence suggested that, maybe, we were not the only ones looking for privacy.

"That's perfect," whispered Lycette behind his back as he led the way. "I'd hate for a sworn vegetarian acquaintance, or worse, one of our teachers, to report we've been seen in this carnivorous palace."

Pleasing film music filled the room, as did the tantalizing aroma of tandoori spices and fresh bread. I inhaled deeply. "I can't get enough of that smell. It's half the pleasure of eating out. Thanks for bringing me here."

"Do you suppose hiding behind that screen is part of the thrill as well?" said Lycette, poking a finger through the screen. We laughed at that idea, but I think it was.

Shortly after we'd placed our order, a turbaned waiter came to our table carrying a large stainless platter filled with the distinctive bright pink breasts and thighs of their Tandoori chicken, the house specialty. Another waiter placed small dishes of spiced yogurt, mango chutney and rice pulao on the table. He returned minutes later with two plain lhassis and iced water.

Through the screen, and across the room, I could see the busy kitchen and the clay tandoor oven where meat and dough were roasted. I saw a turbaned cook push a long metal scoop into the round mouth of his oven and withdraw several steaming naans. He stabbed them with a knife to let the steam out and waved for the waiter to bring one to our table. How long had Punjabi people cooked that way? A thousand years, two thousand? Three? Everything in India was so old.

"Are you in a rush to go back?" I said, between bites of the spiced and marinated pink flesh.

"Not particularly. Why?" Lycette broke off a piece of the steaming naan and dipped it into a small cup of raita, a refreshing yogurt dish that smelled of cumin, coriander and mint.

I pushed my plate aside for a moment. "I keep thinking about the story Anup told me."

"About Prakash's daughter? Laila?" asked Lycette.

"Yes. According to rumors, her family has been hiding her for the past fifteen or sixteen years."

"I guess they meant to protect her from public opinion and the ire of zealous pundits who might want to question her virtue and make an example of her."

I closed my eyes to recall that conversation and wished I had paid closer attention at the time. "Anup also said that a hundred years ago, or even less, public opinion would have demanded that she be put to death for dishonoring her family and her community. Can you believe it?" Just thinking about it, I felt tears rise to my eyes.

"And it wasn't even her fault," said Lycette, nodding her agreement.

"I hate public opinion and the hypocrisy behind it. When I was a kid, my mother and I were ostracized because my stepfather was a drunk. It wasn't our fault either, but people who had been our friends avoided us. They wanted nothing to do with my mom because of him, and nobody would help us when we finally got up the courage to run away. Nobody except one woman. And she did it in spite of her husband's disapproval. But what she did, the connection she made for us, gave us a way out." Overcome by the emotion these memories triggered, I let my head fall to my chest. It was always painful to reminisce about that part of my life. "I don't know what they told Laila to keep her sequestered for so long, but, if I get a chance, I would like to let her know that she's not responsible for what those drunk soldiers did to her."

Lycette shook my plate in front of me. "Eat. Your food is getting cold."

I pushed the tender chicken around with my fork. "I can't help thinking that maybe we could do something for her. Befriend her. Talk to her. Maybe she would listen to us because we're not Indian and don't represent public opinion."

"So, how do you propose we do that?"

"I'd like to reconnoiter Prakash's house. If we're lucky, maybe we'll get a look at Laila. That would be a start. I brought the address Anup found for me." I took a bite of food and followed it with a sip of water.

Lycette stared at me. "I understand you care about Laila, but are you sure you want to do that now? What if we're found out? What excuse will you give Prakash? Are you willing to risk his kicking you out of his class?"

"I could always say we were exploring the neighborhood and taking pictures."

Eyebrows raised, she looked at me uncertainly.

"Look," I said, "all we know about Laila is speculation, and an address. We aren't even sure that she's there, or that she's alive! We have to start somewhere. Are you in?"

"I'm in, of course. I feel the same way you do about that poor girl. It's just that I wasn't expecting to go there today. Makes me nervous."

I was glad Lycette was committing to help me. Sharada had already promised to find out all she could from some of the older teachers at the dance school. Breaking a piece of naan, Lycette asked, "How do you feel about resuming veena classes with Prakash? It's unfair that he was assigned as your instructor at the CCKM."

"I'm nervous, but I have to push on. Hopefully, it won't be a repeat of the last semester."

"Yeah. So rude of him to conduct the classes in Tamil, and so rude to never invite you to play. What was he trying to achieve?" Lycette nodded with conviction.

I tensed at the memory. I'd never felt so invisible.

Lycette tore a piece of chicken off the bone. "Regarding your status as a student, I think you should fight back. Obviously, Prakash couldn't control what happened to his daughter years ago, but by controlling his class and blocking your studies, he can fail you. It might give him a sense of revenge, but it's not right."

I could tell she was plotting an argument. She became pushy when she wanted to make a point. But I needed a clear head to address the disastrous circumstances that had put me in the class of a man who hated foreigners.

Leaning forward over the table, she continued. "To him you're not a student. You're an entitled white girl with a foreign grant." She snorted. "I bet he doesn't even differentiate between the various foreign countries. In his eyes, they are all guilty of imperialism in India. The British are the biggest offenders, of course, but so are the French who settled in Pondicherry, and the Portuguese who practically own Goa."

"So, what do you suggest?"

"You have to change his perception of you. Maybe you should try to blend in a little better in the class. Be less French, you know, more like an Indian girl."

I shrugged. "How can I do that?"

Lycette laid her hand on my arm. "I know that you wear saris, bangles on your wrists, flowers in your hair. I'm not talking about your looks. I'm talking about attitude. In his eyes, you are the student and he is the guru. In this country, gurus are gods. They are the ultimate authority on a subject, and traditionally, students are at his or her mercy. You should try to treat him as such. If you are angry with him, and I know you are, it probably shows in your body language, your eyes, your silent waiting for a chance to participate in his class."

"I can try," I said. I knew, of course, about the status of gurus in India, but how did it apply to me? I was French and this was the twentieth century. We ate silently for a while.

"Do you believe in dreams?" I asked.

"Uh! Yes, and no."

Even though there was no one within earshot, I lowered my voice. Well, I had this strange dream in which I was invited to his house."

"Don't hold your breath," said Lycette, crunching her nose in a sneer.

"Look, could we at least check his residence? I'm dying to find out if Laila really lives there. If we're lucky we may even get a glimpse of her."

"And if we're discovered?"

"If we're discovered, well, we'll have to scramble for a good lie. Let's just do it."

"I still don't understand why you are willing to gamble your music degree, to find a girl you don't even know."

"I just want to repair a wrong, if I can. I know from experience that sometimes you need someone to care enough to pull you from the well life has dropped you in. I feel that it's my turn to help."

We paid the bill, and left. The restaurant A/C had kept the temperature in the 60's but it was 90 degrees outside, and the rings that had been loose on my fingers a minute ago now felt tight. Fortunately, the parking wallah I had tipped had kept my scooter in the shade and we were able to mount it without burning our legs.

It took us a while to find Prakash's house, because it was partially hidden behind a cluster of pink and orange bougainvillea that spread its thorny branches along a four-foot-high wall interrupted by a solid wooden gate. I leaned my scooter against the wall and gave the gate a careful push. It was locked. An old but impressive two-story house stood way back from the street. An empty verandah and a balcony ran the length of it, and its closed shutters gave it a sense of aloofness. It must have been a fine house in its day, but the paint was peeling off and some of the plaster appeared dilapidated.

307

Craning my neck over the top of the wall, I was surprised to discover a vegetable garden. I couldn't recall ever seeing one like this in Madras. It was orderly with leafy rows of green vegetables, and a trellis supporting small tomatoes and sweet peas. There were patches of flowers I recognized: red begonias, star jasmine I could smell from where I stood, clusters of white hydrangea and pink gerbera. Several suspended baskets of orchids hung in the shade of a makeshift awning made out of a white sari tied to four wooden poles, and an orange water hose stood neatly coiled to the side. Who, in that house tended the garden?

It was two-thirty in the afternoon, and the occupants were probably taking a nap. I looked questioningly at Lycette but neither she nor I was prepared to intrude.

In spite of its flat roof, the big house reminded me of an old *mas,* the kind of farm houses I had seen in the south of France, with their sustainable gardens and fruit trees. What surprised me here was the lush flower garden and leafy greens growing side by side. It said a lot about someone in this family.

"Interesting," said Lycette in a low voice. "You can be pretty sure that this garden is maintained by women. Prakash would never view gardening as a proper occupation."

"My thoughts, exactly. And his wife is probably too old for that kind of labor."

"Didn't Anup say Laila had a brother? Assuming he is married, his wife lives here too, you know, joint-family style."

"Maybe they have a gardener," I offered.

Lycette shook her head, "It's more elegant than the work of the gardeners I've seen around. And the T.S. and Kalakshetra employ the best."

"Do you think it could be Laila?"

We weren't getting anywhere. Except for butterflies and bees, the garden was deserted and the house looked asleep. It was time to leave. "Let's go. Now that I know where they live, I'll return to investigate. I need to find out about what's happened to Laila."

The next day I gathered my courage and returned alone to the house. I was scared of running into Prakash, whom I visualized brandishing a lightning rod like some kind of Indian Zeus. But as frightened as I was, an invisible riptide was propelling me forward, forcing me to go. I had to uncover what Laila, the girl Sharada only remembered as a brilliant older classmate, had become after thirteen years. I was only twenty-one and couldn't imagine what thirteen years of seclusion would have done to me. Thirteen years would have been an eternity when I was young.

Rather than wearing jeans, which might have attracted attention to me, I dressed in a sari, applied a red bindi to my forehead, selecting a shade of powder that matched the red found in the border of my sari, a small fashion detail Indian women paid attention to. And then I slipped a short garland of flowers under the top of my braided hair darkened with coconut oil. From a distance, no one wouldn't have guessed I wasn't Indian. I took my camera along. Maybe I would be lucky today and get a shot of Laila to show Sharada. In any case, a camera was useful as a prop because, if worse came to worst, I could always pretend to be taking photos of Prakash's old-fashioned neighborhood.

It was mid-morning, and to avoid taking too many dusty roads teeming with buses, rickshaws and bullock-carts, I took Marina Road that ran along the ocean past Madras University. The century-old institution, with its red brick walls and Mogul turrets, was a strange blend of architecture and was touted as one of the oldest universities in South India. After a refreshing spin along the coast, I rode back into the city and found Prakash's house without any problems.

I leaned my scooter on the far end of the wall and approached the spot Lycette and I had checked the day before. My heart thudded in my ears as I rose on my toes to catch a better view of the garden. At the border of the vegetable patch, a peacock was pecking at some grains, its tail trailing lazily behind it like a folded royal cape. Twenty feet away, a young woman was watering a row of leafy greens, and for a split second, she looked up and her eyes met mine. Was this Prakash's daughter? If it was, Sharada would be able to identify her. She was looking in my direction, water trickling idly from the forgotten hose. I smiled, racking my brain for a way to engage her in conversation so I could take her picture.

"Your peacock is gorgeous! May I take a photo of him?" I asked. For an instant, I wondered if she spoke English, but when she nodded "yes," I understood she did.

My blood was thumping in my ears, as I slowly raised my long lens camera above the wall and focused on the peacock, well away from her. I was holding my breath, praying she wouldn't get frightened and leave. From the corner of my eye I saw that she was following my movements. After taking a few shots of the decorative bird, I lowered my camera and turned toward her. She was tall for an Indian girl. Her oval face and arms looked tanned, but a glimpse of her stomach exposed under her plain green sari revealed she was fair-skinned. She wore no jewelry, no bindi, no necklace, but her large dark eyes, outlined with Kohl, spoke of intelligence and curiosity.

Letting my camera hang from its strap, I brought the palms of my hands together in salute, "Namaste," I said. "My name is Minouche." In the friendliest voice I could muster which was hard because my throat was so dry, I added, "I'm a dance student at Kalakshetra."

She nodded in acknowledgement, which encouraged me to think that, if she was Laila, she had retained the English she'd learned in school all those years ago.

"At Kalakshetra, Sharada is my friend," I said slowly, to make sure she understood.

"You," she said, pointing at me, "are a dancer?" She made a graceful dance gesture with her hand.

"Not yet. But I'm learning." I imitated her gesture and smiled at her. She smiled back.

"May I take a photo of you with your peacock?" To clarify my request, I motioned for her to get closer to the bird. For a few seconds she remained rooted where she was but, as if absorbing what I was asking of her, she moved closer to the peacock. It was a perfect pose. As I adjusted the focus on her, I saw a pale scar crossing her burnished skin at the base of her throat, right where her collarbone sank under the short blouse she wore under her sari. Anup had mentioned she had been raped at knife point and left bleeding in a mango grove. The scar had to be the result of the knife wound inflicted by one of the attackers.

Excitement knocked the breath out of me. There was no longer any doubt about who she was. For a moment I forgot all about Prakash and what would happen if I were caught snooping around his house. I was looking at Laila. I took a photo, and another, and another, afraid she would leave, but she didn't move until the water pooling at her feet touched her bare toes. She jumped back and stepped aside to turn the water off. I thought she would retreat into the house, and it would be the last I would see of her. But she stood up and turned to see if I was still there.

After listening to the rumors Anup had shared with me, I had expected her to be frightened, or possibly incommunicative, but she kept surprising me. Like now, when she bent down and turned the water back on to resume her task. She glanced in my direction from time to time, with an open expression on her face. Not smiling. Not fearful either. Curious maybe?

"Your flowers are beautiful," I said, my arm sweeping over the colorful expanse of her garden. The smile she gave me lit her face and reached her eyes.

311

For being close to thirty–what was she, twenty-six or seven?–she still looked young in spite of an unexpected strand of white parting her thick black hair, which was pulled into a braided chignon. Her graceful body, still lean, reminded me she had once been a dancer.

I had been afraid to come here today because I was scared of Prakash, but after looking into her eyes, I realized I no longer cared what Prakash could do to me. I wanted to let her know I was here for her, to listen to her, and let her know that times had changed, and that she had more options than she knew or imagined, to expand her life.

But the house was waking up. Someone opened the tall shutters shading the rooms from the hot sun, and people could be heard talking. There was a chance they would see me.

I pointed at the house behind her and waved goodbye. "I better go, but I will be back." Elbows locked to her sides, she shyly waved back. Her movement seemed strange to me until I realized she'd probably waved that way to block the motion of her body in case someone happened to see her. After what had happened to her, it was obvious that her family would object to her talking to a stranger.

I mounted my scooter and reluctantly drove away. I would have liked to stay longer. But I feared being caught snooping. I sensed that our first meeting had been successful in initiating a bond. How thrilling to discover that Laila appeared normal and even spoke English. She was lovely, and engaged, caring for flowers, peacocks and green things. Though she'd undoubtedly been traumatized by the rape, she didn't, outwardly at least, act as a victim. Once again, I wondered at what had pulled me into the wake of this young woman's tragedy? A woman hidden by her family. A woman in a green sari. In the back of my mind I heard the voice of the old soothsayer Sharada, Lycette and I had visited a while back. She had warned me *to beware*, or was it *to be aware of,* the color green. What had she meant? Had she tried to warn me to stay clear of Laila, or had she seen, behind her blindness, that maybe Laila was the one I had come to India to meet? As if destiny had a long reach and had found me in Paris to free her?

On the way back from my morning expedition I stopped at a photography shop and dropped off my film to be processed. I couldn't wait to tell Lycette I had finally made contact with Laila, so I drove straight to her place on the Kalakshetra campus. On arriving, I pulled my scooter up onto its stand, and cried out, "I saw Laila!"

Lycette, who had been reading a printed letter inside her modest but cozy student hut jumped to her feet to greet me. "You did?"

"Not only did I see her but, I took some pictures of her. I'll get them back tomorrow."

Her eyes shone with excitement. "I can't wait to see them. How was she?"

"Shy, but friendly, and still pretty," I informed her, as I walked in and sat on the futon she had rolled against the low, indoor brick wall of the hut. "More importantly, she appears to be as sane as you and me." I went on to describe my encounter and share my impression of her.

"That's fantastic. So, what do we do next?"

"I don't know. I can hardly believe we found her."

"No, *you* found her."

"You get half the credit for helping me locate her house," I said. "As soon as I get the photos back, I want to show them to Sharada. We could also talk to Anup and see if he has any suggestions on how to proceed."

"Good idea," said Lycette.

She plopped down in front of her traveling trunk on which sat an expensive Remington typewriter, a Rolls Royce compared to my portable Olivetti. Noting my envious expression, she explained. "I had my typewriter sent from New Delhi. I can live without a car and a big house, but I needed my old Remi." Petting it like she would a cat or a dog, she looked at it fondly. "I have terrible handwriting, and so much paperwork is involved in my divorce."

"I'm so sorry you have to deal with that. Any idea when it will be finalized?"

She shrugged. "Things move so slowly in India. Who knows?"

I noticed the time on the small travel clock sitting by the typewriter. "Oops… Got to run, Rao is coming over for my veena lesson."

"How is that going?"

"Going great. Rao is patient and speaks excellent English. Compared to Prakash, it's like night and day. And he is young. Do you know that he studied with Prakash before the Music College was even established? So, he knows his style and has helped me a lot to fill in the blanks in the course. I also get to hear old stories about the other teachers, including KV. Some are good, some are just gossip, but always interesting."

I mounted my scooter. "I'll stop by tomorrow to bring the photos. And let me know if you need carbon copy paper for your legal correspondence. I got lots of it."

The next day, after getting the photos back, I met Lycette and Sharada at Kalakshetra. Looking at Laila's pictures, Sharada got emotional.

"She was my friend, but I had forgotten how she looked. It has been so long. But it definitely is her. She was always very beautiful. I wonder how she kept herself in shape. You know how our Indian lifestyle does not include much exercise, unless you are a dancer." She laughed. "As we get older, if we're not careful, rice sticks to our waist."

"Do you think she still practices dancing on her own?" asked Lycette, always the dancer.

"It is unlikely," said Sharada, "but who knows?"

"Maybe gardening is her exercise. When you see her flower beds and vegetable patch, you'll see what I mean," I said, pointing at some of the color photos illustrating my words.

As I gathered the photos to put them away, I reflected, "I heard

Anup is at an out-of-town conference. Since he's the one who made me aware of Laila's predicament in the first place, let's plan on sharing with him what I found out when he gets back."

CHAPTER THIRTY-NINE

NOV 1961 - BACK TO SCHOOL

As much as I wanted to return to Prakash's house to try and see Laila again, I found myself unable to go. I was cramming for the coming term exams at Kalakshetra, and at the music college. I was, of course, committed to help Laila, but I also had to focus on getting a degree. So I allowed myself to listen to the small voice in my head that told me that Laila wasn't about to go away.

Tucked inside my mosquito net after dusk, to avoid being eaten alive by the remorseless insects, I stayed up late, reading music history, humming the tunes I had learned to sing, and those I played on the veena. I memorized the Sanskrit verses that accompanied the hand language I had been so keen to study with Sharada, and practiced *sholukatus*, those rhythmical strings of mnemonics improvised ragas and songs were built on.

On November 15, as the Music College was scheduled to re-open, I woke up refreshed and ready to take on the world. Miraculously, and in spite of my overloaded curriculum in having to satisfy teachers in both schools, I'd managed to pass the required tests, and today I was looking forward to mixing with my fellow music students who had been helpful to me in spite of, or maybe because of, Prakash's disdainful attitude toward me. I owed it to them to have stayed abreast of the daily class assignments.

Taking to heart Lycette's advice, I took particular care to wear a tasteful sari and subtle jewelry. I applied kohl under my eyes, a red bindi in the middle of my forehead and combed my hair into a single braid decorated with a few jasmine blooms, as all the girls in the class did. I reminded myself to act modestly and I'd work harder to hide my frustration at being ignored. Prakash was feared as only Indian teachers touted as gurus can be, but I would embrace the guru system rather than fight it.

As my learned neighbor and friend Anup had explained to me during one of our long afternoon discussions, while we listened to his extensive collection of rare Indian records, music had been passed on orally, one-on-one, for centuries. Maybe that's why the distinguished musicians teaching at the College weren't keen on degrees and curriculums. In their eyes, a degree was just a piece of paper. It had little to do with the life-long vocation and devotion expected of a student. But under the solidifying regime of a newly independent India, they were required to modernize their teaching methods and structure the school programs to get government money, which was now their main source of income. Gone were the British who had sought to weaken the Indian spirit by repudiating its ancient arts, but gone also were the maharajas whose courts had patronized musicians and dancers and rewarded the best among them with their own weight in gold and precious gems. Under their rule, a musician of Prakash's status would never have wanted for anything. Students would have come to him begging to be taught. He would have had his pick of the best amongst them, and allowed them to live under his roof as little more than servants in

317

exchange for the privilege of breathing the same air, and listening to his exalted music.

I could see how India's Independence had changed all that. Apparently, some of the younger teachers were receptive to the opportunities offered by schools and colleges, but the older generation scoffed at them. The idea of being forced to teach someone, especially a foreigner, might be as repugnant to an old-school Brahmin as eating meat. No wonder Prakash paid no heed to the college's regulations. In his mind, he was probably doing the college a favor by showing up for classes.

I had been slow to realize that, just because I'd paid a nominal entrance fee to the music college and the musicians on staff got paid to teach, they didn't owe me the key to their rich artistic heritage. Especially Prakash, aka Narasimha, who was by far the fiercest of them all.

That nickname fitted him so perfectly. How could I fail to be intimidated when he looked in my direction, shoved his instrument to the side, racked his throat to gather the shredded leaves and red juice from his betel nut chew, and spit them noisily into a spittoon sitting within an arm's reach? And how could I fail to be angry when he gathered his shawl, instructed the class in Tamil, and left the room without a single glance in my direction, a routine he had sustained for a whole academic year? I had been confused and bitter about such an instructor, but the students hadn't been surprised. His reputation preceded him.

Armed with new insight, I resolved to show him I was capable of the devotion and humility he expected of a disciple; not for his person, for I wasn't looking for a personal guru to rule my life, but I would practice harder than ever and surprise him into acknowledging my dedication. First, I needed to establish some kind of connection with him if I were to graduate his course.

I decided to bring him a present, a delicate six-inch tall sandalwood

318

sculpture of the Goddess Saraswati playing the veena. I had bought it for myself, and part of me hated to part with it, but I knew that giving a present which meant so much to me was the only kind of present to give.

I had wrapped the image in a white silk scarf and waited until Prakash was seated on his mat to step around my veena and lean forward to present my gift to him, right hand extended, left hand supporting my right arm, in as humble a way as I knew how. I had rehearsed the move with Sharada a few times, for it was important that my fingers never come into contact with his skin.

Eyebrows raised, Prakash looked up at me in surprise, and slowly unwrapped the statuette, which he placed in front of him. Time stopped. I didn't know whether to speak or keep silent. I couldn't have spoken anyway, for the speech I had prepared had evaporated. My mind was blank, and I shrank under his thoughtful stare.

He appeared in no hurry to speak.

"So, you are back?" he finally said in English.

I lifted my eyes to his face. I don't know who was the most surprised, him to receive a present from me, or I to hear him speak to me in English.

"Yes, I am back." My mind was grasping at straws. "I never left."

He shrugged, and added in a sarcastic tone of voice, "Well, one never knows with you, westerners. You come for a few days, a few weeks, learn a few things and go back home thinking you know everything about India."

"With respect, Sir, I'm not like that. I've already been here for a year, studying hard, and I plan to work harder to complete the course, but I need your assistance to do that."

"I see." He watched my face intently. Around us, my fellow students were holding their breath. Eyes open wide, brows knitted, mouths ajar, they looked thrilled but worried about retribution. It was obvious that they had never heard of a student challenging this teacher.

"Need my help, hey?" He looked at me speculatively. "Well, we shall see. So, you say you are not like those Americans who live large and try to buy their way into our sacred customs with their Fulbright or Ford dollars?"

"I'm not like them, and I'm not American. I'm French. I don't have a lot of money, and I'm not looking for short cuts. I plan to stay here, in Madras, for another two years to complete my studies."

He turned to the rest of the class. "What are you waiting for? Tune up!"

Obediently, the students started to pluck at their instruments, and a cacophonous splash of notes erupted in the warm air stirred by the two large ceiling fans cooling the room.

From his sitting position on the floor, Prakash turned back to me and bent slightly at the waist.

"*Rumba vanakam* — you know what that means, right? It means "thank you". So, thank you for your gift." He paused. "How is your Tamil?"

"It would be better if people in Madras didn't speak English so fluently," I said, holding back a smile that was trying to escape my lips.

"Well then, you had better get on with it." He turned away from me and called out a scale and a tempo to the class. Bent over our veenas, we all started to play in earnest.

For a moment I couldn't figure out where to find the notes on my strings. I felt jubilant, dizzy. Had I really had this conversation with Old Narasimha, the lion man? This was the breakthrough I had been praying for, ever since I had joined the music college. Mixed with the excitement about this new development, I felt a shiver of fear in the back of my mind. What of Laila? How would I be able to balance my studies with Prakash and my desire to break the shackle of public opinion that appeared to have imprisoned his daughter for almost two decades under the old regime? And how could I encourage Laila to step into the current of an India she had not yet met? I let out a ragged sigh and forced myself to focus on the present.

I caught Prakash's wandering eye watching me, and attacked the tune with renewed fervor.

I rushed home, looking forward to telling Stefan about my big breakthrough. Prakash was talking to me and finally acknowledging my presence in his class. This was big news and bode well for my future at the music college. But Stefan wasn't yet back from University, and not only was I disappointed not to find him, I was sorely annoyed to find his Hungarian friend, Charles, in my kitchen making coffee for a girl who, he told me, was his new girlfriend. He was, of course, using my French espresso set, my coffee beans and fresh cream, and I found myself hanging on to every bit of control I could muster to resist the urge to kick him out of my house. After the stringent admonitions I had directed at him a few months earlier, he deserved to be shunned, but his date didn't.

Charles had already guessed that much, and taking advantage of my unusual leniency, he sidestepped like a boxer into the living room where the girl waited silently.

"Minouche, meet Eva, short for Evelyn. Eva, Minouche and her husband are my best friends here in Madras."

Like hell I was!

She was a tiny thing. At first, I even took her for a child, but when I looked closer I realized she had to be in her twenties. I read self-assurance and intelligence in her blue-gray eyes, and something else I couldn't quite grasp. Defiance?

Fair by Indian standards, her creamy caramel skin, too dark to be white, suggested she might be Anglo-Indian.

She was clothed in a frilly dress boosted by a voluminous petticoat.

To my eyes, the petticoat was wrong and dated her outfit. It made the dress look old fashioned, almost bulky on her. Was she attempting to make herself look bigger than she was, the way a cat's fur stands up when he runs into danger?

She had good legs, but the heels of her long bonny feet stuck out of her high-heeled shoes. Her white purse hung on the back of a chair.

"Nice meeting you Eva," I said in a friendly voice. I had no interest in making her suffer. That was a treatment I reserved for Charles. "Where did you guys meet?"

"At my church," said Eva evenly. "The Saint Mary's First Anglican church holds a social every Saturday afternoon." Her English was very smooth, with a hint of a British accent.

"Really!" I purred. "How great is that!"

I turned around and glanced at Charles. He grimaced impatiently. Maybe he didn't like where the conversation was going, for I knew he had guessed what I was thinking. I had to give him credit. Knowing his chances of dating a Hindu were nil, he had actually gone to a Christian church to pick up an Anglo-Indian girl! How very crafty and devious for the atheist he professed to be.

"So, Eva, what do you do?"

"I'm a secretary for a large shipping company where my father worked before it was annexed by the Indian government," she said dryly.

"It must have been a difficult transition," I said, and meant it. "What does he do now?

"I don't know. He went back to England when I was ten," she said stiffly, a hint of blush rising on her tawny cheeks.

"And your mom?"

"She's a teacher at Bharat Monahan Girls Higher Secondary School. She made sure I graduated from the Madras Secretarial Academy. I type 105 words a minute," she added with pride, and this time, I definitely caught a glint of defiance in her eyes. Considering I hardly typed thirty words a minute on the old Remington typewriter I shared with Stefan, I was duly impressed, and told her so.

The more I studied her, the older she looked. The make-up, the dark nail polish, the short, permed hair. It all looked studied on her. Her pale brown skin, painted and powdered, lacked the elasticity and vitality of my Hindu classmates' complexion enriched by oil baths and Ayurvedic ointments. Her eyes, free of kohl, looked small and plain compared to theirs, but her multicultural background and aplomb fascinated me. This was a slice of Indian life I hadn't encountered before. I wanted to find out more about her hopes and goals. What was she doing with Charles? I couldn't help but suspect she was looking at him as a ticket to the West, for what girl would, or could, fall in love with such an obnoxious burly, pushy, burpy and farty opportunist?

Two hours later Charles and Eva were still hanging out at our house. A soon as Stefan had arrived, Charles, true to character, had worked on Stefan to worm his way into our dinner arrangements.

To my surprise I noticed that Gangan, our sweet, considerate Hindu cook was giving the Anglo-Indian girl the cold shoulder while tending table. Apparently, Eva's pride and defiance didn't count for much in Madras ultra-conservative society, if her social status was lower than my Hindu cook's.

After our two imposed guests had the good sense to retire to Charles' small bungalow next door, Stefan looked at me with a Cheshire cat smile on his face. "I think you're turning into a native. Did you listen to yourself? 'Where do you work? What does your mother do?'"

"Was I really that bad?"

"Pretty much. You sounded just like those Indians we meet at public functions, or on a train."

I shrugged. Turning into a native, couldn't be all bad, and I hoped that new trait would show in my music and dancing as well. Meanwhile, eager to get his reaction about Charles and his conquest, I asked, "So, what do you think about these two love birds?"

"He wants sex. She wants a new passport," he said, rather to the point.

For once, we were in complete agreement, and I found it amusing, until memories of my old self popped in front of my mind like a jack-in-the-box. On the night we had met, Stefan had wanted sex and I had been the girl dreaming to hitch a ride on his dream to go to India. And here we had Eva, ready to trade sex to get a visa to the West, a new start filled with caste-free opportunities she would never have in Madras. We weren't all that different, she and I.

CHAPTER FORTY

JAN 1962 - THE REQUEST

My progress in the veena class was faster now that I had Prakash's attention. He included me in the rounds of exercises the students performed in group or individually, and he stopped me to correct a wrong fingering, or play back any section I may have missed or changed. He was demanding and thorough, but appeared to follow my progress with benevolent curiosity. I was still studying privately with Rao and between the two teachers' inputs, I was feeling in control of the lessons.

When I got to school on that radiant January morning, the Music College was buzzing with excitement. Prakash's daughter-in-law had given birth to a healthy baby boy. The gods had blessed the Lion-Man with a grandson.

"Professor Prakash is already busy preparing a special ceremony for the baby," announced one of my classmates on our way to KV's vocal class. "He will want to give a concert. That means we are going to have some time off." Her cinnamon-colored face, lit by the gold studs in her nose and ears, broke into a satisfied smile.

We entered KV's classroom and sat down, cross-legged on the floor mats. I opened my notebook and was reviewing my notes when KV walked in. To my surprise and the students' obvious curiosity, he called my name and stepped back into the corridor to speak to me.

I stood up and joined him. Though I knew it couldn't be anything of a personal nature, I could feel the blood rushing to my face and was aware of the tingle of anticipation KV's presence always triggered in me. I had stopped fantasizing about him, but his physical closeness still aroused in me a chemistry that I couldn't deny or explain. A tingle in my loins; the hair on my arms rising as if to meet his touch. I took a deep breath, set a blank expression on my face. Maybe I should get ready to hear there was a problem with my progress in his class.

But it wasn't about me. "Professor Prakash likes the photos you took at my wedding," he said, as an opening.

I nodded politely. Everybody had seen the photos of his and Padma's wedding. A couple of them had even been posted in the local newspapers. So, what was the purpose of this conversation? I was doing my best to look casual, which was not easy, for my heart was thumping in my chest like a runaway train.

Unaware of my agitation, KV was explaining, punctuating words with hand language and nods, which in India can mean almost anything. His struggle with proper English was visible and kind of sweet.

"He hopes, maybe you come to his house to take photos during the ceremony for his grandson, in three weeks' time."

"I see." I kept my reserve but felt excitement spark in me. This request opened up a zillion possibilities. Could I really be a guest in the house I had been casing a while ago? I had been so busy with the new semester that I hadn't made any progress in approaching Laila. But now this?

KV interrupted my thoughts. "He see my wedding album," he said.

"He is very, how you say… impressed. You have excellent camera, and are good photographer."

His smooth cheeks were flushed with the effort he made to speak English. His forehead, olive rather than brown, was sweaty, and the three bars of yellow ashes, marking him as a Vishnu devotee, were smeared. Without speaking, I inclined my head in acknowledgement.

He continued. "He not sure you be interested, so he asked me to find out. He also heard the recording from my concert. It be very auspicious if his concert for grandson is recorded too. Something to play for the child later. Again, you have the best machine, so, maybe, you ask your husband's permission and let me know."

"I'll do that," I said. I understood now why KV had approached me, rather than Prakash. He was a former student of the old guru. It would allow Prakash to save face if I happened to refuse.

It was a tremendous opportunity to have a look inside Prakash's house and get close to Laila. But what if something went wrong? What if my camera failed, or the film? Those things did happen. A mishap of that amplitude would certainly wreck my new-found status quo with Prakash, and ruin any chances of graduating in his class.

Still, I very much wanted to do it. I just didn't want to appear too eager. As for asking my husband's permission, a perfectly understandable request in Madras, I coughed to hide the smile pulling on my lips. No need for that. I would instead enlist Stefan's help. I was pretty sure he would enjoy it, as he had the last time.

I followed KV back into the class and sat down, aware of the inquisitive glances of my classmates. As the class started, I allowed my voice to blend with theirs, but my mind kept wandering to Prakash's somber house behind the lively garden. I was going to get an invitation to the exact place where I needed to be, in order to find out more about his daughter. Hopefully, I would see Laila again, and she would recognize me. I felt connected to her, and was hopelessly curious about her situation, but why? What was our connection? Was she the object of the seer's vision about the color green? Green could, of course, relate to Laila's sari, or the lush garden she was growing, but so many other things were green. I was dying to solve that puzzle. And now I'd get a legitimate chance to meet that girl, or rather that young woman, for she wasn't a girl anymore.

Not for the first time, I was grateful for our cameras and tape recorder. These tools were opening doors for me into the sanctum of a very haughty South Indian Brahmin family. I knew that the subjects I photographed trusted me with a piece of themselves, as did the musicians Stefan would enregister, and that it was my responsibility to protect both. I happened to be at the juncture of an ancient culture that was bound to evolve now that the forbidden West was open to it. How long would it be before Indian men gave up their dhotis for blue jeans? How long before the women cut and permed their hair? To photograph and record "the here and now" and preserve it for the future had been my spontaneous desire ever since arriving in India. I was a chronicler. Interestingly, while talking to Rao, I'd found out that I wasn't the only one. Some American, Dutch, French and Indian scholars were recording and compiling songs and dancing, all over the world, and a whole department dedicated to those studies had even been created at Columbia University and a few others, in the U.S. As my French musicologist friend had explained to me, the interdisciplinary field that weaved together the study of music and anthropology within a particular cultural context was now being acknowledged by academia, and I was in a perfect spot to join these scholars.

So, I waited a couple of days to conceal my eagerness at the prospect of that assignment, and then sent word to Prakash that I would be honored to photograph and record the special ceremony and concert he was planning for his first grandson.

Having taken that decision, I started to worry. My classes with Prakash were going so well, I dreaded failing him at any level, especially with regards to those precious family pictures he expected of me. The British had betrayed his trust. The French would have to do better. But first, I needed to figure out what to expect at the child's ceremony. The go-to person for that was Sharada, whom I held as my living and breathing encyclopedia on Indian etiquette.

When, after her last class of the day, I went to her classroom with my questions, she invited me to sit on the grass mat covering the ground at the head of the hut where she usually taught. I lowered myself across from her and tucked my legs under me. I told her how Prakash had invited me to photograph his grandson's *ayushkarma* ceremony.

"What is it like?" I asked. "I surmise it won't be anything like the bris ceremony I witnessed when my Jewish friends invited me to attend the circumcision of their newborn son. I also hope it won't involve total immersion. I'm not keen on watching a baby struggle to catch his breath."

"Nothing like that," replied Sharada. "One of the ceremonies performed is similar to your baptism," she said, "but, instead of sprinkling Holy Water on the baby boy, his head is shaved. We believed that this ritual enhances the life span of the baby."

Enhancing the longevity of a baby's life sounded desirable, but shaving his head had me worried. "What if he jiggles or has a tantrum? Are they not afraid to hurt him?"

Sharada shook her head benevolently, as she would at a demanding child. "It is a common practice. They know what they are doing. They may give him a few drops of rice wine or a wee bit of hashish to make him sleepy."

I bent forward in astonishment, thinking I maybe hadn't heard correctly. "Hashish? To a newborn? Is that even legal?"

"He will not be a newborn. He will be three weeks old. Look, it is done for the baby's sake. Hinduism has a number of rites of sacramental purification, which are performed from birth till death, so maybe the law looks the other way when it is appropriate."

Surprised by her *laisser-faire*, I argued back, "Appropriate? Really?" I immediately felt silly. Who was I to condemn the customs of the country I had chosen to embrace?

"It is only for the baby's sake," she replied, blushing a little, for she was an educator, and part of her job was to teach children right from wrong.

I grinned an apologetic smile at her. "I'm sorry. I shouldn't be so judgmental." I stretched my right leg out and pivoted on my left hip to point my foot away from her, in order to release a cramp that was creeping up my calf. I had another question for her. "Even though I am not a guest per se, and have only been invited to take photos, am I expected to bring gifts to the family?"

Nodding, she thought about it for a few seconds. "I guess it would look good. If you behave like a guest, you will be perceived as a guest."

"What should I look for?"

"Maybe a sari for the new mother?" said Sharada, tentatively. But on seeing me crunch up my nose at that idea, she explained. "Well, obviously you are a student; you would not be expected to buy a silk or expensively embroidered sari. You might consider choosing a simple but lovely cotton sari. I can direct you to some reasonably priced stores if you need me to."

"I'm sure I could use your help with that," I said. "And what about Old Narasimha, sorry, Professor Prakash?" I added with a repentant grin.

"For him, you can never go wrong with a white scarf," Sharada said. "It is formal and ceremonial. And if you can afford it, you may want to look for one with a thin gold border."

Knowing it was probably a stupid question, I bit my lip and asked,

"What about Laila? Would it be proper for me to give her something?"

Sharada looked down and was silent for a beat. "You should not. She is only the baby's aunt, and remember, you are not even supposed to know her. But if you see her there, and if she is receptive, you might try to develop more of a rapport with her. That could be the greatest gift of all for her. An outside friend."

"You knew her before the incident, didn't you?"

Sharada nodded sadly. "Yes. I remember her well, though she was a couple of years ahead of me when I started."

"And when was that? When you were six?"

Sharada beamed proudly. "Five. It is the best time to start a child's training. At that age, children are like rubber. With the right technique, their bodies acquire stamina and form." She gave me a crooked smile, acknowledging the aches and pain I still endured for taking up Bharata Natyam as an adult. "How are you faring with the private dance instructor I recommended?"

I grimaced. "Okay, I guess. He sticks to simple dance pieces."

She bent forward and patted my knee. "You should not blame yourself. You are brave and doing the best you can, considering your age."

Eager to redirect the conversation away from my failed attempt at becoming an accomplished dancer, I asked, "How was she? I mean Laila."

"She was beautiful and talented, but then, many girls have those gifts. What she had, which is rare, was charisma. Our dance director was training her to be a solo artist and the star in our production of *The Ramayana* when she was raped. She would have been famous all over India." Sharada leaned back against the solid base of the hut's wall with a somber look on her face.

"A poster child for Bharata Natyam?"

"Yes. You have to think of it in context," said Sharada. "At that time, the British were on their way out and there was a resurgence of all the Indian arts that had been suppressed for three hundred years. Laila was a symbol of the new India. Her father was immensely proud of her." Sharada suddenly looked tired and seemed lost in her own thoughts. I got the hint. I thanked her for sharing her insights with me and made arrangements to go to the bazaar with her the next weekend to look at saris and scarves.

CHAPTER FORTY-ONE

THE BABY

On the day of the ceremony, Stefan and I arrived just after sunrise at Prakash's house. The festivities would go on all day, but the ritual preparations, the prayers, the building of the ceremonial fire, were all scheduled early on, and I planned to document the preparations. Stefan and I had discussed the way we would handle this assignment, and, like before, decided that he would man the tape recorder while I took photos. He positioned himself out of the way, but close enough to record the priests' anticipated Sanskrit chants. We had brought three long-play Scotch magnetic tapes and five rolls of film, and I hoped we wouldn't run out. Tapes and films were expensive in Madras, but it was an investment worth making, since Prakash, like KV, had agreed that I would keep a copy of the recordings and photos for my own use. I unpacked the cameras and looked around.

An old maidservant sweeping the yard directed me to the main part of the house. The large room I entered was buzzing with the excitement and chatter of women. The familiar scent of coconut oil added to the fragrance of the braided lengths of frangipani flowers they wore in their hair, welcomed me. Two bare windows facing an inside courtyard were pulled half-closed for privacy. Their metal shutters, painted a hideous khaki color, made me wonder, not for the first time if, or why, shutters all over Madras had been coated with cheap, left-over, army paint.

Two interior doors, one on each end of the far wall, opened to the rest of the house. I was not really surprised to see that the large room was devoid of furniture. No armchair and no TV, which most Indian households I had visited were usually proud of. It confirmed what Anup had told me about Prakash's old-world values, and his disdain for Western appliances. No tables and chairs either, which made sense since they didn't use them, and a floor devoid of clutter was also easier to keep clean, and the best defense against rodents, snakes and scorpions.

A lonely trunk stood against the wall between the two windows. But what caught my attention was an ornate veena poised on a solid wooden rack in the far corner of the room. The veena's burnished body and dark dragon head looked old, and reminded me of instruments I had only seen in music history books. I wondered if it had belonged to Prakash's father, whose fame as a court musician was rumored at the CCKM. Did Prakash play it in concerts? Two more veenas were sitting on the ground and the white-washed wall above them was bare except for a large calendar poster of the goddess Saraswati, which suggested this might be the room Prakash used to practice, play or teach. I noticed that the women in the room kept a respectful distance from it.

In the middle of the room, shielded by half-a-dozen chattering women sitting around him, I discovered the baby boy resting on a thickly folded sari atop a flat cushion. Under it, a thin grass mat with a red and green pattern covered the floor, and the handful of color-faded cushions thrown around didn't have many takers as most women were comfortable sitting on the mat. To the side, a large vessel filled with water suggested that the baby had been recently bathed and dried, and now, sitting cross-legged in front of him, an older woman whom I took to be Prakash's wife, was gently rubbing some sweet-scented oil on his plump naked body. I kneeled next to her and introduced myself. I had picked up just enough Tamil to do that without embarrassing myself. I pointed at my camera and the woman nodded approvingly. The sari on which the baby was lying was a light shade of blue that offset his warm caramel-colored skin. He had a full head of dark hair, and a single ray of sun slanting through the half-pulled shutters put reddish highlights in the damp curls that stuck to his forehead in small nervous loops. I decided to take portraits of him right away in case the shaving ceremony happened next. He was a gorgeous baby, with dimples on his cheeks, tiny hands and plump feet. His hazel-gray eyes, heavily lined with kohl, were wide open as he followed the movements of my camera. A gold chain rested against the folds of his fat baby neck, and my heart melted at the sight of him. He was simply divine.

Tired of kneeling, I stood up. "He reminds me of Baby Krishna. What's his name?" I asked the women, squatting around me.

"His name is Raju," answered a young woman in English. "He is my son."

Her accentless English was remarkable. I turned to her and was surprised to see how young she was, even though I shouldn't have been, for I knew that, traditionally, parents arranged marriages in the early teens of a girl's life. She looked to be maybe sixteen and had a slim figure under the graceful folds of her red silk sari. When she smiled, her teeth flashed white against her dark complexion. She smiled proudly at me and explained, "The name 'Krishna' is not given to a first born. It is reserved for the eighth child, because Krishna had seven older siblings."

"Do you plan to have that many children?" I asked, watching how her long eyelashes shaded the black iris of her doe-shaped eyes.

She frowned, and I wondered if my intrusive question had offended her, but then she smiled. "Maybe two more," she said, "but never eight. We have family planning now."

I turned back to the baby and held back my desire to pinch his little cheeks. Indian babies were so pretty. A hundred times more beautiful than any French baby I'd ever seen. In the village, they were every shade of brown, like freshly baked bread, and their dark eyes, outlined in kohl, gave them an incomparable presence. I had questioned Sharada on the use of kohl on babies. She'd explained to me that it wasn't a cosmetic attribute. Rather, parents smeared the kohl around their babies' eyes and drew large black bindis on their forehead in an attempt to make them ugly, to protect them from the jealousy of the gods.

As I focused my lenses on little Raju, I was glad Stefan and I had no children. Preoccupied as we were with studies, and our desire to travel, neither he nor I were ready to be parents. There had been a time when, out of curiosity, I had engaged him in a conversation about future plans to start a family. What he had said at the time had made me think that he probably didn't want children. "Why would anyone in his right mind want to bring a child into this messed-up world?" I had argued that the world we now lived in wasn't as bad as the world he had experienced in his childhood of exodus and wars. His response to that had been even more memorable. "Well, I'm your husband. If you want a child, help yourself." To this day, I hadn't quite figured what he meant. Was he implying that if I got pregnant it would be up to me to raise the child on my own? It made me wonder at how, following his rushed decision to get married before settling in Madras, we had both overlooked discussing the most basic questions about marriage and parenting. Someday we would have to figure all that out together, but with our academic workloads pending, now wasn't the time.

I was getting good shots, photographing the scene from different angles, and that's when I first noticed Laila standing in a corner, her back to a closed interior door. She was part of the female gathering in this room, yet she stood alone. Unaware of being watched, she was tousling the fringed end of an emerald green sari. Was it really her? It had to be. I recognized the svelte tall figure I had seen among the flowers, and the distinctive white strand accenting her long, plaited hair. Except for a nose ring and a wrist-full of glass bangles, I could see no jewelry on her. The vivid green of her sari would have made anyone look pale or grey, but her face and arms were warmed by a bronzy glow, probably the result of long hours spent gardening. The words of the witch flashed briefly through my mind but I dismissed them. I had no time to guess at prophecies. This was a real-life encounter.

She looked longingly at the gorgeous baby being fussed over by the women in her family, and I wondered why she wasn't joining them. Was she shy, or was she mourning the fact that she would never be a mother blessed with the approval and pride of her family? My heart bumped faster in my chest as I directed the lens in her direction, zoomed on her and shot a few frames. Staring at her in the viewfinder, I suddenly saw she was looking straight at me. I lowered the camera and smiled. She smiled back, her sadness forgotten for a few seconds. I put the camera down deliberately and walked in her direction, but she abruptly turned her back on me and busied herself with rearranging the wick of a large oil lamp that stood in the corner of the room. I looked behind me and saw her mother glancing in our direction with concern. I smiled at her and resumed shooting, but my mind kept going back to Laila's separateness. Were her parents expecting that of her? I could understand they wouldn't want her exposed to the judgment of relatives or neighbors. Who knows what they had said behind her back when she had been raped? Perhaps that she had it coming because she was too pretty, too proud, or arrogant? Early on, maybe, but would they still think that fourteen years later, and would Laila resent their earlier discrimination?

For the next hour I got caught up in my assignment and explored the horseshoe layout of the grounds. The priests were assembled in the inner courtyard, separated from the street by a wing of the living quarters. Viewed from this side, every visible ledge was decorated with oil lamps that would be lit at dusk. Festoons of flowers hung from balustrades and balconies, and tall vases overflowing with white hydrangea like the ones I had seen in the garden tended by Laila, marked the four corners of the space dedicated to the ceremony. Someone had decorated the cemented walkways with a chalk design that reminded me of my wedding in Bombay. Though it was not specifically part of my assignment, I spent some time nosing around the kitchen, where three Brahmin cooks were overseeing small cauldrons of rice and vats of coconut flavored curry that made my mouth water. I had left home early with hardly any breakfast, and I was hungry. One of the servants must have read my inquisitive looks, because she directed me to a verandah where a young cook was dishing out hot idlis, the soft pillowy steamed cakes made from rice and lentil batter that he served with sweet chutney on freshly washed banana leaves. Catching up the aroma of fried onions, cumin and ginger, I followed my nose a little further, where some of the guests were chomping on masala dosais, the crisp fermented pancakes filled with spicy potato fillings. In spite of the curried fillings, dosais always reminded me of the rye or buckwheat crepes I used to eat as a child, when on vacation in Brittany. It was too bad that Gangan had never learned how to make them.

"Hey! I tried to find you, but you'd disappeared," called Stefan, who was finishing his meal. I sat cross-legged next to him and signaled to a servant to bring me a *dosai.* I was surprised at Stefan's lighthearted, chatty tone of voice. Maybe it was the satisfied feeling following a delicious breakfast, or maybe it was just easy for him to behave here like we were a happy couple, because that's what people around us expected. It was also a very safe place to act friendly. He could count on there being no demands made on him, no scene, none of the tears to which I sometimes succumbed out of frustration because of our lack of communication. He was all smiles and I found myself proud and happy to be his wife, enjoying his attention and cheerful mood. After exchanging a few details on how we planned to cover the coming ceremony, he left, and I was just finishing a glass of whipped buttermilk when Prakash came over. I jumped to my feet to greet him, and he thanked me for the unwrapped gifts I had deposited on a table, where the guests could admire them. "You did not have to do that," he said in English, fingering in his large, knobby dark hands the starched fabric of the white scarf he wore.

"I wanted to thank you for allowing me to be part of this joyful event," I countered, with a respectful bow.

"Indeed," he said, and left to join a group of dignitaries who were entering the courtyard.

In accordance with the priest's horoscope, the shaving of the baby's hair would take place at 10:53 a.m., and it was only nine o'clock. I had some time to kill and decided to find the garden I had spied over the wall on my first visit to Prakash's house. Following a gravelly alley that ran behind the house, I saw that the peacock I had admired that first time was safely corralled inside a small shed. I wasn't surprised. Peacocks can get quite belligerent around strangers.

The garden was as I remembered. There were no signs of Laila or the peacock, and was soon absorbed in my task, taking photos of a flower I had no name for, when I caught a glimpse of green from the corner of my eye. Laila was watching me. This was my chance to continue breaking the ice. I put my hands together in greeting and waited for inspiration, but I couldn't come up with anything special. After a few seconds I said gently, "How are you today?"

"Fine, thank you," she said politely. She looked intently at my camera and took a step forward when I bent over the flower to get a close-up.

"What are you seeing? Is photography difficult?"

"You can see for yourself. Here." I lifted the strap from around my neck and offered her the camera. At first, she refused it, but her fascination was visible. Coming closer to me, she extended her hand and exhaled, as if surprised by its weight.

"Put the strap around your neck and hold the camera like this," I said, helping her with the strap. "Look inside the viewer, right here, and when you are ready, press this button until it clicks." I could see she understood. She focused on an orchid, and I heard the click of the shutter closing. Like a child discovering a new toy, she laughed with delight, focused on another flower, pressed the shutter release again and handed the camera back to me with an expectant smile.

"Try this one," I said, showing her the zoom button. She took the camera back, put it to her eye and activated the zoom. She exclaimed out loud and stumbled backward, but I was ready and stood solidly behind her to stop her fall. Just then, a hummingbird that had been flying over our heads fluttered above a recently watered gardenia.

"Now!" I said urgently. "Frame the flower with the bird. Quickly… press the shutter release."

I heard the click and hoped she had caught the rare sight of that tiny bird drinking from a flower.

"Ah! *Viyattaku*… This is… how you say…wonderful." Her eyes were full of wonder. She was so excited, she had trouble remembering to speak in English.

She gave me back the camera, and on hearing the back door open, she hurriedly stepped behind a trellis supporting a thick wisteria bush. I watched a young kitchen helper empty a dish of food detritus into a pile of compost by the wall and go back inside. After she was gone, I told Laila in a low voice, "Next time I see you, I will give you copies of the photos I took of you with the peacock, and also of the ones you took today."

She rested her hand on my arm, "Thank you." She lowered her eyes and said shyly, "I do not have any pictures of me since…" She stopped in mid-sentence and a pained, faraway look came to her eyes.

"I understand," I said, feeling like the good witch in a fairy tale. "I'll pick the best ones for you." Looking at her pleading posture, I wanted to hug her and tell her everything would be alright because I believed in my heart that things in life could improve. My life was proof of that. Maybe one day I'd be able to tell her how a friend of my mother had helped her escape an abusive husband and move on to a better life.

I hoped that she would listen to my story and believe, as I did, that it was my karma that had brought me into her world because there was a debt of kindness I needed to repay. Stefan, of course, didn't believe that stuff, and had advised me to keep my nose out of Prakash's family affairs, but if there was a way I could inspire Laila to dare find a path of her own, I would help her find it.

CHAPTER FORTY-TWO

THE CEREMONY

The time set for the head-shaving ceremony was approaching. Reluctantly, I parted from Laila and returned to the front of the house. Stefan was waiting for me in the courtyard where guests continued to arrive.

"It's starting," he said, impatiently. "Where were you? I was look-ing for you."

"In the garden, taking photos." I didn't like his tone and didn't feel I owed him an explanation, but didn't want to start an argument. "Were you recording?"

He shrugged. "Yes, but I stopped. This special Ganesha puja is taking forever. Those priests have been going on solid for the past hour."

Holding the Nagra in front of him, he got up from his lotus position and said, "I read somewhere that, to make sure the Vedas' teachings are never lost, Brahmin priests continue to spend years memorizing it forward and backward."

"Leave it to Hindus to protect their scriptures. But then, Catholic priests still memorize masses in Latin, a dead language they don't even speak."

I unzipped my camera bag to check the unused rolls of film I had stored in it, and pointed at the Nagra. "So, you're done for now?"

He nodded sharply. "What do you think?" Apparently, my question was getting to him. Showing some appreciation might help keep him focused on the assignment.

"Good idea. It would be a shame to run out of tape before Prakash's concert."

His face relaxed, but I was wrong about the source of his irritation.

"Sorry if I sound impatient. I'm afraid I feel a migraine coming on," he said. "I need to go home and take my medication. Will you be okay on your own for a while?"

"Go! I'll be fine. Nothing much will happen for at least an hour."

"OK, then. See you shortly." He slipped the strap of the portable tape recorder around his shoulders and hurried to the spot where his scooter was parked while I busied myself with changing film in my camera.

Our house was only two miles away, but with the crazy Madras traffic, there was always a chance that he would get caught in a small fender bender in front or behind a bullock cart or a water buffalo. As for his migraine, I could only pray that he would nip it in the bud, for I depended on Stefan to record. I could have asked him to leave the Nagra with me, just in case, but we both knew that I couldn't have handled both the recording and the photography at the same time. Moreover, it was an expensive piece of equipment that he felt responsible for. Fingers crossed. I just had to trust he would be back in time.

I was changing film in my camera when a thin and sallow-faced middle-aged woman in a splendid black and gold Benares sari, and her friend, a plump matron clutching a Kashmiri wool shawl around her shoulders, approached me. They had been eavesdropping on our conversation and appeared somewhat surprised we had been invited.

"Are you that foreign girl taking lessons from Sri Prakash at the music college?" asked the matron, her ferret eyes excited with something to gossip about.

"Yes I am."

"British, are you?"

"No, French."

"I saw you taking pictures in the back garden," said sallow-face. "You absolutely have to photograph their orchids. They are gorgeous."

Hoping to put an end to the conversation, I closed the back of my camera with a satisfying click. "I did. And you're right. They are splendid."

The shawled matron rounded her eyes and nodded. "They require a lot of care. Srimati Prakash, our hostess, grows the best orchids in Madras."

It made me wonder. Was Prakash's wife also spending time in the garden, or were the orchids Laila's labor of love? I would have to ask her when I got a chance.

Meanwhile, I needed to get rid of these two busy bodies.

"Excuse me please, but Professor Prakash will be upset if I don't set up my camera."

"Of course, of course," chorused the two nosy matrons, stepping back.

On arriving at Prakash's house this morning, I'd noticed that the large courtyard we'd entered was enclosed on three sides by living quarters. A long blue awning had been deployed on the windowless side of the eastern building, making it look like an outdoor theater where the ceremony would take place. Because this type of event was traditionally under the protection of the elephant God Ganesha, a large plaster statue of him painted in garish colors had been placed on the right side of a knee-high platform. Under the awning, the back wall of the building had been whitewashed and hung with giant framed images of Prakash's favorite Hindu deities. Saraswati, the patron saint of musicians and artists, hung in the center with her veena. To her right, Vishnu, the healer and restorer of the known world, kept a benevolent gaze on the faithful. On the other side, Shiva, the destroyer, ascetic and fierce, stood with a cobra wrapped around his neck. Hanging from the frames were garlands of fresh flowers whose scent blended with the familiar smell of the sandalwood and frangipani incense sticks planted in the rice bowls that lined the bottom of the back wall.

The platform at Lakshmi's wedding had been higher than the one facing me and had allowed for a better view of the participants. I calculated that, even though I owned a powerful zoom lens, I would need to get closer to them to capture the shots. Standing up and moving around was out of the question. It would appear disrespectful and being Prakash's guest didn't guarantee the priests would accept my intrusion. I would have to infiltrate the scene early so they got used to my presence. A row of polished brass oil lamps, like the one I'd seen Laila refill earlier that morning, separated the low stage from the spectators. Upon that platform, bamboo mats had been laid in a U-shape around a ceremonial fire burning in a large metal vessel, and the two old Brahmins Stefan had recorded earlier sat on either side of it. As in other ceremonies I'd witnessed, they were naked to the waist, except for the single white thread crossing their chests. They were still chanting the Sanskrit verses in unison, and, from time to time, they punctuated the verses with the throwing of twigs, herbs, flowers or rice into the fire, and when they did, the flames would change color and rise for an instant, before settling down.

As a courtesy to the guests, grass mats had been laid down on the ground facing the ceremony, and by now, many of the men were slowly gathering in the section reserved for them. The women, many with young children, were already seated on their own side. Camera held low, I walked carefully through the row of seated women, modestly nodding to the hypnotic rhythm of the Sanskrit verses that flowed over me like a monotonous song. I was taller than most women, so rather than sitting in front, I inched my way to a good shooting position in the third row and settled next to a young mother nursing her child under the folds of her sari.

I looked around and saw that Stefan was back, sitting in the first row of the men's section, right next to Prakash, whose large stature and distinctive mane couldn't be missed. He'd set the Nagra and microphone in front of him, and appeared to be explaining the many dials and knobs of our state-of-the-art recorder to him, and a small group of fascinated men looking over his shoulder.

After a moment, I caught Stefan's eye and tapped my forehead questioningly hoping he would understand. He beamed a smile at me and gave me the thumbs up. I breathed a long sigh of relief. It would have been catastrophic if he had to forego the recording of this concert.

Because the awning didn't extend to cover all the guests, many women behind me had covered their hair with the end of their saris to protect themselves from the increasing heat of the sun moving west over our heads. Sunglasses were popular too, and I recalled the baskets of cheap imported eye shades that were sold in front of the temple's entrance, along with glass bangles and bead necklaces.

Prakash's wife was nowhere to be seen until I discovered her in the back, welcoming newcomers. Further down, on the women's side, Laila stood half hidden by a tall potted palm. She was discretely surveying the crowd. Not mixing with the guests seemed to be her choice. She obviously had no desire to deal with their curiosity or pity, and appeared poised to take flight if necessary.

Nothing new happened for a while and my legs were starting to fall asleep when a young man wearing sunglasses approached the consecrated space. He carried the baby and was followed by his wife, whom

346

I recognized from my morning photo session. Smoothing the bamboo mat with his feet, he lowered himself to the ground to the left of the fire, his crossed legs forming a love basket for the child. Pointing at the young man with her chin, my neighbor said, "Sri Prakash's son."

I aimed my long lens in his direction and adjusted the focus carefully, preparing to take a few shots of father and son. The sweet tableau made me smile. The young man was at ease with his son, who was awake and clearly agitated by all the goings on. Fascinated by the flames leaping in his line of sight, the baby jiggled and, reaching up with his tiny hands, he knocked off his father's sunglasses. I had just zoomed on the young man and was surprised to see that, highlighted by the ceremonial flames, his eyes were hazel gray. Anonymous in a row of seated women, I could stare at him without drawing attention, and saw now that Prakash Junior looked nothing like his father. He was handsome. Hiding behind my camera, I focused on the baby. I couldn't see his eyes, for he was turned away from me, but I clearly remembered noting this morning that they had also been different, lighter inside the raccoon mask made by the kohl make-up. At the time, I had taken it to be just that, an eye-color that would change as the baby grew older. In France, I had known babies whose eyes had gone from amethyst to blue, or even brown. I had no idea if the same change applied to Indian children.

I stretched my neck to get a better look. I was puzzled. Light eyes were rare in South India, especially amongst Brahmins who didn't inter-marry. Was there in his ancestry a light-eyed Afghan or Kashmiri beauty? But I'd no time for tales of ancestries. I had to pay attention to my assignment. It wouldn't do to disappoint Prakash if I wanted access to Laila. The ceremony was picking up momentum, so I emptied my mind to focus on the improvised theater where the event was unfolding.

For the next hour I tried to remain centered on the job at hand. As predicted, and to my great relief, the shaving of the baby's head took

347

place without incident, and I got some beautiful shots of the now bald cherub. Gone was his thick head of hair and the damp little curl I had photographed in the morning.

Following the ceremony, the priests were thanked and paid with honor gifts and money, the fire was abandoned, and the platform swept, so the musicians could set up for a late afternoon concert featuring Prakash, and other musicians from the Music College. Having heard that KV would participate, I looked for Lakshmi, his young wife, but she was nowhere to be seen. I wondered if her absence had to do with her new role as stepmother to his children, or if she had been barred from joining us because of her menses, during which time Brahmin women were barred from kitchens, as well as social and religious functions. Lakshmi had been so elated on the day of her wedding. Next time I saw her, I'd have to ask her about married life in her in-laws' house.

I had warned Stefan not to run out of tape, but saw now that I only had one roll of film left for the concert. Fortunately, it would start later in the afternoon, so we would have time to go home to rest, recharge the batteries of our tape recorder and cameras, and pick up more film.

That afternoon break went fast, and when we returned, we found the courtyard more crowded than before. Apparently, word about the concert and Prakash's generous offerings of food had spread, and the place was buzzing with anticipation. Free to circulate in the crowd, I decided to photograph the guests. It might please Prakash to see who'd responded to his invitation.

When the concert started, I saw that many of the college's students and staff were standing in the back of the audience. Feeding off the empathy and enthusiasm of their audience, the musicians were exceptionally spirited. Stefan was back at his place close to the performers to capture the music, and I rejoiced at the thought of adding that special recording to my growing collection of classical Indian music.

By the end of the concert, I was tired. It had been quite a long day. I thanked Prakash for his hospitality and told him it would take a few days for the photos to be developed and the recordings copied. While Stefan secured our equipment on the back rack of his scooter, I looked around for Laila, but Stefan was waiting for me, and I had to leave.

On getting home, I helped Stefan store the gear as we always did, and thanked him effusively for his help, because without him, I couldn't have completed my assignment. Stefan accepted my thanks as his dues and, citing a residual headache, he begged off any further conversation, and went to bed straight away.

I'd been dying to talk to him about Laila, but knew it was ill-advised. When I'd first spoken to him about her, he had strongly objected to my meddling into Prakash's affairs.

So here I was, tired but buzzing with all the impressions I'd collected during the day. I checked the time. Seven o'clock. I drank a tall glass of cold water and decided to call on Lycette. The sun had set, and the cooling air was redolent with the smell of the flowers planted along the path linking the T.S. to Kalakshetra.

I ran into her coming home from an evening dance class. Her practice outfit, stained with sweat, was slowly drying as we walked together to the student hut where she lived alone.

I was relieved and excited to find her. "I saw Laila again today. I've so much to tell you."

"Can it wait until after I take a shower?" she asked somewhat warily, lifting her single tress off her neck to let the night breeze dry her skin. "I'll be better able to focus on what you bring."

"Sure. Go ahead, I'm not going anywhere."

Lycette grabbed a dry towel, some fresh clothes and a toilet bag and went back out to the communal showers the school provided. I turned on her portable fan and sat on a floor mat in the sparsely furnished room. A glossy Spanish Vogue magazine rested on a bolster, and I paged through it. Spanish had been my second language in school and the ads and stories were pretty easy to follow. Ten minutes passed and Lycette returned, fresh and smiling. She hung her towel to dry on a coat rack set inside the door, and threw her damp dhavani and blouse in a hamper.

"So, tell me about your day," she said, applying some camphor insect repellent on her bare feet before passing the bottle to me.

I told her about the baby and the morning ceremony, and then I described my encounter with Laila in the garden.

"You were so lucky to find her alone. And she talked with you?"

"Not much, but enough to find out that she loves gardening. She was quite friendly."

"Tell me more? What did you talk about?"

"She asked about my camera, and what I was seeing through the lens, and whether taking photos was difficult."

"So, she's genuinely interested in photography?"

"So it seems. So, I handed her the Nikon, and showed her how to set the focus."

I rubbed some of Lycette's repellent on my feet, hands and neck and returned the bottle to her. "She was fascinated and proved to be a fast learner. She actually took photos of her flowers." I smiled at the memory. "She was quite proud of herself and asked, very shyly, if she could get a copy of the shots she took." I paused for a moment thinking about her other request. "She also hoped I'd give some photos I took of her. Apparently, she hasn't been photographed since the...incident." I found it hard to use the word rape.

We both paused for a moment.

"Maybe you can find a way to get her involved with photography," said Lycette. "She could take lessons. That might encourage her to get out of her house, and look around for new subjects."

"It crossed my mind. Prakash would have to be brought in the loop.

I wonder what he would say."

"Do you think he owns a camera?" she asked.

"I doubt it. He's old-school, and doesn't trust foreign made things."

"Maybe you can find one for her, and locate a manual she can read," said Lycette.

I sighed. "You're right. But first let me develop the photos of the ceremony and show them to Prakash and his family. We'll take it from there."

Lycette walked me outside. The air was warm and humid but the sky, high overhead, was velvet black and studded with a zillion pins of light. Some of the closest stars were so white they looked like real diamonds refracting prisms of color. Inside the brightness, I looked for green, and once again wondered if Laila's favorite color had anything to do with the old witch's oracle.

CHAPTER FORTY-THREE

DINNER INVITATION

The following Sunday, Sharada, Lycette and I called on Anup, to share with him what we had discovered about Laila. He certainly deserved to know, considering he was the reason we had even found out about her earlier trauma. When he heard that her reclusive lifestyle appeared to be mostly by choice, he shook his head wisely.

"That is good news," he said. "I'm glad to know that her home is a safe place rather than a prison." He nodded. "I have always wondered if, to this day, her parents felt guilty for failing to protect her when she was young."

I tried to imagine life in those pre-independence years. There had been a lot of political unrest in India. "Maybe they should have forbidden her to take shortcuts through the mango grove," I said, remembering that Anup had told us that's where the rape had taken place.

"Or maybe they should have instructed their son or a servant to accompany her to school," said Sharada, somberly.

Norma exhaled a long sigh of relief. "I wonder how many years it took her to recover emotionally. She must have been terrified to leave her house."

"I would imagine," said Anup. "After recovering from her physical injuries, she probably could not face her fears of the violence she had run into as a child. Her parents were right to keep her indoors, and shield her from the curiosity and gossip of people, even in their own family."

"That's probably why she's been hiding for all these years, but tell Anup and Norma what happened last week," said Lycette.

"Prakash had asked me to take photos of his grandson's Ayushkarma," I said, "and, my taking photos of the flowers in the garden caught Laila's interest. Maybe because I was a new face, and a foreigner. Or maybe because she'd seen me a few weeks back when, after talking with you, I reconnoitered her house to try and catch a glimpse of her. In any case, I think it was time for her to open up to someone. It triggered a spark of friendship. I was taking photos, and she got interested in the process, especially after I invited her to try taking a few photos herself."

"And how do you think Prakash will react when he discovers you have befriended his daughter?" asked Anup.

"It remains to be seen. Her mother almost caught us talking a couple of times, and she appeared concerned that my curiosity might upset Laila. But Prakash never saw us together."

"Hum, hmmm," said Anup. "So, what are you girls up to? Going to continue pulling Laila out of her voluntary seclusion?"

"That's why we came to talk to you. We could use your advice."

We brainstormed for another hour and decided that the best option would be to get Laila more involved with photography. But to do that, I would have to clear the way with Prakash, which was a scary proposition, since my final degree depended on him.

Following the ceremony, I had handed the rolls of b/w films I'd shot to Azam, an enterprising photo technician with a small lab on the T.S. Campus. Azam was a Parsi widow, a polio survivor with a shrunken leg she hid under her white sari. Developing and enlarging so many photos would have cost me a fortune, had she charged me the amount expected of tourists and foreign residents, but to secure my business, she'd made me an offer I couldn't pass up. In exchange for my selling her two of my best cameras at a reasonable price when I left Madras, she would develop all the photos I took for the cost of the paper and developer. It was an incredible deal for me, and a way for her to acquire some highly professional equipment which, if imported, would have cost three times their value.

On getting the contact prints back, I selected the best pictures, including the ones Laila had taken in the garden, and asked Azam to enlarge them. Because she only developed b/w prints, she had sent the Kodacolor slides to a lab she knew in Bangalore. All I had to do now was wait.

A week later, I was still waiting for the b/w enlargements and color slides when Prakash stopped me in the school corridor after class.

"My wife and I would be pleased if your Mr. Stefan and you would stay for dinner when you deliver the snapshots to our house. You will let me know when they are ready, right?"

"Of course. Hopefully it will be soon."

Even though I was thrilled to note the change in Prakash's attitude toward me, I couldn't help but bristle a little about his labeling my photos as snapshots. They would be anything but, considering the large prints I planned to feature in a deluxe album. As for bringing Stefan along, I would rather have avoided it. I was afraid he might interfere with my taking advantage of that dinner to suggest to Prakash that Laila might enjoy taking photography lessons, but Indian etiquette required that we both attend. It wouldn't be proper for a married woman to go out alone at night.

Later that day, when I went home, I found Stefan in his study, ensconced in an ornate wooden chair he had bought from one of the T.S. guests leaving Madras. Bare feet wedged between two piles of musty-looking books from the MU library on his desk, he was rocking back and forth on two legs. Lassitude and frustration distorted his handsome face.

"Round and round with the same *merde*. For God's sake! How many ways are there to describe God or discuss dharma? I'll never find any answers in those books! All they want to do is talk, talk, talk about it."

He dropped his feet onto the floor, slamming the chair on its four legs. "I'm sorry, but I have had it with Mahadevan." He wagged his head from shoulder to shoulder, like an Indian. I repressed a smile his perfect Indian impersonation had triggered.

Professor Mahadevan was his tutor at Madras University. In the early days of my stay in Madras, before joining the music college, I had attended one of his seminars, mostly to check out what being a university student felt like, as opposed to being an achy and sweaty dance student. He was a mild-mannered and scholarly type of man, with a narrow chest, rounded shoulders and thick glasses that kept sliding dangerously down his shiny, round nose when he lectured. I quite liked him. "What's going on with him?" I asked.

"Just that he's commenting on commentaries. It's an endless circle of second-hand information." He sighed and looked up at me. "But you didn't come here to talk about me. What's on your mind?"

"We've been invited to dinner at Prakash's house."

"Dinner? When?"

"When we deliver the photos, which reminds me, I need to bring you up to date on what Sharada, Lycette and I found out and discussed about Prakash's daughter Laila."

"Oh, really! And where was I when you held that meeting?" His tone of voice was resentful.

"You were out," I lied. "And frankly speaking, I know you don't approve of my involvement with Laila."

"That's because, as you say, I don't approve of your involvement in matters concerning your instructor's family."

Repressing my distaste, I pushed down my frustration at his pompous, controlling ways and temporized. "You may have a point, but a few of us feel differently, and I'm here to ask whether you're with us or against us."

"What does that mean, exactly?"

"That means that if you're with us, you will support our efforts to create some kind of avenue to improve her situation."

"And what if I don't?" He scowled and looked at me belligerently. "In case you've forgotten, I'm your husband and am entitled to have my say about it." He poked his right index finger at my chest. "I'm also a sensible guy making sure you don't compromise your music degree at the CCKM." His face wore a smirky expression I'd never seen before. Was he threatening me? Coercing me to do things his way, or else? If I had learned anything from my mother's unfortunate marriage, it was that one should always defuse threats before they become blows. And what better way to ward off a threat than use one of my own. There were a few things I could throw at his face, but I refused to play that kind of game with him. We loved each other and were supposed to work things out, not play dirty with threats. He was watching me, probably expecting me to defend my involvement with Laila, but I remained silent. I just stared at him and waited.

I guess it worked, for after a while he relented. "Ok, sorry. I'll go with you to that dinner. What do you call Prakash in school? Narasimha? I guess I'll be there to protect you from the man-eating lion." He gave me his boyish smile. Apparently, his obnoxious threats were forgotten.

"Thanks." I let out a sigh of relief and turned to go.

"Hey, when will that be? I need to order tapes to make copies of the recordings. I'm out."

"The date hasn't been set yet, so, don't worry. I too need time to get the photos back."

On the day the enlarged prints were delivered to me, with a note that the slides would arrive in a couple of days, I carefully unwrapped the brown paper package and spread the photos on the large dining room table. Warned by messenger, Lycette and Sharada were on their way over. Stefan was out and could see them later.

On seeing them, Sharada bent over them and exclaimed: "Those are beautiful Minouche. You did a great job."

"Yes, those are spectacular. What about the color slides? When are you getting those?" asked Lycette.

"In two days."

"Great shots of the baby. The mother is pretty too. I do not think I ever met her," said Sharada.

Lycette chuckled. "Wow! Prakash's son is really handsome. He doesn't look anything like his father, which is definitely a good thing." We all had to agree.

She reached over the table to take a closer look. "Did you notice his eyes? I know this is a black and white photo, but they look lighter than the people around him."

Intrigued, Sharada looked over her shoulder.

I held up the photo in the light. "Yes, I noticed. I'd say his eyes were some kind of hazel gray.

"And the baby's eyes?"

I thought about it for a few seconds. "I have a feeling his eyes were not dark either. At the time, I thought it was normal because I know

357

that babies' eyes change color before they grow into toddlers. His will probably darken too."

"Light eyes can be found in Northern India, but are very rare in South India, especially amongst Brahmins who do not inter-marry," said Sharada, waving off a bee that was flying around her head, attracted to the jasmine garland she'd wrapped around her chignon.

"This is India," said Lycette. "Think of all the invasions that took place through the centuries. The Aryans, the Greeks, the Persians, and most recently, the Brits. Everything is possible."

I gathered the photos in a neat pile. "Well, regardless of his eye color, I think he's very attractive. His young wife must be proud to have landed such a prize. Not all girls are that lucky."

"True," said Sharada. "And some girls, like Laila, will never marry at all. Do you think she will ever talk about what it means to her?"

"I doubt it," said Lycette, soberly. "At least, not any time soon."

"We'll have to be patient with her and create situations in which we can talk with her away from her family," I said. "If we can restore her self-confidence, and help her figure out her options, she'll start thinking outside of the walls she's erected around herself."

I pulled out the large photo album I had purchased, and they helped me organize the prints in order before affixing them on the waiting pages with the small and ornate sticky corners I had chosen.

The following day, at school, I let Prakash know that the photos were back, but that Stefan was still waiting to receive the magnetic tapes he'd ordered to make copies of the concert.

"The concert recording can wait," said Prakash. "Please, come to my house on Friday, and bring the photos. We are eager to see them. Dinner is at 6 p.m."

CHAPTER FORTY-FOUR

FEB 1962 - IN THE LION'S DEN

On our way to Prakash's dinner invitation, we rode tandem on Stefan's Lambretta scooter. Dusk was approaching. Clouds of insects and mosquitoes had left the cool shelter of the trees that protected them during the day, and now hovered noisily over the road in a pre-blood-letting dance. When we arrived at his house, Prakash suggested we eat before looking at the album. I had been so focused on the photos that it took me by surprise and made me wonder whether Prakash was hungry, or just a good host. Nonetheless, I welcomed his invitation to eat first as the smell of cumin and Masala spices wafting from the kitchen was tantalizing. We were invited to sit on floor mats, behind the freshly washed banana leaves that would be our plates. Helped by Laila, Prakash's wife went back and forth to the kitchen and served the food. The thin grey hair that didn't completely hide her scalp gave away her age, but I had to admire how, feet pulled together, back stooped in half without apparent strain, she ladled the vegetarian curry and dhal on our leaves. I already knew there was no point offering my help; both women would eat after we did, as custom required.

We finished eating and were offered *pan*, the traditional after-dinner digestive consisting of a rolled leaf seasoned with lime extract, shredded coconut and betel nuts. It was quite a mouthful and not quite to my taste. I chewed in silence for a while, tucked it in my cheek like a chipmunk, and finally, invoking my need for a breath of fresh air, I stepped out in the garden and spat it in the bushes.

When I returned, I brought out the photo album I had put together. For a better look, Prakash and his wife moved a coffee table to the middle of the room under a bright single bulb hanging from the ceiling. They soon were absorbed with the album, and it gave me a chance to slip to Laila an envelope containing smaller copies of the photos I had promised her.

On reviewing the large images of the elaborate Ayushkarma ceremony he had held for his family and friends, Prakash was beaming with pride. He also appeared very taken by photos of himself posing with the priests and the various dignitaries who had attended the function. But when he reached the back of the album where I had featured several photos Laila had shot in the garden on that day, especially one of a hummingbird hovering over a gardenia, he did a double take. "What are those?" he asked.

In spite of my resolution to tell Prakash about his daughter's interest in photography, I hesitated. How was I going to explain that, in hopes of finding Laila in her garden, I'd sneaked through their puja room, a private place of worship where they kept a small altar decorated with fresh flowers and incense?

"Those are photos taken by your daughter," offered Stefan unexpectedly. He glanced at me, inviting me to continue, which I did.

"She seemed interested in my taking photos, so, after your grandson's ceremony ended, I looked for her around the house, and, when I found her in the garden, I showed her how to use my camera to take a few pictures," I said, skipping over my snooping through their private quarters. "She's a fast learner and has a good eye for photography."

"Is that so?" Prakash turned to look at Laila, who was leaning over his shoulder to take a closer look at the graceful black-and-white shots she had taken of some orchids. Her eyes, bright with excitement, betrayed her surprise and self-satisfaction at seeing her work printed. I nodded encouragingly at her, hoping she would take this opportunity to talk to her father about studying photography, but she didn't speak.

As if reading my mind in in the ensuing silence, Stefan jumped in. "Looks like you might have your very own photographer right here, in the family," he said. "All she needs is some instruction and practice."

I felt rather than saw Laila's intake of breath. As if encouraged by Stefan's comment, she stepped forward and looked at her father, eager to hear what he might say.

"Hmmmm," muttered Prakash in a voice that held no praise. When he turned his good eye on her, waiting maybe for an explanation, she backed away and leaned against the wall behind me.

"Go on. You don't have to be shy about talking in front of us," said Stefan to Laila, in an encouraging voice.

I was surprised Stefan had dared address Laila directly, and for good reason. Prakash looked at Stefan curiously, as if wondering what a foreigner knew about the etiquette a daughter had to follow when addressing her father, especially when her father was a Brahmin. "In our culture, we value shyness and modesty in a girl," he said, tartly.

Unruffled, Stefan nodded and smiled, and I felt a little spike of jealousy at the apparent ease with which the two men carried on a conversation. But I shot Stefan an encouraging glance and continued to unpack the projector he had retrieved earlier from the scooter's saddlebag.

Laila had retreated into herself, and to fill the silence, I commented on what I was doing. "One of the cameras I used held film for color slides. I brought a projector so you may see them and select the ones you want to print. Color prints are expensive, and you may not want to print them all." Pointing to a picture of Lord Krishna hanging on the room's back wall I asked Prakash, "Would it be all right to move that image out of the way so we may use that wall as a screen?"

"I will do it," he said. Leaning on his right hand to push himself off the floor, he got up and carefully took down the framed poster of the Blue God playing his flute. Carefully, he placed it out of harm's way by the door. I helped Stefan push the low table against the opposite wall, and set the projector on it before plugging in an extension cord he had thought to bring.

When that was done, Laila helped her mother and father settle in front of the table, and she then sat down with them, careful not to block the machine's powerful light. I turned on the projector, and the unadorned whitewashed wall changed into a perfect screen.

Unlike the sober black-and-white prints we had viewed, the projector splashed the wall with bursts of vivid colors. In many of the photos, the ceremonial fire and the lanterns hanging from trees lit the faces of my photographic subjects in dramatic ways. At first, it was a bit of a fashion show, the men proud in stiff white kurtas and dressy long scarves bordered in gold, the women displaying their best jewelry and posing in expensive silk saris. As I kept advancing the slides, Prakash and his wife and daughter chatted in Tamil, exchanging comments, I didn't understand, but from the look on their faces, I wondered if they were making snide remarks about some of their less favorite relatives or guests.

As color slide after color slide lit the wall, an expression of wonder crossed Laila's face when she turned to me. "Do you think I could take colorful photos like these?" Her voice was filled with excitement.

I smiled at her. "Yes, you could, with a good camera and the right film."

Reaching for a fresh *pan* which he placed expertly inside his cheek, Prakash grumbled. "I bet good cameras cost a fortune."

I was pretty sure that remark was aimed at me, and I silently appealed to Ganesh, my favorite Hindu god, to protect me from Prakash's possible displeasure at my having sought out his daughter and bonded with her over photography. But, regardless of any repercussions, I had to keep my eye on the real issue, which was to welcome Laila into the twentieth century. I could still picture her eager expression when I'd handed her my Nikon, and her excitement on capturing the sight of a hummingbird as it landed on a flower. This passion was waiting to be part of her life. But to own it, she'd have to break through whatever held her back in her parents' house.

"Photography is for rich people," added Prakash. While staring at me, he'd spoken in English, and loud enough for me to hear it. Hands clenched at my side, I waited for the sky to open up and fall over my head. He was probably going to tell me to mind my own business, and not give his daughter expensive and fancy ideas for what, in his eyes, could only be a useless hobby. I held my breath. But the moment passed. The tray of slides was now empty and the projector went dark. Prakash scratched his throat and spat a fresh jet of red saliva into an old coffee can his wife had placed under the low table.

The room was silent, and I shivered with nervousness. I thought of Anup, Lycette, Sharada and even Stefan. Had all our concerted efforts to break Laila out of her seclusion been for nothing? As I was putting away the color slides, I noticed Prakash's wife having a quiet conversation with him in Tamil. Towering over her without raising his voice, he appeared resistant at first, but little by little his broad shoulders relaxed. "Let's talk over coffee," he said hospitably, inviting us to return to the middle of the room and sit on the floor again. His wife smiled conspiratorially and handed me a pillow for my ankles. I guess she could tell I wasn't comfortable in a lotus position. I smiled back at her. She appeared subdued around her husband, but woman-to-woman, I felt that she approved of me befriending Laila.

After his wife returned from the kitchen with cups of steaming Madrasi coffee and a tray of pistachio-scented sweets, Prakash cleared his throat. "Thank you for taking such beautiful photos of the ceremony, Minouche. My family and I are grateful. I would like to print all the color photos, regardless of the cost. It will be a priceless souvenir for us and for my son and his family." Turning to Stefan he added, "I understand you are making copies of the music tapes but need some more time. There is no rush. I will be happy to pay for the copies when they are ready." After a long minute during which I wondered what next was going to come out of his mouth, he turned to Laila and asked, "So, is it true that you took these pictures?"

Shyly, Laila raised her eyes to him. "Yes, *Appa*, Minouche showed me how to do it with her camera."

Finally ready to finally listen to her, he nodded encouragingly, "And when was that?"

"When she came to the garden, Minouche let me hold her camera. She showed me how to look into the little window…"

"The viewfinder," I corrected, with an encouraging smile.

"Yes, the viewfinder," said Laila, nodding in my direction. "She showed me how to look into it to frame the flowers. It was not hard, and when the hummingbird landed on the gardenia I pressed the little shutter-button. I was not sure I had caught it on the photo! Oh, Appa! It is so fascinating."

Noticing that the toes of his right foot were peeking from under the edge of his dhoti, Prakash pulled on the long scarf he wore to cover them. "Well, I can see that this photo business made a strong impression on you," he said.

Laila, who was sitting on the floor a few feet away from him, edged forward. "Appa, please, can I study photography with Minouche? Can I?" she said, urgently. "I have not wanted anything so much since… you know…" she didn't finish her sentence. She didn't need to. She stared intently into her father's and mother's faces and added, "There are so many things I have been missing out on. Kalakshetra for one. I would like to call on Sharada. Minouche told me she is teaching the senior dance students now. Maybe I could watch, or even join her class sometime. You know how much I loved dancing." Her face was flushed with excitement. It was as if she had suddenly woken up from a long sleep, like in some fairy tales I had read as a child. She straightened up and said resolutely, "I am no longer afraid to leave our house, especially if I can have a friend like Minouche with me." She turned to me, "I could go to Kalakshetra with you, yes?" She let her head drop to her chest and when she looked up, her eyes were filled with tears. "Appa, there are so many things I want to do. I… I…"

I looked at her face, shiny with sweat. She appeared to be hyperventilating and I worried she might faint. I gently patted her shoulder, and she took several long breaths that seemed to calm her down. I looked at her sitting in front of her bigger-than-life father, her slim figure wrapped in the green sari she seemed to favor, her glossy dark braid almost touching the floor, and tears came to my eyes. She was twenty-six, only six years older than me, and my heart ached in my chest at the thought that she had stayed in hiding for thirteen years, afraid to face not only physical dangers, but the nightmares they'd left in their wake. Thirteen years without friends, without the dancing that had been her passion until then. She was in the prime of her life but didn't know it. I so wanted her to come out of the cocoon her parents had woven around her, and see for herself how much had changed in India in those thirteen years. A new government. New institutions. New laws. The departure of most things British, except of course their monuments and their railways. She would no doubt find a bigger, freer world than what she remembered, which brought to my mind the vivid memory of how Paris had suddenly opened up for me after my mother and I had escaped my stepfather's tyranny. From her sitting position,

Laila bent forward at the waist and reached out to touch her father's feet, as I had seen devotees do to their gurus, and to deities in temples.

"There, there," said Prakash. He bent over to rest his hand on her head, like a blessing, and switched to Tamil, and though I couldn't understand his words, they sounded loving. Maybe he was finally able to let go of the dishonor his family had been subjected to. He probably would never apologize for the overprotectiveness he had smothered her with, but his face was lit with something akin to wonder, an expression I could never have imagined on him.

Turning to Stefan and me, he said, "I have not heard my daughter talk like this for many years." He paused for a moment, took a long breath, and resumed. "As a young girl, she was always reaching out for new things, new lessons, new instruments, new choreographies. This is the first time she has shown interest in something outside of her life with us, here, at home." Prakash's wife was crying soundlessly into the free end of her sari, and the hair on the nape of my neck stood up in the room's palpable electricity. I turned to Stefan, who discreetly nodded to the door behind us.

I jumped on his suggestion. "Thank you for trusting me to take the photos of your grandson's ceremony. It was a great experience for my husband and me. I also want to say that I'm very glad Laila is opening her heart to you," I said. "You have a talented daughter, sir. Let me know if I can be of any help." Smiling warmly at Laila, I nodded at our hosts. "I think we'll go now."

Stefan and I stood up, quietly slipped the projector and photo trays into a leather case, and made for the door. Prakash's wife joined us, and brought her hands together in a formal Namaste gesture before letting us out in the front yard where our scooter stood under a single tamarind tree. Coming from the house, I couldn't help but notice the row of stumps lining the fence surrounding the house like sentinels. Prakash's wife, who had walked to the property gate with us, said in halting English, "Many mango trees here, before. Good ones. With juicy, sweet smelling red mangoes. My husband…" with her hands she showed how the trees had been cut down. I nodded my understanding. No wonder Prakash had destroyed those trees that would only remind Laila of being ravaged on a bed of crushed mangoes and blood.

Wrapping my left arm around Stefan's waist, I straddled the scooter, waved at her, and we rode away. What had just happened? Hopefully, a door had been cracked open for Laila. I couldn't help but hope she would find the courage to push it open further and step into a new era of possibilities. I knew that Lycette, Sharada and I would be there to help her find her footing. I took a long breath of the night's cool air that felt good on my clammy skin. Staring into the dark shadows bordering the road, I thought I saw a face. A kind face. The face of the woman who had held a door open for my mother and me, when we had no money and nowhere to go. I remembered how the streetlights abounding in Paris had suddenly burned brighter after we were given a key to our very own hostel room. Maybe that's why I'd been so obsessed with helping Laila reclaim her place in society. A gift, such as that woman had given us, had to be repaid.

As we sped across the long Adyar bridge, I laid my cheek against Stefan's back, grateful for his timely interventions this evening. I looked up into the sky. It was black as ink, but the edge of a yellow orb was poking the eastern horizon and a touch of soft moonlight began to inch its way along the road, graying the shadows. In a couple of days I'd be back in school and would face Prakash in his veena class. Meeting the man and father behind that intimidating guru persona had been a stressful, but also a touching experience. He had shown such great hospitality and kindness to me, and more importantly, he'd wholeheartedly embraced Laila's breakthrough. I could hardly believe it had actually happened. I suspected that he would continue to enforce

Maryvonne Fent

the strict teacher/student relationship in the classroom, but I no longer minded. I knew the lion-man had a heart.

CHAPTER FORTY-FIVE

A CIRCLE OF FRIENDS

In spite of the successful outcome of our visit with Prakash, I was restless over the weekend, and, aware of Stefan's earlier warnings, I wondered about a possible fallout from my involvement with Laila. I had witnessed an intimate moment between father and daughter, and though I was thrilled that Laila had come forward with a request and an agenda of her own, I was not entirely convinced that her father appreciated my part in it. Not only was he a Brahmin, he also was a strict guru, and I fully expected that, in the classroom, he would quickly restore the teacher-student barrier I had breached.

As these thoughts fought for dominance in my head, I also became aware that I was desperately curious about Laila. Had she really broken through her cocoon, and been granted her wishes? I contemplated not going to class on Monday but knew in my heart that I had to face my fears head on. There was no turning back. I'd only be delaying the inevitable.

On Monday I dressed carefully in a pale magenta cotton sari, slipped seven glass bangles on each wrist—one for every day of the week–and threaded jasmine in my braided hair. Filled with uncertainty, I slowly drove to school, took my time parking my scooter in its regular spot, and joined Prakash's veena class at the last minute. For the next hour, I did my best to blend in, head bent modestly down, eyes glued to the frets of my instrument. When, without getting up, he asked me to stay after class, I nearly had a heart attack. My heart was beating so fiercely in my chest that, for a moment, I thought I might pass out. Was he going to unleash some punishment on me for meddling in his affairs?

"I hope your weekend was fine," he asked, rather formally without looking at me.

"Yes. Thank you." Feeling very much a foreigner, and a woman in a patriarchal country, I reluctantly sat back down. I was dying to move away before I found out I had made the biggest mistake of my short academic life.

Letting his good eye stare straight at my face, he said, "I have been thinking. The way you approached and befriended my daughter was rather brazen."

I felt numb and could think of nothing to say, so I looked at my feet to avoid his stare. Here came the axe, and there was nothing I could do to stop it.

He cleared his throat and I heard him say in a quiet voice, "It was also brave. You knew I might get angry with you for nosing into my affairs. And what of your studies then? You tell me. You would have needed to find another school."

I lifted my face to him. Uninvited, tears were trickling down my cheeks. They rolled down my chin and onto my neck, but I refused to acknowledge them.

His voice softened a touch. "No need for tears," he said. Even though he hadn't touched me, he wiped his hand on the scarf ever present over his left shoulder. For all I knew it could have been the scarf I had given him. "I do not intend to punish you. In fact, I was only praising your courage."

So that was it? Deep inside me, I realized he needed to submit me to that show-down in order to save face. My tears were proof that, though I had made a dent into his family armor, he was again in control. Considering all the possible outcomes, I decided I deserved his remonstrance.

"I-I'm so-sorry if I intruded into your family matters," I stammered. "It was not my intention." And out of nowhere I blurted out, "I heard what happened to Laila, and I hoped to make her see that it's not too late to learn new skills, to have friends and have a productive and happy life. She's still young. Hardly older than me."

Allowing a gruff smile to cross his face for the first time, Prakash straightened his back and, cleaning the strings of his veena with a rag he kept next to him for that purpose, he said, "I do not completely under-stand what happened, but your visit opened my heart. When I looked inside, instead of the hatred that had been there all these years for the British soldiers who defiled my child, I found my daughter, as she was fourteen years ago. I suddenly realized how lonely she had been." His voice caught in his throat, and he coughed to hide his emotion. "I can see you know what happened to her. Everybody knows, but it is hard for people to understand how that devastating experience left her trau-matized physically and emotionally. She became fearful of everything. Remaining homebound was her choice."

I nodded to acknowledge his words, and he continued. "Saturday night was the first time she told me she wanted to go out. Make friends again. I believe you are sincere when you say that, maybe in this new India, it is not too late for my daughter to have a better life. Since she wants to learn your photography, I was hoping you can make time to give her lessons? In exchange, I would give you some extra veena assignments."

First, I was stunned, then elated. Of all the things he could have said, I hadn't expected such a direct overture.

"I'd love to," was all I managed to answer.

"That would be perfect. You can talk it over with your Mr. Stefan."

Extra veena assignments from him? I didn't need to confer with Stefan to know it was a deal I couldn't turn down. Laila and I would both be getting what we wanted.

"I would be glad to share whatever photographic skills I have acquired with Laila," I said. "Extra veena lessons from you would be a blessing, but that would be too much." I bit my lips, wishing that I had not succumbed to that automatic response in which one is expected to refuse a cookie twice before it's finally accepted. So, praying that he would insist, I smiled at him, "I like Laila and hope we can continue to be friends."

To my great relief, Prakash lifted his right hand in a commanding manner. "I insist on the veena lessons," he said. "You are going to need a lot of help to pass the final exam when the time comes."

I flinched. Was my mastery of the veena really that precarious? Keeping my concerns in check, I answered, "In that case, I'm sure my husband will agree to that arrangement. It's very kind of you."

"Very well then."

I joined my hands and brought them to my sweaty forehead, acknowledging him as my guru. "Namaste".

"*Namaskar,*" he replied with a satisfied grin. He then got up and left the room.

I could hardly believe what had just happened. Had the man who'd ignored me for a whole year really offered to coach me privately?

I cut the next class, a drumming lesson, and stopped at the T.S. office on the way back home. Borrowing paper and pen, I wrote short notes for Lycette, Sharada and Anup, in which I asked them to meet me for lunch at noon, at Ranga Villa. I had news. It cost me half a Rupee to have a messenger take the notes to them.

It was only 9:30 a.m., and while waiting for them, and to make room for our meeting, I moved my instruments into my study and fluffed the floor pillows in our living room, the square and sparsely furnished room I used for my music lessons and dance practice. Gangan's daughter had come earlier that day to wash the porous floor tiles, cooling the room as she cleaned it.

Gangan offered to go home to the village to have his wife cook some vegetable *samosas* and *masala dosais* for our lunch. I accepted. His wife was a much better cook than he was, when it came to savory fried food, and I wanted to avoid frying odors in the house. For refreshments, I would serve fresh coconut water cooled in our refrigerator, and later offer delicious Madrasi coffee Gangan would buy at the market and bring back in a large glass jar.

After weeks of worrying about Laila, I was in a party mood, a fact Gangan couldn't quite grasp. He kept looking at me furtively and, in doing so, bumped into furniture and jumped when I called him. I could see he was wondering what had gotten into me. I wanted to hug him and tell him that everything would be okay, but that would have embarrassed him to no end. Hugs, or even touching, were totally out of the question between mistress and servant. It was, of course, ridiculous in my eyes, but it kept everyone on an even keel in our small society. Still, only if to stop him worrying, I needed to give him a clue.

"Good news today from my music teacher. That's why I'm inviting my friends."

His face lit up and I saw his shoulders relax. "Very good, Sir. Very good."

I guess I would never convince him to stop calling me sir.

Lycette arrived on her bicycle. "So, where is everybody?" she asked.

"Stefan should be here any minute, and Sharada too."

"So, Stefan is now part of the "Free Laila Campaign?" she said. She stared at me questioningly, her mouth turned into a derisive pout.

"He actually helped a lot when we went to Prakash's house for dinner. As you know, my husband's opinion counts as *my* opinion in this town. Anyway, the other night, he covered my back and kept the conversation with Prakash open and neutral when I froze. I don't think I could have gotten through the evening without him. I think Prakash would have swatted me aside like a bug."

Just then, Sharada showed up on foot and left her sandals by the door, next to mine and Lycette's. She came into the living room and chose to sit cross-legged on a thin mat rather than the pillow I offered her. Soon after, the familiar sound of a scooter engine roared up the road, coughed, sputtered and died. Stefan rushed in, and I stopped him for a second to tell him that things were all right between Prakash and me. He looked relieved at the good news and went into his study to drop his satchel. When he returned, he lowered himself on the floor next to me.

A few minutes later, Norma and Anup emerged from the jungle path, followed by Rishu who, no doubt, had been double-dipping for milk and treats at their house. "We are returning your cat," said Norma, with a grin.

It was Anup who had given me information when I despaired of ever being in Prakash's good graces, and I was glad to give him credit for telling me about Laila. "I have more news," I informed them, as they pulled pillows off a chair they'd been piled on, to sit on the floor.

Soon the house was alive with chatter. It wasn't a party, but it felt like one and made me happy. It had been a long time since I'd heard laughter in my home. My guests settled down, and, on the floor next to me, Gangan set a tray with a bucket of ice, a tall pitcher of coconut water, and some glasses which I filled and passed around.

The smell of fresh samosas and potato-filled masala dosais wafted deliciously from the kitchen and when Gangan brought them in, along with small plates and a bowl of green chutney, they disappeared in minutes. He proudly retrieved the empty platter. The rumors were true. His wife made the best samosas and dosais in Adyar.

"So, what happened? Tell us," said Lycette, impatiently.

"What did you learn about that poor girl?" asked Anup, taking control of the gathering. Even when seated, his tall stature, long white mane and thick salt-and-pepper eyebrows inspired respect, and Stefan looked surprised, but he didn't comment. I remembered now that he hadn't known of my previous conversations with Anup.

I brought everyone up-to-date on the past few days' events, starting with the Ayushkarma ceremony and Prakash's invitation for dinner on Saturday night to deliver the photos I had taken. I recounted how we had looked at the large album together, and how surprised he had been to discover in it some shots taken by Laila. "I think that those photos are what prompted Laila to open a dialogue with her father. At first, he seemed to view photography as a hobby for rich people. He wasn't making the connection between Laila using my camera to take a few shots, and her desire to seriously study photography, but her enthusiasm won him over. And when he started really listening to her, she surprised him by revealing that she was ready to leave the protection of the house she'd relied on all these years, and venture into the world. She even mentioned her desire to visit you at Kalakshetra," I said, to Sharada, who brought her hands to her mouth in surprise. "At that point," I concluded, "I got a little emotional, and Stefan and I packed up and left."

People in the room were quiet, maybe attempting to recreate in their mind the scene I had just described. After a minute I continued. "As you can imagine, I started to worry that maybe I shouldn't have been a witness to that emotional breakthrough. Laila was obviously using our presence to make her case. In a way, we are part of the new world she now wants to join. But I kept thinking that, in the eyes of her father, I was the intruder."

"You were," said Stefan, under his breath.

Looking in Stefan's direction, I acknowledged his remark. "I didn't want to admit it, but you were right about that, and he could have been angry at me, and kicked me out of his class. But when I met with him this morning, I learned that my secret intrusion into his life had been forgiven. Not only that, but I think he's seen the light about Laila. He'll support her in regaining some autonomy. And he asked me to give her photography lessons."

There was a round of applause and congratulations in the room. In perfect Indian fashion, Anup's head bobbed enthusiastically. "Well done!"

Sharada waited for the din to calm down and said, "So this happened Saturday night? Why did you wait till today to tell us about having dinner at Prakash's?"

"Because I had no idea what would happen this morning. I was prepared for the worst." As I said that, my hand went involuntarily to the finger of my left hand where a faithful coral image of Ganesh, the elephant God, sat in a silver setting. I had bought that ring for myself, during a short pilgrimage to Madurai Temple, and had been wearing it ever since. Ganesh, after all, was the lord of wisdom and success, the remover of obstacles and patron saint of artists. I felt sure He was protecting and guiding me, in the same way my prayers to the Virgin Mary had protected me from harm as a child, by diverting my stepfather's violence away from me. I sometimes wondered if what, at the time, I looked upon as small miracles, were more simply an expression of my faith in a positive universe.

"Now that we know that Laila and her father are discussing the future, I may speak to my brother about filling the part-time assistant librarian post that just became available," said Anup. "We might start by offering her just a few hours a week to get her out of her house. Minouche, you are the only one who has spoken to her recently, do you think she could handle it?"

"Honestly, I don't know... I know that she's an experienced gardener and has shown interest in photography, and that she speaks good English. Other than that, I still know little about her."

"But you'll be able to find out more when you teach her photography," said Lycette.

Norma, who had been listening quietly, perked up. "Maybe, her duties in the library could be tied to the topics she's interested in. For instance, have her catalogue botanical works and dance books."

"Good idea," said her husband. "The small salary she would receive would also give her a sense of independence. And she could save it toward buying a camera."

"Or chocolate!" said Sharada, surprising us all.

Lycette slapped her knees and added, "Or those delicious coconut meringues they sell in town."

"Oh! I love those," Stefan said. He had been so quiet during our discussion, that I had almost forgotten he was there.

"And we could take her to a movie," said Lycette, looking at Sharada and me.

Sharada was frowning in concentration. "I have an idea which I will need to discuss with Kalakshetra's director," she said. "Laila knows dancing better than any of my advanced students. If she is up to it, I would like to invite her to assist me in a couple of classes and see how she does."

"That might appeal to her," said Norma excitedly. It was a rare show of enthusiasm in a friend I valued for her gracious reserve, a quality that had kept me from complaining about Stefan around her.

"Just take it one step at a time," said Anup with finality. "For now, it is enough that she understands she has options. It will slowly change her view on life, and the rest will flow from that."

I kept silent, happy to sit among my favorite people, feeling grateful for their past support and warm presence. Together, we had reignited Laila's life flame and pushed open a door for her. Except for my encouragements and some photography lessons, my role in Laila's emancipation was mostly over. I knew the rest would be up to her.

One by one my guests slipped on their sandals, and I saw them off before sitting in an old cane armchair we kept on the front porch. The heat was oppressive. It bounced off the gravel path fronting our house, and Rishu, who had been sleeping on the front steps, woke up and lay down at my feet, in the shade. I was vaguely aware of Gangan picking up the remnants of our lunch when I heard a crystalline crash followed by a short cry in Tamil. Probably a broken glass. No big deal. They were cheap and easy to replace, so I chose not to interfere. Gangan would insist on taking care of it himself. So, I was surprised and upset when I heard Stefan's admonishing him in a curt tone of voice, and poor Gangan mumbling an apology. Stefan's outburst at that trivial loss was not warranted and it dispelled the happy mood my circle of friends had created around me.

I yawned. I suddenly felt tired, unsettled. Why should I feel that way when things were going so well? Laila was on her way. Our grants provided all we needed and more. And in spite of this uncalled-for incident, Stefan and I had been getting along better these days. So, why the weariness? Why that unexplainable feeling of loss when all I needed to do was study and focus on my next step?

CHAPTER FORTY-SIX

MAR 1962 - THE MUSIC FESTIVAL

In the weeks that followed, I made rapid progress on the veena. The added classes I was getting from Prakash were making a marked difference.

My study schedule was busy, but I was happy to pick up Laila and spend a couple of hours a week with her, at the beach or the T.S. campus, so she could practice how to focus lenses, work with the ever-changing natural light, and use a light meter. Later, I planned to take her to the Mylapore Temple to capture inspiring stone sculptures of dancers, and goddesses, but not yet. I didn't want to expose her to a crowded situation until she felt she was ready for it.

Meanwhile, Stefan had fallen back into a demanding routine as he prepared for a final in June, three months from now, but we'd made plans to take a trip as soon as it was over.

Looking back, I still couldn't understand the reasons for the apprehension I had experienced after Laila's big breakthrough. So, I put the memory of that unsettling feeling behind me as a moment of stress and exhaustion.

On March 15, the winter weather was bright and temperate, and the heavy dampness and mildew-filled weeks of monsoon appeared months away. As I stepped outside into the garden and breathed in the invigorating smell of all the green life around me, I reflected that I'd now been living in India for over two and half years. Longer than I expected when I'd first arrived. My chest swelled with my breath, in tune with this perfect moment.

During a lesson, yesterday, Prakash had reminded us about the yearly music festival to be held in Madurai at the end of March. The music college would close for a week, as most of the musicians on staff and many of the students would attend. I was looking forward to the drive down there on a bus chartered by Kalakshetra, whose senior students would also attend.

According to Lycette, driving from Madras to Madurai would take nine hours. Anticipating how hot the day would get, our departure had been scheduled at 4:30 a.m. Way too early if one liked sleeping in, but it was the Indian way. The earlier, the better.

When I told Stefan about my plan to attend that music festival, he was less than happy. "I wish you would change your mind about going. I need you to attend the French Consulate reception with me on that date. You know how important it is for me to have a presence there, as I wait for a French passport."

I smiled encouragingly. "So, go! You don't need me for the Consul to notice your presence. I remember he quite liked talking with you."

Nervously shaking his head, Stefan said, "That may be true but he might also notice your absence, and think there is a rift between us, which would look bad for me and my passport application," he said. "You know how gossip starts."

"On the other hand," I said, in the most persuasive tone of voice I could muster, "it's a perfect opportunity for you to boast how my presence at this most exclusive South Indian music festival puts France on the map. Because, for sure, I'll be introduced to important pundits as the French student from the CCKM."

"Do you think he'll care about that?"

"He should. That's good public relations work, and it's free," I said, chuckling.

But Stefan was not amused. "I can see that your mind is made up."

"Well, it would look really bad for me if I were not present at that event. Prakash reminded me personally, and my teachers and classmates will all be there, as it's the most important music event of the year. What would it say about me if I blew it off?"

We had left it at that, and on the appointed day, I got up at 4 a.m. and sneaked out of the house without waking Stefan who had been up past midnight studying. I couldn't help but wonder if his unwillingness to see me go away for three days was only caused by the status of his passport application. I knew, of course, that being a stateless Polish refugee was very demoralizing for him. The French immigration bureaucracy was hopelessly slow, and I understood his impatience. But he had never made a show of needing me to secure his papers before. Maybe something else had triggered his reluctance to see me travel with my friends. Could it be that he was concerned about my increasing show of independence?

The chartered bus was new. It sped smoothly on the recently resurfaced road, and the discreet purr of its engine was soothing and didn't disrupt conversation.

Sharada, and the twelve girls she was chaperoning, sat in the front portion of the bus with Lycette and me. The two middle rows where we'd stowed our bedding rolls separated us from the boys who sprawled lazily in the rear. I noticed the two sides exchanging furtive nods and glances.

"That's what flirting looks like in Madras," said Lycette, with a smile. She made it her business to know everything that went on in Kalakshetra. "Look at Ambigai. She's in love with Raman, the boy in the very back row."

Observing the young people made me feel light and happy. Happier than usual because I was on the move and on my own with a sense of freedom I hadn't experienced in a while. Maybe being alone was empowering because I had walked out of my house on my own terms. It was bizarre, but I almost felt a few years younger. I wanted to giggle and recycle silly jokes.

"So, how did Stefan take your decision to join us?" asked Lycette, in a low voice.

"He called on my spousal duties, and my responsibility to accompany him to a function given by the French Consulate tomorrow, but I didn't give in, even though it was strange to push my personal agenda ahead of his. A first for me."

"I know what you mean. I went through that process several times," said Lycette. "Three times actually, one for each of my husbands. I remember watching the leash stretch and fray, and waking up one day to find it was severed."

I wasn't sure how strong my emotional leash was and didn't want to examine it. Right now, I was feeling whole and happy.

"I'm just learning to fly," I sang, and flapped my elbows like wings. We started laughing.

After a while, the excitement died down and we all stretched and rested as best we could. By 6 a.m. we were starving and stopped to eat a breakfast of vegetable *samosas, idlis* and buttermilk at a roadside stand. Many of us refilled thermos bottles with strong coffee before getting back on the bus, satiated and ready for a real nap, since we wouldn't arrive to our destination until two in the afternoon.

When we reached Madurai, it was buzzing with traffic, even though the festival was not due to start until the next day. Buses, lorries, taxis, motorcycles, hand-pulled rickshaws, bicycles and excited men, women and children filled the streets.

"Last time I attended this festival," said Sharada, "a dozen chariots and floats were marched in procession and blessed before the festival's official opening. Minouche, I hope you brought your camera. Few outsiders get a chance to witness this event."

The bus had come to a standstill, and I lowered my window. Around us, the statues of Hindu gods half buried under heady flower garlands were already being paraded on antique wooden floats. Their decorated wheels were so huge they dwarfed the twenty or more men pulling the chariot structures with ropes as thick as the ones I had seen on ships.

"I don't know why Indians call them chariots," said Lycette. "They look more like shrines on wheels."

At the sight of two elephants, outfitted with thickly gilded and embroidered blankets that also covered their foreheads, I grabbed my camera and got a few shots of them pushing a chariot towards the center of town, where the famed Meenakshi Temple rose like a graceful mountain of carved stones.

As we came closer, the excited voices of the people filling the street washed through the open bus windows. I was overwhelmed by the general commotion and sighed with relief when the bus, having finally managed to bypass the temple, pulled into a calm street and stopped in front of the old boarding school we were to stay in.

The front of the building was not elegant. It was dark and looked like a decrepit fort, with narrow windows cut into thick stone walls. The entrance, a massive medieval-looking double-door, was reinforced with forged iron bars and hinges resembling some I had seen on images of British garrisons.

We alighted from the bus and entered. The boys were directed to another wing of the school. In contrast to the severe façade, the classrooms, and especially the dorms, were spacious and clean. They were free of furniture, except for lockers and bare sleeping cots, as students and visitors were expected to have their own bedding. Large windows overlooked an open verandah that was bordered by slender columns covered with climbing vines and bougainvillea. The length and edge of the verandah abutted a broad flight of worn steps leading down to a wide, flowing river.

After dropping off our bags and bedding, and with Sharada's approval, we hiked our saris up and ran down a dozen stone steps to dip our feet in the river that submerged the lower treads, and splash cool water on our faces and necks. A couple of steps continued under the surface of the water. The river bottom was soft and silty.

Sharada called for attention. She had an announcement to make. "Listen girls, we will be going to the Meenakshi Amman Temple for a prayer ceremony in an hour. After that we will eat dinner in a facility hosting other schools and institutions attending the festival. Curfew is at 9 p.m., which will allow you enough sleep to get up at 4:30 a.m. to bathe."

"Teacher," said Chandra, raising her hand, "I did not see any showers near the dorms."

"Who needs showers when you have a river?" said Sharada. "And…"

"But is the river safe?" interrupted Chandra, peering nervously at the wavelets licking her feet.

Lycette splashed water in Chandra's direction. "I have it from a reliable source that no croc has been sighted near this school for the past hundred years," she said, with a wink at Sharada.

"Pay attention," said Sharada. "Yes Chandra, bathing in the river is safe as long as you do not do anything stupid." At that the other girls smirked, and Sharada called them to order. "As I mentioned earlier, you girls will bathe first, starting at 4:30 a.m. You will need to be back in our dorm by 5 a.m. to let the boys bathe. And, no peeking please!" At which, all the girls giggled.

Getting back in the dorm, I dried my feet and unfolded my bedding on one of the cots. I fluffed my pillow and lay down for a short while. It was wonderful to have nothing to do except be. No classes, no homework, no arguments, no cook to supervise, no errands, no irritating neighbors. I felt myself float up and then down, down... and fell asleep. When Lycette nudged me awake half-an-hour later, the girls were smoothing their braids and changing into fresh saris. I hurried to do the same.

We got back on the bus and it dropped us close to the Meenakshi Amman Temple, a shrine dedicated to Lord Shiva and his consort, the Goddess Parvati. I already knew it was supposed to be one of India's architectural marvels but I was not prepared for its grandeur or size. The fortified west gate, a gigantic tower entirely covered with the carved figures of dancers, musicians and gods, loomed over me, making me feel small and insignificant. It reminded me of some pictures of the famous Khajuraho temples I had seen in a book.

"Madurai has been around in one form or another for 2,500 years," said Sharada, sounding like a tourist guide. I guessed she had been doing some reading while we were resting. "It was an important commercial center and traded with Greece and Rome as early as 500 BC."

Awed, a girl whispered, "Are you saying that this temple is 2400 years old?"

"No. The original temple was so rich, it became a target for warring neighbors," answered Sharada. She checked the brochure she held in her hands: "It says here that it was burnt down more than once, but was restored in the 1600's."

Most of the temples I'd visited had four *gopurams*, the elaborate towering structures that characterized South Indian temples. Usually, one for each of the entrances facing north, south, east, and west. But this fabulous temple counted ten of them. From where I stood, some of these gopurams appeared to be more than a hundred feet tall, and two of them were either gilded or covered with real gold.

After checking with Sharada that I wouldn't offend anyone by taking photos, I got my camera out. The monumental size of the edifice made it hard to find a good shooting angle, and I turned my attention to the curvaceous figures of heavenly dancers, whose bodies carved on stone pillars were darkened and smudged by the touch of a thousand hands.

Soon we entered a small interior shrine and settled quietly on the right side of the room, sitting cross-legged on the floor behind the women who had preceded us inside.

Bare-chested priests, whose heads were artfully shaved to leave only a topknot of hair on their shiny skulls, sat on the floor to the left of the hall. Behind them, an assembly of male musicians, all Brahmins, swayed in time with the Sanskrit verses intoned by the head priest leading the ceremony. They added their trained voices to the chanting, and I felt the hair rise on the nape of my neck and on my arms.

The powerful rhythm of the chanting had put me in a kind of trance, and Sharada had to tap my shoulder to signal we had to leave.

"It's so beautiful," I murmured. "I don't want to leave."

She smiled indulgently. "Do not worry, you will get more of it before we return to Madras."

"Are all these musicians performing at the festival?" asked Lycette, who had rejoined us.

"I believe so. Most of them anyway," whispered Sharada, bringing her finger to her lips to shush us.

Turning away from her, Lycette asked in a hushed voice. "Do you know any of them?"

"The fair-skinned one in the front row is my vocal teacher at the CCKM," I said, a little too casually.

"Ooh!" exhaled Lycette behind her hand. "The one you had a crush on? He's quite handsome."

I ignored her comment. Seeing KV among his Brahmin peers made me realize how absurd it had been for me to even fantasize about him. But as French poets had rhymed for centuries, *le coeur a ses raisons que la raison ignore.* The heart claims reasons that reason ignores. It certainly had been true of me.

Directing Lycette's attention to another musician, I whispered, "The stiff old Brahmin to his left, the one with the white topknot, teaches *gottuvadyam* at the college, you know, the slide-veena."

"Ah! I recognize him," said Lycette, as we continued to whisper behind our hands. "I heard him in concert. I am surprised he's here. I heard he never rides in a car or a bus. In fact, he is famous for walking everywhere he goes."

I slapped my upper arm to kill a mosquito that had landed on it. "Well, unless he started walking three months ago, he obviously broke his rule," I joked. "I should ask Anup about him. He would know."

"I used to think our neighborhood was kind of boring, you know. But between the T.S., Kalakshetra and the music college, there are lots of interesting characters," said Lycette. She sat still for a moment, then, leaning toward me, she tapped my arm. "By the way, I meant to ask you. How come Laila didn't come? Was she invited?"

"She was. Sharada invited her, but Prakash declined the invitation. He didn't think she was ready to be part of a crowd. Maybe next year."

We stood up and retraced our steps through the temple grounds, circumventing a large water tank where pilgrims were performing purifying ablutions. For now, I was content to follow a surge of people under the west tower, through the open gate and into the street.

The day's heat had abated and a cooling breeze made the evening pleasantly temperate as we entered a large tent erected against one wall of the temple. We were invited to sit down on long straw mats that had been rolled out in parallel rows.

As was the custom, several Brahmin cooks and helpers walked back and forth between the rows, sprinkling a thin stream of water over our outstretched right hand to rinse it. it was a civilized gesture that always thrilled me. They proceeded to serve a plain but traditional South Indian meal on freshly washed banana leaves. Water was ladled into tall tumblers, accompanied by short tin goblets of thinned buttermilk. I was starving, and dove into the food with my fingers, a skill I'd finally mastered.

By the time we returned to our dorm, around seven o'clock, I was exhausted. The windows opening to the verandah had been closed, leaving the air inside the large room warmer than outside. The ceiling fans hanging from the high ceiling spun but did nothing to lower the temperature. I was hot, and tired, and worried about waking up at 4:30 a.m. Hopefully, someone would pull me out of bed.

As I finally nodded off, wondering what it would be like, in a few hours, to bathe in a river under the stars, it occurred to me that, apart from answering Lycette's inquiry this morning, I hadn't had time to think about Stefan. I wondered if he was missing me.

CHAPTER FORTY-SEVEN

THE RIVER

"Time to get up!" Sharada's voice reached me through foamy layers of sleepiness. I opened my eyes and saw her standing by the dorm's door. Turning my head, I glanced toward the high windows that bordered the verandah. I expected to see stars, but the moonlight pouring in was so bright I blinked, momentarily blinded. Jumping up from the cot on which I rested, I stumbled on the bottom edge of the green sari I had slept in, and found my way to the verandah door that stood open. A giant moon hung against the grey velour sky, its round face so close I wanted to rise on my toes and stretch fingers to touch it. Magic was in the air. Everything felt possible.

The breeze carried the faint smell of smoke from cooking fires burning upwind, and below me, the river that had been greenish the day before, had turned into a quicksilver stream.

I stepped outside, and stood at the top of the stone steps descending to the water. It made me think of Benares and its famous ghats which I'd seen in books. Here too, there was no beach. A scattering of sari-clad girls who had completed their bath were climbing the steps back to where I stood, and it occurred to me that they looked like music notes on a staff. It made me smile.

The night air was balmy, and as I descended to the middle of the steps, I observed the moon-washed line of trees visible across the river that wasn't as wide as the Ganges, but wider than the Seine in Paris. Further down, Arya, one of Sharada's advanced dance students, was just starting her morning ablutions. She slowly stepped in the river, filled a small brass vessel she carried with her and, holding it with both hands, poured the water over her bowed head. She repeated the process over her shoulders and breasts. Eyes downcast, she appeared to be praying, her lips moving to the rhythmic stanzas of Sanskrit verses that rose and fell like the beating of wings of an invisible bird. The tangle of bangles on her wrists and the gold chains I had seen around her neck shone white in the moonlight, while the wet sari draped over her toned dancer's body gave her the appearance of the voluptuous sandstone figures carved on the nearby temple walls.

In this light, she looked like an apparition, and I stared in fascination as she finished her morning bath and returned to a step where she had left a dry sari.

She peeled off the top part of her wet sari and wrapped the end of the one she had brought in reserve around her waist. The wet one slithered to the stone floor. She swiftly pleated the six-yard-long length of green cloth against her stomach and threw the end of it over her shoulder. The switch was so flawless I might have missed it if I hadn't been staring at her. She then untied a knot in her hair and let her thick braid snake down to the small of her back. She bent down, gathered the wet bundle and prepared to head back up. Aware my staring might embarrass her, I looked the other way.

At that moment, I sensed a shift around me, as if gravity had ceased to root me to the ground. I was feathery light. Under the moonlight, the sweep of steps descending into the river was suddenly animated with faceless translucent figures, and I became aware of a glow over the river. Exhilarated and frightened by the strangeness around me, I closed my eyes, waiting for the baffling sensations to subside.

On hearing Arya start up the stairs, the silver toe rings on her feet heralding her passage on the worn stones, I turned around and opened my eyes.

I froze in confusion. The woman facing me wasn't Arya. It was a stranger, but there was something oddly familiar about her.

"You've returned," she said.

I felt the heat of her presence. The tendrils of her voice, that sounded soft and musical, enveloped me. With a shock, I realized she hadn't spoken aloud in English or French. Her words simply hummed in my mind and I understood her.

I stared at her in surprise and my breath caught in my throat for, in the milky moonlight, her eyes were hazel-green, like mine, and her sari the same shade of green as mine. Her moist skin glowed golden in the moonlight and light shone around her like a halo. As quick images flashed in front of my eyes, I saw that she was the embodiment of everything I hoped to become. She was essence of woman. Was it a goddess I was looking at?

I wanted to know what she saw when she looked at me? Did she see my eyes, hazel-green like hers? The lime-green color we both wore? The deep calluses veena strings had dug into my fingertips? She observed me intently and her eyes lit up with laughter when she asked, "Don't you recognize me? I'm you, in another lifetime. Tell me, what are you here to learn this time?"

What was I here to learn? Intuitively, I knew she wasn't talking about love or marriage. It had to be about the paths I had discovered in India. Dance and music. Music and dance. I admired dancers, but music was ultimately something that defined me better. It alone threw light on me, unlike dancing or theater.

"It doesn't matter," she said voicelessly, looking into my eyes. "You can do it all because it is already in you. Several centuries ago you were born here into a wealthy family. You were an important patron of the arts, but you never received the gift of music or dancing. So you've returned to learn and fulfill that dream, and take our culture back to the West." She turned her palms to me and blessed me. "Meditate," she said. "Remember who you are."

I was seized with vertigo, falling through the layers and layers of lives from which I stemmed, as if a trap door had been sprung under my feet. Feeling faint, I closed my eyes for an instant and when I opened them, the moon's reflection was shimmering on the empty stone steps where, a moment earlier, a spirit, or a goddess, had stood to offer me a message.

A few feet below me, Arya lifted the bottom of her sari to continue her climb back to the dorm. As she passed me, I reached and touched her arm to reassure myself. Her skin was cool and solid under my hand. She turned her head, and I met her eyes. They were brown in the milky light.

"Minouche!" I heard my name being called. It was Lycette, descending the steps two at a time to where I stood. She adjusted the damp scarf wrapped around her head and handed me a large towel. "Here. You'll need it when you get out. The boys will be here soon, and you won't get another chance to bathe until tomorrow morning." She stared at me. "What's with you? You look like you've seen a ghost." She took my elbow, helped me down the steps and led me to the water's edge. "Hurry up," she said.

How long had the vision lasted? A few seconds? Minutes? I was reeling. What had I seen? What did it all mean?

I let my sari drop to the ground and submerged myself in the river. The cold seized me like a giant hand squeezing the air out of my lungs. I shivered and heard my teeth clatter. Blocking the chill from my mind,

I pushed away to the middle of the river, turned on my back and floated down the slow current for a few minutes, swimming back and floating down current again. Eyes locked on the paling sky, I searched for answers.

"Minouche! Get out! Now!" Standing on the riverbank, Sharada was waving at me. "Please, stay with the group. The water is safe near the steps, but there is no telling about the current if you swim away."

I obeyed and swam back. When I got out, the air was warm on my naked body and the steps slick under my feet. I quickly wrapped the dry towel Lycette had brought me around my shoulders, grateful for her thoughtfulness, and picked up the crumpled sari I'd slept in off the steps, Suddenly, I was shaking from head to toe. Everything around me looked different, more familiar. Had I really been an Indian in a previous life? I certainly felt at home in Madras. Were there even such things as previous lives? Obviously, there were if you were a Hindu and believed in reincarnation. But did I believe in reincarnation? My head was a hopeless jumble of questions that needed answers, but that would have to wait. Right now, covered with goose bumps as the sky lost its glory and morphed into pre-dawn grey, I felt very much alive, and mysteriously protected.

CHAPTER FORTY-EIGHT

REINCARNATION

Back in the dorm, my companions were adding the finishing touches to their dress, choosing their jewelry, combing and re-braiding their hair. I was doing my best to concentrate on the choice of a fresh sari and blouse, but I felt disconnected from the goings-on around me. Outside, the boys had arrived for their morning ablutions. Splashes and hoots could be heard, and Sharada had taken a seat near the windows, making it impossible for any of the girls to peek at them.

I dressed quickly and lay back down on my bedroll. I closed my eyes. What had I seen and what did it mean? I couldn't make sense of that experience in a rational way. I must have been dreaming, for there were no such things as apparitions. Yet, I had run into a mysterious being. And in my heart, I wondered if it was Saraswati–the Hindu goddess of music, art and wisdom–who had communicated wordlessly, mind-to-mind with me.

She'd told me I'd come back to fulfill my dream of learning music and dancing which I'd failed to master in a previous life. It was a seductive theory, but still, just a theory. I couldn't deny my strong affinity for India. It was almost as if Stefan had only been the incentive for me to get here, and there were days when I thought that I belonged here more than he did. Days when my love of everything Indian sustained me when confronted by his self-centeredness and controlling ways. But in spite of missing my mother and my friends, I'd never considered returning to Paris. Madras felt familiar under my feet, as if I had walked its streets and prayed in its shrines for a lifetime. And the sensuous stirrings that seized me at the sight of the temples' erotic carvings were guileless, free and open, unlike the Christian teachings I had received as a child. So maybe it was true. One may travel from life to life, and maybe return to a cherished place.

Sharada's voice pulled me out of my reflections.

"Let us go, girls. Breakfast is waiting for us in town. We do not have a bus, so we walk."

That suited me fine, for the words of the goddess, or whoever it was I had seen, kept turning in my mind like a hamster on a wheel. Letting the other girls go in front of me, I sought Lycette out and linked my arm into hers as we descended into the dew-covered street. In a low voice, to avoid being overheard, I asked, "Do you believe in reincarnation?"

Lycette looked at me. I could see she was surprised. Eyebrows raised, she shook her head and quipped, "What kind of question is that so early in the morning? Why do you want to know?"

The sun was rising and a small pond at the foot of a crumbling wall glowed like a mirror. Boulders from the wall had rolled down and come to rest in the still water where they lay, half submerged among water lilies and lotus leaves that floated like flat round trays. A water buffalo sloshed slowly in the shallows, nibbling lazily on flowers and leaves.

"Never mind why. I asked you first." I didn't want to discuss what had happened to me. This was not the right place or time, but I was dying to hear other people's thoughts on the subject.

A man who had been riding slowly alongside us on a bicycle,

abruptly rattled his throat and spit a jet of red betel nut juice sideways into the pond, missing the moist black muzzle of the buffalo by a few inches.

"Phew! Watch where you spit!" Lycette shouted, indignantly. The man snickered and pedaled on, leaving our group behind.

"*Desgraciado! Basura loco!*" she swore after him in Spanish. The girls in front of us giggled.

I liked that about her. She was never afraid to speak her mind. So why was she procrastinating in answering my question?

"Tell me. What makes you ask?" she finally said, in a half amused, half puzzled tone of voice that made me think she wasn't taking me seriously. As casually as I could, for I still felt somewhat under the spell of the apparition, I repeated, "Just asking if you believe in reincarnation. Do you think there's such a thing?"

She smirked. "I hope not," she said, in a sarcastic tone of voice, "because when I die, I don't want to run the risk of being reborn as a Chinese farmer breaking my back in a communist paddy field, or worse, come back as a dog or a donkey."

Sharada, who was walking behind us, tugged hard on Lycette's sari. "You are being quite blasphemous, Lycette."

We slowed our pace to let her catch up.

"Not really," said Lycette. "What is blasphemous about not wanting to come back as a girl someone may want to trade for a camel or several goats? I like who I am now, and when I'm done, I'm done."

"You are imagining the worst-case scenario," said Sharada. "But if you live an honorable life, follow the precepts of your religion and acquire good karma, who knows? You might return as a greater person."

"No thanks. I intend to do all that I can in this lifetime. I don't need, or want, an extension."

Obviously tired of the exchange, Lycette excused herself and rejoined the girls who had moved ahead. I wasn't overly surprised.

Mysticism had no attraction for her. I fell into step with Sharada.

"What about you, Minouche?" she asked, turning to me. "Do you believe in reincarnation?"

"I'm not sure, though sometimes, I feel like I've lived here before."

Sharada's dark face was alive in the morning light. The diamond on the side of her nose scintillated like a tiny star brightening the pure white of her eyes around charcoal black irises. She held up the palms of her hands in my direction to interrupt me, and I saw the deep indentation of her lifeline, running like an ochre river in the pink flesh. A lifeline for this one life, I thought.

"I too have felt that way before, but it is easy for me to accept it as more than *just* a coincidence," she said seriously. "I believe in karma, so I accept that I may have visited other places in other lives."

"As someone else, or as your same self in a different life?"

"Sometimes I think I may have been someone else, but it could just be my imagination," said Sharada, with a shrug.

"What if someone told you that you had lived in Paris before, and had been an important painter, or dancer there? Would you believe it?" I pressed on, the goddess' words fresh on my mind.

"I think it would depend on who told me. It would have to be someone special. Someone I could trust. I also think I would pray and meditate on it to try and find a resonance of truth in me," she said.

We had arrived at the large and festive tent where breakfast was being prepared. Sharada excused herself to greet some of the dignitaries and musicians she was acquainted with, and, noticing that Lycette was engaged in a conversation with some girls from Kalakshetra, I turned back to explore the adjoining park that had been chosen as the concert grounds. I was surprised by the mega size of the stage and the colorful canvas roof covering it until I remembered the dance and drama performances scheduled for the last day of the festival. The backdrop depicted a giant image of the God Shiva as Nataraja, the divine dancer depicted with many arms. I loved the stories about Nataraja, whose dancing had coalesced star dust to create our universe.

Behind me, the area appeared big enough to accommodate thousands of people. It was an impressive sight. I came close to the stage to admire a tall set of peacock-shaped oil lamps. They were beautiful, made of heavy brass and probably on loan from the temples. They smelled like ghee, the clarified butter used to fuel them. Images of gods and gurus lined the edge of the stage, their frames smothered with thick garlands of marigolds, frangipani and jasmine, whose fragrant scent rose on the cool morning air.

A couple of curtains hung like banners on both sides of the stage. Somewhere behind the giant backdrop of Nataraja that was propped center stage, I heard what sounded like a veena being played, but it wasn't a song. What resounded in the still morning air was the insistent plucking of two single strings, like someone fine-tuning an instrument. *Pling, pling, pling... plong, plong, plong... pling, plong... pling, plong.*

I climbed the rickety steps to the stage, walked behind the backdrop and found myself face to face with Prakash. He was alone, finessing the tuning of his instrument. I stayed and observed how he worked to move one of the frets a smidgeon to the right where it needed to go. He continued massaging the hard wax the fret was set into, sounding the corresponding note and listening to its intonation without ever looking up. His concentration was total. I coughed to get his attention. "Namaste, sir. I look forward to hearing your performance later tonight."

He sucked on the chew stashed in his left cheek and glanced at me with his mismatched eyes, which had so unsettled me the first time I sat in his class. He nodded a silent greeting before bending over the neck of the veena to perfect his task, and I realized that there were no technicians or repairmen around. Apparently, each musician was responsible for his instrument.

I turned around, found the steps, and nearly fell off in my haste to rejoin my group in the breakfast tent.

After we'd eaten, Sharada gathered her flock and made an announcement. "It is now 9 a.m. and the concerts start at 3 p.m. So, let us meet at the bus in ten minutes. We will ride into town for sightseeing and some shopping and come back here for lunch. Remember to stay together. This festival attracts thousands of people, and you don't want to get lost in the crowd."

"Yes teacher," answered the girls in unison. Every time I heard them say that, I felt l was back in elementary school, on my way to a museum maybe, a trip we often made on Thursday afternoons.

After lunch, we returned to the school. Walking around in the hot dusty street had taken its toll on me, and I was ready to lie down and rest in anticipation of the many concerts scheduled on that first day of the festival.

I was deep in sleep when Lycette pulled on my foot and woke me up. "It's two-thirty. Let's go," she said. I hastily straightened my hair and drank a tall glass of water from a large clay jug someone had placed on a table by the dorm's door.

With Sharada's permission, Lycette and I left the other girls behind and made our way to the concert grounds where we elbowed our way into the growing throng to find a good vantage point on the floor mats that had been laid down for the first fifty rows of spectators. The late comers would need to bring their own mats or sit on the grass.

After a long wait, the festival began with pundits praising their gods, their gurus, and the artists. In Tamil, with an occasional sprinkling of English, long-winded speaker after speaker extolled the merits of Tyagaraja, a legendary Karnatic music composer who saw music as a means of experiencing the love of god. In good Indian fashion, several generations of musicians had declared him a Holy Man, and small shrines dedicated to him had sprouted in homes and schools all over

South India. Finally, some minor acts took the stage, and after they left, I felt the audience's anticipation rise, as the restless crowd got louder.

I spotted KV on the side of the stage and assumed he would be performing soon. Following my eyes, Lycette had seen him too. His fair coloring, slender youth and full head of black hair stood out among all the shaved heads. "What's so special about him?" she asked, puzzled.

"I guess it's the way he delivers the simplest tunes. When he opens his throat to find a note, his eyes always close, and he seems to enter a special place." It was hard to describe what it was like for me to watch his lips and feel their shape around the notes. I was mesmerized. I became the notes. I became music.

Lycette nodded. "If you look around, lots of those music pundits are old and quite rotund. He represents the new generation," she said. "I can see why you'd have a crush on him."

I let out a sigh. "It was absurd, of course. I was married and a foreigner, but music is a powerful conduit for longings, and when I daydreamed, it didn't matter that he was shorter than me, and a Brahmin, or that he was a widower with four children under ten. All the girls in his class had a crush on him too, which he didn't seem to notice. He paid the same amount of attention to each one of us, unaware of the magnetic attraction his students experienced in his presence."

And now, sitting a few feet from the stage as we waited for his performance, I became so fidgety that Lycette laughed. "There is nothing wrong with attraction. Attraction is good. It means you're alive."

I was grateful for her non-judgmental assessment. "I guess."

"Nothing wrong, as long as you don't act on it."

I flashed back to KV dropping a full glass of water on my living room floor when my fingers had, accidentally or intentionally, I can't really say, brushed his hand. I felt myself blushing. Lycette laughed, more of a snort than a laugh. "Keep in mind that KV is probably an ordinary man in other areas, you know, like eating, conversing, and in bed."

"Yeah, yeah. I know. But when he sings, I'm spellbound. I think we all are. That's his gift."

My last statement led me to think about Stefan. What was his gift? He was smart, and curious, and endeavored to be good, and do good, as his mother had taught him, and as the Hindu teachers also expected in the ashrams he visited. In spite of the migraines he suffered from, he showed an enormous capacity for studying, but it didn't seem to serve him well, judging from the way he complained about the nebulous material offered at the university. Chief among his criticisms, he deplored the fact that Krishnamurti's enlightening teachings weren't on their curriculum.

Little by little, the day's heat subsided, and the sweet smell of the coconut oil women used on their hair, rose to my nostrils. When I'd first joined Kalakshetra and had stood at the back of the class behind the twenty perfectly oiled braids of the dancers in front of me, that smell had made me nauseous. Nowadays, it smelled like home. But was it the "now" home, or a past home? In my mind I envisioned the green-eyed apparition and her summons. Had it really been a glimpse of me in a previous life? Who was I now? What was my gift? Was I a dreamer hoping to introduce a glimpse of India's artistic past to the established and often jaded stages of Parisian schools, concert halls and theaters?

I stared at the playful smoke rising from the oil lamps that lined the stage. It curled up and climbed into the cooling evening like the music filling my heart and my ever-circling thoughts.

CHAPTER FORTY-NINE

APR 1962 - HOME SWEET HOME

The Music Festival turned out to be an amazing display of South India's traditional performing arts, instrumental and vocal, as well as dancing and choreography. Three thousand years of Hindu identity had been represented in the performances of the most famous musicians in the country, and after bathing in the almost delirious atmosphere of the event for four days, I was more than ever inspired and committed to be thoroughly proficient on the veena, whatever it took. I would master that unique instrument and unveil its ancient music to the western world. What a gift that festival had been.

Exhausted but still exhilarated by my experience, I was impatient to share the highlights of my trip with Stefan, but it was early afternoon and when I got home, he was out. Gangan was out too and wouldn't return until it was time to prepare dinner.

I emptied my travel bag into a basket. The washing woman would have a lot of saris on her hands when she came tomorrow. Rishu purred and rubbed against my legs, edging me slowly toward the kitchen where his empty dish sat. His clever manipulations never ceased to make me laugh. I looked for the imported bag of dry kibbles I had purchased in an English store and refilled his bowl. His single-mindedness deserved a reward.

I took off my clothes and added them to the pile of dirty laundry I had brought back. The shower beckoned, hot and cold water, washcloth, soap and shampoo. As romantic as my bathing by moonlight had been, I was dying for a thorough wash and scrub.

Tepid water rushing from the sun-warmed pipe was delicious on my tired body. After a minute, I turned on the hot water to shampoo my hair and rid it of the coconut oil my classmates had convinced me to use, for that extra shine they loved, and to protect it from the sun.

The water was draining slowly, and I saw that a small ball of hair was blocking the drain. I picked it up and was surprised to find three long black hairs tangled with mine. Puzzled, I pulled one of them out and admired the thick glossy strand. It definitely wasn't one of mine, as my ash-blonde hair was soft, often unmanageable, and barely that long. I wondered if the washing woman had taken advantage of my absence to wash her hair in our bathroom.

Having servants in Madras was a strange business. The cook didn't sweep, the sweeper didn't wash clothes and the washing woman refused to touch a garden tool. As a result, I, who had been at the bottom of the food chain in Paris, had to have four domestics, all procured through Gangan. Though he was vague about it, Stefan and I were pretty sure that all were related to him. This was the way things worked around here, and I liked the idea that the money earned contributed to the welfare of Gangan's extended family.

Ignoring the used towel that hung on a hook behind the door, I reached for a fresh one on the linen shelf. My favorite bath towel, a soft length of powder-blue terry cloth large enough to wrap around my body like a sarong, was missing. Where was it? I didn't recall sending it to the laundry. I looked around but goose bumps were perking up on my arms and breasts, so I grabbed a regular towel to dry myself off.

Refreshed and dressed in a loose pajama bottom and a T-shirt, I retrieved a couple of letters from France that had been left on a corner of the dining room table. One was from Stefania, Stefan's mother, probably written in Polish as she didn't know French well enough to write in it, the other from Maman. I left Stefania's letter for Stefan to open, and eagerly snatched Maman's letter. To enjoy it better, I settled cross-legged on the covered floor mattress that served as a low sofa in our living room and slid my index finger under the envelope flap to open it. Stirred up by my return, Rishu was getting the crazies at the edge of the mattress, clawing at the colorful length of fabric that covered it and pushing his front legs under it.

As always, I was touched by the tenderness of my mother's words and the articulate way she expressed her feelings. Growing up during the depression, she had been taken out of school at fourteen and placed as an apprentice in a dry-cleaning store, a toxic job that had put bread on the table while her father searched for work. But the hard life she'd been dealt hadn't dampened her lyricism, and though she was no artist, she always drew sprigs of lily-of-the-valley in the margin of her pages, a trademark I remembered from my earliest childhood. I loved her letters. She had a way of entertaining me with ordinary news, telling me how one of her colleague's four-year-old son had fallen in the Luxembourg Gardens decorative pond while competing in a mini-sailing boats regatta with other children, or how Francine, my school friend, had come to see her with a black eye and no good excuse for it. Some of the passages in her letters reminded me of the best authors I had ever read. She wasn't afraid to express her feelings with words and pictures. Thinking of her warmed my heart. It was good to know I was loved so fiercely and unconditionally, and I resolved to write her back before I got too busy.

A jingly noise caught my attention. Rishu was chasing a shiny object he had teased from under the bedspread, sweeping it wildly across the tiled floor, bouncing it between his front paws, all the way back to the mattress on which I sat.

I bent forward and picked up his noisy toy. It was a tiny round bell, similar to the ones I wore around my ankles when I danced, but smaller and lighter. Mine had been selected by Sharada and mounted on a soft leather anklet. I threw it back at Rishu, finished reading Maman's letter, and walked to the kitchen for a glass of cold water from our small refrigerator. I caressed its smooth white enamel surface fondly. It was a late wedding present sent by Brigitte and my friends. The presence of this refrigerator had a big impact on our daily life, and seeing how proud of it Gangan was, one would have thought it belonged to him.

After being away for four days, I was rediscovering my surroundings in a different light. My home was welcoming and comfortable, and I was looking forward to Stefan's return to tell him about my astonishing vision and, maybe, boast a little about the famous people I had met.

With time on my hands, I entered my study. I was anxious to review last week's lessons. Piles of notebooks and textbooks on music and dance welcomed me. My veena sat on the floor next to the D.H. Lawrence and Huxley novels I had bought to improve my English. I saw my anklets on the windowsill where I had left them. I checked them both to see if any of the bells had fallen off, but they looked intact. The portable Olivetti typewriter sat on my desk with an unfinished letter to Brigitte. The room was a mess, but it was my mess, or better yet, my nest, and I loved to burrow in it like a mouse burrowing under leaves.

But my eagerness to study evaporated. I suddenly felt too tired. The Music Festival's accommodations had been adequate, but less than comfortable and I longed for a nap on a softer bed; My earlier desire to acquire a king-size bed for our bedroom had been quashed long ago. There wasn't enough space for such Western extravaganza. So, per Norma's savvy suggestion, I had settled for two single mattresses, fitted with washable slipcovers, and pushed against each other over two slender charpoys solidly strapped together. The result wasn't overly soft, as the mattresses rested upon the taunt straps characteristic of these native cots, but they were better than a bedroll stretched over the bare one I had slept on three nights in a row.

Without bothering to undress, I lifted a corner of the mosquito net Gangan had tucked in earlier after making the bed. I slid longingly on the cool mattress and breathed in the subtle scent of freshly laundered bedding. I closed my eyes. Turning on my stomach, for I had never learned to sleep on my back, I embraced my pillow. It was wonderful to be home. I let my body relax, my neck and shoulders, my arms, the small of my back, my legs, the arch of my foot, my forearms. Last, I made a conscious effort to relax my fingers, which were always tapping rhythms or practicing air veena. Stretching, I slid my left hand into the small space between the two mattresses, but stopped when my fingers came upon a foreign object caught into the straps supporting the mattress.

Intrigued, I pulled on it, but it was caught in the straps supporting my mattress. I toyed with the idea of leaving it there, whatever it was. I was so comfortable, I didn't want to move, but curiosity got the better of me. Had I lost one of my rings? It felt bigger and flatter than a ring. I rolled on my side and lifted the edge of my mattress to fetch it. I was surprised to see it was a cheap piece of jewelry in the shape of a crescent moon. I could see it was part of a set of ornaments dancers usually clasped in their hair; *Chandra*, the moon to the right, *Surya*, the sun, to the left. Along the part, they usually clipped an ornamental chain that ended with a fake gem that dangled below the hairline. I had such a set, except mine was of better quality.

What was a dancer's hair ornament doing in my bed? Suddenly

I wasn't sleepy anymore. My pulse accelerated and I shivered with tension. A bitter taste rose to my mouth as I reviewed all the little things that had puzzled me ever since coming home today; the long glossy hairs in the shower; my missing towel; the little bell Rishu had found under the bedspread in our living room, the fresh bed sheets and now, the cheap jewelry under my mattress.

Had Stefan used my absence to bring an exotic dancer or a prostitute into our home? In our bed even? It couldn't be any of the Kalakshetra dance students I knew. Their reputation was impeccable. So, who could it be? The question hung over my head like Damocles' sword. I was afraid of the answer. My hand flew to my chest to stop the pounding of my heart and I scrambled out of bed. Feeling sick, sad, and betrayed, I retreated to the living room to think things through.

By the time Gangan arrived to fix our dinner, I was angry. Anxious to test my suspicions, I called him to the bedroom. He walked in hesitantly, head lowered, hands fussing with the bottom hem of a long white shirt that hung over his dhoti, in Madrasi fashion.

"Good afternoon, Gangan. I couldn't find my blue bath towel," I said, in a voice I tried to keep neutral. "Do you know what happened to it?"

"Gone to laundry Madam."

"How come? Wasn't it clean?"

He stared down and didn't answer. I waited a beat and called his name. I wanted to see his eyes.

"Gangan, did you make the bed this morning?"

"Yes, Madam."

"Have you seen this piece of jewelry before?" I showed him the crescent moon.

"No Madam."

"Are you sure?" He bowed his head again and refused to meet my eyes. "Gangan, please look at me."

He finally raised his eyes but the look on his face was troubled. His lips were pinched tight, as if he were afraid to let out a secret; his head bobbed from side to side and his bony shoulders were hunched away from me. He edged toward the door.

"Please Madam, I know nothing. I am only cook. Maybe Master knows something. I go to the kitchen now and prepare dinner." He let go of his shirttail and almost tripped over himself going out the door.

His comment cleared my vision. The morbid curiosity that was pushing me to grill him was misplaced. He had nothing to do with whatever may or may not have happened in my absence, and if I read his body language correctly, whatever he knew was making him angry too, and probably scared of losing his job.

Sleeping, or even resting, was no longer an option. I sat down with a book but discovered that reading wasn't an option either. Daylight faded and I sat in the dark, dreading the confrontation, which I knew was unavoidable.

My mind was racing. How does one measure guilt? I'd fantasized about another man, but there were indications that Stefan had gone a step further and acted on his fantasy. Was fantasizing that much nobler than having sex? I wasn't even sure that he had. I was just assuming at this point, going round and round in my head with all the clues I had discovered. And what idiot leaves a trail of evidence like that behind?

I retrieved the foreign hairs from the trash basket in the bathroom and looped them carefully around my finger. I then waited until the dinner table was set and placed the lock of hair, the crescent moon, and the small dancing bell on a folded white napkin in the middle of Stefan's plate.

I sat, staring at them, weighed down by the knowledge that those three unremarkable artifacts held enough power to change my world.

The muffled cough of a scooter engine petered and died. I heard the front door open and close.

CHAPTER FIFTY

HOME NOT SO SWEET

Stefan walked into the dining room. He had a smile on his face. "You're back!" he exclaimed. He sounded pleased. He dropped his books on a corner shelf and bent over my chair to kiss me on the cheek. Instead of confronting him right away, as I had rehearsed in the past three hours, I let him kiss me but didn't respond.

Eyes averted to the floor, Gangan shuffled back and forth between the dinner table and the kitchen. Part of me wanted to get the drama over with, demand an explanation from Stefan, yell at him and damn him to hell. And I wanted to scrub away the ghost of his lips on my cheek. They felt foreign and dirty.

"So, how was your trip?" he asked.

I looked up at him. He wore all white, which amplified his dark tan and tall figure. His light blue eyes were bright under windswept hair. How ironic that he should ask questions about my trip now, the first time in months he'd showed interest in what I did in my free time.

I was seeing him as if from far away. He was so handsome that my heart shrank with dismay. Not so long ago, I'd loved him so much I would have jumped from the top of the Eiffel Tower to save his life. And now what? Where would we go from here? My mind searched for the words that had to be spoken. I wished Brigitte were here to give me courage.

Stefan was in such a good mood that it took him a whole minute to notice I hadn't responded to his greeting. He sat down at the table and had started to pour us both a glass of freshly squeezed lemonade when his eyes fell on the white napkin in the middle of his plate.

"What's that?" he asked, pointing to the crescent moon, the tiny bell, and the loop of hair. "Something from your trip?"

"I wish it were," I said. My voice was so heavy with dread, that he stopped pouring and did a double-take between the proffered objects and me.

"What is it?" he repeated, sounding genuinely curious.

"Just what you see, a cheap crescent moon, an ankle bell, and some long dark hairs."

"What is it doing in my plate?"

"Maybe you could tell me where they come from?" I croaked, my mouth dry with apprehension.

"How would I know?" His voice was getting tense and suspicious.

"You should know. I found them in our house."

Gangan, who had come to the door with a steaming dish of fried okra, looked at us and retreated quickly behind the kitchen door, almost dropping the oval dish in his haste.

"In the house?" He paused, apparently gathering his thoughts. They must be Eva's, Charles' girlfriend. They came over while you were away."

"Good try, but I don't think so. Eva has short, permed hair. She also is Anglo-Indian and a Christian. Those baubles came off a cheap Indian dance costume, not the kind of dancing Eva would engage in," I said.

"In that case, one of the servants left those behind," he said smugly, before taking a large swig of lemonade.

"I wish it were true," I started. "If only…"

"It is," Stefan interrupted.

To Stefan, I must have appeared dead calm. Not that I was trying for that, but I didn't know how to express the battle raging inside me. All I could do was stare alternately at his face and at the garden behind him. That made him nervous. His right eye started to twitch. He combed back his hair by running his fingers through it. Too loudly, he said, "Shall we eat? Gangan, bring the food!"

The bossy edge in his voice made me grind my teeth. That did it. A nice Stefan was hard to deal with, but a bossy one was an animal I was determined to wrestle into the dust. I thought back to the alarming days of silence he had imposed on me on a whim, and how I had finally broken down his barriers with a heated ultimatum. I needed anger right now. I needed to remember who I was, just as the goddess in my vision had instructed me. "No food yet," I told Stefan. "Hold the dinner, Gangan," I commanded, as the cook entered the room.

Gangan mumbled under his breath and turned away once more. I looked at his retreating back and leaped off my chair to follow him into the kitchen. "You better go home, Gangan. I will serve the food when we are ready, and you can clean up tomorrow, alright?"

"Madam be okay?"

His brow was furrowed with worry for me, but also for himself. I could see he understood that our fighting could bring an end to his job and ruin his whole family. "Everything will be okay," I said, reassuringly. "We'll eat later. First, the Master and I need to talk. You go home now."

I touched his bony shoulder to calm him and felt the tremor traveling his thin body. Maybe he hated confrontations as much as I did. I closed the kitchen door behind him and turned back.

Sparing Gangan the brunt of the coming fight had given me time to enter into my new skin. I felt stronger, taller, and determined to get to the bottom of whatever had taken place in our home in my absence.

"What's with you?" said Stefan, accusingly, when I walked back into the dining room.

"What's with me is this." I approached the table, hand stretched out to count on my fingers. "Four things. First, you could explain to me how this," I pointed to the trashy hair ornament, "ended up under my mattress, in our bed."

Stefan started to speak, but I raised my hand to stop him. I was finding my stride. He wasn't going to derail this conversation.

"Second, tell me why I found long black hairs in the shower drain? And third, where is my favorite bath towel, the one my mother sent from France? Gangan said it went to the laundry yesterday, but it was clean when I left. Finally, I won't even bother to ask about the cheap dancing bell Rishu dug out from under the living room cushions."

Having said my piece, I leaned against the wall, crossed my arms across my chest like a shield, stared at him and waited.

He sagged in his chair. His eyes lost their shine. His smile turned into a grimace when he started chewing on the inside of his left cheek. The man I now saw wasn't quite as handsome as the one who had walked through the door full of sunshine and confidence.

"So what! We had a party."

"Who had a party?"

"Ashok, Charles and I, and some students from the University."

"Ashok?" I had met Ashok a few times and found the sight of him unsettling, with a skull that was too big for his short body, giving him the appearance of a dwarf. Worst of all, I loathed his small porcine eyes that lit up and leered as if undressing me.

"You already know what I think about Charles, but why hang out with Ashok? He is not even a student. He is a full-grown man who just hangs out at the University."

"That's because he can't afford to pay the regular fees, but he audits a bunch of classes."

"I bet he does!" I said sarcastically. "So, you threw a party in our home?"

All of a sudden, Stefan gave up the pretense. Smart enough to know he was busted, he looked at me defiantly and spit out: "Yes, we had a party. I'm fed up with the phony philosophical bullshit they dish out at the university. Tired of it. We decided that, for a change, it would be fun to get drunk and raise hell."

"You mean, Ashok-the-low-life challenged you to break the rules that we promised to keep in order to live in this house on the Theosophical campus? As for Charles, who also swore to obey these rules for the privilege of living next door to us, I can't believe he went along."

"Well, he did. I guess we were both tired of obeying other people's rules about what to eat, what to drink, what not to smoke. Aren't you?"

"I do get cravings for meat once in a while, but I don't roast a pig on the porch. I go to a restaurant," I said, feeling righteous. His vehemence surprised me. I hadn't known he felt that way.

"We were just going to have a few drinks and let off some steam. We were indoors, for God's sake. Nobody needed to know. So, we decided…"

"We?"

"Okay. Charles, who didn't need a permit to buy it, got the whisky. The guys brought a bunch of food. Ashok brought some ganja, and I guess it got out of hand."

"That still doesn't explain how some dance ornaments got under my mattress. You did entertain girls in our home, didn't you? Who brought girls?"

"Ashok knew…"

"Well of course, it makes sense. Ashok-the-low-life-ganja-pusher-pimp procured girls! How many?"

"Two dancers. They were his cousins, for God's sake." Stefan's tanned face was turning a muddy shade of gray, and beads of sweat pearled and rolled off his hairline.

"I bet they were. I bet they also were prostitutes, because no dancer I know would entertain a bunch of ganja-smoking drunk students," I blurted, feeling hurt and vindicated. My indignant outburst remained unanswered, so I went on. "How stupid can you be? They probably came from the slums. And of course, Ashok arranged for you to pay them. So, how much did it cost you?"

"Forty rupees," said Stefan. "Ashok said it would help their families." The ordeal was exhausting him. His eyes were glazing over. I could see he longed to escape me, and retreat into the safety of his own mind. I pushed on.

"Forty rupees! That's one week's salary for Gangan. And I'm pretty sure those girls only got to see four or five rupees each. The rest of the money went into your friend Ashok's pocket. Money for school, of course," I added with a smirk.

My mind was in overdrive. Did agreeing to pay for girls mean he wanted to sleep with them, or did he really believe they were there to dance? Had the girls been called after he was drunk, or had it been pre-planned? I, too, was tired of this confrontation. Like in a war, there were no victors. If that weekend had been planned in advance, he was a total hypocrite. But if things had just happened as he claimed, one leading to another as situations sometimes do, he had been a thoughtless and credulous idiot, and I felt almost sorry for him.

It had been, what? Two days, and so far, no one had raised an alarm, but the prospect of Stefan being found out made my stomach ache. After all the stern warnings he had given me about living up to the conditions imposed by the T.S. when I'd first arrived, it was almost ironic "Do you realize we might get evicted if anyone finds out what you did?"

Stefan stared at me without answering. I think he was looking at his transgression from a brand-new point of view. We lived in such a privileged place, surrounded by a gentle jungle, minutes from the ocean. Had he even considered what it would be like to move to a crowded, radio-blasting neighborhood where the population density was fifty times what it was on this heavenly campus?

I was sure he would be devastated to lose our house, but above and beyond that, the words "prostitutes", and "slums" suddenly seemed to hit him. A hypochondriac by nature, he was clearly struggling with the implications of this sudden line of reasoning.

I pressed on. I knew I had touched a raw nerve. "I suggest you make an appointment with a good doctor. If they were who I think they are, who knows what purulent or incurable disease those sailor-friendly dancers may have gifted you with."

He looked sick, and I saw him blanch. As much as I hated him for what he had done, part of me felt sorry for him. I studiously refused to let it show. "Our bed is all yours tonight. Tomorrow, I'll have Gangan separate the cots and set one of them up in your study." And then I said, "From now on, I want to sleep alone."

He didn't protest. I wasn't finished.

"And you better tell your pimp friend that if I ever see his face around my house, I'll find a reason to have him arrested."

Neither of us was hungry after that. The mere idea of food turned my stomach. I went to the kitchen and put the prepared food into the refrigerator. When I returned to the dining room, Stefan had retreated to the safety of his study and his books.

After that, I couldn't stand the thought of staying in the house with him. I needed a place to think and figure out a way to organize my life so as not to derail my studies. I may have lost a husband, but I still needed my degrees. Now more than ever.

I thought of asking Norma and Anup if I could spend the night at their house, but decided against it. They were sure to ask what we were fighting about, and I couldn't tell them without putting our house in jeopardy. As much as I liked and trusted Anup, he was the brother of the man who had made an exception for us when he had allowed us to live on the T.S. campus.

Undisturbed by man or beast, for Stefan hadn't reappeared, and Rishu had chosen to fall asleep on a fat burgundy cushion, I grabbed my travel bag out of the closet where I had relegated it only hours ago, threw in my night clothes, a shawl, my toothbrush, a couple of books, and headed to Lycette's. The irony wasn't lost on me, but Lycette, who had been Stefan's heartthrob before my arrival in Madras, was the only friend I could count on to keep her mouth shut. She also was older than me by a few years, and worldlier by a long stretch. Maybe she would help me figure out what my next step should be.

I used bungee straps to secure the bag on the back of my Lambretta scooter and took off. The fresh evening air dried the flow of tears that had started rolling down my cheeks.

Did wives leave their husbands when they acted like teenagers and did something stupid? I took comfort, if any comfort was to be found, in the fact that Stefan was not having an affair. What he had done was dumb, but it would have been different if he had fallen in love or had been lusting after a specific woman.

I swerved to avoid a man walking in the lengthening shadows and realized I had forgotten to turn on my headlights. It scared me and made me focus on the road. I'd better think about what I was doing, or I might get into much more trouble.

I arrived at Lycette's hut and I was disappointed to find the door locked and Lycette gone. Out to dinner probably. I parked my scooter, dropped my bag against the short mud wall, and sat against it. Had I left Paris and traveled 5,000 miles to end up squatting in the dark to the loud thumping of my angry heart?

The chirping of crickets and croaking of frogs were reassuringly familiar, but I shivered at the thought of what creatures the nearby nocturnal mangrove was sure to conceal. My imagination was running wild. Frogs ate crickets and cobras ate frogs. A citronella candle and a box of matches sat on the ground a few feet from me, as if waiting for my visit. I lit the candle, took the shawl out of my bag, and threw it over my arms and feet, feeling very small and very much alone.

CHAPTER FIFTY-ONE

PICKING UP THE PIECES

By the time Lycette came home, two hours or so later, I had fallen asleep outside her door. If she was surprised to find me there, she didn't fuss over it. She opened the door and prepared a small platter of almonds and dark Belgian chocolate, a treat she knew I liked. We munched on the snacks while she listened to my heated rundown of what had happened at my house while we were at the Music Festival. She didn't interrupt me once.

"What an idiot," she said, when I had emptied my heart to her. "I'm so sorry you've had to go through that. Absolutely stupid but typical male behavior," she added, shaking her head wearily.

"What do you mean by typical? Are you saying that all men enjoy whoring when their wives are away?"

She extended her hand, palm turned to me, to fend off my outburst. "It is disturbing, but what we're talking about is herd mentality. Young men doing what young men do when there are more than three of them in a room. That's all."

"Disturbing doesn't come close," I said, my eyes swelling with tears. "It's... disgusting... sickening... revolting and utterly vulgar."

She waited for me to calm down. "Look, you're my friend, and I feel for you, but it's not the end of the world. You'll get over it."

"It doesn't change the fact that I can't stand the thought of Stefan ever touching me again." I shivered and wiped at my eyes with the edge of my shawl.

"I totally agree that you shouldn't have sex with Stefan until he has a clean bill of health, which may take several weeks or months. That, in itself, should be punishment enough." I thought I caught a glint of malice in her eyes, and I couldn't help but crack a tiny smile. "As for 'never again,' I don't know. Marriage requires forgiveness and some-times compromises. Not that I was ever very good at those."

"But he made love to a prostitute in our bed," I cried out, with renewed rancor.

"No, most probably, a prostitute serviced him in your bed. He didn't make love to her. Listen, you just told me he was drinking and smoking dope. From what I know about him, he is neither a drinker nor a ganja user. Have you ever seen him get high or drunk?"

"No. Alcohol gives him migraines, and he sure as hell doesn't smoke anything that I know of. As a matter of fact, he used to lecture Viktor, his godfather, about the evil of chain-smoking cigarettes."

"He would."

"It's just that I expected Stefan, the dedicated philosophy and yoga student he claims to be, to think and act on a higher level."

"Well, gurus have their demons too." She smirked. She and I had often made fun of Stefan's guru-like proclamations.

"Kidding aside, he always works so hard to avoid migraines, I would never expect him to defile his body this way."

"Yes. Me either," she said. "Stefan drinking and smoking ganja? Very unlike the person you and I know." She looked pensive. "He must have been on a real bender."

"I hope he woke up with a killer hangover." I spat the words out like hot pebbles. "But I hate to say he didn't look any worse for it today."

"They probably had the party over the weekend. He's had a day or two to recover."

That made us laugh, but I was far from feeling tolerant about the whole thing. Silence settled between us as Lycette got into some pajamas printed with wild horses and gauchos with lassos. It looked like something she might have brought back from Argentina.

Meanwhile, introspection was raising doubts in my mind. "I don't know. Maybe it's my fault for not being a better wife."

"None of that. This is not your fault," Lycette said. "Listen, I have two brothers and I've been married three times. I can assure you that Stefan's actions have nothing to do with you. He loves you. He just did something stupid."

"Of course it has to do with me. He chose to have sex with someone else."

"Look, Minouche, he just had a spell of testosterone gone mad. Men run into that condition once in a while."

"Testosterone gone mad?" In spite of myself, I burst out laughing.

"I'm not kidding." Her face was serious. "Getting drunk, doing stupid things, and getting in trouble is a recurring condition for men. My brothers taught me that. I'm just surprised Stefan never did anything like that before."

"Maybe he did. I just never caught him at it! God knows what he was up to before I came."

Lycette shook her head gently. "Don't go imagining things. I can assure you he was always a very proper gentleman, except for his tendency to lecture whoever he happened to be with." She paused, turned around and pointed at a travel trunk she used as a bench against the wall. "Hey, look, I've got this bottle of Cognac I keep for medicinal purposes only... of course. Let's have a shot," she whispered, "but keep it quiet. You don't want to get me kicked out of the school."

She got up, fetched a can of Coca Cola and some ice from her mini-icebox, popped open the can and split its content into two glasses. Giving me a conspiratorial look, she dug a bottle of Remy Martin from the bottom of the locked trunk and poured a generous shot in both glasses.

"To us. To women who are wiser, smarter and keep their hormones under control and their panties on," she said, toasting me. "Even though, in your case," she continued with an impish smile, "what was it you were telling me? Some daydreams about your voice instructor? I know, daydreaming is what we girls do, but you, Minouche, have a wild imagination. That could get you in trouble too, you know."

I chased off that suggestion with a wave of my hand. Infantile stuff. I couldn't even remember what I had been raving about. In view of my real-life drama, my fantasies about KV had evaporated. I could hardly recall what his voice sounded like.

I took a sip of the Cognac and Coke. Not only was alcohol forbidden on the Kalakshetra and T.S. campuses, it was unlawful in Madras and in most Indian states whose government imposed prohibition. We were breaking many laws and I didn't give a damn. I let the tiny bubbles tickle my nose and sighed. It was delicious.

"Wicked wonderful! Thank you, I promise not to tell!"

The drink reminded me of my mother, who had toasted me with a shot of Cognac the night she'd told me, without reproach, that she'd figured out I was no longer a virgin. That was only three years ago. Why did it feel like three centuries?

"Look, we both need some sleep. I have an early dance class tomorrow, and it's late," Lycette said, as we finished our drinks.

She rinsed and dried the glasses, hid the Remy Martin bottle back in the trunk, which she relocked, and spread the travel bedding she had dug out for me on the hut's concrete floor. I knew its comfort would be spartan at best, but considering that the alternative would be to return home, I was grateful to Lycette for her hospitality.

I lay on my back. The thatched roof of the hut was high above my head. I imagined the night sky above it, filled with other worlds higher still, as if to give me room to breathe and grow.

I woke up to the sound of Lycette foraging around for her notebooks.

"Hasta luego," she said from the door, reminding me she had spent most of her childhood speaking Spanish. "Mi casa es su casa. Got to go. What about you? Don't you have music classes today?"

"Later this afternoon," I replied sleepily. "Thanks for everything."

"You're welcome! Hang in there. Things will sort themselves out," she said and was gone.

I burrowed under the sheets. I didn't want to wake up. I didn't want to think about yesterday. I didn't want to think about the future. I wanted things the way they were before. However unsatisfactory they had been, I wanted them back. I pulled my knees under my chin and went back to sleep.

When I woke up, sunlight flooded the floor and lingered on my bundled body. I was hot. I kicked the sheets off and stretched. The window in the hut's wall to my left was open, and tendrils of jasmine swayed in the morning light. I breathed in the fragrant breeze as it flowed through the hut, cooling my sweaty skin.

I turned on my back and stared at the tiny white flowers. Behind them, high in the sky, white clouds glided smoothly, effortlessly, and silently on an unknown path. I imagined I was one of those clouds, pushed by unseen currents. Maybe it was okay not to know where the path would lead.

In the meanwhile, what was I going to do about Stefan? Long-term plans felt nebulous. Maybe the best way to deal with married life for now was to approach it one day at a time. But sweeping what had happened under the rug didn't feel right. I needed to focus and make some decisions. I wasn't about to forgive him for what he had done, not any time soon anyway, but though I was loath to admit it, some of the things Lycette had said made sense. Like for instance her treatise on testosterone gone mad. I wondered if she'd been right when she'd said that none of what had happened was about me. Perhaps I'd stopped being attentive to what Stefan had to say long ago, even though I knew part of his attraction to me had to do with my being a good listener. Still, I wasn't willing to let him off the hook.

And then I had to think about our grants. My grant rather, for this morning I didn't care what might happen to his. I had to consider what would happen to me if we decided to separate. Would it affect the Paderewski Foundation's decision to extend it? I needed it for three more years to get a degree. Would they be inclined to support us separately? And if not, what would I do alone in Madras, without any source of income?

Panic rose in me. Last night's drink and an empty stomach were starting to make me nauseous. I found it hard to breathe.

I needed to focus on something I could control. Something I owned, and the only thing I could think of was my music. I had a goal and deadlines to save me from drama, chaos, and confusion. Relief and motivation flooded through me. I would do whatever it took to become the first foreign undergraduate to get a diploma from the Central College of Karnatic Music.

I straightened my clothes, picked up my bag, found my sandals outside the door, mounted my trusted scooter which made life so much easier for me, and headed home. By now, Stefan should be on his way to class, if he did go. It was already 9 a.m., late in a country where people loved to get up before dawn. I would change and pay a visit to Rao, my friend and private music coach, to schedule a more intense tutoring program. I would also bring him up to date about the music festival which he had been unable to attend due to some personal problems.

When I got home, Stefan's scooter was gone, which calmed my apprehension. I wasn't ready for any kind of follow-up discussion after yesterday's sordid confrontation.

Gangan must have heard me driving up because he came to the porch. He looked relieved to see me. The toothless smile he gave me— he was missing several front teeth on his lower jaw—warmed my heart. It reminded me I was accountable for my actions, present and future. They affected many people's lives. Being a memsahib carried its own load of responsibilities. I smiled at him.

"Morning Gangan. I'm starving. Can you prepare some breakfast for me?

"Yes, Sir," he said, happy my appetite required his services.

"Quickly, please. I've got some errands to run."

Looking alarmed, he stopped and stared at me questioningly. I couldn't very well open my soul to him or dump my troubles on his thin shoulders, as I had with Lycette. Still, he needed to hear something from me.

"And Gangan, don't worry. Things will be alright."

"Yes, Sir."

"Make some fresh coffee, will you? And please, don't call me Sir."

"Yes, Sir… Madam."

My reassurance brought back some spring in his old legs, and he trotted to the kitchen where I heard him throw a handful of charcoal on the brazier to boil water.

I took a quick shower, dressed up a notch in a moiré cotton sari whose eggplant color changed hue when the light played on its pleats. I put up my hair in a careful chignon and applied kohl to my eyes and a little rouge on my lips. My actions were deliberate. I wanted to look good and walk with my head high. I had to believe that Stefan's breach of trust hadn't been about me. If he chose to make a fool of himself, I wouldn't let it affect me. Easier said than done, but I was working hard on believing it and my dressing up was part of it.

I quickly ate the poached eggs and toast Gangan had laid out on the dining table, emptied a second cup of coffee and was about to leave when I saw the mailman coast to a stop in front of the kitchen door on his antique bicycle. He proudly rang his distinctive ding-dong bell twice to alert Gangan, and handed him a letter.

"From France," Gangan said, eagerly handing me the letter. He knew I was always happy to get mail from home.

It was from Viktor and addressed to Stefan and me, so I opened it and started reading. I shook my head in dismay. Stefan had repeatedly invited Viktor to visit, and now Viktor was giving us the date of his arrival, two weeks from now.

At first, I couldn't imagine a worse time for a family visit, but on second thought, maybe it was a good thing, as it would dictate our sleeping arrangements. Furthermore, Stefan would spend most of his free time with Viktor while I worked on my projects. And it would force us to be polite with each other and present a united front. I don't think either of us was ready to entertain the older man with the details of last weekend's deeds.

I left the open letter on the table where Stefan was sure to find it, and went looking for Gangan. I needed to get the new sleeping arrangements organized right away.

"Gangan, I want you to break down the double cot in the bedroom, and put my cot with my sheets and pillows under the window in my study."

"Yes, Sir… Madam."

"And move the other cot into the Master's study today. He will be sleeping there."

"Yes, Madam." Gangan's eyes grew large with misgivings.

"Can you ask the gardener to help you move the extra cot out of

the storage area and put it in the bedroom. You'll have to make it ready
for a guest, an old gentleman, who will be arriving from France in a
few days."

"Yes Madam. For a guest..." I could tell he wanted more information, so I pointed to the letter. "Our relative is coming on vacation." He
seemed relieved to hear that explanation. While talking I had walked
to the bedroom door. "The double mosquito net won't be needed for
now, so you should store it."

Gangan nodded his agreement.

I continued. "Next, you must go to the Theosophical Society
commissary and get three individual mosquito nets, extra linen and
blankets. Do you think you can handle that by yourself? Today?"

"Yes, Madam. I go to the office now, and get the nets. Gardener
not here today. I think one house boy come help me move the cots."

"Excellent. Should I give you a list?"

"No, Madam. I remember."

"Thank you Gangan." I gave him a reassuring smile, placed the
letter announcing Viktor's visit in full view on the dining room table
and left. There really was no rush to ready the bedroom for his stay, as
he wouldn't arrive for another two weeks, but I was eager to distance
myself from Stefan and refused to worry about how he would react
when he came home and found our territory redistributed under
my command.

CHAPTER FIFTY-TWO

VIKTOR

It had now been five weeks since Stefan and I "faisions chambre à part" as French people snidely would put it. Simply said, it meant that we no longer shared a bed. And three weeks since Viktor had arrived in Madras to enjoy his long-awaited vacation.

Viktor's loving presence had made it easier to settle into a kind of semi-normal home routine. He had, of course, protested when we had assigned the bedroom to him, but we had been able to convince him that, considering our class schedules and our need to access our individual small offices filled with books and music instruments, it was in fact the simplest solution for Stefan and me.

The front door opened and slammed against the wall. Rishu jumped to his feet and rushed outside. Viktor walked in with a smile on his face.

"Ah! Minouchka. Here you are. Sorry about slamming the door."

He looked tanned and handsome, an old man in a light blue sport shirt and white slacks with a full head of barely graying hair. Our vegetarian diet, combined with his daily walks and swims, had brought a spectacular improvement to his health. His wheezing was almost gone, and he had lost some of the flab accumulated by years of confinement in his Paris apartment.

"Stefan gave me an excellent tour of the Madras Museum."

Through the open door I saw Stefan parking his scooter. He walked up the steps onto the verandah and into the living room, looked at us and hesitated, as if waiting for an invitation from me to join the conversation. Getting none, he announced, "I have to catch up on some reading before dinner," and retreated toward his study.

Viktor turned toward him with a huge smile on his face. "Thanks, *Stefaniush,* for a wonderful afternoon. Enjoy your reading while Minouche and I catch up. We'll see you at dinner." He turned back to me. "Where were we? Ah, the Madras Museum. Do you know that it's the second oldest museum in India, established in 1851? The building is magnificent, and has a brilliant archeology department."

"Really! I haven't been there yet," I said. "I much prefer to see artifacts on location."

Viktor nodded enthusiastically. "You should really take the time."

"So, what else did you do?" I asked.

"We went to the travel agency to book my return flight for next week."

That took me by surprise. I didn't want him to leave so soon. First of all, this vacation was important for his health, but hidden under all the possible reasons I might give him was the most important to me. I wanted to put off living alone with Stefan again. I had to talk Viktor out of it. "Why so soon? You didn't have to do that. It's only been, what? Just three weeks?"

"By the time I go it will have been a month," said Viktor.

"Look, you should take full advantage of the cost of your flight. It's not like you can fly here twice a year."

"Well, I don't want to impose on you two. You need your space, and," he paused with raised eyebrows, "your bedroom, maybe?"

He cocked his head, waiting for some kind of acquiescence or explanation.

I looked over his shoulder. Stefan had closed the door to his study and was out of earshot. I hadn't intended to discuss our problems with Viktor. Confiding in Lycette was one thing, but telling family and friends what Stefan had gotten himself into would certainly qualify as a betrayal and would spread unhappiness all around. I didn't want that for Maman, for Stefan's parents, and especially not for Viktor. On the other hand, revealing a few of the things that had happened between Stefan and me might show Viktor why his presence was so beneficial to us, and maybe change his mind about leaving.

"Right now, Stefan and I need time to work out some problems, and your presence is helpful."

"Hmm… I see. And what would those problems be? Can you talk about it?"

I shook my head without answering.

"Obviously," he added with an apologetic smile, "I'm not well versed in feminine psychology, but I may have some insight into a young man's head."

That shy suggestion that his homosexuality might make him a better judge of character where men were concerned made me smile in spite of myself. If anything, I thought that his sexual orientation might in fact give him better understanding of me. Still, I hesitated. What I had to say would damage his image of Stefan, his beloved godchild and favorite student. But there was no way around it.

"I know you think of Stefan as a brilliant human being with untapped potential, but to tell you the truth, he's made some stupid choices recently. Your presence defuses my anger about it and makes it easier for us to live under the same roof."

"That bad, hey?" Viktor rocked gently in the chair he had pulled next to mine.

"Bad enough to have him sleep in his office. So, don't worry about depriving us of our conjugal bed!" I tried to make light of it with a weak chuckle.

"I see." He remained silent for a while. "It pains me greatly to ask, but, is he having an affair?"

"No. Just a stupid party with some MU male friends who brought drugs, alcohol, and some disreputable dancing girls into our home while I was away at a music festival. And Stefan had the gall to entertain one of these dancers in our bed."

"Ooh! That doesn't sound like the Stefan I know."

"Nor I, but there are lots of things you don't know about him." I paused and hesitated. How much should I say to get my point across without completely shattering Viktor's image of him? "You've mentored him for a long time, and know that he can be stubborn, self-centered and rather indifferent to the distress he causes. But he was never like that with me. When I first met him, he was attentive and supportive, but now, I'm not sure I know who he is anymore."

"Intellectually," said Viktor, "he appears to be the same, brilliant, inquisitive…"

"Intellectually, maybe. But behind that façade I can't find the lover I met in Paris. I know he was always eccentric and a little bit of a loner, but on the whole, he behaved like a normal person. Someone who celebrated Christmas and birthdays, someone who knew how to have fun, laugh and make friends."

"How is he different now?" asked Viktor grimly.

"For one thing, and for me it's huge, he has to control everything. Starting with our wedding, which he planned without consulting me; with the choice of my dance classes which he again arranged without my input; there is also the use of our money and even his concerns about my weight." I realized that I was getting heated about the subject of control and hesitated. Was it too much to tell Viktor about Stefan's campaign to control my physical appearance? To this day, the thought of it made me so irate that I carried on. "Do you know that he put a scale on the table for three months and weighed every bite I put in my mouth? I'm still amazed I let him do it. If he tried that now, I think I would scratch his eyes out."

Viktor shifted uncomfortably in his chair. "A scale, you say? Why in the world would he do that?"

"Why?" I said, with a shrug and a sigh. "Because he wanted me to be thinner and look like a model or a dancer."

Viktor didn't look amused. "What did you do about it?"

"Nothing. I just ate on the sly. But I was angry and got sick. Some unidentified fever that caused me to lose ten pounds in a week."

"Ten pounds?" A pained expression crossed his face.

"You should have seen how delighted he was with my new looks. Never mind I was so weak I could hardly attend my dance classes."

"What was that thing you said about birthdays and Christmas?"

"Oh, that! He just decided that they were stupid celebrations and refused to get involved. It made me feel so lonely on those occasions." I knew I should stop there, but the dam was broken. "One time he didn't talk to me for several weeks. I was going crazy wondering what I had done, but it was just some kind of psychological experiment he had undertaken without my knowledge. He was just using me as a guinea pig."

"But why... why would he do that?" said Viktor, deep in thought. I could see the wheels turning behind his intelligent forehead.

"Look," I said, "the list could go on. Bottom line, I'm still figuring out what to do."

"I see. I see." He looked miserable.

What had I done?

"What happened to our Stefan?" He was distraught, and his hand went to his shirt pocket and patted it, probably looking for a cigarette pack. He had given up smoking to stay with us, but after listening to me he looked like he needed a smoke. I guessed that, right now, a strong *Gauloise* cigarette would have done the job.

"It would be great if you could stay longer," I said. "Not just for us, but think about yourself. If you go home, you'll probably fall back into eating the wrong food, smoking and not exercising, and will lose the health benefits you gained living with us in the last three weeks."

I had said enough, or maybe too much.

"I don't know child. I'm not sure it's a good idea. I hate to say it but it's up to you two to sort things out."

"I agree, but in the meantime Stefan and I both enjoy the neutral zone your presence offers. And I enjoy your affection. It helps me keep calm around him. So, please, stay a little bit longer."

"Whether or not I can change my tickets, which I'm not sure I can, I have to think about all this before I make up my mind. I could tell there was something amiss between you two, but I had no idea. No idea."

I got up and embraced him, his unshaved cheek scraping mine. I didn't mind. It felt good. It was the only hug I'd had in several weeks.

CHAPTER FIFTY-THREE

MAY 1962 - THE SHARK

Yesterday's conversation with Viktor had alleviated some of my frustration, but I felt guilty about unloading my grievances on him as I had. I'd exposed the godson he idealized as a controlling and insensitive person, and I'd told him that his golden boy had tarnished his image by entertaining a prostitute in our bed.

Too late I realized that my venting had been tough on Viktor who valued honesty and loyalty above all, but I now had to live with what I'd done and rebuild what I could. Some of the youthfulness he had regained around us in the past three weeks had evaporated. He was quiet, avoiding both Stefan and me, and, as far as I knew, hadn't made up his mind on whether to stay on for a bit longer or leave as planned the following week. As I watched him pace silently from room to room, his back appeared to stoop under the burden of his disappointment. In my heart, I knew I owed him an apology and invited him for a walk on the beach. Rather than the shortcut I usually took to the beach, I followed a wooded path that opened up near the fishing village.

It was approaching eight in the morning and a thin marine haze hanging between sea and sky slowed the rising heat.

Chattering like crows, the fishermen's wives stared seaward into the gauzy glare and waited expectantly for the day's catch. Naked children ran lightly back and forth at the edge of the water, daring the sea to lick their toes, and the smooth ridges left earlier on the sand by the retreating tide were now trampled by their small dark feet.

Our progress along the beach was silent and slow. Viktor looked tired and we sat down on the sand to watch the return of the catamarans.

"I'm sorry, I really am, to have caused you pain," I said, as a peace offering.

"Don't be. I'm upset, but maybe it was for the best that you reminded me that our Stefan is not a saint."

"Still, I should have found a different way to confide in you."

"I've thought a lot about what you said, and if it's true, so be it," said Viktor. "For years I have closed my eyes to the flaws in his character. When he was my student I chose to ignore his attitude and his flippant answers, the kind he would use with me to win an argument."

Viktor turned to me, a pained expression veiling his eyes. "I know he can be cruel to the people who love him. When he was a student at the Polish college near Paris, I had to remind him to write home, as if he were a child. I knew how precious his letters were to his parents and how proud they were of him."

I had met Stefan's parents before leaving for India, and despite the language barrier, I had enjoyed our visit, thanks to his brother who spoke French and was as open and friendly as Stefan was inscrutable.

"They are simple people, and a little bit in awe of Stefan," I reflected, letting a handful of sand run through my fingers. "For most of their lives, their concern has been survival, and here comes a son who is looking for nirvana."

"I wonder what they really think of that," said Viktor, with a puzzled smile. "They probably worry about how such studies will allow him to support a family, which has been the main preoccupation of their lives."

"And nothing they can do about it. In their eyes he'd either be a wise man or a nut case. Of course, you and I know the two are not mutually exclusive."

"Unfortunately," Viktor chuckled. "So, what are you going to do? Stay? Move out? Go home? Kick him out?"

"To be honest, it all depends on the fragility of my grant if we split up. I can't jeopardize what I'm working on. I need to know for sure what the Paderewski Foundation would do if they found out we were planning to divorce."

"A fair question considering that Stefan and you are their poster children. The success story of a poor Polish emigrant married to a French girl of supposed Polish descent..." A teasing smile floated on his dry lips.

"Don't remind me," I said, closing my hand over a fistful of sand. "I flew under their radar at the time, but I would hate for them to investigate my fake family tree."

"I have given your problems a lot of thought, and hate to surmise, but do you think Stefan capable of tipping them off if you left him?" he asked.

I had. "Such vengeful action would rather be out of character for someone on a spiritual path, and it might endanger his own status. But then again, one never knows."

We fell silent. Close by, the fishermen's wives and children milled around or sat in groups, except for a young woman who came forward to greet me. Her feet, long and slender, were heavy with worn silver anklets, and her toe rings glistened through the salt and sand coating her skin. I remembered speaking to her before. Her name was Mira.

Far beyond the breakers, the sails of two catamarans bobbed up and down. Viktor and I got up and joined the waiting women. Mouth stained red with her betel nuts chew, Mira pointed at the sea and launched into an explanation, but her English was too hard to understand. On seeing that I wasn't catching on, she used hand language, like a dancer, to mime how the two boats had sailed out together and parted beyond the breakers, and how a net had been dropped and stretched between them, out in the deep where the fish hid.

Now the two catamarans were returning. When they were near enough, the men who had remained in the village swam to them, grabbed the ends of the net and swam back to shore. One arm-length at a time, they started pulling the net in.

By the time the catamarans were beached, the whole village had gathered around them. The women's saris, bleached and torn in places by age and sun, swelled and flapped in the wind like sails, a bouquet of reds, purples, yellows and greens that contrasted vividly with the dark and stark ropy stick figures of men clad in the barest of loin cloths.

Heavy with water, fish and sand, the enduring net of corded twine was dragged away from the waves which were hungry to reclaim what was theirs. Seagulls and children buzzed around in anticipation of a meal. The length of the net was pulled open revealing the first layer of the catch. A quick prayer of thanks to the gods was carried on the wind, and the spastic, hapless fish heaved their final breath as the women began to line them up by size on freshly washed banana leaves.

Suddenly, the onlookers jumped back, pulling the children away with them, and pandemonium broke out as a five-foot shark broke free from under a blanket of algae that had concealed it at the bottom of the net. Snapping its jaws, it lurched frantically to free itself, tearing at the mesh with a triple row of gleaming razor-sharp teeth.

Viktor, who had been watching the net, rushed forward to help the fishermen contain the beast inside of it. The mighty fish was jerking, jumping and slapping the ground with its powerful tail. The men had it almost contained when its open jaws ripped through the net and closed, inches from the leg of a child who had snuck back into the line of men to get a closer look. On instinct, Viktor picked up the child and shoved him out of harm's way to where the women and I stood, before grabbing an oar lying at his feet and shoving it into the shark's maw. The oar broke. The shark writhed free of the net and started to flap and roll on the sand, closer and closer to the water line.

Transfixed, I watched as Viktor, looking tall as a Viking, helped the small and wiry fishermen in their attempt to grab the beast's murderous tail. By now the shark was desperate to slip into the sea. It heaved and reached, but the men, intent on the profit it would bring the village, continued to block his escape. A boy was sent to his father's hut and returned with a metal-tipped spear. Muttering a prayer under his breath, the head-fisherman pounced and stabbed the shark through its left eye. It jerked one last time and stopped moving. When they were sure it was dead, the excited villagers approached to take a good look at it. The bravest children kicked it.

Boastful now that the crisis was over, the men surrounded Viktor. Assaulting him with a stream of Tamil, they slapped his back excitedly. Viktor appeared to be enjoying the moment, and for a second, I got a glimpse of the man he must have been before the war, a tall, powerful athlete loved by all.

Detaching herself from the women's group, the mother of the child whose leg had nearly been torn off approached Viktor. The men stepped back as she quickly touched Viktor's feet, and then her eyes, muttering a prayer of thanks, and in the midst of happy chatter, the villagers resumed their various tasks. The head-fisherman carved out the shark's fin and placed it on a clean banana leaf Mira had brought him. I looked questioningly at him.

"For China restaurant," he said in English. "China people pay good price."

I nodded. "What about the rest of the shark?"

"Too big for one man carry. We take to market on bicycle. We cut there, and sell. And we tell story how foreigner helped kill it. People much love stories."

We waved goodbye to the villagers and turned back toward our stretch of beach. To my surprise, Viktor was clenching a lit bidi between his lips. He pointed to the native hand-rolled cigarette.

"I know I'm not supposed to smoke on campus," he said guiltily. "But nobody said anything about having one of these on the beach." His eyes twinkled with mischief. If the bidis hadn't smelled so foul, I might have smoked one too, for the presence of a shark caught close to where we swam daily had shaken me.

Viktor gave a little laugh. "Life and death, Indian style," he said, pulling the strong smoke deep into his lungs. "Those men back there were incredibly brave to hang on to that shark."

"So were you. You could have lost a leg or an arm!"

He grinned. "If the Nazis didn't manage to kill me, no shark will. So, where were we, before all that excitement started?"

"Making life-altering decisions," I said with a sigh.

But the shark incident seemed to have reduced my problems to petty neurosis. "I think I have lost enough time wondering what to do with Stefan, whether or not he would rat on me and what the grant Foundation would do if we split. I don't want to take a chance to ruin my stay in India. The way I see it, my priorities are to get a music degree, so I'm going to concentrate on that and move on. Our marriage is wounded, but it might heal if I don't go in for the kill."

Viktor looked back and pointed with his chin. "Not like the shark?"

I shuddered at the image. Viktor nodded thoughtfully and blew the ashes away from the tip of his bidi to keep it lit. "That was a bad joke," he said. "Sorry, Minouchka." After a few seconds he added: "I think your plan is sound. Keep your eyes on the prize and leave some room for a possible reconciliation."

Behind us, the fish were being stacked between layers of leaves and laid into baskets. We watched as some of the women got in line to get their share. They placed the baskets on their heads atop a cushion of leaves and started at a trot in the direction of the market. Today, after their big catch, they looked content. I sighed, thinking how simple their lives looked from where I stood.

"I never wanted things to turn out this way," I said, turning back the way we had come. "I don't know where we went wrong. Life is not fair."

"No, life is not fair," said Viktor, rolling what was left of the cigarette in his fingers until all the tobacco had disintegrated into a fine dust. "Look at me. I lost everything and ended up in a concentration camp. But life goes on. I'm still here. I'm alive." He wiped his hands clean of ashes on his shorts, an unconscious gesture I had observed many times when visiting him in Paris. "So, the man you love has changed and has let you down. The question is, do you have what it takes to make it work until you get what you want? For me it was staying alive one more day. In your case, you want a music degree, and maybe a loving husband?" he added hesitantly, looking at me under bushy eyebrows. "Am I right?"

"Yes. As you know, I have no special skills and will need a degree to secure a job with a future, like the teaching position my French friend Nellie Caron assured me I might get at the *Centre d'Etudes de Musiques Orientales*, in Paris, if I graduate from the CCKM." I kicked a beached heap of algae with my bare foot and buried my toes into the cold damp sand under it. "As for a loving husband, I guess it's up to him."

"So, focus on that. Let Stefan work out his own demons. Maybe they won't affect you in the same way anymore, for you too, have changed. You now have the upper hand in this relationship. Can you stand dysfunctional love for as long as it takes? In the end you win and take home the makings of an academic career." He stopped and looked at me, and when he spoke again, there were tears in his voice:

"You know I love you both like my own children, so I hope that in time, you'll forgive Stefan." Shyly he added, "and never forget old Viktor."

"Forgive Stefan, maybe... but forget you, never. You've been like a father to me too," I said, planting a kiss on his cheek.

One thing my discussions with Viktor had made very clear was that the continuation of my grant was central to my goals. The best way to secure it might be to follow the route of least resistance. Sometimes, that's how a war was won, the way the Russians had defeated Napoleon by burning every village and retreating as he advanced into the steppes until winter engulfed him and his army.

I knew I had what it took. A chill of excitement went through me as I contemplated my new game plan. No confrontation, no scenes, no drama, no tears. Which was great because I hated all that. Stefan and I needed to talk like two reasonable people about what we wanted to get out of life, and come to an agreement on how to live side by side peacefully, respectfully, as we helped each other achieve our goals.

CHAPTER FIFTY-FOUR

INTROSPECTION

The next morning, looking tired and bedraggled, Viktor waited for Stefan to leave to tell me that he'd decided to keep to his original travel arrangement. For one thing, he was worried about letting slip in front of Stefan that I had talked about the flaws in our marriage. I tried to reassure him that it was unlikely, but is was no use. He made it clear that he longed to step out of our problems and go home to his simpler life. As he had so well said two days ago, "It was up to us kids to sort things out."

I knew he was right, but I cringed at the thought of another sit down, or preferably, a beach conference with Stefan. Talking under the open sky, as the soothing climb and retreat of the waves tuned to my heart beats always felt easier.

Where would I start? I too must have gone amiss, somewhere, sometime. Where had I gone wrong?

Looking back on my life, I'd never been one to let someone make decisions for me, especially momentous decisions that were bound to affect the rest of my days, but on arriving in Bombay, I had not questioned Stefan's plans to get married. Maybe I'd been overwhelmed by India, or blinded by vanity. Flattered to be the chosen one. Chosen above all. Chosen above Lycette, on whom I knew he'd had a crush. Chosen over exotic Indian brides whose parents would have benefited from a match with a Westerner. Why had I signed away my independence and my life just like that? It had been irrational.

Two years later I questioned that decision. I wondered if, maybe, I had never forgiven Stefan his sleight of hand, his assumption that, because I'd come, I was just there for the taking. Yet, I'd given him every reason to believe I would happily marry him. I think I loved him, but had I really been in love with him for himself, or in love with his charisma and exotic life history? Had I subconsciously looked at him as a key to a better future? If that were the case, I was no better than he was, because it took two to grow or ruin a relationship.

Maybe I should have done something about livening up our empty, silent evenings. Overridden Stefan's objections to getting a record player, and found ways to get radio reception. The programs would have been in Tamil or Hindi, which I didn't understand, but it would have filled the house with voices and music. It would have made it easier to live with clouds of insects that drove me under a mosquito net soon after sunset; easier to bear Stefan and his silence, his moods, his migraines and his books; easier not to miss my tribe of bohemian friends, the renegades who used to populate my Paris nights with flamenco music, sangria and bitter espresso coffee.

In hindsight, I should have shown more appreciation for the Theosophical Society campus we lived on. Maybe I had spent too much time complaining about what it lacked rather than appreciating what it offered. It was safe, lush, green and cooler than most other neighborhoods in Madras, even if it was insular and lacked the restaurants, the blast of movie music, the relentless ebb and flow and spicy smells of the bazaar, the women's saris turning crowded streets into garish tableaux.

And now what? Divorce was not an option. The society we lived in didn't endorse it, and if we separated, I would be the one losing face and status. When it came to marriage, Indians were not so different from the French. Men ruled. Women endured. Well I didn't plan to endure for the rest of my life, but I refused to expose myself to the ensuing gossip and financial problems.

Was there a way for our relationship to move back to that state of friendship we had shared in Paris before that civil ceremony which, now, looked very much like a marriage of convenience? A document that allowed us to live together under one roof in the Theosophical Society. The marriage that had probably helped me get my grant and would help Stefan get a French passport. The marriage that had pleased our parents, professors and neighbors.

I was exhausted by the conflict and desperate to make things look normal around us, and though I couldn't imagine being intimate with Stefan, it struck me that I would have to ask Gangan to move our cots back into our bedroom after Viktor left next week. I could imagine them, side by side, but under separate mosquito nets, a sight I would spare Viktor. Poor Viktor. I wished I hadn't caused him so much distress, but our conversation had clarified some of the issues in my mind. When all was said and done, the one thing I needed to preserve with Stefan was traveling. Boarding buses or trains alone in India was hard for a woman, and not always safe. Moreover, Stefan and I were at our best when traveling together, and the lengthy holidays our schools offered would give me time to do some serious fieldwork which he, too, enjoyed. I knew from experience that traveling caused him to forget about his books and fall contentedly into a tour guide mode, which made interaction with him easy.

My goal now was to do what I could to resurrect our friendship and find a way of living and traveling together.

CHAPTER FIFTY-FIVE

JUN 1962 - NEW MORNING

On the day of Viktor's departure, the taxi arrived early. I was sitting in the verandah, waiting for Viktor to finish getting ready when the cab's aggressive bulb horn silenced some of the jungle voices as it stopped in front of Ranga Villa. A family of crowned sparrows and paddy field pipits fluttered to safety, and the crotchety rogue rhesus that kept a watch on Rishu and our kitchen window in hopes of a quick bounty, swung his muscular grey body onto a higher branch of his home tree. Crows airlifted heavily from the tamarind tree where they were resting, and smartly assessing the cab for what it was, unleashed a deafening cacophony of protest.

Viktor emerged from the bedroom, carrying a beat-up leather suit-case secured with a belt. I had become used to seeing him attired in light-colored tropical shirts, white slacks and sandals, and was saddened at the sight of the old grey suit, white shirt and dark tie he wore.

Even though we'd had the suit and tie dry-cleaned, the shirt washed and starched, and the shoes resoled and spit-polished, those clothes took away some of his re-acquired youthfulness, and reminded me of the huffing old professor stinking of cigarette smoke who had landed in Madras a month earlier.

I wished he could have stayed forever. His presence gave me a sense of family I had rarely shared with Stefan. Viktor was someone kind to talk to over coffee in the morning. I could discuss innocuous things with him, without ever fearing trick questions or judgmental repartees, which often was Stefan's habit. He was someone normal whom I could call a friend and loved, like I had my grandfather. I had tried my best to convince him to stay a few more weeks, but he had been adamant about going.

"I have to resume teaching. I've already taken a one-month leave of absence."

I stared into his eyes, looking for a reflection of the bitter grievances I'd shared with him. "You know that I need you here."

"My students are the ones who need me. You, Minouchka," and he pointed a nicotine-stained finger at me, "will manage."

Maybe he knew me better than I did. I wanted to be loved and protected, but I was perfectly capable of taking care of myself. He, on the other hand, was the only philosophy professor at the Polish College of Les Ageux, near Paris, a school that had been Stefan's home for four years and was well known to the Polish intelligentsia in France.

"I do believe Poland will be free again someday," he said, eyes burning with a fervor I could see, but not explain, in someone who had survived so many wars. "I have to do my part to prepare the next generation for the homeland, whenever it comes."

There was no arguing with Viktor when he raised the flag of patriotism. He was looking to the future, and I suddenly felt a little vexed to be relegated to his immediate past. He made me promise to write often, and in a low voice asked me to keep him informed of my tenuous relationship with Stefan.

"The taxi is waiting. You ready?" said Stefan, emerging from his study and slipping on his sandals.

Stefan greeted the driver, a tall Sikh wearing a bright orange turban, and the man came in and took Viktor's old suitcase in his right hand. Surprised by its lightness he tossed it to his other hand. Obviously, he wasn't used to people traveling light. He nodded appreciatively and gently placed the suitcase in the middle of his new taxi's spotless trunk before holding the door open for Viktor.

Gangan waved from the front porch and wiped his nose with a corner of his dhoti. Eyes moist with tears and mouth open in babbling gratitude, he held in his hands a fat bundle of Indian rupees Viktor had handed him on his way out. "Here. That's for you. I won't need it in France."

Stefan sat in front with the driver; Viktor and I sat in the backseat. In spite of the early hour it was already getting muggy, and I lowered the window to let in a stream of fresh air. I had decided to wear a dress for the trip to the airport and regretted it at once, for the purple vinyl upholstery was hot and sticky under my bare legs and thighs.

The plane was on time, and our goodbyes rapid, which was providential, as I was prone to tears and didn't want to make it harder than necessary for any of us.

The ride back to Ranga Villa was depressing. Slouched against the passenger door in the back seat where he had joined me, Stefan stared silently out of the window. Slumped against the opposite car door, I fought the anxiety that churned in my stomach at the prospect of the discussion we needed to face to move on now that Viktor was gone.

After we got home, lunch was even worse. Neither one of us was hungry. I became fascinated with dissecting the curried okras on my plate and counting the grains of rice it took to make a perfect circle around them. Stefan had brought a newspaper to the table and let his food go cold.

Gangan was scurrying around the kitchen door, worriedly watching our slow progress with the meal. He looked so upset at our lack of appetite that I lied to him and told him we had gotten a bite to eat at the airport. Stefan's eyebrows rose at my excuse, but he wisely chose not to contradict me.

We were a miserable bunch. All three missing Viktor and distraught at losing the neutral zone he had provided for us.

Folding the newspaper and throwing it on the table Gangan had just cleared, Stefan said under his breath, "I'm going to miss the old guy."

It was an understatement, but coming from someone whose concern for the outside world appeared confined to his own shadow, it was huge.

"I miss him already... I wish he'd changed his mind and stayed longer," I said.

I was not entirely surprised when Stefan cleared his throat and, looking as casual as he possibly could, asked: "So, what are we going to do about our bedroom now that Viktor is gone?" Turning away from me, he reached down to pet Rishu, who was rubbing against his leg.

From the corner of my eye I saw Gangan leaving for the afternoon. He would be back to prepare dinner. Meanwhile we were alone.

"Don't you think that we should first talk about what happened?"

"You mean my partying and getting drunk with the guys when you were away?"

"No. I mean you bedding a prostitute in our bed. I guess that was the last straw for me, but there is more to it. A lot more."

"What do you mean?" said Stefan. Alarm narrowed his clear aquamarine eyes, those eyes I had fallen in love with, not so long ago.

For the first time it occurred to me that he, maybe, had no clue about all the small and large particulars that had driven a wedge between us, before his final transgression alienated me from our conjugal bed. I dreaded having to lay it all out for him, but it had to be done, so we could both move forward. So, I told him how his frequent judgmental remarks had made me feel inadequate. And how his aloofness and unexplained disappearances had caused me to cry and sorely miss my friends in Paris. Most of all, I told him how much I resented his need to control every aspect of our married life, from what I ate to the clothes I chose to wear, to his uncalled-for intrusion into my dance instruction curriculum at Kalakshetra and, more importantly, our fighting about my decision to shift my studies to music.

At first, he listened, disbelief showing on his face. His eyes started to blink with suppressed tears as I pointed out how lonely he had made me feel, me who had given up everything I knew to be with him. But I soon realized he wasn't going to take it lying down. He shoved his chair back, and I cringed at the screeching noise it made on the tiles. Mouth down-turned, he said dryly, "Once married, isn't a woman supposed to accept her husband's decisions? That's the way it was in my family, and after we got married, I assumed you'd trust me to make the right decisions for you, and for us."

Was this how the discussion was going to go? Stefan lecturing me on how a wife should act? I closed my eyes. Looking back over our married life, maybe I should have been a better wife. More compliant for better and for worse, as I'd promised. But I couldn't. What I'd learned from my mother's unhappy marriage was to watch out for myself and never let a man dominate me. Her misery had marked me in a way that was more potent than my wedding vows. Still, it was hard not to feel doubt. By challenging Stefan's authority, was I undermining the self-confidence that served him so well with everyone else? I couldn't help feeling guilt at the realization that maybe I was taking something away from him. Another betrayal of sorts in a long list of losses he had endured since childhood.

"Maybe you should consider that what marriage meant for your father no longer applies to us," I said. "In his role as head of the family when you were sent to Siberia, your father was expected to make all the decisions. It was war time, and, as a government official and a soldier, he was more suited for it than your mother. But these are different times, and you're not responsible for me, nor are you responsible for what I study, or do, or eat." I reached for his hand over the table. "I still care about you very much, I hope you know that. And no doubt, I'm probably to blame too for our failures," I admitted. "Anyway, that's beyond the point." I took my hand away.

"So that's it? You're giving up on our marriage?" He bowed his head. "I guess you got that from your mother," he said, staring at the floor.

I knew he felt under attack and chose to ignore the barb.

Getting no reaction from me, he lifted his eyes to mine. "That dig about your Mom. That was uncalled for. I'm sorry."

"Look. When we met, I never expected you to be the marrying kind. That's why I was so surprised when I arrived in Bombay and you had the whole thing planned out and ready to roll without even consulting me."

"The marrying kind?" He allowed himself a small chuckle. "It's true. I never planned to get married. It was all about Maurice laying the way for us to stay at the Theosophical Society. It seemed like the sensible thing to do. And Miss Petit wanted to protect you. She worried that you were terribly young and unprepared for India." He paused and stared at his hands. "She thought that you would find the unexpected betrothal romantic."

I sighed at the memory of their kind hospitality. "I understand Maurice and Miss Petit wanted to help us, but they went too far."

Reaching down for Rishu, Stefan grabbed him by the scruff of the neck, sat him on his lap and rubbed him behind the ears. Within seconds, Rishu began to purr. "Maybe they did," he said, "or maybe I gave them a false reading. I've been torn between my desire to have a family of my own, and my search for enlightenment for as long as

I remember. Both are demanding paths. After you became my wife, I found myself conflicted, and sometimes resentful to be burdened with the responsibility of another human being. It's my problem. I'm sorry you suffered the consequences." A couple of reluctant tears escaped from his eyes, but he wiped them impatiently with the back of his hand.

It was a response I hadn't expected, and it made me sad that we hadn't talked more often of what ailed us over the past two years in India. "I understand and respect your struggle. I suspected as much. But in order to move forward, don't you think we should make the best of what we have? Two grants, a home, a cat, transportation, a handful of servants, the prospect of a solid degree each, and each other."

"What do you mean by *we have each other*?"

"Just that. We have each other and can be a team. I believe that, in our hearts, we both know our marriage is in trouble. Maybe we can rescue it. I'm not sure. But for now, no one else needs to know. Especially not the Paderewski Foundation and the Theosophical Society, for obvious reasons. So, for your sake and mine, we need to present a united front."

He swallowed hard and was silent for a while. "It's a lot to digest in one sitting, but I think I understand." He stared outside and let silence envelop us. After a long pause he asked, "So, what now?"

I blinked away tears and sat up straight to speak the words I had prepared, but was loath to deliver. "Now that Viktor is gone, I have instructed Gangan to return our two charpoys to the bedroom. But you'll understand if, for now, I prefer to keep them apart under separate mosquito nets."

Without answering, Stefan got up and started to pace back and forth on the verandah. Then he came to a halt in front of me and rested his hands on my shoulders. "You have to believe me when I say that I'm sorry. I never meant to hurt you." He straightened up and resumed pacing in front of me. "That party was a stupid idea. I was just so tired of studies that are going nowhere, and all the do's and don'ts of this campus. You know that I don't drink, but after a few shots I was game for anything to happen that night. Not to hurt you, but to liberate myself, to feel myself being alive."

I understood his feelings and could sympathize with him, as long as I ignored the nautch girl incident. So I waited, and when he sat down again facing me, I gathered my courage and broached the ideas my conversation with Viktor had generated. "Look, what if we could just roll time back and remember how happy we were in Paris. And how I just came to India to be with you? Do you think we can do that? Just be the dreamers and seekers we were in Paris."

Looking into my eyes, his voice constricted by emotion, he said, "Maybe for me the bottom line is whether or not you still love me?"

I shrugged. "Love is such a big word. Do we really know what it means? But I understand friendship and caring for each other. There is so much we still can do together." I got up and joined him. "We can help each other fulfill our goals, get our degrees. You still want to get your Masters at MU, right?"

"Yes. I keep hoping I'll find some hidden wisdom around the bend."

"Listen, India is rich with ashrams and holy men. If you don't find what you're searching for in Madras, you may find it elsewhere. Don't you want to travel as much as we can?" I looked into his eyes and smiled. "We travel well together and working as a team, you can continue to help me record classical and tribal music, which will help with my degree, and I can do my best to help you with yours. Let the past mistakes be gone, mine as well as yours, and let's be the best friends we can be."

A hesitant expression broke on his handsome face. "We should certainly try."

On hearing these words, I was flooded with such relief that it threatened to turn into tears. I *so* wanted to make things better, and it appeared as if we might be able to escape the heavy cloud we had lived under for the past five weeks. I turned to a calendar hanging on the wall and pointed at it. "We have a two-week vacation coming up in August. Not enough time for a trip to Nepal, but maybe a long enough break to go to Khajuraho, that famous eleventh century temple we always wanted to visit?"

Stefan laced his fingers through the wire mesh screen that enclosed the verandah, and stared at the lush gentle jungle surrounding our house. I saw him bend down and pick up a parchment-like object which I recognized as a piece of discarded snake skin. Reptiles did that sometimes. They weaved through the clean metal mesh to shed their old skin. He opened the screen door and dropped his find outside. Turning to me, he nodded.

"That's a great idea. And if we go through Calcutta, maybe I could arrange a meeting with Sri Ramramji, an Advaita Philosophy professor at Calcutta University who is on our curriculum at MU." He paused. "Is there anything else you'd like to do?"

His concern surprised and pleased me. He wasn't in the habit of asking for my opinion on anything. I felt a surge of optimism. Perhaps he really wanted things to change.

"There is only one thing I need to do before we go on vacation," I said. "I promised Laila to take her to Mahabalipuram, down the coast, to take pictures. Her father bought her a camera, and she's eager to use it to start building a portfolio."

His eyes softened. "I never told you, but you did a great job reaching out to her."

The compliment surprised me too. But maybe now, with the burden of matrimony lifted from his shoulders, he could relax and really talk to me.

I stepped to the verandah screen and watched Loulou, our resident Rhesus, swinging from branch to branch on his favorite tree. He landed on a large limb and stared boldly at me. I wondered if he felt, as I did, that the tension of the past few weeks was on its way out. At least I hoped it was. Knowing Stefan as I did, I was surprised he hadn't pushed back harder against my complaints. But maybe it would come later, as he processed our discussion. I hated to think about the various challenges we might still face in keeping our new arrangement as quiet as possible to ensure our grants, and continue to enjoy our lovely Ranga Villa. Part of me also wondered how long he might willingly accept our new sleeping arrangement. Had I gone too far? Would love and desire ever fill my heart again? Only time would tell.

"What would you say if we drove to town for dinner?" said Stefan. "I haven't been hungry in weeks, but suddenly I'm starving." He smiled nervously, "Chinese food or tandoori chicken?"

I felt a true smile curl my lips, and stood straighter, as if years had fallen off my shoulders too. "Chicken tandoori and mango pickles, please. And bring a map, so we may start planning a trip or two."

BIO

Maryvonne is French and grew up in Paris. While studying classical Indian dancing and music in India for five years, she was a guest of the King of Nepal and met the freshly exiled Dalai Lama and his entourage in Northern India. On her return to the West, she taught in the US at Wesleyan University and UCLA. While teaching Indian music to her American students, Maryvonne discovered a taste for rock-and-roll, taught herself to play the electric bass, and exchanged her saris for platform boots.

Her daughter, born in New York, empowers children through the arts, one project at a time. Her American husband is a talented songwriter and recording artist. He brought two sons and a hybrid wolf puppy–Barewolf–into their lives. They live in Hollywood, where Maryvonne shares her time between writing, playing the bass and enjoying her growing American family. After twelve unforgettable years, Barewolf passed on. She now has two cats

Maryvonne has published *The 35¢ Dowry*, the first novel in the Mango Blood series. She has also published short stories and has translated a French thriller (*Les Yeux Sans Visage* by Jean Redon) and several screenplays to be optioned for movies. She's currently starting work on *The Dancing Foot*, the final tome in the Mango Blood series.

SOON TO BE RELEASED

In *The Dancing Foot*, the sequel to *Mango Blood*, we follow Minouche's coming of age as a wife, a musician, and a spirited young woman whose adventures and encounters in India, Kashmir, Sikkim, and Nepal, will forever change her view of the world, and her life.

THE DANCING FOOT

CHAPTER ONE

It was six in the morning, and I was tightening the straps on my bedroll when Stefan returned from the train station, where he had gone to pick up information and a train schedule for our trip to Khajuraho, the eleventh century temple we were headed to. "Bad news," he said, lips pressed in an annoyed grimace. "I underestimated how long it would take to get to Khajuraho by train."

"How long?" I asked, with a sinking feeling. We had already spent thirty-four hours on a train since leaving Madras for Calcutta four days ago.

"Twenty-one hours," said Stefan, dropping the train tickets he had picked up on the unmade bed. "And whatever route we take, we'll have to change trains at least once."

"Ouch! That hurts," I said. "Any other option?"

"We could fly to Lucknow—a six-hour flight—then take a local train to Khajuraho. We would be there in eight hours."

"Can we afford it?"

"We could, but it would affect our budget for the next three months. So, I got us train tickets. We'll just have to bear with it."

"All right then."

"By the way. Good idea, buying these magazines yesterday. It will make time go faster."

Twenty-one hours. India was a huge country. It made me appreciate anew the stoic behavior Indians exhibited on the lengthy railroad stretches we'd shared. Hopping from one capital to another in just a few hours, which I'd enjoyed in Europe during my hitchhiking days, was far behind me.

I was packed, but we still had a few errands to run. "When does the train leave?" I asked.

"At nine. It gives us a couple of hours."

To save time, we asked for our hotel bill before quickly going to the next-door market to buy a few ripe mangoes and some bananas, which we planned to wash with soap in the hotel bathroom sink before leaving. We also got some Rich Tea biscuits and ginger nut cookies, cashews and almonds—my favorites—and several large bottles of water. In a south Indian Brahmin restaurant across the street, we ordered some spicy Masala Dosas, and wrapped four of them in the wax paper a helpful waiter provided. The hot coffee and chai sold in train stations would be boiled, and therefore safe to drink.

We caught our train at Calcutta's Howrah Junction. The third class we were traveling on was crowded, but after several stops in small towns with forgettable names, we were able to claim more space on the wooden bench we sat on. Around us, the villagers' complexion— for there were not many city dwellers traveling our way—was lighter than in Madras, and the tight legged pantaloons and long kurta they wore over it, were often gray with dust and age, as was the plain turban most of them donned.

I hadn't found any books in the newspaper stand we had visited last night, and the English language magazines I'd bought reminded me of some of the worst gossip magazines I'd seen in London. I wasn't in the habit of reading these kinds of publications, and was surprised to discover a hardly veiled slant against women and girls in their ads. In them, wives decked in gorgeous saris were encouraged to excel in the kitchen to keep their husband happy. No career ads or higher educa- tion articles for girls. There were also some frightening accounts of violence in East Bengal villages, in which rape was described as some kind of rural community justice. Side by side with these horror stories, pictures of glamorous Bollywood actresses competed with images of Goddesses advertising chewing tobacco. It was all very strange, but I forced myself to read them cover to cover, including the offensive ads, of which there were many. I'd often suspected that, living inside the Theosophical Society, with its gentle jungle, peaceful gardens and gated campus, had sheltered me from the visceral and crowded rest of India. I hadn't seen or understood what was happening out there. It was high time I looked beyond the fence.

We were going west, toward the parched plateau of central India. As more and more passengers got off to catch north bound trains headed toward the fertile lands irrigated by the Ganges and its tributaries, we eventually had room to open up our bed-rolls. It gave us a chance to catch a long nap before transferring to the local small-gage train that would take us to our final destination.

We reached Khajuraho at six am. By then, there were only a few of us left on the train, a few locals and a handful of tourists. We were so excited about visiting that famous landmark that, rather than taking the time to check-in at the guesthouse where we were booked, we secured our luggage in a locker, keeping only our cameras and two bottles of water. Cycle rickshaws were waiting for those of us heading to the imposing group of monuments I could see in the distance.

The air was crisp and cold, and a red sun ascended slowly behind the tallest of the superstructures waiting for us. After so much anticipation, I was curious and impatient, but nothing could have prepared me for what lay in front of me after the rickshaw climbed a small grassy hill and stopped.

My jaw fell open. The closest temple, dominating a cluster of further shrines, rose up, massive and regal. We paid the rickshaw driver and advanced toward a worn flight of stairs guarded by the sitting figure of Nandi, which I knew to be Siva's sacred riding bull. Beyond it, ancient steps, tall, chipped, and worn, led to an immense stone platform on which the entire temple rested.

In spite of its weight and monolithic build, the structure looked light and airy. A mountain of lacy carved pillars, crowned by seven ascending roofs, danced against the rosy sky. On approaching the bottom wall, I saw that, at eye level, it was carved with horizontal friezes depicting detailed and animated scenes of battles with horses, camels, elephants, and the favored weapons of the times. It also portrayed images of soldiers engaged in rape, and bestial sex, that were so disturbing to me that I hurried to the next level, leaving Stefan behind.

If your loins are stirred by these sights, the temple had whispered to me, *leave them behind.*

It struck me that, for the last thousand years, this temple was doing more than housing a shrine. It was taking initiates and non-initiates on an extraordinary exploration of their senses, and heart, and mind.

Open your heart, whispered the gracefully crafted walls as I moved on to artful friezes depicting various stages of human love from playfulness to passion before evolving into devotion.

Learn, do not judge, warned the temple about the erotic dance of godlings and sages quenching their lust for human mates.

Be, hummed in my blood as I ascended higher levels along the dancing walls where Hindu gods reveled in platonic and orgasmic bliss.

Renounce, it finally said in the detached and enigmatic smile of Brahma the Creator, who, with Vishnu the Preserver, and Shiva the Destroyer, ruled the world from the heights of the shrine.

I stopped where I was and waited, as the sun rose higher in the sky chasing the morning chill. Where was Stefan? Absorbed in photography, probably. A few women walked past me, and I got a whiff of the jasmine garlands they were carrying to the inner shrine. After a few minutes, I decided to follow them.

The small sanctum carved inside the heart of the temple was sunk in almost total darkness. Abruptly sightless, I shivered, my head and heart buzzing with the messages I had received. After the caressing heat of the sun, my whole being was shivering in the austere chill, and as my eyes adjusted, I saw that the room was devoid of sculptures and decorations. It was musky and empty except for the phallic image of the Lord Shiva embodied by a tall black stone. Above it, folded bats hung on the ceiling dreaming their dreams. It was a place where the smoke of sandalwood incense wafted lazily in the motionless air; where butter lamps gave a short yellow glow and a bare hint of heat to ward off the sepulchral bleakness. A place where a stark single stone enthroned in the room, adorned with holy saffron markings and fragrant strings of jasmine flowers, felt cold and moist to the touch. This place was too dark and too cold. I suddenly longed for the flamboyant stained-glass windows of old cathedrals, in which the sun brought to life the stories of medieval saints and knights. My heart was beating hard in my chest as my hand followed the thick wall, until I found the narrow exit cut into the stone. I blinked into the light. My eyes teared and adjusted to the brightness of the outside world, and my skin reached for the healing touch of the sunlight it craved.

Still no trace of Stefan. Rather than waiting for him any longer, I found my way to the worn stairs and descended into the grassy clearing surrounding the temple. I walked a little way, and sat in the shade of a lone leafy tree to contemplate what I had felt and learned. My legs ached, but my mind was ablaze, and, as I sat there, facing this eight-hundred-year-old temple, an other-worldly sensation seized me, and I became one of the dancers stamped on its walls, braving the heat, the dust, and the deluge of a hundred monsoons; I caught a glimpse of the changing dynasties and delighted in the displays of a thousand court dancers and musicians honoring the patronage of gold-laden Rajahs. I survived the pillaging and the fires of Moghul wars, and witnessed the industrial revolution, the riots, the non-violent movement, and the first man on the moon. The breath of many gods caressed my stone body. Eight centuries were nothing but the blink of an eye in Shiva's dreams.

My throat constricted with tears as I came to. What was I looking at? A stone sentinel? A mirror reflecting my soul? Somewhere in the back of my mind, priests were chanting *neti, neti*—neither this nor that—in rhythmic Sanskrit verses.

That's where Stefan found me, half an hour later, sleeping against the tree. "You should be careful, there might be scorpions and snakes in the grass." He turned around and pointed at the smaller temples beyond the edifice we had visited. His eyes shone with excitement. "Can you believe this cluster?" he whispered under his breath. "And we've only visited one."

More people had arrived. Whole Indian families trailing children and grandparents were studying the ribald bottom friezes before ascending to the more artistic display of the higher levels. Stefan turned to me. "So, what do you think of Khajuraho?"

I glanced at the formidable structure. "I think so many things...

Like, whoever commissioned the building of this temple had a vision. They wanted to illustrate the Kama Sutra in stone, and more. And apparently they succeeded."

"I am no prude," he said with a shake of his head, "but, even I was surprised by the gore, the rapes, the bestiality and violence depicted in the battle scenes. I'm astonished that parents allow their children to see it."

"Me too. Maman would never have exposed me to that. Do you know that, at the movies, when actors kissed, my grandpa used to cover my eyes?" I smiled at the remembrance.

He cocked his head. "I think there is a lesson in the way the temple reveals itself. Maybe it's meant to frighten and educate people by showing them what happens in times of war, and what to look forward to in an era of peace and faith."

I considered that. "It's a nice thought." I took a moment to consider. "These battle scenes were awful, but as I kept going up and around the temple, I really enjoyed the physicality of the sculptures. Stone bodies in 3D, rather than words on a page. The depiction of gods and humans entwined in ecstasy moved me." I made a face, "I believe I'm a little jealous of the dancers and musicians living on these walls. Maybe I came to India nine centuries too late."

"Who knows. Maybe you *were* here in another life," said Stefan with a dramatic wave of his hand.

I let his words sink in. "Ah! Reincarnation? Are you serious?"

"Who knows?" He dug into his equipment bag, brought out one of his cameras and fed a new roll of film into it. "What I know is that we need to find a spot to take a long shot of the temple before more people arrive. Right now, the light is great on the eastern walls. Did you notice how the shadows animate the dancers?" He reached down and pulled me to my feet. "Come on. We better get going."

Ready or not, I too wanted to play with my camera. I would only get two-dimensional images, but they would forever remind me of the voices I had heard in the shade of these whispering walls. Few sculptures were level with my eyes and, as I worked my way around the temple for the second time, my neck started to hurt, but still I took photo after photo. There were so many picture-perfect shots calling me.

Finally, heat and hunger drove us back to the rickshaw stand, and after a quick stop at the train station to pick up our bags from the lockers, we headed out to the guesthouse. We were relieved to discover that food was available for a few rupees, and after a restoring meal of rice and vegetable curry, we decided to take a nap.

We returned to the temple in the afternoon, and were rewarded with a beautifully lit western wall. After taking more photos, we strolled to the minor shrines standing close by, but none were as enchanting as the first one, so we returned to our favorite temple and stayed there until we ran out of film, including the two extra rolls of Fuji color negative we'd bought from the manager of our guesthouse.

Later that evening, sitting cross-legged on the bed, Stefan spread his map of India in front of him. "I wasn't sure how long we would need to stay here, but short of building some scaffolding to photograph the high frescoes, there isn't much more we can do here." He looked into my eyes and smiled. "You were right, we travel well together, and working as a team we can both get what is needed for our studies. Photos for your ethnomusicology papers and more philosophy materials for mine. I can't wait to meet Sri Ramramji, the Advaita pundit, when we go back to Calcutta." He paused. "Is there anything else you'd like to do here?"

His concern surprised and pleased me. He wasn't in the habit of asking for my opinion on anything. I felt a surge of optimism. Perhaps he really wanted things to change.

To be continued in *The Dancing Foot.*

Check out my website at maryvonnefent.com and find me on
Instagram, Linkedin and Facebook for pictures and news.